THIRTY-THREE CECILS

De Morier, Everett, author.
Thirty-three Cecils : a novel / Everett De Morier.
Philadelphia : Blydyn Square Books, 2015.
©2015
pages cm.

ISBN 978-0-9857055-6-5 (ebook)
978-0-9857055-7-2 (paperback)

1. Erie, PA — Fiction. 2. Binghamton, NY — Fiction.

Published by Blydyn Square Books, Philadelphia
www.BlydynSquareBooks.com

Cover graphic design by Paul Prizer/Paul Prizer Design Group, Inc.
www.PrizerDesign.com

Book interior design by Kim Shinners/EJB Publishing Services,
www.EJBPublishing.com

THIRTY-THREE CECILS

A NOVEL

EVERETT DE MORIER

To Lawrence Wayne De Morier,
You were a much better father than I was a son.

Contents

Prologue

The Box

| Present Day |

The most painful aspect of editing and preparing this book for publication was the unavoidable, yet necessary, task of making Arlene Kellerman aware that the box she sold in her yard sale for three dollars—the same box this book is based on—sold for $2.5 million just a few months later.

Everything else was easy.

Once I sat down with Mrs. Kellerman, once I could finally verify where the box had been for the past twenty-plus years, then all I needed to do was compile both journals from the box into this book and return Diane Sawyer's phone calls.

It was truly that easy.

I'd like to tell you that it was my brilliant skills as an editor that made this book what it is. I'd also like to describe the painstaking hours it took to whip the journals into readable form. But those would be lies. This book was already written when Blydyn Square Books purchased the journals. It simply had to be put into electronic format, organized, edited slightly for grammar and spelling (while keeping the unique voices of the authors intact to the greatest extent possible), and then sent to the presses.

On the promotional side, the mixture of hype and curiosity drove crowds to get to this book long before it even hit the market. Presales alone actually qualified this book as a bestseller before its release date. All this excitement was flamed by the massive twenty-plus-year search for the journals, the intrigue of the actual events the book describes, the numerous unanswered questions from police and the public, the nine pending multimillion-dollar lawsuits, the missing money, and, of course, the questions concerning the deaths of both Walker Roe and Riley Dutcher.

Any book touching on even a few of these subjects would have a big market, which is why this is not the first book to be published concerning Gopher Ink, the company that Walker Roe and Riley Dutcher formed only days before their deaths. Since the original events took place in 1992, the subject of Gopher Ink has been the focus of eleven books, four documentaries, numerous websites, and two feature films. The best of these were based on research and interviews; the worst were merely collections of public records and sensationalized speculation.

But the truth—what actually happened and why—has never been known, at least not until now. So a book that provides answers—answers instead of speculation—about what happened to Walker Roe and Riley Dutcher has long been anticipated but was never realistically expected.

Walker Roe and Riley Dutcher's reluctuance to speak during the creation of Gopher Ink, as well as the seizure of all available documentation by the Roe family, meant that there has been little firsthand knowledge before now to help answer any of the questions. However, the answers begin and end within the pages of these two uncensored journals.

But one question remains: Where have the journals been for the past two decades and how did they get from the hands of Walker Roe and Riley Dutcher in 1992 to Arlene Kellerman's yard sale?

Because we know that Chris Hogan owned the box the journals were found in—and was the recipient of the $2.5 million auction price paid by Blydyn Square Books—we need to begin with him, in order to trace the box back to Gopher Ink.

Due to the ongoing lawsuit between Chris Hogan and Danny DelRizzo, Hogan was unwilling to be interviewed; however, Danny DelRizzo was more than willing to speak on the subject.

According to both Danny DelRizzo and Arlene Kellerman, the discovery of the journals occurred as follows: On the morning of her yard sale in April 2014, Arlene Kellerman carried the cardboard box in question out from the basement of her Erie, Pennsylvania, home for the first time in over seventeen years and placed it in the area of her yard sale where a yellow sign read "Odds and Ends." She sat down in her lawn chair, sipped a cup of coffee, and talked to her sister Ruth while she waited for customers to arrive.

Danny DelRizzo, then a junior at nearby Gannon University, was on his way to meet a friend to play tennis when he drove past the yard sale and pulled over to browse. When Danny saw the box, he was immediately excited and did not try to bargain on the price. He paid Mrs. Kellerman the three dollars she was asking and placed the box in the trunk of his car. Mrs. Kellerman placed the three dollars in a coffee can that she was using to hold change. She walked back to her chair, sat next to her sister, and commented on how difficult it would be to get rid of her deceased husband's things.

That day, Mrs. Kellerman made a total of $467.25 from her yard sale. The big-ticket items included her late husband's golf clubs, lawnmower, and tools. Mrs. Kellerman was moving to a retirement community, so she would not need a lawnmower or tools. And she hated golf.

Immediately following his tennis game, Danny DelRizzo brought the box back to the house he shared with his three housemates. The box contained a Saint Pauli Girl bar light, a few old computer disks, liquor supply books, various owners' manuals, and several spiral notebooks. He placed the bar sign on a nail that was already on the wall of the living room and plugged the light in. He was pleased with his bargain bar light and placed the box the light came in on the floor of his bedroom closet.

The Saint Pauli Girl light shone brightly for the remainder of the semester, while the journals remained in Danny's closet.

With the semester complete, Danny DelRizzo began to prepare to go home to Harrisburg, Pennsylvania, for the summer. He pulled the box the Saint Pauli Girl light came in out of his closet. He unplugged the light and was planning to place it back in the box when he noticed that the box was far too big to be the original box in which the light had been packaged. He discovered that he could easily put the light in the trunk of his car by itself and save space. Danny made a quick survey of the box; he saw the instruction books, the old disks, and the notebooks and determined that the box contained nothing of value. He tossed the box on the front porch, a staging area where garbage was often placed until it could be taken to the dumpster later.

According to DelRizzo, this is where Chris Hogan found the journals.

"Chris is a real packrat and computer junkie," DelRizzo stated. "He was always prowling through our junk to see if there was anything he might want."

Chris Hogan spotted the cardboard box and pulled out the old floppy disks and the four notebooks. He left the rest of the items in the box.

It makes sense that, given Chris Hogan's interest in computers, he would gravitate toward the computer gear, but why did he take the four notebooks from the box?

"Notebooks are for notes, man," Hogan said proudly during the press conference held after the sale of the journals to Blydyn Square Books. "I thought they were notes from a class, so maybe they were from a class I might be taking next semester. Or from a class that someone else might take. So I took them."

This act of taking the notebooks, as well as the disks, led to Hogan's $2.5 million windfall; the journals of Walker Roe found on the disks would have been incomplete without Riley Dutcher's handwritten notebooks.

Upon returning to his home in Altoona, Pennsylvania, for the summer, Chris Hogan placed the disks in one of the many vintage computers he owns and found that four of them contained liquor inventory information. He erased them, freeing them for resale (in the geek world, the old disks are becoming collectible). Then he opened the fifth disk. It contained only one file: a Microsoft Word document entitled *Thirty-three Cecils.*

Hogan was intrigued by the title and read the file.

"I had heard of Walker Roe," Hogan told reporters during the press conference. "But it didn't click to me what I was reading. I just started reading and couldn't stop. I got about forty pages in and started to Google some of the names and saw all the articles and stuff about it." He smiled. "Then, I looked at the notebooks and read them, too." His smile widened. "And then, wham! I figured it out pretty quick."

Upon his discovery, Chris Hogan made Danny DelRizzo aware of what he believed he had found.

Chris Hogan's father, Seth Hogan, located an organization called the Ritzer Group out of Pittsburgh that could authenticate that the journals were the real thing. During the wait for the results of the analysis, the relationship between Chris Hogan and Danny DelRizzo became strained.

"Hey," DelRizzo stated, "Chris never would have had those journals if it wasn't for me, and he was being a real jerk about it."

Early emails from Hogan to DelRizzo stated that, although DelRizzo had thrown the journals out and they would have been discarded if Hogan had not rescued them, the two were still friends and housemates and DelRizzo would receive something from the sale.

Replying emails from DelRizzo asked specifically what *something* was, and several emails stated that by *something*, DelRizzo had assumed Hogan meant *half.* Soon, emails and texts showed that even before the journals were authenticated, the idea of only receiving *something* had angered DelRizzo. He began to threaten legal action to get the journals back. Because of the threats, Hogan's offer of *something* was soon retracted.

The journals were authenticated in September 2014 and sold to Blydyn Square Books for $2.5 million. A $5 million lawsuit was soon filed by

Danny DelRizzo against Chris Hogan. The cornerstone of the suit claimed that because the box with the journals in it was still on the porch when Hogan found it, and not in the garbage, the journals were technically still in the house and therefore still the property of Danny DelRizzo. DelRizzo was suing for the full value of the journals as well as legal costs.

This lawsuit led *Newsweek* columnist Martin Koehler to write, "Even twenty years after his death, Walker Roe is still pissing people off."

Soon after the journals were analyzed, Arlene Kellerman was sitting in the Carol Center at the Glenridge of Parlor Ranch, a retirement community outside of Sarasota, Florida, when she saw a report on CNN that the Walker Roe and Riley Dutcher journals had been located, authenticated, and purchased at auction for $2.5 million.

"Wow," she said to Mrs. Ralph Willet, a fellow resident. "That would have been nice to find, huh?"

I met Mrs. Kellerman at her retirement community. She took the news about the box's value reasonably well. After a long period of silence and after drinking one very large glass of red wine, Mrs. Kellerman merely posed a question.

"Ya know," she said, smiling, "I wonder if that kid would sell the box back to me for *four* dollars?"

So, how did the box get from Gopher Ink's offices at the Wanamaker Studios building on the Erie waterfront to Mrs. Kellerman's basement?

The answer is, through her late husband, Jeffrey Kellerman. Mr. Kellerman had converted the basement of their Warren County home into a bar, complete with a pool table, jukebox, dartboard, vintage video games, and a myriad of beer and liquor advertising collectibles. He was always on the lookout for new items for the bar and on a trip to Mega-Liquor Warehouse, he found one.

After the purchase of Mega-Liquor Warehouse from the estate of Walker Roe, the new owners, Lee and Martin Womath, placed a collection of various items from the old store up for sale: specialty bottles of beer, liquor gift boxes, beer posters, liquor and beer signs, various advertising materials, and a box containing the Saint Pauli Girl light. According to Jeffrey Kellerman's credit card records, he purchased the light and the contents of the box for twenty-five dollars. He brought the box home and placed it on a shelf behind his bar.

One can only assume that Jeffrey Kellerman planned to rearrange some things and make room for his new bar light. But this never occurred. Kellerman died from a massive heart attack just fourteen days after purchasing the Saint Pauli Girl light. The box would remain under the bar, untouched, for seventeen more years.

The jukebox, the Pac-Man and Ms. Pac-Man video games, the pool table, and the dartboard would all be split up between the Kellermans' two sons, Brad and Charles. Neither Brad nor Charles Kellerman wanted the Saint Pauli Girl light, however, so Arlene Kellerman brought the box up from behind the bar and placed it in her yard sale.

That is the history of the box. Now, to the book itself.

The book you are about to read begins with the journal entries of Walker Roe. At the time they were written, in 1992, Walker was somewhat well known as an award-winning cartoonist and filmmaker, but was primarily known for his public indictment on fifteen counts of fraud and counterfeiting. During his sensationalized trial, in 1988, it was proven that he had bilked his company, Ten Tuesdays, Inc.; defrauded three Erie banks; and counterfeited over sixty thousand dollars' worth of currency. After completing seven months at Lewisburg Prison Camp, Walker Roe returned to Erie, Pennsylvania, to put his life back together and to rebuild his relationship with his two young daughters.

This is what the public knew about Walker Roe. But Riley Dutcher, the other founding partner of Gopher Ink, was unknown. The media descended on Dutcher after he saved Walker Roe's life on July 28, 1992. Information on Dutcher prior to the time the two men met and throughout the formation of Gopher Ink was extremely sparse.

Until now.

Previously, the public had speculated about what drove the two men to form the company and what the company's goals were. The public speculated incorrectly. We were also wrong about what bonded the two men together. We were wrong about their characters. We were wrong about their motives, what they were striving for, what they feared, and what they loved.

We also now know who killed them.

Walker Roe and Riley Dutcher were murdered while leaving Russ's Diner in Erie, Pennsylvania, on September 1, 1992. Upon the discovery of the journals, in 2014, Blydyn Square Books made excerpts available to the authorities. This information led Erie police to collect further evidence, which allowed them to make their first arrest in the double murder of Walker Roe and Riley Dutcher—over twenty years after the killings occurred.

With the journals located and a suspect pending trial, the task of organizing and editing this book began. The original intention was to translate these journals into narrative form, matching Roe's journal with Dutcher's to create a storyline depicting the sequence of events. This concept was quickly abandoned.

Journals are personal accounts of thoughts and emotions, and it would be impossible to view the events these journals describe in any way other than directly through the individual writing styles and the words of the two men who wrote them. We then thought about framing the journals with public records, interviews, and timelines, allowing the journals to add the meat that had long been missing from the complete story. Then we decided against that approach.

We also considered providing media frameworks between journal entries to give the reader articles and background information on the events in the journals, along with maps of the locations mentioned. This idea, too, was quickly abandoned.

Besides the few newspaper pieces that were originally clipped out and inserted in the journals by either Walker or Dutch, no outside pieces will be provided here. Numerous books have been written on the subject of Gopher Ink, based on the media coverage. This book will not be one of them.

The journals will be presented here completely, and besides adding chapter numbers, names, and dates to identify the writer and when the entry was written, the journals will be presented exactly as they were originally written, with very few, if any, alterations.

As a warning to the reader, these journals do not wrap up in a neat, tight bundle as most readers like books to do. This book ends in the middle. It ends before it should have, just as the lives of Walker and Dutch ended. And when these journals end, not all the questions will have been answered. In fact, more questions will be produced because these journals allow us only a little bit of insight into Gopher Ink, outside of a view into the hearts and minds of its two creators.

The journals will end just as these two men and Gopher Ink ended—quickly and unexpectedly.

Martin Garrett
Editor
Blydyn Square Books

JOURNAL 1

Walker

CHAPTER 1

FINDING EDDIE

| JULY 6, 1992 |

One October, back when I was respectable, I traveled to Fayette, Mississippi—to research the backdrop for our newest documentary, the last real film I made before my counterfeiting and bank fraud activities began to pique the interest of the FBI and other federal agencies—where I had to interview a witch. I say I *had* to interview a witch, but that's a lie. I didn't *have* to interview her; I *wanted* to interview her. The witch had nothing to do with the film we were making, but Malcolm Clyde, my local producer, had told me about her and I was curious.

And in complete honesty—and I have no experience with honesty, so I'm winging it here—I also need to clarify that she wasn't exactly a witch, or at least I don't think she was. I can call her a witch because Clyde had called her a witch, so there's a loophole where I can use the term and still tell the story truthfully. The individual in question made her living as a fortune teller, and in Clyde's Southern view of folks, this made her as much a witch as Glenda and all her sisters. This particular witch's name was Opal Boggs.

This is true. Her name was Opal Boggs, which is an ideal name for a witch, and she made her living reading cards—not tarot cards but regular playing cards. She had only one eye and chewed tobacco. Clyde reluctantly drove me over soggy Mississippi roads that shot around rotting clapboard farmhouses until we arrived at Opal's squat cinderblock house. Her home was on a slight hill, as all witches' homes should be, and it was guarded by an army of rusting appliances. We went inside and Opal read my cards, which was the real reason I wanted to meet her.

Now, it's important to note that *nothing* Opal told me about my future came true. Nothing. Catherine and I didn't stay married forever. My three young daughters did not all grow up to be beautiful young women because Rachel was killed four months later when a truck hit her while she was riding her bike twenty feet from our front door. I would think any self-respecting fortune teller would have seen *that* one coming. And the film we were making did not become a financial success, but instead became evidence toward the thirteen felony, fraud, and counterfeiting charges against me. This led to my arrest, my trial, and, after being splashed all over television and the newspaper, left me humiliated, bankrupt, and divorced.

But one thing Opal said, one thing she told me, she nailed. Man, did she nail it. While arranging cards across a rickety card table, while spitting brown tobacco globs into a Folger's can that sat near her foot, Opal stopped. She wiped her lip with the sleeve of her flannel shirt. She looked down at the six of clubs on top of the king of diamonds, then mumbled, to no one in particular—especially not to me—the seven words that still echo in my head.

She said, "He sure do disappoint people, don't he?"

There was a pause. I swallowed. Then she flipped another card and continued.

And the award for insight goes to Opal Boggs.

He sure do disappoint people, don't he?

Yes, I do. And not some. Not many. All. There is no one, not a single person, who has been spared. There is not a director, not one of my children, business partners, friends, investors, no one I have not completely and utterly disappointed. All came to me and all were turned away worse off for it—from my daughters waiting for lunch and having me tell them that every Burger King in Erie was closed because I couldn't write another bad check and didn't have enough cash for a kid's meal, to my production company wanting to know why their check bounced.

These were the trusts I broke. These were the lies I told. These were the wounded souls I preyed upon.

Lawyers. Friends. Creditors. Clients.

Neighbors. Family. Clergy. Cops.

He sure do disappoint people, don't he?

And that's where I am now. On the other side, but still in it. Free, but still cuffed. Resolved, but on my way back down into the mine and writing this—writing anything—for the first time in years. Beginning again and attempting a redo. Working toward full disclosure, the truth, all of it, no matter how much the old scabs are torn open and the fresh cuts bleed. Just to see if I can.

Because I have this idea. A hopeful idea. This Grinch has a wonderfully hopeful idea—of how I can stop it. And that's where I am now.

The confession and catharsis I'm attempting will come. Eventually. And I will lay it all at your feet, dear reader. I'll give the details that led to my arrest—which, unless you were somewhere in the Danakil Desert, humming with your hands over your ears and your eyes closed, you've heard something about.

And although I was a bit preoccupied when the great media machine descended on me, I have since caught up. I have spent countless hours in the library reading old newspaper microfilm from that period of time—there is a sickening pleasure in hitting pain-rewind—and I believe I've read most of them.

The basic ones—Creator of the children's classic *That Walrus Is Not On The Guest List* arrested for bank fraud and countefeiting; Four new counts added to Walker Roe case—are fine. Accurate and simple. But some of the others—Walker Roe sentenced up to a Thousand Tuesdays—are just plain silly. They're trying to play on the name of my company, Ten Tuesdays, Inc., but a thousand Tuesdays is almost twenty years. The most I would have gotten would have been twelve. It's very sloppy journalism—after all, it's not lenience I'm looking for here; it's accuracy. Continuity.

In the end, I was far more famous as a forger then I ever was as a cartoonist or filmmaker, having just enough success to warrant being hanged publicly. But it was also the story itself. You have to admit the concept was good. The creator of the cartoons and films about ethics and morals, about kindness and goodness, going on to defraud banks and counterfeit currency is newsworthy. The keynote speaker on subjects such as power and perseverance robbing from his own company is good stuff.

And the aspect that made it truly juicy was—I did it. I did it all. There was nothing I was accused of that I didn't do.

If you followed the trial, though, you will see that I did fight. But I was fighting in proxy. I was fighting for Catherine, Abby, and Liz. I was fighting so there would be something left of me and something left of our home to give to them. If it were just me, I would have asked for stiffer sentencing and requested that flogging and thumbscrews be involved, so great was my self-loathing.

And in the end I was purged and made clean; I served my full sentence, leaving me without any need for parole or conditions, and I came out on the other end clean—no home, no income, no family, no more good name.

I will discuss more of this as soon as I recover from what I've just written, and possibly I'll be able to write about Rachel's death for the first time. But I want to get to the other part now, the true reason I began writing this after all these years. I want to talk about the thing, the idea, this nagging concept of change, of reprogramming—I know that you don't want to take self-help advice from me, and I don't blame you, but I believe this idea has some merit, if I can only coax it out a bit.

Here's the concept. Let's say there is a prisoner; we'll call him Eddie because Eddie seems like a solid prisoner name. Eddie is going to escape from prison. He gets out of his cell, he gets outside the pod, and then out of the building, and makes it over the wall into the woods. Now, because Eddie is a detail-oriented type of guy, he manages to quickly ditch the orange prison jumpsuit and get into some street clothes. He gets a little cash and is a few hundred miles away before the guards even know he's gone. Eddie is very good.

Now, Eddie is a disciplined man and once he is free, he does not make contact with his sister in Toms River, New Jersey, or his childhood friend in Middletown, New York, and he doesn't even attend his mother's funeral six months later. He cuts all ties with his past. But Eddie does not have a duffel bag full of money in a bus locker somewhere, so he'll have to make a living, and for the sake of the example let's say Eddie gets a new identity and gets himself a job.

So, with all that in mind, here is the question: Will Eddie be caught?

Answer: Yes.

Why? Because without even realizing it, poor Eddie will begin operating according to his programming, and if the police are looking for him, they will find him. And when they do, Eddie will be making a living as a mechanic, like he did before. And he will be on a dart league, like he was before. And he will be a member of the Moose Club and he will order Gallica rose bulbs from a catalog and drink Mountain Dew and follow the Detroit Tigers. All just like he did before. And even though his name is now Brian Landers, he is still Eddie and if the police follow his profile, they will find him and they will drag his sorry backside back to A-block. Why? Because as disciplined as Eddie is, he never changed his programming. He never rewired. He is still reacting and thinking and living just like the Eddie the police were looking for.

Now, some would say that this programming is just who we are, our personality. Then, in Eddie's case, he needs to get a new personality because that's all that's keeping him from going back to prison. And for that one percent of us who have everything exactly as it should be, sure, go ahead and call it your personality. But what if this *personality* is stopping us from taking better care of our families or making more money or being content or obtaining a personal relationship with God or just plain being happier? After all, this personality of ours didn't come in a box. It was shipped to us over ten, twenty, forty, sixty years, being whittled and formed by each experience and fear and belief and desire. A trillion tiny thoughts, a million tiny events chipped away and made us, us.

We take the same route home from work. We sit in the same seats during lunch. We go to the same garage when our car doesn't work and we order the same pizza on Saturday night. Is that our personality? Is that what makes us, us? Pizza and car repair?

Here is example two. Let's say you are at the airport heading to Chicago for an important meeting for the standard big promotion, big contract, big life kind of meeting. Your boss is anxiously waiting for you to call him the nanosecond the meeting is over. This is one of those big, big deals.

Now, what would happen if before boarding the plane you cashed in your ticket and instead of going to Chicago you went to Key Largo and didn't check your voicemail and just decided to lie on the beach for a few days? What would happen?

Many things. And you can be fairly sure that your life would change. At that moment, life would change very quickly.

Now, why do we assume that in moments like that we can screw our lives up pretty quickly—get on the wrong airplane and an entire career is shot—but that we can't make good things happen just as quickly? Who says? Again, you do not want to take self-help advice from me. I am only writing this to try to understand the paradox and begin working it out for my own selfish use.

Example three: me. Walker Roe. Forty-year-old ex-con, burnt-out filmmaker, cartoonist, counterfeiter, forger, divorced father of three girls—one in heaven and two down here. I'm the guy who still, years later, shows up in jokes that begin, "*Walker Roe dies and shows up at the pearly gates and Saint Peter . . .*"

At any point along the path—at jail, at my arrest, at the divorce, at the bankruptcy—any time along that line, a fuse could have popped, a wire could have sizzled, and I could have changed.

People do have epiphanies. In Sanskrit, the word is *darsana*: a sense of instantly seeing or beholding, a ripple so great that the cosmic reset button is triggered. It does happen. I've interviewed people who've experienced it.

But it didn't happen to me.

I was emptied. I was hollowed out, cored, and left emotionally dead, surviving only on what rations of shame and self-hatred I could gather. But I continued. I continued as I was before. What little was left of me remained—a smaller version of the original, transcription errors and all, badly wired, programmed erratically, but remaining intact.

And, therefore, we can assume that I will make the same mistakes again. I will react to the same stimuli, I will come to the same conclusions, I will make the same decisions using the same pattern of thoughts and goals and self-serving fear as I did before. In effect, I will somehow do it all over again. Maybe not on the same scale—I doubt I will be given the tools to make as big a mess as I did before—but with enough time I will act selfishly enough and irresponsibly enough that my children or my ex-wife or others I have not yet met will be harmed.

Simply put, I will disappoint more people.

The point is that if I do not rewire, then this is inevitable: This . . . will . . . all . . . happen . . . again.

That's the gnawing idea. That's the thought that has been scratching inside me and has led me to finally start writing after all these years. A human being may be able to act differently temporarily, to change his or her behavior for a while, but the wiring will always be there.

Now, you may *believe* that a toaster is truly a radio, but when you plug the thing in, the coil will get red-hot and it will crave a piece of bread. So you leave the toaster unplugged and as long as it remains cold and useless, you can simply keep on believing that it is a radio.

And up until the very moment that you plug it in and press down the lever—it is.

Chapter 2

The National Agency for Little Girls Who Won't Eat Their Chipped Beef on Toast

| July 9, 1992 |

Denning Arms Apartments—or as it is better known by its nickname, *Divorce Court*—is a mid-sized apartment complex in the southern part of Erie, Pennsylvania, and is the transitory *pro tempore* for many of the fresh ex-husbands and new ex-wives who migrate through the Erie County family court system. It is also my home.

According to Bugby—and I'll get to Bugby in a minute—almost half of the newly divorced humans in Erie County spend at least a month or so at Denning Arms. In other words, if you live in Erie County and become divorced, there is a fifty percent chance that you will return to Divorce Court, the apartment complex, after leaving Divorce Court, the legal institution.

Divorce Court, the apartment complex, is well aware of its appeal to the formerly married and has positioned its product accordingly. There are no leases on the apartments to frighten away those who cannot predict what the first few months of divorce will bring. This is also attractive to those who anticipate a quick end to Sheila's romance with the beer-truck driver and a fast invitation to come back to the split-level in Waterford or Union City. Divorce Court is also located near the two necessities for the newly divorced: (1) K-Mart. You can get everything from furniture to food—nothing too permanent or expensive—just in case Sheila calls and you need to move back home quickly; and (2) Booze. Bugby, who owns

Divorce Court, the apartment complex, also conveniently owns Mega-Liquor Warehouse, which is just one block away.

Divorce Court, the apartment complex, has a playground behind building D for those weekends when the newly divorced children visit. When an outsider first sees the playground, the eye is drawn to what looks like far too many benches circling the playground like wagons preparing for a Comanche attack.

"That's so newly divorced Ken can sit and talk with newly divorced Barbie," Bugby told me. "While displaced Zachary and displaced Britney play on the seesaw. *Wishing well.*"

Wishing well is a phrase that Bugby adds to every third or fourth sentence he speaks, unconsciously. A verbal tic.

I met Lester Bugby on the day of my release from prison—we had communicated by letter before that, and he was the bridge between me changing my address from Lewisburg Federal Prison Camp to Divorce Court, the apartment complex. We became friends shortly after we met and we've remained friends ever since.

Bugby has thinning hair and a propensity to wear jogging suits no matter what the weather or occasion. And as I've already mentioned, he adds the phrase *wishing well* at the end of most paragraphs he speaks. Now, at first, I heard the phrase as *wish-you-well,* or *wishing-you-well,* but I soon realized it was *wishing well.* And because the phrase *wishing well* is not often used in casual conversation, this tic of his is extremely noticeable.

In order to understand the history of Divorce Court, the apartment complex, you must first understand the history of Lester Bugby.

First off, no one calls him Lester; he's simply Bugby.

Bugby was born in Sedalia, Missouri, in 1930. He is the only child of Victor Bugby and Sonia Denning Stephenson Bugby, a Midwestern beauty with long brown hair, high cheekbones, and the strong glare of the wealthy. Denning Arms is her namesake.

"Only because *Sonia Arms* sounds like a frickin antacid," Bugby said. "We named the hotel Denning and I named the apartments Denning. *Wishing well.*"

I have seen old photographs of Sonia and in each picture she has the same fractured smile, the same glare that reaches out to you, leaving you with the sensation of having just been ordered to do something but you can't remember exactly what that is. This is an appropriate response since Sonia Stephenson was spoiled to the core and, although she may not have received everything she ever wanted—how many of us do?—she *did* receive everything she ever asked for.

Sonia Stephenson was the fourth child born to Edwin and Lena Stephenson, and the only one to survive. The three previous children had lived anywhere from a few months to a year and then all experienced a sudden high fever and blisters on the skin and died in a single night. Sonia was fairly healthy for the first year of her life, and then, three days after her first birthday, she came down with the blister sickness that had killed her brothers and sister before her.

Edwin and Lena Stephenson had called for the doctor, who hoped it was not the mystery illness he had seen in Sonia's siblings, though he soon realized it was. He made Sonia as comfortable as possible and prepared the parents for the worst: Sonia would be dead by morning.

The Stephensons kept a vigil all night in their daughter's nursery, praying, crying, hoping. The next morning, they approached the crib slowly, hoping to avoid the sight of another dead child for as long as they could. But when they arrived at the crib, they saw two things they were not expecting. The first was that Sonia was alive. Very much alive. The second was that she was standing up on her own, something she had not yet done.

Sonia looked around her crib as if she had just arrived there. Her breathing was heavy and she was covered with a glossy coat of sweat, but the blisters were gone. And upon her face was the glare: the Sonia glare, the expression she would keep for the rest of her life, the one that is captured in those old photographs.

"The joke was," Bugby told me, while pouring Johnny Walker over ice and adding Coke, "she had sent death on an errand and it got lost on the way back. She wasn't sick another day in her life." Bugby sat down in his La-Z-Boy across from me, the sound of the ice in his glass mixing with the swish of his jogging suit. "Never. The old man said she never even got a cold all the time he knew her and even when she died, she just died. *Wishing well.*"

Sonia had wrestled death and had wounded it to the point where it retreated. Temporarily.

If Sonia had been spoiled before that miraculous night when she defeated death, her spoiling took on new levels afterward. Sonia had every material need a young girl could want: ponies, dolls, pedal cars, trips, swimming pools. She grew up healthy and spoiled and beautiful.

Then came her coming-out party.

Sonia Stephenson's coming-out party was *the* event of the season. The Stephensons' home was large, but Edwin had added a great room onto the back of the house, at Sonia's insistence, several years earlier to be used especially for this event and then, later, for her wedding—two events in which Sonia was very interested and of which she had every microscopic detail planned.

On the day of the party, after guests were ushered in, Sonia stood at the top of the formal staircase and waited for her introduction.

"I would like to formally introduce," Bugby had said to me in his best attempt at a proper Midwestern accent, "Miss Sonia Denning Stephenson."

A small orchestra played and Sonia made her way down the stairs, each step allowing her formal gown to flow all around her as if she were dressed in water. The room was full of wealthy landowners and neighbors who clapped and gaped lovingly. Sonia stepped down the final step and joined the large group of applauding people. She smiled her trademark smile, bowed to her parents, bowed to the guests, and then turned to bow to her long line of suitors. And then she stopped. Along the wall of the formal staircase were several softback chairs. These were where Sonia's suitors would sit and wait to dance with her. This was where the suitors would rise and acknowledge her and then each would have a dance and one of them she would marry; she had decided this long ago—by the end of the evening, she would know the man she would marry. This was not a common tradition; it was simply what Sonia had decided to do.

And, after taking only a few steps toward the chairs, Sonia stopped, transfixed. The chairs for her suitors were empty. Except for one.

"It's a typical Sonia thing to have blocked out the fact that frickin World War I was going on at the time. It didn't concern her until then. Sedalia was not that big of a place, and every eligible kid was drafted. Except my old man. He was a year too young to be drafted. *Wishing well.*"

Victor Bugby stood at his cue, looking upon the young Sonia Stephenson. He stood in his suit that was two sizes too big and his shoes that pinched his toes, but he stood and smiled.

"The old man was crazy for her and had been for years," Bugby said. "So he thought he'd go and at least get a dance with her. He knew that when everyone came back from overseas he'd never get close to her again, so this was his only chance. *Wishing well.*"

But Victor Bugby got more than a dance. Sonia Stephenson despised two words: *no* and *wait*. Sonia wanted to be married next year, and she *would* be married next year. She danced with Victor three times, and during the third dance, she told him to ask her to marry him.

"She even told him what to say and how to say it." Bugby laughed into his drink. "The old man had to go to her father during the party and ask—I can't remember exactly what it was, but it had a lot of *sirs* and *requesting permission of your daughter's hand,* yadda-yadda-yadda."

Sonia and Victor were married one year later in the same large room where they had first danced together. They honeymooned in New York City and, in a true test of Sonia's timing, they arrived in New York on the day the war ended.

If Sonia had regretted her decision to marry Victor instead of waiting until more eligible men returned from the war, she didn't acknowledge it. She went straight to work on having their ranch built. With Sonia's dowry, Mr. and Mrs. Victor Bugby purchased a large tract of land and began building a home and a commercial farm.

Victor did not know anything about farming, but he took to it because he wanted to please Sonia. Sonia ran the books and proved to be a brutal negotiator. Soon the Bugbys had one of the most successful farms in Missouri.

"And eventually Sonia became pregnant with me. *Wishing well.*"

If Sonia had a fault, a mental misfiring, like Bugby's *wishing well* tic, it was war. It wasn't the war itself; it was the concept that there was something out there so big, like a war, that could run over her plans and not even stop to apologize. The war had interfered with her coming-out party and now, when her little boy was 11 years old as her business was booming, another war might take her husband away. So Sonia decided to change her odds.

Although her family was wealthy, they had no true political pull, so there were no skids to grease to ensure that Victor would not be drafted. He couldn't even use the loophole that he should be exempt because he was running a farm, because it was a large commercial operation with a dozen or so hired hands.

But Sonia wasn't taking any chances. She came up with a plan to keep Victor out of the war—to keep the war from taking what was hers.

"Not because Sonia was so in love with him," Bugby said. "Or maybe she was, but the big part of it was that he was hers and nobody was going to take away what was hers. *Wishing well.*"

One night after dinner, Sonia presented Victor with a thick envelope and instructions. He was joining the Coast Guard. He was joining the Coast Guard and they were selling the farm and moving to Erie,

Pennsylvania, where he would be stationed. She had purchased a small hotel there that she would run until he returned.

"The old man didn't say anything. He just smiled and nodded. He would have done anything for her." So the Bugbys sold the farm and they set off for Erie, Pennsylvania.

"She didn't care. She never looked back." Sonia quickly began to look around the growing city of Erie. After the hotel, she purchased a dock, a diner, and a television repair shop. Sonia's business acumen was so sharp that these businesses prospered immediately.

A few years later, Victor had completed his tour with the Coast Guard and returned home. And in Sonia's last example of her mixed-up timing, she died exactly one week later.

"She died in her sleep," Bugby said. "And when the old man held her he found blisters under her clothes, like the kind she had when she was little. It was like the sickness had finally caught up with her. I've spoken to doctors and I don't know if that's true or not. She probably just died. *Wishing well.*"

Victor Bugby was devastated after the death of his wife. He didn't start drinking or gambling or fall into a depression, but he simply didn't know what to do. He didn't know what to do without Sonia telling him, so he would ask everyone, anyone, for advice—from what clothes to wear in the morning to what food to eat at night.

Victor did the best he could to run the businesses but soon realized he did not possess Sonia's business ability. He did, however, have the insight to sell the businesses while they were still profitable. All but one. The hotel.

The Hotel Denning was Bugby's childhood home. He was raised there. He helped his father check in guests, made reservations, carried bags, served food, and sat and visited with salesmen and families and sailors, all in the large parlor his mother had insisted on having. Every night, that parlor would fill with music and stories and laughter and warmth. He and his father lived in the house that Sonia had insisted upon, in the back of the hotel, but they spent most of their time in that parlor.

"It was a great time for a kid," Bugby said softly, looking past my shoulder and down the hall. "We always had guests. It was like one big, always-changing family. I loved it. *Wishing well.*"

The Hotel Denning remained an Erie landmark until the fire of 1978 wiped out all the buildings and the surrounding area. No one was hurt, but the hotel was destroyed.

"I was in the navy when it burned," Bugby told me.

Victor Bugby was depositing the fire insurance check at the Chase Bank of Erie on Flathing Street on March 3, 1978, after spending a morning with friends asking their advice on what he should do next, when a lone gunman walked into the bank. The thief got away with three thousand eighty-three dollars—and the life of Victor Bugby. The gunman was never caught.

Bugby always stops the story here and changes the subject. He may come back to it, but he never tells it without stopping, so there is a gap of time that goes unfilled. I'm not sure when exactly Bugby built the Denning Arms apartments after he got back from the navy. I only know that he built it on the original site of the Hotel Denning—on the site where he had lived with his father and laughed with guests in the large hotel parlor, on the site where Sonia Bugby had demanded that a hotel be placed.

I'm mentioning all of this about Bugby for a few reasons. First, because Divorce Court, the apartment complex, is my home and Bugby is my friend. Second, because in some perverse way I feel connected to Sonia and Victor and the Hotel Denning because I live here. And third, because right now, Bugby is missing.

It's not unusual for Bugby to be missing. Over the three years I've known him, he's gone missing four or five times: simply gone without a word and gone for a few weeks. Bugby has nothing to do with the day-to-day operations of either the apartments or the liquor warehouse, so he could be gone for months while everything kerchunks along just fine without him.

Now, the first time Bugby went missing—that's missing since I've known him; I'm sure there were plenty of times before that—was triggered when he read an article about this man who built a ship in the Canadian wilderness in the 1930s, miles from the nearest water, with the hope of getting back to Lithuania or someplace. Bugby bought a plane ticket and flew to see the ship, which was still rotting in the Canadian bush. He was gone a week that time.

One other time was after we were eating breakfast at the Broadway Diner and he saw in the paper a story about a flood someplace in Mexico that wiped out half a village. Bugby left that afternoon without a word and spent three weeks helping the town of Barra de Navidad rebuild.

Bugby's only been gone a few days this time, so who knows when he'll be back? He could be anywhere from Japan to Jersey. He could have heard a song, or seen a commercial, or read a gum wrapper, and that triggered the need to visit a polar ice field or help a widow in Paraguay harvest her crops.

Who knows?

I have my girls tonight and it's tradition to eat with Bugby on Thursdays. I have my girls three nights a week, or more—Catherine is wonderful about this—but on Thursdays we eat with Bugby. If Bugby isn't back by tonight, we'll do something else for dinner, but this has become one of our traditions and the girls will be disappointed.

Now, the Thursday tradition—I can't remember how it started exactly; Bugby just asked us over one Thursday and we kept going back—it's always the same. We walk over to Bugby's apartment around six. He greets us at the door and shuffles us into his dining room, which is packed with old mahogany furniture from the original hotel. He assures us that this week, this meal, will go better than the last one.

"I have something special for you tonight," he will announce. We'll sit and the girls will smile at each other. They will smile the way you do when you know something strange is about to happen but aren't sure exactly how strange it will get.

"I know what happened last week," he'll say. "So I've been thinking about this and I know you're going to like this one. *Wishing well.*" Bugby will then disappear and return with plates of food he knows the girls hate—plates of food that *everyone* hates—and he'll set them on the table. He'll set out fried liver or boiled pig's feet. He'll bring out chitlins or cow tongue. Once, he brought out a tray of barbecued chicken feet—don't ask me where in Erie you go to get barbecued chicken feet or how many defenseless chickens had to give their lives for the gag, but he did it. The girls will shriek and wrinkle their noses. They'll giggle and hide their faces and squirm and shake their heads.

Bugby will sit down and stuff his dish towel into the neck of his T-shirt to protect his jogging suit from stains. He'll cut himself off a large piece of tongue or scoop himself a healthy serving of chipped beef on toast. Then he'll lift a portion to his mouth and just as the first bite is about to be eaten, just as he is about to take in the horrible concoction, he will happen to look over at the girls and see that they are not eating.

"What?" he'll say in mock surprise. "Oh no. No, not again." The girls will laugh. Liz will pull her T-shirt over her face. Abby will giggle and move in close to me. "You don't like chipped beef on toast either?" The girls will sputter and smile and hide behind me and each other.

"I can't believe it," he will say, pulling his dish towel napkin from his shirt and tossing it angrily away. "How can you not like chipped beef on toast? It's good. *Wishing well.*" But the girls won't budge.

Bugby will rise from his chair. "I've been cooking all day!" he'll yell, and then he'll turn to me. "Why didn't you tell me they don't like chipped beef on toast? I thought all little girls liked chipped beef on toast. *Wishing well.*"

He'll lift his hands toward the sky in wonderment. He'll turn back to the girls in shock. "I go to all this trouble to make you a nice meal of chipped beef on toast and you won't even eat it?" He will storm out of the apartment. He will come back in and look for his car keys. He will sulk and mumble and try to find phone numbers for the correct government agencies to report little girls who won't eat their chipped beef on toast. He'll rant about what rude children he has in his home. What ungrateful children. And the girls will giggle and laugh and hide behind me.

Then, when he can take it no more, when he sees that he has once again failed, he'll announce defeat. "Well. You can't go away hungry." Bugby will pick up the bowls from the table and walk toward the kitchen. "I'll go see if I have some peanut butter or something." And he'll walk away mumbling—*I just can't believe it, perfectly good chipped beef on toast.* He will quickly return with one of his homemade pizzas or his baked pasta or his stuffed pork chops or one of the many other things he makes that the girls adore—all still hot from the oven. As all good props should be.

Then there will be more giggling and squirming.

"Okay," Bugby will say, tucking the dish towel back inside his shirt. "Next week I'll make you something you'll *really* like so we won't have to eat this stuff. *Wishing well.*"

And we'll eat and laugh. We'll speak in strange voices and we'll tell stories. We'll sing and we'll wonder. Just like in the parlor of the Hotel Denning. Just like a family.

I'll share the girls with Bugby on those Thursday nights, but the rest of the time I have them, they are mine exclusively. This—and I know you know this—is not because I am a good father. I am not.

Since the invention of the father, I am one of the most defective models ever to have come off the production line. I have robbed my children when I should have been building their future. I have lied to them when I should have been inspiring. I have embarrassed and humiliated them when I should have been instilling pride and integrity. I have shot them up with fear and squandered their birthright and gutted their name. I know all of this.

What I am is a selfish father. I did not return to Erie after prison because my daughters needed me; I returned because I desperately needed them. I returned because I can't belly laugh unless the three of us are belly laughing together. I can't sleep unless we are all collapsed on the three couches of my living room, with the television blaring in front of us. I can't read unless I am reading to them or they are reading to me. I can't see the tail of a firefly or hear the sound of a truck horn or the music of a windshield wiper properly unless we are all examining it together, marveling at it.

My best friends are eleven and nine. My girls. And although they would endure it if I vanished today, I would simply wind down and stop without them.

My oldest daughter, Abby, says it best: "You're not like a real dad." She giggles as the car bounces side to side to the beat of "Werewolves of London" as oncoming cars look on with caution. "You're like a twelve-year-old. With a license."

And I suppose there are worse things to be than a twelve-year-old with a license.

In fact, most of those worse things, I've already been.

Chapter 3

Far Below Prescott Mansion

| July 10, 1992 |

The *Erie Times News* is delivered daily to my door at Divorce Court, the apartment complex, building C, apartment 6, and has been each morning for the past two years. I eagerly await its delivery and poke my head out to the landing at least twice before the weird kid with the bangs slumps up the three flights of stairs and tosses the paper, which lands somewhere between the fourth step below my door and the spot directly at his feet. I've actually watched him look at the paper when it lands at his feet and then slump back downstairs without even trying to throw it again.

The *Erie Times News* is an important aspect of my daily ritual, a ritual that has nothing to do with reading the paper and everything to do with scanning it. I am scanning for two words and a picture: for the word *Walker* and the word *Roe* and for my mug shot. I am looking for me.

Each morning, I gather up the paper, which sometimes has unfolded and dominoed down a flight or two of stairs, and then I begin the examination for my name and my nefarious picture—no article can be complete without that mug shot. Any day that I do not find any mention of myself in the paper is a minor success, and in a world where there are no major successes, minor *is* major.

Now, I am currently working on a one-hundred-twenty-day record of not finding my name or picture in the pages of the *Erie Times News*—it would have been longer, but there was a piece a while back about a local real-estate mogul being investigated for fraud and, of course, I was mentioned in the sidebar.

When the paper finally arrived, I scooped it up and walked it in, past Liz and Abby who were getting ready for the day, and spread it out on the kitchen counter to be studied in a forensic manner. The initial scan showed no mention of me. *A possible one-hundred-twenty-one-day record, ladies and gentlemen; this is unofficial so please hold your tickets until the results are confirmed. Pause, pause, pause—flip, flip, flip—confirmed. The crowd goes wild.*

Yes.

One hundred twenty-one days for the newspaper, and about forty days for television—there was an E! channel piece on celebrity scandals that I caught while channel surfing one night.

Now, as far as hate mail goes, it's probably ten or maybe twenty days tops. I get negative mail all the time. I suppose I could change my address—I still keep the same PO box I had for every cartoon strip I wrote—but I won't. Most of the mail is from Clyde, my old producer, and Clyde-assisted others, so I don't count them, but occasionally I will get a letter from readers who tell me how disappointed they still are. Some of them, I actually respond to. I never respond to Clyde's. Legally, I know he's not allowed to contact me but I take some sick pleasure in knowing that someone hates me so much and that his hate has remained constant for two years. The other letters will stop eventually, but I imagine Clyde's will continue long after we have abandoned mail for video watch phones.

Now, the purpose of my newspaper ritual is not as self-absorbed as you may think. I do it to ensure that I haven't done anything stupid today, that there is no additional damage caused by the stupid stuff I did before—that some spark hasn't flamed up years later, causing a huge Walker Roe fire in Texas or Madrid. And since I have not yet discovered how to rewire myself—in fact, I have barely started to work on it—I also have not disappointed anyone new, so there is a vacuum of virtue by lack of depravity, which means there still is a chance of someday growing up to be a good father. One of those real, non-twelve-year-old-with-a-license type of fathers. The type of father who worries about his daughters' math grades, not about them hearing the women a few spaces behind them in the grocery line point to him and remark, *Hmm, I wonder if there's a picture of Daffy Duck on the twenty-dollar bills he's using,* while others in the line snicker or look away. At those times, I always pretend not to hear. Liz will look back—she isn't sure what's happening—but Abby always takes my hand and moves in closer, as if to protect her father from grocery-store bullies.

I close the newspaper and toss it in the garbage, reveling in the paradox that not long ago I would have read this same paper and actually been disappointed if I *didn't* see my name or picture in it—at that time, it would have been a publicity photo instead of a mug shot. I would walk down our driveway at the house on Tibett Terrace to get the paper and eagerly look for an interview I had given or if some recycled old news had been made new again by a press release I sent out. Standing in my T-shirt and shorts, I'd wave to busy neighbors on their way to offices in Erie, then leisurely head back in to my own office.

I spent the first forty years of my life trying to get my name *in* the newspapers and it looks like I will probably spend the next forty trying to keep it *out.*

With the newspaper properly checked and a new indoor world record safely in hand, I turned my attention to the rest of the hectic morning. It's Friday and that's always a crazy morning for us. I have to get the girls up and fed and to day camp now that it's summer and then get myself to work and then pick the girls back up at Catherine's for the weekend—they stay at Catherine's until I get out of work.

In the center of the living room of the apartment at Divorce Court, the apartment complex, the ladybug-shaped tent shuddered. Liz had recently discovered modesty and has begun getting dressed inside the tent that the three of us slept in last night. We tried sleeping in the bathtub again; this is a goal of ours, but we just can't make it all night without giving up and heading for the tent.

At Divorce Court, the apartment complex, building C, apartment 6, Abby and Liz have a real bedroom with two beds and end tables and matching lamps. They never sleep there. Instead, we all sleep in the living room, either in the tent or on the couches—we each have a couch of our very own. When the girls are gone, I sleep on a couch, too, partly because I miss them and partly because I never bought myself a bed. The second bedroom holds my clothes and all my encyclopedias and books, but besides that it's really just a big play room.

The living room has three couches that we each picked out ourselves. These couches frame the walls. Mine is a black faux leather monstrosity that squeaks and sputters when you sit on it. Abby's is a dark red overstuffed cloth couch with large cushions that we lift partially up and down as if the couch is trying to eat us. Liz has this white furry model that resembles some strange stuffed creature. Liz's couch is always the dragon or the cloud city or the unicorn when we play. These couches are where we sleep and play and eat—we try to eat on Abby's or my couch since white fur is not exactly stain resistant—and read and talk. And since no adult besides Bugby ever comes in here, Divorce Court, the apartment complex, building C, apartment 6, looks more like a furniture showroom or a teenager's clubhouse than a place where real people live.

This is home.

Liz crawled out of the ladybug tent that sits in the small space that is devoid of couches in the center of the room.

"Done," she said. Her hair flopped in front of her face and she blew it out of her way. She had successfully changed into her school uniform, with all the buttons done and her shoes on the correct feet. Her hands were stretched out to her side as if she had just completed a perfect three-point dismount and the judges were compiling her score.

Because God has a sense of humor when it comes to children, Liz looks like me—she is small and compact with black hair and dark eyes, and Abby looks like her mom—willowy, tall, and graceful.

I have not mentioned what Rachel looked like—Rachel, my daughter who was killed—and I'm not going to speak much of her now. In fact, I may not mention her again at all. But I will tell you that Rachel was Elizabeth's twin. Her identical twin. So, I'm sure the first thing you're thinking is, when I look at Liz, do I see Rachel? People always ask me that question, so you have a right to ask. The answer is no. When I look at Liz, I see Liz, and as wrong as it is, as morally reprehensible as it may be, I rarely speak about and try not to even think of Rachel, and if you could wipe my mind clean of every Rachel thought, if you had a way where I would forget her very existence, I'd ask you to push the button and do it. I'd beg you to.

"Dad," Liz said, her hands still outstretched.

I looked over and took my cue. "And the crowds go wild here at ladybug stadium where Miss Elizabeth Roe has just emerged from the giant ladybug after defeating the enemies of the princess and also landing a perfect backwards somersault."

"Thank you." Liz bowed to the imaginary audience and blew slow-motion kisses to all. "Thank you. Thank you."

"And then Miss Elizabeth Roe is attacked by a giant space squid," Abby said, sticking her head out of the bathroom, her mouth still full of toothpaste. "And the blast makes her . . ." She spat toothpaste into the sink. "It leaves her standing in her butterfly underwear."

"Dad." Liz pointed to her older sister.

"Stop teasing your sister with imaginary space animals that embarrass her in front of her imaginary audience."

Abby laughed and spat again. "I imaginary apologize."

"Good." Liz went back to blowing kisses to the crowd.

"Hey." Abby wiped her face on the Sleeping Beauty hand towel and walked toward the couch to retrieve her backpack. "Ya know what I was thinkin'?" Abby stopped to wrap her soft brown hair behind her and tie it with a cloth-covered rubber band. When she does tasks like this on her own, grownup tasks like putting her own hair in a ponytail, I can't believe how old she's getting. She's eleven already and I wonder how many more years it will be before she'll think sleeping on a red sofa in the living room is no longer fun. How many more years will it be before she's older than I am? More mature than me? How many more years until she will no longer protect me from my past but instead use it against me? When she brings home a boy I don't like and there is a fight and I hear the words, *Yeah, well at least he didn't go to prison?* Door slams. Car engine starts.

"I was thinkin' about Abercrombie."

"Yeah, Abercrombie." Liz smiled, grabbing her own backpack from her couch.

"Where's he been?"

"Abercrombie? That's funny, because I was just reading about him in the paper," I said.

"Abercrombie, Abercrombie, Abercrombie." Liz chanted the name as I held the door open and ran through the morning checklist: paper, breakfast, teeth, book bags—check. Liz marched out the door after her sister and we all headed down the red-carpeted stairs of building C. "Abercrombie, Abercrombie," Liz continued.

The story of Abercrombie began when Liz asked me once why she didn't have a little brother. Instead of me saying, *Well, sweetheart, because Daddy went to prison and Mommy married your teacher,* I told her that she did have a little brother but he was a little different and he lives here with me. He sleeps in the walls of Divorce Court, the apartment complex, and his name is Abercrombie.

Abercrombie is small and grayish and has suction cups at the ends of his fingers and cones where his ears should be. Abercrombie can walk up walls and slither down drains and hear the sound a bug's wing makes on a distant star.

Abercrombie can use his suction-cup hands to hold on to speeding airplanes or to catch bullets. His bug-like hearing can pick up events an hour or so before they actually happen, and, if it wasn't for Abercrombie, Divorce Court, the apartment complex, would have been cinders long ago.

It's great having a famous son.

Over the past few years, Abercrombie has battled the Butter People of Zool, when their ship crashed behind the playground. He has outsmarted the Countess of Backward Clocks, Chicken Rodriguez, Big Daddy Dog Walker, and a myriad of other made-up villains whose names and reasons for wanting to destroy all of Erie only Abby can now remember—her memory is great for stuff like that.

Liz stomped off the last step as if trying to teach the ground a lesson.

"Everyone knows," I began, holding the door open as my daughters stepped out into the morning, "that the most trained and most cunning fighters in the world, the strongest and most daring protectors, the most stealthy spies and the most vicious warriors known to mankind . . ." We arrived at the car and we all poured in. I allowed the girls to be busy putting their seatbelts on before I spoke my next line: ". . . are the gophers." I opened my mouth to continue and allowed Liz to interrupt me.

"Gophers?" Liz laughed. I can always count on Liz to come in right on cue.

"Of course," I said, looking to Liz and then to Abby. "What? You're kidding me, right?" Liz's freckled face was scrunched up in disbelief and Abby had her, *Go ahead, I'm waiting* smile on her face.

"Of course, gophers. What are they teaching you at that fancy private school of yours?" I sighed. Then, acting annoyed at the need to stop my story and go over what I assumed my daughters already knew, I resumed.

"For hundreds of years, gophers have protected humans against evil. They are perfect fighters. Subtle. Quiet. Unassuming, but powerful. Bloodthirsty but loyal. And very, very dangerous."

"Gophers?" Liz asked.

"Sheesh," I snapped. "How do you think we won World War II? How do you think we landed on the moon? How do you think we get the cream inside Twinkies?"

"Gophers?" Liz answered.

"Exactly," I said.

"So." Abby smiled, crossing her arms. "What do these gophers have to do with Abercrombie?

Yeah, I thought. *What do they have to do with Abercrombie?*

"It's not that simple," I answered, stalling. "Gophers are wild, vicious beasts. They would tear your throat out as soon as look at you. The reason gophers are our protectors is that a device was created years ago to allow one person, only one, the gift to communicate with the Gopher Queen."

"There's a gopher queen?"

"Of course there's a gopher queen." I looked out the window and allowed the moment to build. "And since this device will allow only one human being to talk to her, it's very important that it's the *right* person. A person who is not only good, but strong. A person who is smart as well as fast, with reflexes of lightning and nerves of pure steel."

"Let me guess," Abby smiled smugly. "Abercrombie?"

"Abercrombie?" I huffed. "Are you crazy? The Gopher Queen will only talk to a female. A woman. She'd tear Abercrombie to bits if he tried it."

"Then who?" Liz asked.

"There's only one person who has used the device for years to form a partnership with the queen." Another moment passed. Then I looked into the rearview mirror to emphasize my point.

"Brave women have died trying to speak to the queen on their own, thinking they were strong enough, brave enough, to approach her."

"We saw gophers at the zoo." Abby smiled, not in a mocking way, but in a *You can handle a minor challenge like this* way. "They just sat there and didn't attack us."

"Pffff." I snorted. "Those are drone gophers. Peasants. Anyone can handle them. They're not fighting gophers."

"So, who's the brave lady who knows . . . who knows where this gopher thingee is?" Liz asked.

"There is only one person alive who is that strong."

"You said that. Who?"

Another moment fell for effect.

"Mrs. Dreesly."

"Mrs. Dreesly?!" Abby laughed. Liz followed.

Mrs. Dreesly is an old woman who lives in building A. She is approximately one hundred fifty-seven years old. She collects salt and pepper shakers and always calls me Brian.

"Yes." I paused for effect. "Mrs. Dreesly."

I began . . .

In a secret control room far below Prescott Mansion . . .

Lila Devamore leaned against her cane and looked up at the large computer screen that covered the front wall of the control room.

"There." Lila pointed to an area of the world map. The technicians, seated in a row of monitors and keyboards, quickly adjusted the satellite's lens to zoom in on the area where Lila was pointing. The image became larger.

"Closer," she said. There were more clicks and the screen zoomed in further, but it revealed only water—and plenty of it. "Once more," Lila said, and the screen changed once again, showing a craft moving quickly over the water—a ship that cut effortlessly through the moving surf.

"It's a ship!" a technician yelled out.

"Not just any ship." Lila turned and slowly climbed the stairs in the middle of the room. Her joints cracked and moaned until she arrived at the large leather chair in the back and sat down with a slight harumph. *She leaned forward on her cane and frowned at the screen. The image zoomed in again and then stopped. There was a collective gasp from the technicians as if all the air from their lungs had been startled out of them at the exact same time. A bubble of silence was followed by worried mumbles.*

On the screen, the ship could be clearly seen, along with its flag: a vulture clutching a minute hand. It was the insignia of the Countess of Backward Clocks.

"Hello, Ida," Lila Devamore whispered to the image on the screen.

"But she . . ." one technician started to say.

"Maybe it's not her?" another technician nervously asked.

"Oh, it's her." Lila leaned harder on her cane and stared at the image. The ship mocked the waves that pounded against it and cut through the water of Lake Erie like an attacking shark.

"Why is she there?"

"What does she want?"

"If she's there . . ." Lila pointed with the black knob of her cane to the display showing the ship's coordinates. "She wants the device that will allow her to speak to the Gopher Queen. She's always wanted it."

The agents all looked at each other. No one wanted to be the first to correct Lila.

"Ma'am," one of them said reluctantly, "there are only two people in the world who know where the device is. The president and the king of Toline."

Another technician typed on a keyboard and then checked a display. "And neither one is currently anywhere near that ship's location, ma'am."

"No," Lila said, leaning back in the chair and pulling a phone from her belt. "She's not after the location of the device." Lila began to dial. "She knows who the last person was to have it. The person who's had it for the last sixty years." Lila put the phone to her ear. "She's after Dreesly."

Lila listened as the phone rang. Then a soft series of clicks and whistles could be heard on the other end.

"Hello, Abercrombie," Lila said. "Busy?"

We arrived at Holy Cross Day Camp and I pulled into the dropoff lane and waited my turn.

"Do more," Liz yelled.

"Tonight," I answered.

"Where's Abercrombie now?"

"You'll see."

"I hate that Count . . ." Liz stopped herself. "I don't like that Countess of Backward Clocks."

We pulled up inside the yellow-painted block that signaled it was safe to drop off here. The girls undid their seatbelts and reached forward to kiss a hand or an elbow or whatever body part of mine was closest and then hopped out of the car. They walked toward the school and I coasted slowly until they were inside the building. Then I drove away.

The distance from Holy Cross to Mathis and Corbin, my employer, is only four miles. I could say that I chose my job because it was close to the girls' school/day camp, but really, it was just luck. After I was released from Lewisburg, I simply made a list of all the potential employers that answered one question correctly: *Will you hire me?* Those who answered this question incorrectly, I refused to work for, and since there was only one company that answered correctly, the decision was easy.

Mathis and Corbin is the fine publisher of educational textbooks since 1941. It was started by Elijah Corbin and Lawrence Mathis. There is very little information on these two in the company literature, only that the company is managed by a private holding company in Toronto—nothing on the history of these two men, just that Mathis and Corbin was formed in 1941.

I asked Bugby about Mathis and Corbin once—if either of them had ever stayed at the Hotel Denning or if his father had ever had any dealings with them.

"Someday," Bugby said, smiling, "I'll tell you a few stories about Elijah Corbin. *Wishing well.*" And then he added, "It's interesting stuff." So, either Bugby has some information that's too juicy to dish out all at once—stories that need to marinate a bit—or he had never heard of either Mathis or Corbin and just wanted to see how long I would chase the breadcrumbs.

Mathis and Corbin's corporate headquarters—and its one and only facility—is in Erie, Pennsylvania. We're talking textbooks here, not trade publishing, so there is no need to be located on New York's Publishers Row. Here, if the right agent does not have lunch with the right editor,

Introduction to Life, Earth, and What's All Around Us: An 8th-Grade Earth Science Primer will still go kerchunking out of the presses and will still be purchased by schools and ignored by fourteen-year-olds across the nation.

The four-mile trek from Holy Cross to Mathis and Corbin was fairly uneventful—don't try using the stuck-in-traffic excuse in this part of the world unless there's five feet of snow outside, and in Erie, Pennsylvania, five feet of snow does occur, sometimes even in the winter. I pulled into the parking lot twenty-four minutes early.

In the three years I've worked here, I've never been late. Not once. This is easy when I have the girls and drop them off only four miles away, but I am even earlier on the days I don't have them. In three years of winter storms that dump a foot of snow an hour, in three years of power outages where you need to take cold showers in the dark, I have never been late. And considering I've never had a job you couldn't do from home while wearing pajamas and a Buffalo Bills baseball cap, I think that's pretty good.

But in actuality, it's simply another example of the wacky way I am wired—not an actual line of code, since I'm still identifying those lines, but an interesting wiring response. A wiring riddle.

The first few months as a new employee of Mathis and Corbin, I consciously came to work early for several reasons: to display a good example, to allow my coworkers additional desensitizing time—to show them that although I am that convicted felon you've read about, the chance of me sneaking up on you while you are taking your lunch nap and removing your kidney for a quick black-market sale is minimal—and to guide myself through the workday routine, a schedule all my inner clocks are unaccustomed to. In the before-time, I would wake at four A.M. and write and block out camera shots until around nine or ten, then quit for the day. Catherine and I would have the entire day to ourselves.

I was early for work the first few weeks here, and then for the entire first month. And then for the entire first year. Each day, the collection of early days piled up, until just one day late would topple the whole stack. Each day, each day, each day, one more, one more, one more, and now it will only require one, just *one* day, to—WHAP!—bring it all down.

I've talked to many people—and had psychiatrists and counselors interview me—about *the seal.*

The seal is what is referred to in psychological circles as that moment when you cross a moral or physical boundary: that first murder, that first infidelity, that first time siphoning off from the company's pension fund.

Do you know what happens immediately after that first time? Do you know what follows just after breaking that seal and stepping over that moral line?

Nothing. Nothing happens.

You are not struck by lightning. Sirens do not wail toward you. The finger of God does not flash down from heaven to smite you down. Nothing happens. You've crossed that line and you've survived—because no one gets caught the first time, or at least no one gets caught *right away* the first time. And once it's done, once nothing happens, the second time is easier, and then the third, and soon you're in a pattern where you don't even think about it any longer. The next thing you know, you are making mental notes such as *After burying the hitchhiker's body in the woods, remember to stop at the store and pick up Cocoa Puffs and cheese slices.*

That's why rehabilitation is so difficult—because the seal has already been broken; we have lost our crime virginity. If they could surgically mend the thing back before they kick us out of prison, our odds would increase.

So here's the insanity. If I am late for work once, that seal, that unimportant seal, is broken. So I can be late again. Then again. Then maybe I sneak out of work early once. Then maybe I have a few days where I don't show up at all. And since that seal is broken, what's the reason to keep other seals intact? Maybe reaching this deadline is no longer important or plagiarizing these few pages is no big deal. Then I lose the job and I lose the girls and then I start to do stupid things out of desperation—because desperation is what fuels most sins and what powered my own.

Now, here lies the quandary. Is all of this superstition, or boundary patrol? Is it discipline, or obsessive-compulsive disorder? Because an alcoholic can never drink again, should a pathological seal-breaker such as myself never break another seal? And because I don't know the answer to this, I will not take the chance. This particular seal will remain intact for as long as I can possibly keep it that way.

Now, these ramblings about seals and moral boundaries—you shouldn't take them too seriously. It's just introspection mixed in with cartoonist backwash, an occupational—or former occupational—hazard. It is the ability to take minor observations and retool them so you will spend $12.95 to purchase a Walker Roe videotape of these thoughts and think me brilliant for identifying them. *Don't pay any attention to the fact that I have not come up with any new ideas or concepts in years, folks; just turn your attention to the human-nature trivia I have laid out for you in the center ring.*

But, if nothing else, this all emphasizes that the odds are that *this*, *now*, is provisional. Temporary. A finger in the dike and it won't be long before someone discovers there is no music coming out of *this* toaster. You can "fake it until you make it" for just so long, and unless a change, a real rewiring change, occurs, I'll be popping toast all over Erie.

I was sorting all this out as I walked through the cool air of the lobby of Mathis and Corbin. The receptionist, Ann, wasn't in yet and I walked past her empty desk to my cubicle.

This cubicle where I work now was actually my second choice. Jenny Locke, head of human resources, told me there were three cubicles to choose from when I first started—one located directly behind the receptionist's desk and two others in the middle of the bull pen, and I could have any of them.

"This one will be fine," I told Jenny, dropping my laptop bag on the chair of the cubicle right behind the receptionist desk. This front cubicle was open and exposed; it could be seen by anyone in the glassed offices to the side, by most of the bullpen behind it, as well as by anyone coming into the lobby. *I've got nothing to hide here, folks,* it screamed. *I'm not in a secluded corner sacrificing farm animals or making calls to my bookie.*

Jenny frowned and looked at the cubicle I chose.

"You know," she said, noticing that this cubicle was not only the first cubicle to be seen by visitors walking in, but was also close enough for me to jam a shiv into the ribs of the receptionist, "I just remembered, Raymond was going to take this one." She shuffled me back to a different cubicle, somewhere in the middle of the bullpen, visible but away from visitors and away from the temptation to shank secretaries.

"Okay," I said enthusiastically. "Great." And I moved into this cubicle and have been here ever since. Incidentallly, the cubicle directly behind Ann is still empty.

I sat down and bumped my mouse awake. The display on the desk lit up. I began the routine of checking messages and looking at my schedule.

There were only three meetings today: two pre-production meetings and one pub-board meeting, which made it a light meeting day. Some days, you went from meeting to meeting and the cubicle was simply a place to keep your lunch.

Pre-production meetings are planning meetings, launch meetings, when a book is preparing to fly from the nest toward schools and libraries across the nation. And pub-board meetings are where all departments get together to decide on new books. If pre-production is the wedding, then pub-board is that candlelit dinner where Mildred tells Harold she wants to have another baby.

I slogged my way through my emails and faxes, and I smelled Phoebe before I saw her—not *her* so much, but her coffee—and when I looked behind me she wasn't at her desk. The smell was definite, though. Phoebe didn't like the mocha-latte-cappa-choca coffees that most Americans drank. She liked Cuban or East African coffees—thick black motor oil that you could grout a stone path with. I turned back toward my screen just as Phoebe was pulling her hand away from the cup she was attempting to leave on my desk without being spotted.

"Ah, shoot," she said in her thick Brazilian accent. "Another second or two."

Phoebe was tall and thin with skin the color of the coffees she liked. And, like Bugby with his jogging suits, Phoebe was always wearing some sort of floppy turtlenecky sweater thing. Summer or winter, some piece of loosely woven wool that looked as if it was minutes from unraveling and turning back into yarn sprang up from whatever blouse or dress she was wearing and hung slack around her neck.

"I told ya the next time I went to Cisar's I'd bring ya a cup." She leaned into the wall of the cubicle, wrapping her fingers around the warm cup she held. "So ya can see what yer missin' with that silly stuff ya drink."

Phoebe was born in the city of São Félix, in Brazil.

"That means Saint Felix," she had once told me. And it was there at the university that she had met her husband, Elan. After being married only a few months, Elan was offered a teacher's assistant position in the United States at Behrend College in Erie. It didn't pay much, but part of the compensation allowed him to attend classes and work on his Ph.D. So Elan worked and attended Behrand and Phoebe worked at Mathis and Corbin, policing for dangling participles and patrolling for misplaced modifiers.

I pulled the lid off the coffee cup and the fumes hit my eyes and nose, causing me to blink and jerk away.

"Oh, stop it now," she snapped.

I held my breath and took a small sip of the hot liquid.

Once, in college, my housemates and I had bought beer called Pig's Head Ale. It was three dollars a case. The greatest thing about this beer was that if you could choke one down, if you could actually finish just one bottle, you would skip the whole drunken process and move directly to the hangover; you were nauseated and had a headache, you were throwing up and had chills. It was the most economical beer there ever was.

Sipping this drain fluid of Phoebe's reminded me of that. If I could drink an entire cup of it, there would be no need for it to contain caffeine because I would be awake and alert all day just trying to get the experience behind me as well as trying to get the taste out of my mouth.

"Is this stuff legal?" I grimaced.

"Of course."

"I mean, in this country?"

"What's wrong with ya?" she said. "It's good." She said it in the same way that Bugby said those very words when he was trying to get the girls to eat barbecued chicken feet. Phoebe slapped my shoulder and walked back to her desk and I continued answering messages and updating schedules.

Of course, what I did not know then and would not know until the following morning when I read about it in the *Erie Times News*, was that right at that moment, give or take a few minutes, when all my thoughts were on the day ahead and what movies the girls and I would rent that evening—as well as how to dispose of the cup of Phoebe's coffee with minimal environmental impact—was that more then twelve hundred miles away, the Canadian police were pulling from the Shubenacadie River the body of Lester Bugby.

Chapter 4

The Curse of the Zombie Paperboy

| July 11–12, 1992 |

A tidal bore is simply stubborn water. Rude waves. It is a white herd of liquid that slams against the natural egress of a river—which is flowing downstream to meet it—but the bore wants to go that way, the wrong way, up a one-way river, and it forces its way into the natural flow of water, determined to get past it. The bore is a gang of liquid that shoulders and punches and leans through the current as it climbs back, miles back. The bore, this creature comprised only of water and might, travels upstream as fast as a man can walk until it finds itself back where it came from. It is water swimming back to spawn. Twice a day, the bore fights the river, and twice a day, it wins.

I was naive to such events before researching how Bugby had died. But understanding these things was essential to understanding even the thinnest version of what had happened to him.

This piecemeal approach was the only way to know, partly because that series of phone calls that is normally triggered when tragedy strikes—*Ted? I'm sorry to bother you this early but did you see the paper? Your cousin Lester died*—did not occur. Bugby was the last of his bloodline, with no family, even distant, left alive and no close friends that I knew of. The police would not have answered any questions—even if I had been brave enough to call—and I couldn't call the newspaper because I was currently involved in my own quixotic war against the media. So, the only avenue was to take what the *Erie Times News* gave me and figure out the rest on my own.

And that's what I did. That Saturday began, as all days did, with the reading of the *Erie Times News*.

It was early and the girls were still asleep in the ladybug tent. I looked out the front door peephole twice. Nothing. The weird kid with bangs hadn't arrived yet. I was turning to get another cup of coffee when, responding by instinct—that sense of feeling a new presence rather than seeing it—I looked back through the peephole. There he was, slowly slithering up toward the landing. I studied him as all curious people study something strange and wild, through the safety of wood and glass—*As you can see, the Slumping Banged Newsy is slowly climbing the stair formation in front of us. He will soon extract a paper from his pouch and drop it, a sign of territory as well as a hope for a nice Christmas tip. Oooh, there he goes. And now he'll head back down the stairs. It is rare to capture this on film. How very exciting . . .*

I watched the weird kid with the bangs slump back downstairs and waited—not really sure why—until he was out of sight and I heard the building door shut behind him. Then I opened my door and retrieved the paper, beginning the scanning ritual as I walked back in.

It's a beautiful day here at Keep Your Name Out of the Papers Stadium, folks, and as the judges make their way to the booth we have a possible one-hundred-twenty-two-day record . . .

Signal stop.

Go back.

Go back.

I flipped back two pages, allowed my mind to take me to what it was trying to show me—like Lassie trying to let me know that Timmy had fallen in the well—and there it was.

The piece was short. A blurb, really, more than a piece.

Body of Erie Man Found in Canada

By Jules West

Staff Writer

Saturday, July 11, 1992

Erie businessman Lester Bugby, owner of the Denning Arms Apartments, the Mega-Liquor Warehouse, and Denning Self-Storage, was found dead in the Shubenacadie River of Nova Scotia, Canada, at 8:00 A.M. on Friday, July 10.

> Canadian authorities are working with the U.S. and Canadian border patrol to determine how long Mr. Bugby has been in the country as well as investigating his death.
>
> Although Mr. Bugby was not registered with any of the rafting groups in the area during the past week, he was found wearing a rafting life vest and safety helmet.

Now, there are moments in life when time is elastic, almost liquid, and we speed up while everything around us remains constant. When Rachel died and I received the call to come back from the business trip I was on, the three-hour plane ride from New York to Erie lasted close to nine years. Pain can do that. And when pain is dammed up, it becomes septic and when you are strapped in a plane while your daughter is lying dead and all the world, except you, is near her, that poison can make time stop completely.

I once did a cartoon version of the Kübler-Ross Model for an educational film. It tells about the five stages we pass through during grief: denial, anger, bargaining, depression, and acceptance. With my quitting, negative, *surrender first and then get details later* personality, I always skip all four stages and move right to acceptance. And then depression.

When a mere phone call told me my daughter was dead four hundred miles away, offering no proof or corroboration, I accepted it. And when a three-by-three article on page four told me that my friend was dead twelve hundred miles away, I accepted that, too.

I just accepted it.

You can do nothing. You can ask nothing. So that is what you do. You wait and you bleed and you apply just enough pressure to keep that bleeding from killing you.

I read the short article in the *Erie Times News* a second time; *Your friend is dead and that's all I'll tell you,* it said.

I looked at the ladybug tent in between the couches and there was no movement; the girls were not awake yet. I looked back to the article. *Bugby is dead and you should call Catherine before telling the girls,* it said this time.

I looked at the clock and decided I would give Catherine another hour before waking her. I could control when Abby and Liz received this one piece of bad news. I sort of messed up on that *Oh, by the way, Daddy's been arrested* one. More waiting. And I read the piece one more time. *Yes, you are now alone, you self-involved bastard. I knew this would have to involve you somehow. Don't worry about your dead friend, just how this involves you, right? How does . . .*

And I shut the paper.

Now, that hour between reading the article and calling Catherine was actually two and a half months long—shorter than that, really, because I didn't wait the entire hour and called just forty-two minutes later—so two months long. And I didn't realize until I had called Catherine just how goofy it all sounded.

"Your landlord died?" Catherine said, barely awake.

"Yeah, in Canada; the guy we always have dinner with on Thursdays."

There was a pause. "And you want to take the girls to Canada?"

It was early. Catherine was never her true self until 10:00.

"No, I just found out he died and wanted to tell the girls."

"Tell them," she said sleepily. "That you'll have to move?"

"No," I said, and then wondered if I *would* have to move—*there we go again; the body isn't even cold yet and you're worried about renting a U-Haul.* "I just want to go ahead and tell the girls that he died, but wanted to make sure it was okay with you before I did."

Catherine had long ago given up on me shocking her. So, having her ex-husband call her at 8:15 on a Saturday morning to ask if it was all right to tell the girls that Daddy's landlord is dead didn't even tickle the tote board, so to speak.

"Sure, Walker," she said patiently. "Whatever you think is best."

After getting off the phone with Catherine and while the girls were still asleep, I walked into the other bedroom and hit the encyclopedias.

When I looked up the Shubenacadie River—I had to go back and get the *Erie Times News* in order to know how to spell it—the entry mentioned the tidal bore. *See also Tidal bore, North America.* Then I spent the next twenty minutes educating myself, reading articles and accounts of the Bay of Fundy tidal bore. When this was done, I had a hunch and grabbed last week's *TV Guide* and looked up the listings for PBS—Bugby's favorite television channel; he complained that Discovery only had three series anymore.

It didn't take long.

At 8:00 P.M. the previous Monday, when Bugby would have been on his last Jack Daniel's and Coke, there was a program on called "Lunar Fingers: The Mystery of the Tidal Bore."

That was it. Bugby had seen the program at 8:00 P.M., probably booked the tickets with his travel agent—who was accustomed to receiving calls from him at all hours—that night, and left the next day. I had waved at him early Monday evening when I was coming in, so it couldn't have been before that.

When my thirty minutes of distraction were over, my own tidal bore of grief hit me for the first time. I just kept trying to picture in my mind the tidal bore that ran up the Shubencadie River from the Bay of Fundy, wondering if Bugby got to see it before he died. And for the first time in over two to three years, even with my two girls just a few feet from me, I felt alone. I felt completely alone. And frightened out of my mind.

I went to the closet and opened the door and looked at the stacks of shoe boxes, some too painful to ever open again, and picked up the box that was third from the top. Toward the bottom of the box, under movie tickets and drawings and pictures, was a letter.

A few weeks before I was to be released from Lewisburg, I had written to the management of the Denning Arms Apartments and three other apartment complexes in Erie. It wasn't standard procedure to need to ask permission to live in an apartment complex, but I knew my situation was unique and I wanted to be honest and not try to sneak my way in. I also didn't want to get settled in with the girls and then a few months later get evicted when they realized who I was—and why there was a CNN truck in their parking lot.

There were four ads in the *Erie Times News* for apartments that looked big enough for the girls and me. I sent all four a letter stating who I was and that I was moving back to Erie upon my release and would like to see the apartments listed. Three of the letters came back the same way—*We are unfortunately rented out at this time; however, we can put you on a waiting list, blah, blah, blah.*

Although Bugby had nothing to do with the day-to-day operations of Divorce Court, the apartment complex, when my letter came in they must have run it up the food chain a bit and asked his opinion. When I received Bugby's letter, it was different from the others. His was one short and simple paragraph.

I opened the letter and read it. It was handwritten on Bugby's personal stationery.

> Dear Mr. Roe,
> Do you like chili? I make some real nice chili. Why don't you stop by my place, Denning Arms Apartments, you know the address, building B, apartment 4, on the Thursday when you get out and we'll have some chili and talk?
> Bugby

I remember reading it for the first time and then reading it over and over. I remember seeing Bugby's neat, tight scrawl, seeing his stationery with his address and wondering what the significance was of the small stone wishing well in the upper-right-hand corner of the paper. Even before I met him, this letter meant possibility. It meant hope.

The day I was released, I pushed through the few press trucks waiting for me and met with Bugby before I even saw the girls. We ate chili. It was great chili and we talked and laughed and were friends before I left.

There was stirring now in the ladybug tent. Abby popped her head out, her hair sprawling over her face, and headed for the bathroom. A few moments later Liz followed. They both came over to sleepily hug me good morning—a nice tradition; I'm not sure how it began but I'm not complaining—then they flipped on the television and collapsed on their respective coaches.

I tried to wait until they were awake, but couldn't. I walked in and turned the television off. I sat with Abby and told Liz to come over, telling them I had something we needed to talk about.

I told them what I knew. That sometime on Tuesday, Bugby went to a place in Canada called Nova Scotia. There was a tidal bore there that he wanted to see. Abby leaned on my shoulders with her eyes closed and Liz sat across my lap with her eyes only half-closed.

I stopped stalling.

"I don't know much," I said. "Just that he's not coming back." They didn't move or stir. "He died up there."

A full three seconds passed as the information filtered through their half-awake brains, and then Abby sat up and looked at me. "He died?"

"Yes."

"How?"

"Don't know yet. In a river."

"He died?" Liz asked, wanting to make sure that her answer was the same as her sister's.

"Yeah. I don't know much else."

Abby fell into my arms. She cried. She cried and I tried to. I tried to bellow out great barks of crying, to will the tears to come. But none did. The tears hadn't come for Rachel and they wouldn't come for Bugby. I couldn't give either one of them even that much.

"He was so nice," Abby wailed into my shoulder. "He was so nice to us." Her cries became louder. "He was so nice. Like a gram," she sobbed. "Like a grandpa."

As I looked over to Liz, she was silent. She had moved off of Abby's red couch, and was standing a few feet in front of me, just staring. A defiant stare. An angry stare. She said nothing, just slashed holes into me with her eyes. Her shoulders were drawn, her fists were clenched, and her head tipped slightly forward as if she were ready to charge. She stood there for several minutes. Wordless. Then she turned and went back inside the ladybug tent.

Time moved at a half pace for the rest of the day. It was as if we were trying to run through maple syrup and kept getting tangled and tripped and stuck. We stayed in the apartment. We watched TV. We did our laundry for the week and folded it, but we did so without singing the folding song. Abby and I played some chess but we didn't taunt each other like we normally do. Liz spent the day inside the ladybug tent.

That night we all walked outside to go get pizza and all three of us looked toward Bugby's empty parking spot at the exact same time. Then, just a moment later, we all looked up at the closed curtain of his dining room window.

"Are there ghosts up there now?" Liz asked.

"Ghosts?" I hit the remote key to the car and we all piled in my Corolla. "No way. Abercrombie wouldn't allow it."

Liz buckled her seatbelt. "Abercrombie's not real."

I turned back and waited for her to meet my eye. "It's a story, honey," I said. "It's just like any other story. It's as real as you . . ."

"But if he was real he could've . . ." She looked away then looked back at me. "He could've . . ."

She stopped. She looked up at the apartment window and then back to me. And then, after eleven hours of holding it in, after eleven hours of embracing anger instead of grief, Liz cried. She bawled. Then Abby started to cry. They both unbuckled their seatbelts and crawled in the front seat on top of me. I tried to cry. We held each other and we stared at Bugby's dark window. We thought of Bugby and laughed and told stories and we realized we weren't really hungry after all. We fell asleep in the front seat and woke up long after the dark had rolled in. Then we sleepily walked back upstairs.

The next morning, the girls were asleep on their couches instead of in the ladybug tent and I tiptoed gingerly around the apartment as I waited for the weird kid with the bangs to deliver the *Erie Times News*. But this time I was looking for more information on Bugby, not caring if I showed up on every single page.

The weird kid with the bangs was later than usual. What's wrong with that kid anyway? Not only is he later each day but he moves as if he had committed some horrible sin centuries earlier and must now spend eternity delivering the *Erie Times News* until the curse is broken. Slumping forward zombie-like, never talking—and I've stood right in front of him and said good morning and he's just walked around me—never looking up, with his hair covering all but the bottom of his nose and his zombie mouth. After a year of his being my paper boy, I couldn't tell you what his face looked like or if he even had one. In fact, if I saw him walk into apartment 5 below me and shoot the new guy who lives there in the face with a bazooka, and if he stood in the police lineup erect with his hair out of his face, I wouldn't be able to identify him.

The clothes look the same, I'd say. *But I can't be sure.*

Through the front door's peephole I saw the weird kid with the bangs shuffle up the stairs toward the second landing and eerily pull a newspaper from his zombie pouch. I opened the door and closed it softly behind me so as not to wake the girls and headed down the stairs to meet him. Fueled with remorse and lack of sleep, I was determined to lift the hair out of his face and look into his eyes—willing to risk the possibility of being beaten up by a beer-bellied father in a Foghat T-shirt, but hoping this act would break the zombie curse and set the kid's soul free.

The weird kid must have felt this and the zombie part of him retreated—or maybe he was just extra tired this morning—because he dropped the paper three steps below the second landing and headed back down the stairs: a new long-distance record. At this rate, the paper will soon be arriving at noon each day and I'll have to walk out to my car to get it.

At that moment, two thoughts flashed in my head at the same time. I've written in a few of my books the theorem that states that the mind can only grasp one thought at a time. This is simply not true; well, technically it might be. If we held a nanosecond stopwatch, we could see that one thought fell into the hole and then was pushed to the viewing screen while the next thought fell in the hole, but this is so fast it doesn't matter. When I've been cornered and had to shoot off rapid-fire lies to save myself, there have been sixteen, thirty thoughts juggled up at once, all on the mental viewing screen at the same time.

And right then, right at the landing while picking up the *Erie Times News*, two thoughts flashed up, both at the same time. The first thought was that I didn't need to wait for the weird kid with the bangs to deliver my paper later and later each day. I'd buy the paper from the box if needed, but the zombie paperboy had to go.

The second thought was that Bugby would not have a funeral. There was no wife or family to bury him. I wasn't sure what they did to Americans who died in Canada and had no one to claim them, but I was pretty sure it involved a vault and a shipping container.

I walked back up to the apartment and opened the paper on the kitchen counter. Bugby had migrated from page four to page one below the fold.

Erie Man's Death in Canada Still Unclear
By Jules West
Staff Writer
July 12, 1992

On Friday, July 10, Canadian authorities found the body of Erie resident Lester Bugby in the Shubenacadie River of Nova Scotia, Canada.

What is unclear at this time is the reason for Mr. Bugby's sudden arrival in the area as well as his purpose on the river.

According to authorities, Mr. Bugby made flight reservations the night before he left, on Monday, July 6. He flew out the next morning on Flight 4325 from Tom Ridge Field in Erie to Philadelphia, then from Philadelphia to Boston, and then from Boston to Halifax, Nova Scotia, arriving at 8:43 P.M. Mr. Bugby then rented a car and drove 37 miles north to the town of Shubenacadie, population 906, and checked into the Whispering Pines guest house.

Whispering Pines confirmed that Mr. Bugby had made his hotel reservation the night before his departure from Erie, that same Monday evening, and that he was planning to stay the entire week.

What has authorities baffled is that although Mr. Bugby was not registered with any of the rafting groups in that area during the past week, he was found wearing a rafting vest and safety helmet. A raft was found further downstream and local authorities are speculating that this may have been the raft Mr. Bugby was using.

"The Shubenacadie is a class A river," says Sergeant Martin Checleau of the Canadian River Authority. "We do no allow

> anyone without a class A license to operate on this river. Anyone who disobeys this law is just asking for trouble and we will arrest them for their own safety."
>
> It is unclear at this time what Mr. Bugby's intentions were on the river. Both Canadian and river authorities are reviewing the case. Canadian authorities are also asking anyone with information regarding the reason for Mr. Bugby's traveling to Canada to contact the Erie Police Department.
>
> Lester Bugby was the owner of the Denning Arms Apartments, the Mega-Liquor Warehouse, and Denning Self-Storage. He was 62 years old and was unmarried. He resided alone at the Denning Arms Apartments.

In the lexicon of media, this was called a trolling piece. A feeler. It's like a test hole drilled through the surface in hopes of finding pockets of lies or deception or sex that can be profitably mined and brought to the surface to sell. This was chum in hopes that something big and ugly would come to feed.

I reread the article and studied it harder. The writing style was succinct and simple, and since I did not recognize the name Jules West—she had written the first blurb on Bugby as well as this one—I assumed that West was either new to the paper or had finally worked her way up to a byline. She was probably given this piece as an errand, a part in the chorus, but it ended up as two pieces.

Tomorrow would be the true test. If tomorrow's story on Bugby was also written by Jules West, then the paper saw no true future in the story. There'd been no national interest in it and it would eventually die. However, if a new byline appeared under tomorrow's piece, let's say tomorrow's article is by Mark Godfrey or—heaven forbid, Cassandra Barry—ahh, now that would change the game a bit. Then the paper would have hit a pocket of collusion. They would have smelled something.

I hate to bother you, jackass, but your friend is dead here and . . .

I shook my head and closed the paper, breaking the self-defense mechanism that drew me in—at Rachel's funeral, I spent four hours with a notebook trying to list every teacher I had from kindergarten up and was so involved in the project that I completely forgot that Rachel was lying dead forty feet in front of me.

The spell was broken and I returned to Divorce Court, the apartment complex. And Bugby was still dead.

Faith—possibly not the correct term, but it's the one I will use—allows us to plug in knowledge and see the outcome. Faith lets us picture the people we love safe when we are not around them and imagine that our favorite team will go all the way this year and that by this time next year we will be thirty pounds lighter. We believe these things and see these things and hold them until we are forced to let them go.

It is a version of this faith, a stronger version, that provides me with a few nuggets of truth.

The first is that Bugby saw the tidal bore before he died. I know this to be true.

I can see him riding his raft with the bore underneath him. I can see the insanity all around him dimmed by the shine on his face. He probably laughed aloud a few times, a crazy cowboy-type scream, the way we yell out when we can't hold in the joy any longer or we'll just burst.

Whatever had happened to him had occurred after that moment. After his face was wet with surf. After he had ridden the bore and was glad to be alive and on the Shubenacadie. After he had done at least a part of what he had traveled twelve hundred miles to do, done what he was planning to tell me about when he returned. Then it happened.

I absolutely knew this.

"Dad?"

Abby and Liz were awake now, standing on the other side of the kitchen counter and gazing up at me.

I realized I was smiling and wondered if the girls thought that strange, like heading to bed wearing scuba flippers. Or smiling twenty-four hours after learning your friend is dead.

We moved to the couch and sat down in a large worm pile of arms and legs. I told the girls about the Bay of Fundy. I told them about Bugby riding that monstrous wave like a man on a white beast. I painted pictures of him happy and fearless and determined.

And then I reminded them about Uncle Walter. When he was dying, alive only because of tubes and pills and shots, if Uncle Walter had had the chance to spend the last day of his life healthy and strong and on a big Canadian tidal bore with the sun shining in his face and the monster waves underneath him, would he have taken it?

"Yup." Liz smiled. "Uncle Walter was crazy, too."

We stood there for a few minutes telling happy stories about Bugby. Then we began the hustle of a Sunday. Showers, packing, getting dressed and out the door to be at Catherine's before nine—another seal I've never broken—to be ready for church at ten.

I made a quick breakfast. The girls packed. There were showers and hair brushing and some laughing and some tears. We headed out the door and into the Corolla and soon it would be four whole days before I saw them again.

"Abercrombie, Dad," Liz said, snapping on her seatbelt.

"Yeah," Abby added.

"Ahh," I said, turning onto State Street, grateful I had thought of the next Abercrombie installment before receiving the news about Bugby. I began.

Herloge, France, April 23, 1942

We watched the Germans pile out of the factory and into the village of Herloge like an angry mob . . . and not just soldiers but SS and special troops. The village was destroyed and empty but the Germans were after something there, bombing and shooting and checking in every building and under every brick pile and hole. . . . And I will tell you this, whatever the Nazis were looking for in Herloge that day, Hitler wanted badly. Very badly. And you know something else? I don't think he found it.

Lieutenant Aime Chamoui
3rd Division Cuirassée de
French Second Army

"We need more time to . . ."

Another explosion hit before Ida Burch could finish her sentence. This time, the blast hit just outside the roofless building the three women were hiding in. This burst took part of the outside retaining wall with it and left a crater in the street just beyond it.

Lila Devamore leaned over the package as the last explosion hit, protecting the device wrapped inside Dreesly's backpack against the fragments of rock and debris that fell. She found herself instinctively protecting the device now instead of doing her job: to destroy it.

This was not how she had pictured all of this. The Women's Army Corp was a way to be involved in the war and not just as a nurse—not to clean up after the dead but to prevent death—but this? The other WACs were operating teletype machines or sorting mail, not working months as a German factory worker and then spending weeks to get close enough to the device to destroy it—not take it, but destroy it.

And it was all Burch's fault. All of it. It was always little Ida Burch's fault, and once again she had the three of them on the run and being shot at.

"Our orders are clear, Burch," Lila had said only an hour before as she watched Thelma Dreesly set the explosives to destroy the unit. The device the three women had spent months getting close to now stood only a few feet in front of them. Finally, this would all be over. They could set the charges and the timer and get safely out of the building before it went off.

"But the power of it," Ida had argued. "We can win the war if we take it."

And then there was the broken row of glass tubes that Ida Burch accidentally bumped into, which alerted the guards, which meant there was no time to destroy the unit and they were forced to take the device with them—forced to run from the building, through the tunnels, away from the whistles and the dogs and the searchlights and the German soldiers who followed them from the factory and fired at them, finally cornering them in this empty village of Herloge.

The German troops were getting closer now. Moving in. There was another loud explosion. Then another, followed by the ta-ta-ta-ta-ta-ta and then the rat-rat-rat of shells fired at random to spook their prey out of hiding. The Germans were checking building by building now and would find them soon, Lila thought. They would take their prize back and kill the three of them and their mission would have failed.

"We don't have any more time," Lila yelled out. Another explosion hit. Then there was silence. They could hear the grinding of tanks.

"Tanks!" Dreesly yelled.

Thelma Dreesly wiped the grit from her eyes and pulled the map from her side pocket and studied it. She ran her finger quickly along the surface of the map until she found what she was looking for. "There," she said. "If the wine cellar is still there, then the tunnel they used to bring the wine in may be there, too. It leads out of the village to the north road."

"We need more time to study it," Ida Burch said, reaching for the pack that contained the device. Lila yanked the pack away from her and stood, strapping the pack tightly on Dreesly's back.

"Let's hope you're half as fast as you used to be, Thelma."

Thelma Dreesly adjusted the straps of the pack even tighter.

"Just try and keep up," she said with a smile.

They waited for the next explosion and then Lila pushed Ida Burch out into the cloud of dust in the street. Dreesly was already several feet ahead of them and running fast.

They ran through Herloge, hiding in the dust and shadows when possible. Thelma Dreesly was now ten full steps ahead of them and weaving in and out of the clouds of dust and debris.

Then they were spotted by the German troops.

"Dort sind sie!" *a soldier screamed. Then others repeated it:* "Dort sind sie. Dort sind sie." *There they are. There they are.*

The three women raced down a narrow alleyway just as bullets tore into brick and stone around them. They darted through the alley and made it into the basement of the building Thelma was looking for seconds before shells tore apart the ground behind them.

"Don't stop!" Liz snapped.

"We're here," I said, pointing out the fact that we were parked in their driveway—or Catherine and David's driveway, or theirs and Catherine's and David's driveway; I've always been confused about how that works. I shut off the car.

"Ida Burch becomes the Countess of Backward Clocks, doesn't she?" Abby unbuckled her seatbelt.

"She does?" Liz asked, not old enough to have acquired her sister's ability to predict where I'm going with a story.

"You'll see."

"And the device they have is the one that lets people talk to the Gopher Queen, right?"

"It is?" Liz said.

"You'll see."

"Tell me."

"You," I said, opening the door, "will see."

Abby huffed and got out of the car. Liz followed.

We unloaded the car and carried in bags and backpacks and books and pillows.

8:56 A.M. I made it before 9:00. Another seal unbroken.

I stayed at the house for four minutes—the minimal amount of time needed to be polite, yet not enough time to drown in my own self-hatred and guilt—the equivalent of Frosty the Snowman going into the greenhouse with Karen to get her warm and then expecting to be able to get back outside before he melted.

I spoke to Catherine about Bugby and told her the girls were upset. Then I talked to David about his plans for the summer—teacher's life, having the summer off—and then, just when my lungs felt like they would burst with guilt, just before Professor Hinkle was ready to slam the greenhouse door and reduce me to a pile of mush with a pipe and hat, I kissed the girls and told them I loved them and that I'd see them in four days and that they could always call if they needed me and to obey their mother and David and then I ran back to the car as fast as I could.

On the way back home an urge hit me and I found a pay phone and had directory assistance connect me to the *Erie Times News*. A few buzzes and clicks and pushing of number three for this and number two for that and I was soon talking to a real, live person.

"Circulation," the human voice answered. "This is Charlotte, how may I help you?"

"I'd like to cancel my subscription, please."

Charlotte asked some questions and then looked up my information. "We're very sorry to lose you as a customer, Mr. Roe. May I ask the reason why you're canceling?"

Well, the zombie curse your delivery boy has may affect my daughters and I've stopped scanning for articles on my scandal and time in prison because my friend was killed by the tidal bore and if I need more information on that, I'll just go to the library.

There was silence.

"I'm moving."

"Oh," the young woman said. "We can just change your customer information and your delivery service will not be interrupted."

Can I just get the articles on Bugby delivered and nothing else? Do you offer a Bugby special?

More silence. "No, thanks," I said. "I'm moving to Spain."

Charlotte told me that she's always wanted to go to Spain and then I got off the phone and thought of what I just said—not the moving to Spain part but the moving at all part. Moving to someplace else in Erie. For the first time actually living somewhere other than Divorce Court, the apartment complex.

Before, the idea of not living near Bugby was unthinkable, but now the thought of the girls and I staying here without him was even worse.

Without Bugby, this was just an apartment. Without Bugby, this was just Divorce Court, the apartment complex, where you have new neighbors every three months. Without Bugby, there will be no more Thursday night dinners. Now, this is not where the old Hotel Denning used to be but merely the place where Bugby isn't.

What if the girls and I could have a place of our own? Instead of having their mom's real house for four nights a week and a clubhouse for the other three? Dad's place: the apartment of couches and ladybug tents. What if we could have a *house* full of couches and ladybug tents?

I made two more calls on my way home. One was to a realtor and the other was to the first funeral home directory assistance connected me to—the funeral home was more complicated than I thought because I had to get Bugby's body released to me. I started that process and then dropped off a check on my way home. The eight thousand I had in my savings would cover the funeral, I hoped; bankrupt people can get mortgages a day out of bankruptcy—I know this because I still get mail that has that exact phrase in bold letters all over it—so I could do both. Hopefully. I could pay for the funeral and the closing costs on a small house. Somehow, I could do both. If not all at once, then I could at least pay for the funeral and then save up for the closing costs.

I owed Bugby and this was one debt I wouldn't weasel out of. It's what I could do for him and by doing it—what? Rewiring? No. But one step toward . . . toward something. Penance maybe? Balance in the universe?

And that's where I am now. Sitting here on a Sunday night, no closer to rewiring than I was a week ago and now minus the only friend I had outside of the girls and writing all this. I'm expecting at any moment that the phone will ring and I will hear Bugby's voice ask—*Ja eat?* And then we'll be down at Oscar's Bar, eating clams and drinking beer and laughing. *Wishing well.*

But not tonight.

Tonight I will eat alone. And I will need to become accustomed to this.

Chapter 5

Bug. Bee

| July 17, 1992 |

We buried Bugby today. We had him flown in from Nova Scotia and sent to Wintergreen Funeral Home—the one on Norcross, not the one downtown—and the funeral was today. Bugby lay in state wearing one of his jogging suits—the red one that Abby picked out—and there was a respectable crowd there; small, considering how entrenched Bugby's parents were in Erie's history, but still respectable. A nice crowd. And we buried Bugby at Lakeside Cemetery in his family's plot.

The Bugby family plot was squared off by a wrought-iron fence and gate and one large marble stone that had the word *Bugby* carved deeply in its glossy stone face. Inside the fence were the headstones for Victor Bugby, Sonia Bugby—Sonia's stone, a pointed monument fifteen feet high, is still the highest marker in the cemetery today, and this made me smile—and Lester Bugby, who is now buried next to his father. There was also another stone inside the Bugby family fence. This one read *Clara Popodeus, 1898–1944* and on the bottom was carved *Beloved Friend.*

Abby and Liz cried, but I couldn't. Then I took them home to their mother's. It wasn't my night to have them, and I knew they didn't want to walk past Bugby's dark window anyway.

The girls wrote a card, a letter written with red magic marker on green construction paper, that we put in an envelope to leave with him. In the letter we wrote:

Bugby. Bugbee. Bug. Bee.
Wishing well. Wishing you well. Wish you well.

We love you. They love you. I love you.
Bye Bugby.

And they signed their names.
And I signed my name.
And we placed it in the casket.

CHAPTER 6

LOADED BUTTER BEANS

| JULY 19, 1992 |

There's an interesting process that begins—that starts another process, actually. Well, it's not the process but the results that I wanted to write about. It's more of a . . .

Sheesh.

No, that's not true. The only thing I want to write about is how much I miss Bugby. I am honestly shocked at how much I miss him. That's what I should be writing about, not my findings on butter beans. I knew I'd miss him but I never knew it would feel like this. Alone again. Missing him reminds me of Rachel and then I wonder if I miss Bugby more than I miss Rachel and then I feel bad because I shouldn't miss my friend more than I miss my own daughter and then . . .

AGHHHHHH.

Forget it. Just forget it. Or at least just forget it for now.

I'll write later.

No more today.

Chapter 7

Reunion

| July 22, 1992 |

Well, here's something to write about.

The "Walker Roe staying out of the newspaper run" is officially over and will be for a long, long time. I'm front-page news again, both local and national, and it's the same for TV. My phone goes from one call right to the next one, just one continuous ring. It's just like the old days.

And just like in the old days, the police have already been here twice. The last time ended with me promising to drop by the station at 2:00 P.M. and answer a few more questions—*we don't need to get attorneys involved, Mr. Roe,* they said—good, because I don't have any attorneys anymore.

I'm writing this because it's all I can do until I leave to talk to the police. I can't watch the TV without seeing pictures of myself or video of the outside of my building, and since Catherine is driving the girls to her mother's house in Ohio to be away from at least the local pressure, there's no one to call. I can only write this and look out the window at the news vans parked outside my building: CNN, ABC, CBS—hey, where is NBC?

Uh, moron, I hate to bother you, but you're going back to prison. Who cares about NBC?

Oh yeah, sorry.

So I sit here and wait, writing this until it's time to fight my way through the reporters to my car and go speak to the police. So let me bring you up to speed on recent events since I may not be able to write again for a while.

Well, all the excitement started yesterday with a few phone calls. Then the knocks on the door. Then the police. Then wham! I'm a full media sensation again.

I wish Bugby was here.

Sheesh, if Bugby was here, you wouldn't be news, bonehead.

Here are the basics. Two weeks ago, Bugby died. After his death—his *unexpected, under strange circumstances* death—I made phone calls and arranged for his body to be flown back here. I paid for all of this as well as the funeral. I also called a local realtor to start looking for a home to purchase. Do you see where I'm going yet? On the *very same day*, I canceled my newspaper subscription, telling the girl at the circulation desk that I didn't need the paper any longer because I was moving to—remember where?—Spain.

Wait—because it gets much, much better.

Immediately after learning of my landlord's death, I began spending money: money for the funeral, of course, and I began pricing multiple homes to purchase—one in Erie and one in Spain. Now, none of this really matters until we get to this next part, to the glue that sticks it all together.

Ready?

Here it comes.

Bugby left his entire estate, everything, to—drum roll, please—DING! Yup, you guessed it.

Me.

Everything he owned. Everything he had. All nineteen million dollars' worth of liquid and property assets, he left to . . .

Me.

In the three years I knew Bugby, he never mentioned any of this. Never. He asked once about what money I had set aside for the girls for their education and I told him that I had a good-sized insurance policy and that was it. That was the sum total of all our financial discussions. I never wondered who he would leave everything to because I thought he'd be around forever. And as long as he would be here forever, we would, too.

But you have to appreciate the beauty of the storyline. Convicted felon Walker Roe moves into an apartment right out of prison and befriends the man who owns the apartment complex. This friendship becomes so strong that the landlord names Walker Roe the sole beneficiary to his large—much larger than I thought it was—estate. Then the man dies under suspicious circumstances, leaving all his wealth to the convicted felon. And then the convicted felon begins making plans to spend his ill-gotten gain, while the landlord's body is still warm. It's perfect.

And the fact that the press found out about me being the sole heir before I did seems so ridiculous. There was a universal smirk among them all when I said I didn't know.

You've got to admit, it's a great story.

And right now, I get to go tell this great story, again, to the Erie police department. And then they may ask me to spend a few nights with them. Or possibly longer.

I told you that if I didn't rewire, this would all happen again.

And I hate it when I'm right.

JOURNAL 2

DUTCH

CHAPTER 8

| JUNE 13, 1992 |

The first day sober (I don't count Hangover Day) is the best. I mean, it's the effing bomb. You can see I'm writing *effing* because I'm going to stop swearing, too, and I figured this was a good place to start. I ain't going to say, *Gosh darn it, oh good gracious* from now on. Not happening. *Effing* works and I still keep face. It's like a nonalcoholic beer. You still look like you're drinking, not like a wuss with an effing ginger ale with a cherry in it, but you look like a guy with a beer. A type of beer anyways.

So I'm sober today and I'm not swearing. Even if I get hit by the Number 7 bus ten minutes from now, I'll die on one of the best days this year. I'm writing this because I was told to keep track of everything. They told me to do that before but I didn't do it and maybe that's the reason it didn't work before so that's why I'm trying it now. I'm starting this journal and I'm writing to you.

You don't know it, whoever *you* are, but that's what they told me to do last time. I'm not real good at writing things down (I'm not real good at writing neat either—you can tell if you are even able to read any of this effing scratch) but I didn't do it before so I'm doing it now.

I remember that I'm supposed to write this as if I'm talking to a person and I'm not sure who *you* are yet but I guess that part don't matter, just the writing part, so here I go. I'll just talk about today so far.

Like I said, the first day sober is the best. If all the days could be this way, I'd be dry all the time, every effing day, and you couldn't pay me to drink. (That's funny—being *paid* to drink. I'd like to see that want ad. Ha.) But the first few days are a trick—not a mean trick, I don't mean it that way—just something that goes away after a while.

The first day after Hangover Day is clear and bright. (So if you drank on Monday and you didn't drink on Tuesday, then Tuesday is Hangover Day and Wednesday is day one. Got it?) Your brain actually works and it's like someone slipped in while you were sleeping and cleaned your apartment and made you coffee. You go to bed in a filthy blanket with bottles and takeout containers ankle deep and you wake up in clean sheets with vacuumed floors and clean dishes and a pot of coffee with *real* half-and-half next to it, not the powdered crap you normally buy, and you look around the apartment and smile and have a cup of coffee and just suck it all in. Until eventually, well, eff, you eventually go back. Eventually. (It's sort of like taking a vacation to Soberland. It's pretty and nice and you wish you could stay but then you need to go back home. Ha.)

But right then, it's new and clean and non-ordinary and you even think maybe you can even keep it this way. Part of you does. Part of you says, *Hey, if I just pick up and do the dishes and wash the clothes, it can be this clean all the time.* And the other part of you laughs and says, *Just enjoy it, dude. Just enjoy it.*

And that's what I'm doing today. Just enjoying it. I got hope—don't get me wrong, I got lots of hope. But I ain't stupid. Dumb, yes, but I ain't stupid.

What I like about the first day is the newness. Is that a word? It's like I'm from a different planet or something and I was just dropped off here. Everything is ripe and fresh. You can walk outside the same building you've lived in for three effing years and look at it and it's like all the times you've seen it before it was only the picture you was looking at and now you've gotten to see the real thing. *Ah,* you say, *it looks different in real life. It looks nice.*

And it's not just the clearness. It's as if you're a new person. You can sit and make plans and you can see how they could work. You can see how the drunk plans were all effed up and you can't believe you even tried them.

See, you normal people—I'm guessing *you* are one of the normals. I probably wouldn't write to a drunk. He'd never read it, ha. You normal people probably think that a drunk has his drunk times and his sober times, right? Wrong. It's not like that. You have drunk, and then you have that foggy hangover time that connects to the next drunk, but this is the part you normals may not get. It's not the drunken times that do the damage. If I could go from drunk to this feeling I got now, this alive-type thing where my brain is working right? Ha! Sign me up, baby.

Drunk is the sleep. The safe, goofy sleep. It's the hangover (well, it's not really a hangover; pros don't get hangovers, but I don't know what else to call it) where I do all the damage. It's the dots that connect the time from when I walk in from the Belmar and go to bed until I come home from work the next afternoon and head back over again. That's the muddled, foggy, paranoid place I live. Things are safe when I'm drunk. It's the gaps in between when things get real stupid and effed up.

It's, like, during the drunk time your voice is slurred and things are moving around and it's goofy and shifting, like a ride or something, and nobody takes you seriously anyway—not even you. And you would never go cash a check or make a call or nothing because you know you're drunk. But the next day it still seems like a good idea. It still seems good and now your voice isn't slurred and you can walk. The times in between, eff, your voice is clear, your walk is straight, and besides having dragon breath you *look* normal. You *seem* normal, even to you. That's when it happens. It's like giving a ten-year-old who's tall and *looks* a lot older the keys to your car.

Even *you* think things are normal and sometimes it's months until you have a *new* day, like today, that you go, *Ah crap*, and you see all the damage the robot you did when you was gone.

I guess I should tell you about me first. (I'm assuming I haven't met *you* yet.)

My name is Riley Dutcher. I'm thirty-one years old and I live on Mather Street in Binghamton, New York. Most people don't know Mather Street and *nobody* outside of New York knows Binghamton other than as a place you stopped at going somewhere else. *Ah, yes* (I'm trying to do a snobby accent but I ain't good at accents), *we stopped at Binghamton on the way to Niagara Falls, or on the way to a Bills game, or on our way to take our daughter to Cornell.*

Not that I know anyone outside anymore. I used to talk to them when I was in sales but not now. That was a lifetime ago. I'm a garbage man now.

I'm not *the* garbage man. Not the guy who rides in the truck and picks up the cans and takes them. Naw. I just sit in a chair. And I push three buttons.

I work at the Broome County Landfill (they don't like it when you say *dump*; it's not a dump anymore—it's a *landfill*). But I don't go out in the garbage or nothing (I have a hair-trigger puke reflex and couldn't handle that). I work at the gate. The garbage trucks get weighed coming in with the garbage and then get weighed going out without the garbage so we know what to charge them for the garbage they dropped in the landfill. We charge per ton, charge for the garbage companies and regular people to dump their crap. I sit at a desk with a ripped green office chair and push the button coming in and push the button going out. It's easy work and work that I could do hung over or sober. And I've been there for over three years without even coming *close* to getting fired.

See, I don't want you to think I'm, like, a wino or something. Like some guy begging for quarters and sleeping in a Whirlpool box near a loading dock. I have a job and an apartment and a car. Not that I'm above that loading dock drunk; we're the same. He's just more honest about it than I am.

You may want to know if the people I work with know I'm a drunk. (I don't say *alcoholic*. I'm not one. I'm a drunk. Alcoholics are quitters. Not my joke, but it fits. Ha.) Maybe they do. I eat Mentos like they're M&Ms to hide my breath and I shower every day. Most drunks don't bathe and you can smell the booze squirting right out of them. Or they'll wear the same clothes they had on the night before. I shower and wear clean clothes and I don't think you can smell it anywhere on me but my breath, and like I said, Mentos are the drunk's best friend. I can go through four packs of Mentos by three in the afternoon. Easily. And like I said, unless I do something really stupid I don't get real hangovers anymore. I get a little shaky, but no big deal. I can work through even the worst hangover if I was stupid and drank something the night before that I wasn't used to. In my booth there's a bathroom if I need it, but I rarely puke.

See, you have this, like, limit. I drink usually twelve to sixteen beers a night, between 5:00 P.M. when I start, and 9:00 or 10:00 when I'm done and ready to sleep. That usually gets me where I need to be.

If I have nineteen or twenty beers at night, then I'll be in hangover country. I can still operate—like I said, I'm a pro—but there's the headache, the shakiness, the sweats.

I work from 6:00 A.M. until 4:00, which is cool because I'm a morning guy. I can be out drinking until 4:00 in the morning (though I rarely am) and still wake up an hour later, four days a week, Tuesday through Friday. So I get to work. I sit at my ripped green chair. I push the button when the trucks come in and pop my Mentos and push the button when the trucks go out. I usually eat at my desk or from the snack cart that comes in (yes, I eat regularly—not all drunks do, but I do). Then I hop in my Datsun at 4:00 and head home. And conveniently, my apartment building is right across the street from the Belmar, the bar I hang out at. But I can stay drunk at my apartment if Sheri at the Belmar is pissed at me for something, but I don't have cable. Drunks need something to do and if you don't have cable and if I don't borrow videos from the library, then conversation is the next best thing. Then on my three days off, I just start drinking a little earlier and end a little earlier. But nothing too crazy.

That's the drunk stuff, but I should tell you more about me. Like I said, I'm Dutch and I'm thirty-one. Just turned last month. My parents are dead and I've lived in Binghamton my whole life except for a year at Oneonta State University before I dropped out. My parents left me their house but I couldn't make the payments and lost it. I should have sold it when I first got it, but shouldas and wouldas don't jazz me up no more.

I was married once. For about a year. Her name was Grace and she lives in Port Crane now. I don't see her much. I think she got remarried but like I said, I don't see her much no more.

Okay, that's good for now. I'm off today so I'm going to pick up the apartment a little and make some coffee and enjoy the new day.

Later.

Okay, I wasn't planning on writing no more until tomorrow but crap has come up. Serious effing crap. Since I wrote those last words in this notebook a few hours ago some serious effing crap has come up.

Okay, here's what happened.

I stopped writing and closed the notebook. I walked into my kitchen to make coffee. I stood in my kitchen and didn't go any further because there was a bicycle blocking the way. I don't own a bicycle. The bike was just sitting there with the kickstand down in the middle of my effing kitchen, like it was posing for an effing picture. So I stood and looked at it. Waited for the memory to arrive of whose bike it was and how it got there. Nothing came.

I walked around it. It's a silver and red bike and it screams *expensive, expensive*! It has black saddlebags on each side of the back tire and on each side of the front tire. Then on the back there is strapped a sleeping bag and a tent (I looked inside—it was a little tent). And I stood there and waited for the memory to arrive and nothing came. I was here yesterday but I can go days without going in the kitchen and even on Hangover Day I would have remembered seeing a bike.

So I sat down and tried to remember if I was in the kitchen yesterday at all and I don't think I was.

Nothing else came.

I made a pot of coffee. I sat and poured in the powdered creamer crap and drank the coffee and watched the bike. Nothing came. I replayed the last forty-eight hours in my head as best I could. Then the last seventy-two hours and everything was still blank.

I don't black out exactly. There is no memory that is *totally* gone but sometimes there are memories that require, like, a password. I'll walk into the Belmar and Randy will smile his big stupid smile and ask me something like "How's the cat?" and click, the door is opened and I remember it all. This was probably like that. I stared at the bike. It was shiny and pretty and loaded up for adventure.

This was not a bike that was sitting on a porch. This was not the bike of a man who would be in the Belmar for a couple of drafts. This thing was cared for and loaded for a trip. And whoever owned it has now stopped his trip and is probably seriously pissed off.

So I drank my coffee and tried to remember but nothing came. Then I wrote down the information on the bike and went down to the library and started looking in bike magazines. This is where it gets *real* bad. This bike is a Fezzari bike. It's called a T3 and it sells for over three grand! Then you add in the saddlebags, the sleeping bag, and tent.

Eff. (I'm swearing in real life but I'm trying not to on paper.) So, if I had a stolen four-thousand-dollar watch in my apartment it would be the same thing. Or a ring worth four grand or . . .

You don't lose a four-thousand-dollar bike and then run to K-Mart and get another one. You go to the police. Then the police retrace the large effed-up drunken trail that leads right to 1 Mather Street, apartment 3. And I'm pretty sure that there are very few Fezzari racing bikes in the greater Triple Cities area.

"Oh no, officer," I'll say as they push my face onto the effing hood to cuff me. "This is *my* Fezzari racing bike. I've had it for years. Of course I know it costs twice what my effing car did, but I always buy Fezzaris. They're my brand of effing choice."

Eff.

So now you're caught up. I'm going to the Belmar at 11:00 (no, I'm not getting drunk, but maybe they know something about it). I'll go and nurse a draft and wait for someone to say something. I was there Thursday night so if I took the bike it probably happened then. And if I did something stupid Randy will be waiting to be the first to describe it. In glorious effing detail.

This is not good.

June 14, 1992

Well, I don't have much more to tell you. I went to the Belmar but Randy wasn't there yet. Colby was bartending but he didn't say nothing to me about no bike. I nursed a beer and sat down and waited for a casual conversation about a stolen racing bike to build up, but it didn't. So I left and picked up a *Binghamton Press* to see if there was anything on the bike in the police section of the paper. Nothing. Then I checked the lost and found section. Zip.

But I did see these little blue and white pieces of glass on the doorframe of the kitchen. I went to touch them and they jumped from the wall to my hand, like by static. There was more pieces on the bike, too—tiny pieces of blue and white glass.

If I took the bike on Thursday night, then that would have left all day Friday for it to be reported and it could have been in the paper yesterday, Saturday, or at least by today, Sunday.

Then I went back to the Belmar and Randy was there.

I walked in and sat next to him. Waiting. He nodded and asked what was up.

"Not much," I said. "What's going on with you?"

"Same ole," he said, sipping his beer. A second built up. Then another. I waited to see the smirk on his face. "So how's the bike?" he would say, shaking his head and laughing.

But nothing happened. Nothing at all. Randy watched the TV, sipped his beer, and then began a story about what an idiot his brother-in-law is (next to what a loser I am, this is Randy's favorite subject).

I sat my beer down and stood up.

"Where ya goin'?" Randy asked.

And I stood there and didn't answer because I didn't know. I never came in and left before. I came in and stayed. I camped out. I drank. I stood there looking down at Randy and it felt good to be leaving. To be going somewhere. Even though there were probably police cars circling my building, it felt good to be actually going somewhere.

"I've got some things to do."

Randy gave me one of those *What things could YOU possibly have to do?* looks, but it didn't matter.

"See ya," I said.

"Later."

And I walked out into the light.

I drank a draft and a half. That's all. There hasn't been a day in three, maybe seven, years where I drank only a beer and a half. Hell, there probably hasn't been a day when I left beer in a glass for over ten years.

I stood at the doorway at the Belmar. Daylight gathers around the doors of bars. It waits because it ain't allowed in and as soon as you step out it's on you like panhandlers or seagulls. It reminds you that the real world is out here and you're drunk in the middle of the effing day and don't belong to it. But today I was sober. So I *did* belong to it.

I watched the street. I watched the gas station across the street. There was my building behind it. Boxlike, with its long green canopy pretending it was a great New York apartment building. And next to that its twin building, 3 Mather Street. Beyond that? Africa. China. The Netherlands. Places I don't go to or belong to, either.

The places I belong are: from the landfill to Mather Street. From Mather Street to the landfill, with side trips to the Giant supermarket or to Binghamton Savings bank when absolutely necessary. Then back here. That's my world.

"Ya live across the street, if ya forgot," Randy cackled from behind me. "Or did ya forget all them important things ya had to do, too?"

I waved to Randy and stepped off the cement steps to the street, then came here and began writing again. I'm in my apartment now.

The apartment that has *not* been invaded by large, blue-suited men with guns. The bike is still here. I like looking at it.

I can stare at that bike for half an hour and not get bored. No memory comes about taking it but I like looking at it. It's like watching a movie or hearing a story.

Maybe that's why I took it.

The bike is strong and solid. It's prepared. You can take this bike and go and it's all you need. You get tired, you stop. You pitch your tent and you sleep. You get up the next morning and go some more. You can cook. There is a small stove and plenty of dried food in the saddlebags. There's clothes and an atlas. There is a brand-new camera.

The tent is new and has not been used. And on the bike is a sticker from a bike shop in Medford, Massachusetts. Did the guy ride all the way from Massachusetts to Binghamton? According to the atlas in the saddlebag, that's like three hundred miles away.

And this is the part I haven't told you yet. In the back saddlebag, when I took everything out to look at it—was money.

I am holding in my hands ten new one-hundred-dollar bills. Tucked away as this guy's emergency money. A grand for an emergency. Eff.

I fanned the money out and looked at ten of the Ben Franklins. This meant that the bike and contents were worth well over five grand.

You don't lose five grand and walk away. You don't lose five grand and not report it.

As I'm writing this, I keep looking at the bike. It's not the bike itself that impresses me. It's the, like, simplicity of it or whatever. Like I said, you could hop on this bike and go anywhere. With a grand in your pocket, you could go for months. You wouldn't need a hotel room. You have a tent. You wouldn't need gas; you have the power of your own effing legs. You could go anywhere.

I've seen homeless guys try to live on bikes. Beat-up yard-sale bikes bungeed down with tattered blankets and tarps. This is not one of them. This is an adventure. This is an effing journey.

If I were on this bike a few days ago, I wouldn't have let anything or anybody take it. And I wouldn't stop until I got it back. Until I got my adventure.

I don't ever feel guilt. Never. Sheri from the Belmar says I was born without a conscience and she may be right. I feel no guilt about taking this bike (and since I can't remember, I'm assuming I took it).

Hell, I couldn't survive unless I took something once in a while. But I do feel bad because this guy's adventure has now stopped.

That part, I do feel bad about. Unless he's rich enough to walk into a bike store and replace everything effing thing and keep going (which I doubt), I've taken his adventure away. Even if he is rich enough, I have at least effing paused it.

And I'm sorry for that.

CHAPTER 9

| JUNE 19, 1992 |

My favorite thing in the world, the best effing thing ever, is to be awake early and sober, real early, before even the normal people are up, and to be showered and shaved and sober and out into the world.

You're ready to go. You're clean and clear-headed. You are just like the rest of them. In fact, that day you are a little above the normals. You are up and about earlier than they are. You are at the Dunkin Donuts before they are and the day belongs to you. It's your effing day because it goes to the first person who claims it, the first person to make it to it clean and sharp and ready, and today that happens to be you (meaning me).

On calendars everywhere they need to include this as National Dutch Day. My day. And today is that day.

I'm off work today. Day one of my three-day weekend and day seven not drinking. (Please, I do *not* count the draft and a half I had the other day. That didn't even poke a brain cell.)

So seven days sober, not counting Hangover Day. I'm showered and out early, 5:30, out the door. I don't have to be out that early. I don't have to be out at all, but I am. There's something that pushes you out on days like this. On National Dutch Day. You need to show off the fact that you're clear-headed and ready. You want to be in the middle of the normal people that you hide from the rest of the year. Them normal people who are in line next to you getting coffee at Dunkin Donuts, they are all cologned and ready for the day with their ironed shirts and car phones, and you are right there next to them. But today you're not still technically drunk from the night before, popping enough Mentos so your breath don't set off the sprinklers. Nope. Today you look back at them and smile.

Really, an honest effing smile. *Warm out there today,* you say. Just like normal people do.

On normal days (well, *my* normal), you want those people to be gone. You don't hate them; you just want them to be forced to use a separate entrance than you and keep fifteen feet away at all times (ha). But not today. Nope. Not only are you one of them today; you're actually slightly ahead of them. You've gotten up and are running errands and getting coffee before them *and* you get extra points because you are off work today. You could have stayed in bed, but you didn't. You went to Giant at 6:00 and bought groceries. You sat at Dunkin Donuts and drank coffee and ate a bagel and watched the normals file in and out. You are one of them but you are not rushed.

Because today, or at least this morning, is yours. It's all yours.

Binghamton is not a big place. And when I say Binghamton I mean the Triple Cities—Binghamton, Endicott, Johnson City, and let's throw in Vestal, too. They are all connected. Main Street to one is Main Street to the others—except Vestal, but Vestal is weird. It's difficult to go an entire day without seeing someone you know or have known and it's rarely anyone you want to see. You never see those people you'd actually *like* to see. I remember in school there was something, some phrase about sitting in one place long enough and the world will pass by you. Well, it should be, sit at the Dunkin Donuts in Endicott a few hours in the morning and the world will pass by you. I saw everyone and no one I wanted to see (not that there are that many people on the list, but there may be a few).

So that started the day and it didn't really get it going in the wrong direction. Normally, if I saw someone I went to school with or my old neighbor from when I was married (I did see my old neighbor today, weird), it would be like getting jabbed in the gut. But not today. Today it was just a slight poke. Not even that, really—a tap maybe. And I recovered. Like being sober is some sort of antidote or anti-venom (ha). Weird.

I sat at a booth at the Dunkin Donuts in Endicott and read the *Binghamton Press* and there was nothing on the bike in the lost and founds or the police section or anywhere. Which is weird because there is not a lot of news here. I would think a stolen four-thousand-dollar bike with a grand in cash on it would be in the paper. Eff, last year it was front-page news for a week when some guy took a shot at a cow while driving by a farm in Chenango Bridge!

So by ten in the morning, I was pretty much done for the day. I was back to Mather Street and had my groceries put away (walking around the bike is hard; my kitchen is not that big) and my laundry got done and the apartment got clean. There was more of them little pieces of blue and white glass in my laundry, too, and I keep wiping them off the walls but they jump and stick everywhere. And still no one had pounded on my door calling me *sir* and asking if they could ask me questions about a stolen Italian touring bike.

And there it stands. Waiting. Captured like the horse of a foreign prince (ha). If anyone came in, I couldn't hide the bike. This is an efficiency apartment, which is really just a fancy name for a room, a bath, and a tiny kitchen. And I can't stash it no place else because there *is* no place else to put it and if there was, I'd have to get it downstairs and out of the building without being seen. And that's when the sirens would wail and faces would get forced onto car hoods.

So the bike stays where it is for now. It's like a Band-Aid that you're afraid to rip off, so you leave it where it is and hope it'll fall off on its own.

I went through everything in them bike bags and then put everything back in. Clothes—the stretchy bike kind of clothes (pretty big—this guy must be tall)—cooking stuff, maps, tent, sleeping bag, camera, paperback books. No wallet. No ID. No journal or idea where he came from or where he was going. And I still don't remember taking it or even seeing it before yesterday morning.

I even sat on my chair for half an hour with my eyes closed. Breathing in and going back in my mind and slowly playing everything forward. Stopping and making sure it was all recorded. And there was nothing about the bike. I don't remember it. Can you be convicted of an effing crime you don't remember? Oh yeah, no problem, you can.

But I wish I at least remembered taking it because I know I did. Then maybe I could remember *why* I took it. What about it got me going? Then I could decide if I should give it back (not the money—hey, finders-keepers—but maybe the bike).

June 21, 1992

I slept good last night. I always sleep when I'm sober and never sleep when I'm drunk. It's like the booze makes you hibernate or something, makes it like you don't need so much sleep. I'll go weeks with just a few hours a night but not last night. Sober, I crashed. Man, I was out.

I woke up once to go to the bathroom and actually went into the kitchen to see if the bike was still there. I flipped the light on and just looked at it, expecting it to scamper like a cockroach once the light was all over it, but it didn't.

Having this bike is the closest thing to having a roommate (ha). Or a secret. It has to be a secret. I can't tell nobody about it. And still nothing in the paper. That's the weird thing. Nothing. I just don't get it. I feel like calling the paper or the police and saying, *Hey, knock it off. I know you're holding out on this so just print it already and get it over with*. But nothing comes.

Today is the last day of my three-day weekend. Sober still, but still off work. Just when I get the landfill smell out of my lungs I have to go back and refill them.

There was this joke when I first started working there. They would say, *Smell that?* And I'd say, *Yeah*, and they'd say, *Know what that smell is?* And I'd say, *No*, and they'd say, *That's the smell of money*. Then they'd laugh.

I'm still not sure I get that joke. I think I do. Maybe it's just not that funny.

I'm drinking coffee now as I write this. Drinking coffee with the powdered crap in it and looking at the bike. I even got on the bike once but the seat was adjusted real high (I told you this guy was tall). And it has those weird pedals that must click into a special pair of shoes. It's like a racing kind of thing, probably. If I were to keep this bike (and I'm just saying, *if*), the first thing to go would be those pedals. I'd want them regular pedals like I had when I was a kid. Not the clip kind, just regular K-Mart plastic flat pedals. I wouldn't be racing against nobody (except the police, ha). So I'd change to regular pedals. The rest I'd keep as is.

I've never seen this color red before, the color that's on the bike. Not candy apple like an effing muscle car or something but different. And man (ha), does this thing stand out. *Fezzari* written up the cross bar (I don't know what the real part name is), *Fezzari* written up the fork. Not obnoxious like, not like a low rider or an effing pimp car. More like *confident*. It don't have to be quiet.

I think that's cool.

I'm sitting here now drinking my coffee with the powdered crap in it and just looking at the bike (hey, my kitchen is so small I'm practically kissing the thing, ha).

I went out to get the *Binghamton Press* like I told you and still nothing about the bike. That's just crazy. Nothing at all.

If I were to keep a bike like this (just saying, *if*), I couldn't keep it locked up here. It would be like keeping a greyhound in a box. A greyhound needs to run.

I know it's just a piece of metal. I'm not sober enough that I've lost it completely, not yet. It's like I said before. It's the symbol. The simple part about it.

I could just leave. I could just effing leave town. Besides the fact that the police would be looking for me (yeah, besides that part), I could just pick a direction and go. Ride for a while. Stop. Sleep in my tent. Ride to town and buy some beans and some bread. Ha, like a cowboy. Like an effing bike-riding cowboy.

A grand could buy a lot of beans.

A grand could also buy a lot of beer. I'd be set for a while.

I don't have decisions like this to make too often.

But I could just leave. I could. Or I could stay here and get drunk for a long time on some rich guy's dime.

Either way sounds interesting, but one way sounds a whole lot more fun (and I know what you're thinking, that I was talking about the drinking part being the fun part. Drinking is fun like breathing is fun, ha).

June 24, 1992

When I lost my parents' house (well, I didn't lose it—I know where it is; it's just that when I go there different people are living in it, ha), I filled the trunk of my car with a few boxes. Then I filled my backseat and front seat with a few more boxes. Stuff that was my parents'. Stuff that was mine and Grace's when she lived in the house with me—pictures, letters, birth certificates, paperwork. And once the car was full of boxes, there was no room for nothing else. No room for the TV or pots and pans or microwaves or nothing. I probably could have made another trip. They weren't locking up the house until the next day, but I was homeless for a while, flopping on my cousin Marty's couch (and his wife *loved* that, ha). I had no place to store anything so I could only take what fit in the car. The boxes.

My parents had that house for eighteen years and I lost it in less than two. Eff.

So I'm driving around with my dead parents' stuff in my car, no job, no place to stay, and I eventually got the job at the landfill. My cousin Marty loaned me the four hundred and twenty-five bucks for the security deposit I needed for this place (his wife probably would've paid the first year's rent, just to get rid of me, ha) and the boxes went into the closet. I took the clothes pole down and crammed the boxes in there from ceiling to floor and they've been in there ever since. Like a mummy in a tomb.

I have one room, a bath, a kitchen, and a decent-sized closet. I don't think about the closet much since I haven't been in there in years (no point—you couldn't cram a piece of paper in there). But I went in there today. I wiggled a box out. It was so tight, it was like pulling a brick from a wall, and I opened the box on my bed.

You got to be careful when you time travel (that's what they called it in rehab—time traveling—spending time in the past), and I do it when I'm sober and not so much when I drink (maybe that's why I drink, ha). The danger is that once you go back and really get zoning in on one thing, one time period, one day or one week, then you start to change things. Little things at first, like something you said or something you didn't say. Maybe something you said was really stupid, so you change just a word, or how you said it, and now it ain't as stupid or maybe it's not stupid at all and then you save that new version in your memory. Before you know it, you are actually the hero of the scene and them other guys are the ones that ruined everything that day.

I do this a lot. I look back at things and tweak them a little bit and I have been time traveling so long that my memory can't be trusted no more. I've changed things so much that my memories are edited. It wasn't until I went into that first box that I saw some of the raw footage. How things really went.

The first box was one of Grace's and my stuff. I vaguely remembered it, but slowly as I went through things, I guess I remembered, but other things, it was like I was seeing them for the first time.

There were cards, birthday cards, Christmas cards, mostly from Grace. Grace had underlined certain words of the cards and then wrote on them how much she loved me. I don't remember these cards. Then there were cards and letters from when I was in rehab. Cards from

Grace saying how strong I was and that I could do anything I wanted and she'd be waiting there when I got back. Cards from my folks telling me how much they loved me. How proud they were that I was going to lick this thing. There was this one long letter from Grace when we first started dating that must have been ten pages long. She wrote about how kind I was and smart and how much at work she looked around and just waited for me to pass by her desk and once I did it was like she could breathe again and then when I was gone it was like she was holding her breath until I walked by again the next time (her words, not mine). Then there were letters after rehab from Grace. There was a notebook where Grace was trying to figure out all the things we could get rid of—cable, stuff like that—so we could live just on her salary until I got another job. There was nothing in this notebook that said she was angry, or unwilling to do without. In fact, on one page she had my name doodled in the margin with a big heart drawn around it. Can you believe that? There she was, trying to figure out what was the minimum stuff she needed just to live, and instead of being pissed off at me for not working she's drawing a heart around my name (my real name, not Dutch, but Riley. She wrote *Riley* with a heart around it!).

There were pictures of Grace and me. One at her cousin's wedding and she is smiling so much it looks like she was glowing and she was holding my arm so tight, like she thought I'd float away if she didn't. There was pictures of us at a Christmas party and pictures taken by a machine at the Broome County Fair. She's smiling in all of them. She's happy in all of them. I don't remember these pictures.

Each layer of the box was like sediment, like a certain time period had been preserved or something, and I'd remove the pictures and come across the next layer, a layer of smaller notes from a different time. These notes were from later on, when I didn't come home much and Grace would leave me notes on the kitchen table when she'd leave for work in the morning and I was still asleep, after coming in only a few hours before. These notes asked what she had done wrong. One note said that if I was mad at her to just tell her and we'd work it out. There were notes asking me not to shut her out, notes saying that she loved me no matter what and we could work out anything together. There were notes on how she had looked at me while I was sleeping and couldn't believe how much she loved me. There were small notes she would stick in my lunch bag, quick ones that would say *I love you*, with that goofy stick figure she always drew.

It's funny that I remember the stick figure but not the notes. Just like I don't remember taking the bike. But the notes are here. They're in the box, in Grace's handwriting, and I must have put them in the box myself so I must have read them when they were first written. I don't remember them but I saved them. I saved them to read now.

It took an hour just to go through that first box. Layer by layer, going further and further back in time, and I saw an incredible thing: Grace really loved me. She really did love me and she loved me more than I loved her. My memory version was that she took off when things got tough. That's the version I had saved, but that's not the raw footage of what really happened. I let her love me and then I broke her heart. She was this pretty, happy girl that just wanted to be with me. She would have been happy just being with me because . . . I don't know why. And I wouldn't even let her do that. That was too much work for me.

When I was done with the first box, I was stupid enough to pull down another one, and the story there was the same. This time, the box was about my parents and there were smiling pictures of them next to me at birthdays and at my graduation. Pictures of my dad with his arm around me when I was leaving for summer camp and then other pictures with my mom hugging me when I busted my arm when I was twelve. More smiling faces. Happy faces and more pictures I don't remember of moments I don't remember. There were birthday cards and letters. Notes while I was in college from them about how proud they were of me. Notes while I was in rehab that said they were just as proud of me and I sat there and tried to remember this proud thing and all I could remember was their disappointment. How I disappointed them and all the memories I had were of avoiding them because the disappointment was so intense.

There was a card from my old buddy Terry Ellis with some pictures he had of when we was kids. The pictures were in a birthday card and he was going to give it to me on my twenty-first birthday party at my parents' but he had to mail it after I didn't show up. In the card Terry wrote, *Remember when we thought 21 was old?* In the back of the card, Terry joked about me not being able to make the party my parents had for me at their house and about how the snow must have been much deeper on the West Side of Binghamton than it was on the East Side (obviously, this was the lame excuse I had given my parents later when I finally came home). My parents had a birthday party for me and I called and said I couldn't make it. I was probably in a bar someplace.

There was a stub to a cashier's check for fifteen thousand dollars when they took a second mortgage on the house to pay for my one failure of a year at Oneonta State. There were other loans on insurance policies and retirement plans later on when I got in trouble and needed quick cash.

And I sat there and let these moments percolate. I deleted all the edited ones in my brain and let the real ones, the clean and true ones, settle in. And then I hit save.

How do you normal people stand moments like this? The pain is so intense. I'm crying now and my head hurts. Feelings like these are exactly what people like me work very effing hard to avoid. It's the reason we drink.

And I don't know how you normal people get through them any other way than being stoned and wasted.

Chapter 10

| June 27, 1992 |

I have three messages on my answering machine but I haven't listened to them yet. They're probably from Randy, wondering when I'll be back in the Belmar so someone will actually talk to him (ha), but I haven't been to the Belmar and I still haven't had a drink yet. I've been running some errands and thinking about stuff.

That's another thing you don't need to do when you drink: all that thinking stuff you normals do. We drunks like having our thoughts given to us, like prepackaged foods. TV was made for drunks. I can sit there for hours with a stupid grin on my face, plastered out of my mind and so happy because all of them thoughts are being spoon-fed to me and I don't have to think about nothing, and if the TV show is supposed to make me feel a certain way, then that feeling is already chewed up for me, too, and delivered right to my brain.

When you're sober, you have to go and get thoughts for yourself and actually cook them and put them in bowls and put them on a plate (ha, that's pretty funny). So I've been thinking a lot lately, since I have no choice (it's one of the downers about being sober).

I looked through each one of the boxes in the closet. I cried and slept, then woke up and kept going. Box by box. Going back into the past and seeing the way it all really was. Looking at what was real and what I thought was real. What was important and what was garbage, and the funny thing is that most of what I thought was important was garbage (and I'm a landfill guy—I should know garbage, ha).

And I saw it all. I had parents that loved me. I had a good childhood. I had a wife who loved me and just wanted to be with me. I had friends. I had coworkers. I had neighbors. And I hated the very thing that they liked: me. And because they liked me, I hated them for it.

I know that sounds weird, but in my brain it all makes sense. On paper, it probably sounds pretty crazy. I was never good enough for me. But for them, I was fine just the way I was.

There's a couple of things you can do when you realize something like that. The first one is, you can walk across Main Street and sit down to next to Randy and get as effing numb as possible as effing fast as effing possible. Because now you've got a new reason to drink. Because it's all gone and you're not going to get your wife back or your parents back or your friends back, and you can't go back to that twenty-first birthday party and actually show up this time. People that loved you are gone forever and you're never gonna have others that will care about you that much. You had something special and cool and rare, and you spat on it all. Yup. That's about it. And if that ain't enough reason to spend the next few years crying in your beer, then I'm effing sure I can find a few more reasons in those boxes. You can sit and drink with your shame and your guilt, and Randy will help make sure you chew it up right and get it all down.

That's the first thing you can do. The other thing is, you can take all the good memories—those good people that loved you—and put them memories back in your brain where they belong. But this time, you don't stuff them down in some hidden corner. You put them all out in a nice frame (ha). And every time you look at them in your brain, you see that you ain't as much of a bozo as you thought you were because these people loved you a lot. And you start to see the reasons they loved you. The things and traits that maybe you haven't remembered that you had. You start to push all that guilt and crap back and remember the good stuff.

The second way is harder to do, but it's not as hard as I thought it would be. Right now, it seems like it would actually be harder to walk across the street to the Belmar, but I'm sure that will change and it will get easier soon. Now, with all them good memories in frames in my head, there is one thing left that's even harder to do.

Give the bike back.

I know. I know, it's crazy, but I've been thinking a lot about the bike. A lot. And I know what I want to do. I want to be on a bike with a sleeping bag and a tent, and I want to go. Not running away, not hiding, but out in the open, proud and happy like all those pictures and notes said I could be. Running simple-like, just needing some money for food here and there and seeing what the world past the

Belmar and Main Street is really like. So, the first thing I need to do is give the bike back.

I want *my* adventure. I don't want to steal some other guy's, and if I keep that bike, that's just what I'd be doing. And then I'd be looking over my shoulder. I'd be taking something that ain't mine and, from now on, I don't do nothing that makes me want to beat myself up, nothing that those framed pictures in my brain would disapprove of. Everything I do has to be something I can live with, because it's all going out in frames on the shelves, whether it's good or bad. No more boxes.

(Ha, Sheri, looks like I found my conscience, huh?)

And here is the even harder part. I need to give the money back, too.

Eff, I can't believe I'm writing this. Yes. I need to give it all back and get my own money for my own adventure.

So the big effing question here is how the eff do I do that exactly? I don't know where I took that bike from. I thought about walking the bike to the police station and saying I found it and turning it in. Yeah, I thought about that for about three effing seconds. The cops wouldn't believe it. Nope. And I don't want to just dump it, either. I want the guy to get his adventure back, but since I don't know who he is and where I took it from, that's kind of hard.

Then I thought of just leaving the bike at the police station steps. Like they used to do in them old movies where there would be a baby in a basket on the orphanage steps. But there are probably cameras all around the police station and they'd see me. Then I thought of sending a letter to the police and stashing the bike someplace and telling them where it was, but that just sounds stupid.

So that goes back to the police station idea. To somehow get it there with a note, maybe saying it was found and that the police should find the rightful owners.

Hey, what about the paper? The newspaper? Would they turn it over to the police? I don't want to just drop it off at a bike shop because they might keep it.

What about a church? What if I left it at a church? They would call the police, wouldn't they?

Let me think about that (that's what we sober guys do—we think about stuff, ha). Leave the bike with a note on it at a church telling the minister that the bike is stolen and needs to be returned to the police.

Maybe.

July 1, 1992

We took in almost a thousand tons of garbage today at the landfill. I don't normally pay attention to that stuff, but that's a lot. We are permitted for, like, twelve hundred or so, but a thousand tons in a day is a pretty busy day. All that garbage is weighed, goes in, and gets squished down by big loaders that ride over it and push it down as far as they can so more and more garbage can be stuffed in there. At the end of the day, it's covered with this giant tarp machine and then pulled back the next day and it starts all over again. And Mount Trashmore gets bigger and bigger.

And I pushed my three buttons and watched the trucks come in loaded, get weighed, dump, and then come back empty and I weighed them again. I wonder how many tons of garbage I've weighed since I've been there.

Eff. Is this what you normals think about when your brain ain't soaked with booze? I need a hobby (ha).

I scoped out my church and I'm dropping the bike off tonight. The church is the Union Bible Church. I looked at a bunch of churches and I chose this one because it's small and the bike won't just get stuck in a corner until one of the nine hundred ministers fills out the right form. And it's in Endicott so it's far away from my apartment (just being careful as far as evidence against me, ha) and this church is off the road and up a hill so the bike won't be seen by nobody from the street and it will be safe until the church opens. But the big reason is they have a prayer meeting tonight at 7:00. So I'll get there before 6:00 and drop off the bike and they should get it right after that. I already have the letter written that I will stick in an envelope and tape the envelope to the bike. On the envelope I wrote TO: UNION BIBLE CHURCH and on the note I wrote (I don't got a computer and I don't want to print it at the library and have the librarian see it, eff, so I hand-wrote it) in big block letters: WE STOLE THIS BIKE AND ARE SORRY. IT'S REAL VALUABLE AND PEOPLE ARE LOOKING FOR IT. EVERYTHING IS IN THEM SADDLEBAGS THAT WE TOOK INCLUDING THE MONEY. CAN YOU GET THIS BIKE TO THE POLICE SO THEY CAN GET IT BACK TO WHO WE STOLE IT FROM? THE POLICE WILL KNOW WHO IT BELONGS TO. THANKS.

Ha. I used the *we* instead of the *me*. Let them think it was a bunch of kids or some vicious bike-stealing gang (ha). So, the scary part is getting the bike out of my kitchen, in effing daylight, to my car. Getting it into my car. Driving down Main Street, Binghamton, then Main Street, Johnson City, then Main Street, Endicott, then to the church. Then getting the bike out of my car and propped up by the front door of the church and not letting nobody see me or the bike. And then getting back.

Eff. That's it?

Yup, that's it.

I just got home from work and will wait another hour or so and then take the bike back. I have the backseat down and I measured it to make sure the bike'll fit. This is the part I'm the most nervous about. The front of my effing building is like a fish bowl. Even if you were at the Belmar and happened to be looking out, you'd see me roll this bright red bike to my car. I should wait until dark, but that means the bike won't be found today and I want to give it back soon. Maybe it ain't too late for this guy and he can continue on his trip.

I don't know.

And I've been planning stuff, too. Once the bike is gone, that's the first step. Then I need to start saving up, maybe selling things, like my car and stuff. Quit my job, get the security deposit back from the apartment. If I get a thousand bucks or so for the car, that will give me fourteen hundred or so to buy a bike (not a Fezzari, ha—just a good but cheap bike), a sleeping bag, and a tent, and still have some pocket money. I get excited when I think about it.

And everything depends on getting the bike to the church and not going to jail. That would put a crimp in everything (ha).

So I'd better get ready.

I've been sober for eighteen days now and have been thinking a lot about that, too. When I was in the boxes, there were pictures and notes and stuff about college and after. Being at the bars with friends, getting stupid. I loved that. I loved being part of a group and hanging out all night. For years I did that, even after I got married. Nothing was more important than that group. Then I started hating myself and pulled away from the group. But I still loved the booze, until finally the group was gone and it was only me and the booze. And here's the weird thing I found out. It never was about the booze. It was always about the people, but I gave up the people and thought it was the booze I needed.

Effing weird.

It's all weird, just like rehab was weird. In rehab, you had to put this heavy thing on, the thing called being an alcoholic. You had to admit it and show everybody you were wearing it. That you were an alcoholic. This embarrassing, heavy, ugly thing and it will always be with you and it'll never go away. Alcoholic. I always thought that was weird. If this powerful thing had held me and I was too much of a wuss to fight it, what's the point? I'm not more powerful than alcoholism, so just give in and get used to it. And these guys were real unhappy that they were in rehab, and do you blame them? They've got this monster on them, this curse that would never go away, like being a werewolf or something. They're beaten before they effing start. The lowest point in their whole effing life and they get beat down even more and are told to put on the alcoholic coat and walk around with it and not to take it off.

I don't feel like that now (but maybe I will later, I don't know). I feel, actually, pretty good and I'm only eighteen days sober. Excited. And ain't that what you're supposed to feel when you start something new? Excited? When people want to lose weight they don't make them say how fat they are. They encourage them and tell them they can do anything if they work hard enough, right? And I don't know if I'll ever drink again but I am pretty sure I won't get drunk anytime soon. Not because I'm strong or anything—I ain't—but because it doesn't sound fun. (And the next thing I could write could be about me getting wasted tonight, so I'd better watch it, huh? Ha.)

I'm giving the bike back, though. If nothing else, I'm giving my roommate, the bike, back and setting the tall guy that owns it back on his trip. On his adventure.

I stood inside my apartment holding the bike right next to me and I stared at the back of my door. I stood there and looked at the door and listened out to the hallway. I was afraid to open the door and go out. I pressed the intercom button to listen for anybody coming in the front of the building, then I stood there some more. As long as I stayed inside, I was safe. As long as I kept the door shut, I hadn't done nothing illegal. I stood by the door, then backed the bike into the kitchen, then rolled the bike back out again and stood by the door again. Then I opened the effing door and rolled the bike out into the hallway.

The door slammed behind me with a klunk and I was out in the hallway moving toward the steps fast, trapped in the hallway where anybody could open their door and see me. The bike rolled toward the steps with that click, click, click sound a bike makes. The sound hit my ears like gunfire, so effing loud, and even if you were in your own apartment, you would know somebody was in the hallway with a bike.

I got to the steps and the late afternoon sun from the street shot through the front doors and lit up the carpeted steps. And I was on the steps, lifting the bike (which was a lot lighter than I thought it would be with all the stuff in them bags), and then carried it down the seven steps to the first floor. Now I was on the first floor and rolled the bike, click, click, click past the super's apartment and toward the front door with the click, click, click beating in my effing ears.

Now I opened the door and if you were coming in the building, you'd see me. Right there you'd see me. I opened the door and walked through and was in between the two doors where the mailboxes are, trapped in a glass cage between the two doors.

This is the feeling I hate. The feeling of being afraid, this worry, this knowing. This effing shame. This is the feeling that I'm leaving behind and after this I will never, ever, ever, ever feel this way again because I will never do anything that makes me feel this way again. I will never be an effing rat running in the gutters and running away from the effing sun.

The outside door opened and I rolled the bike out to the stoop. I had thought this part out and lifted the bike to the street quickly and then rolled it around the building to the alley between my building and building #3 and leaned it against the wall. Okay. Good.

Mather Street is a one-way street going toward Main Street, so you got to come down Edwards and Walnut when you drive in to find a parking spot in front of the building. Sometimes it takes a few times around the block to find a spot nearby. Last night, I came out here several times. Moving the car up and up Mather each time a spot was free until I was got the car right in front of #3 Mather next door and right by the alley.

I walked over to where my car was waiting, got in and started it up, and backed it right into the alley and left it running. This way, I could load the bike in the alleyway instead of on Mather Street where every car going by on Main and Mather or anybody on the stoop of the Belmar having a cigarette could see every effing thing.

With the backseat down, the bike fit on its side through the hatch. Then I covered the bike with an old sheet and an old New York Giants blanket and got in. Then I pulled out onto Mather Street.

Done. Effing done. The hardest part was over and now all I had to do was get the bike to the church before the prayer meeting. My letter was already written and under the seat.

The rest would be easy. I smiled and backed the car out onto Main and got to the corner of Mather and Main and waited at the stop sign for the traffic to thin out. I was sitting there so relieved, so relaxed at the hard part being over, that I didn't hear Randy shouting to me from the Belmar stoop where he was smoking a cigarette. And I didn't see him leave the stoop and walk across Main Street toward me. In fact, I didn't see Randy until he was already across Main and in the effing West Side Mini-Mart parking lot and walking toward my car. Then I saw him. Then I heard him. Then I effing panicked.

In about ten seconds Randy would be at the car. He would be looking in and see the bike. I yanked the car into the Mini-Mart lot toward the fence away from him. I turned the car off and got out of the car, moving toward Randy quickly, trying to make as much distance between him and the car as possible.

"Hey," Randy yelled, placing a hand over his eyes to block the sun. "I thought ya was dead."

"What's going on?" I said.

"What's going on? What's going on with you?" Randy said, moving behind me so the sun was now in my eyes instead of his. "I left ya like ten effing messages. Ya okay?"

"Yeah, I'm fine."

"Where ya been?"

"I've been around."

"No, ya ain't." He laughed. "Cuz I been around and I ain't seen ya there." Randy slapped my shoulder and took a step around me, looking me over for damage. He smelled of Budweiser and Marlboro Lights. "Everything okay?"

"Sure."

"Everything okay at work?"

"Yeah."

Randy looked up and smiled. "Okay," he said, slapping my shoulder again. "Ya had me worried, pal. Come on, I'll buy ya a beer." Randy moved around me and looked at the traffic on Main, trying to judge when would be a good time to cross.

I was this close to giving the bike back and I knew I couldn't just leave the bike in the car and I couldn't wait until tomorrow because there would be no one at the church. It had to be *now* if I wanted this thing to be over with.

"I gotta run an errand," I said.

Randy looked at me like I said I had to go do brain surgery or that I had to have a quick dinner with the governor.

"An errand?"

"Yeah, I'll be back in twenty minutes."

"Ya sure you're okay?" he asked again.

"Yeah. I'm fine."

"Okay, then I'll go with ya on this errand and we can talk." He began walking toward my car.

"Okay," I said, pulling out my car keys and trying to keep the panic out of my voice. "But I'm going to church."

The word *church* stopped Randy cold, as if I'd said there were poisonous snakes in my car. He looked at me and even took a half-step back away from my car.

"Church?"

"Yeah, I won't be long."

Randy stopped again. Then he took a full step backwards. "If you're not back in an hour I'm going looking for ya," he said, pointing at me with his one index finger that was broken and never set straight.

"Okay." I smiled at Randy, realizing for the first time that Randy looked just like Chef Boyardee. The same round red face, the same white hair and mustache. All he was missing was the chef's hat (ha).

"And I want to hear about all this stuff ya been doing and make sure you're okay."

Randy walked back across the street without waiting for me to say anything. He walked back and slipped back into the safety of the Belmar. I got in my car and pulled out onto Main Street.

I smiled as I drove and even laughed at the sight of Randy stopping and being so effing afraid of church. Then I stopped laughing and wondered when was the last time I was inside a church. Then I smiled again at Randy being worried about me and wondered if he was really worried or just didn't want there to be an empty seat next to him at the bar. Then I thought about all them people in the box of letters and pictures that cared about me when I thought they didn't and I wondered if Randy was one of them, too.

I drove slow (probably too slow) down Main Street until I rolled under the Binghamton arch, the one that separates Binghamton from

Johnson City, and then drove down Main Street, Johnson City, slowly through all them lights until I could see the Johnson City arch and Lane's Deli. I wondered when the last time I was at Lane's was and thought about running in and getting a fish and chips when I was done but then remembered I had to meet Randy and figured I'd just eat at the Belmar.

I went through the second arch and was on Main Street, Endicott, then past the Endicott bridge and the park, over the viaduct and past Enjoe golf course, and then there was the church. The little red building up on the hill. The end.

The one thing I didn't like about the church was that I had to drive up the hill a bit, up the church driveway and into the lot before I could tell if the lot was completely empty or not. If there was cars there, they could see you and you couldn't just drive by. I drove up slowly and the lot was empty. I drove the Datsun around the back of the building then I pulled out the bike and leaned it against the car. The Giants blanket got caught in the wheels but I got it out and walked the bike over to the main door with the note already sealed in the envelope and being carried between my teeth.

The click, click, click of the bike was barely noticeable out in the open and I rolled the bike to a flat stoop on the side of the building. There was a main entrance in the front of the building, but when I cased the building before, there was a sign that said "Use Other Door." Besides, the bike would be seen here as soon as you pulled into the lot. I taped the envelope to the front door instead of the bike, then stopped. I pulled the rag I had in my back pocket and wiped down every inch of that bike and the last of them blue and white glass pieces jumped off the bike and onto the rag. Would the police try to get fingerprints? I dunno, but paranoia has done well by me so far (ha). Then I got back in the car and headed down the lot. I had just pulled into the feed store parking lot across the street and had put the car in park so I could wait until I saw a car go in, when four seconds later a blue Toyota hit its signal and drove up the short incline into the parking lot and over toward the building. Perfect timing.

I pulled out of the feed store parking lot and headed back to the Belmar to meet Randy.

Done. Done. Done, done, done, done, and done.

I was clear of the bike and I would never need to do anything like this again. I was free and on my way to my own adventure and the man whose adventure I took could have it back now. I had dates on a calendar when I would leave and a plan in a notebook and I was pumped up and excited for the first time, eff, for the first time in a long time (ha). And it was very possible that I had a friend waiting for me in a bar. It was very possible that Randy *was* my friend, after all.

Life was pretty effing good.

CHAPTER 11

| JULY 6, 1992 |

It's been five days since I've written you and I've been in the effing newspaper twice since then. Ha. No, I ain't kidding. Not in thirty-one years have I been in that paper (well, my wedding announcement was in there but I think that's it, ha).

Hold on, I need to get a cup of coffee.

Okay, I'm back (ah, coffee with real half-and-half and not the powdered crap—yes). A lot to tell you, so I'll start with the newspaper.

Twice in same week (ha)—isn't that a trip? So here's the first article. I taped it below. Wait'll you see this!

Thieves Ask Church to Return Stolen Goods
Endicott, NY
By Wayne Donnavan

When Alvin Stickles, member of the Union Bible Church, arrived at the church on Monroe Street this Wednesday evening to prepare for 7:00 Bible study, an interesting sight awaited him. Resting against the outside church door was an expensive Italian touring bicycle, complete with four full saddlebags packed with clothing, camping equipment, and cash, and accompanied by a note.

The handwritten note stated that the bicycle was stolen. The people who had taken the bicycle were sorry and were asking the church to help by returning it to the police. The note went on to say that there was cash in the saddlebag that belonged to the owner, and that the police were looking for the bicycle and would be able to get it back to the rightful owner.

Stickles immediately called the Endicott police. They arrived at the church to investigate.

The bicycle has been identified as a Fezzari touring bicycle and is estimated to have a retail price of over $3,000. With the cash and assorted gear, including an expensive camera, a Walkman, camping equipment, and clothing, the overall value of the stolen bicycle is estimated to be close to $6,000, making this an interesting story of redemption and change of heart—with one small exception.

The expensive touring bike was not stolen, or at least, it doesn't appear to be.

"We have no report of a bike like this being stolen," says Sergeant Paul Lorenzo of the Endicott Police Department. "We ran this through our national database and found nothing. A sticker was found on the bike mentioning a bike shop in Massachusetts. However, that shop has been out of business for almost two years. The list of stolen bicycles is very extensive, but this is a very specific item and it does not match any stolen claims from the past two years."

The bicycle remains a mystery. Many people are questioning if it was truly stolen or if the whole incident is just an elaborate joke.

"If it's a joke," laughs Sergeant Lorenzo, "I don't get it. This isn't a Schwinn; it's a very expensive item. We've got to assume for now that it is stolen and try to find the owner. Or try to find whoever stole it and ask them a few questions."

Sergeant Lorenzo states that the police will continue to investigate and asks for anyone with information on this matter to contact the Endicott Police Department.

Can you effing believe that? When I eff up, man, I do it big. I was hoping to know, to finally know, whose bike it was. So I could remember. Any hint might help me remember, but I don't even get that. I've returned the bike and no one . . . ahh, eff. Never mind.

And I wanted to hear about the guy who took it and read about how he was going to get back on the bike and head for California or Vermont or wherever. I wanted to see his picture. I wanted to know that he could go now and that I didn't stop him.

Nothing.

And I wanted to remember taking the bike. I wanted to remember taking it so I could forgive myself and move on with *my* adventure. My trip. Nope again.

I remember coming in the night before (sort of) and then I remember finding the bike in my kitchen. What kind of a drunk am I anyway that I can't remember the simplest effing thing about that bike?

So are the police, like, after me now? Like the effing paper said, are they looking for me (or my large bike gang that stole it, ha) to try and figure it out? I dunno. But I read the newspaper piece a hundred times. I laughed and I cut it out and taped it here for you to read. Pretty funny, huh?

I wiped down the bike for fingerprints. I guess you might find fingerprints on the camera or some of the stuff inside if you wanted to look, but I ain't got no record to match the prints with, so who knows?

Anyways, I want you to read the second piece about me. Two days later, *this* article was in there, and this one is really good. (No, I'm not being sarcastic, it really *is* about me and it's really good. Ha. You'll see.)

Binghamton Man to Begin Yearlong Journey
Binghamton, NY
By Brandon Mosely

According to the National Statistics Manager, the average American spends three weeks planning a one-week vacation. This means we spend three times as much time planning the trip as we do enjoying it. However, this amount of time is often required to finance the trip, schedule time off of work, reserve airline tickets and hotel rooms, and generally prepare for that one week of vacation.

Based on this statistic, Binghamton native Riley Dutcher would need to spend the next three years planning his one-year journey across the United States and back. However, he has spent only hours over the past two weeks planning it and will be leaving on July 18.

"Well," Dutcher jokes, "since I have no money, since I quit my job, since I am selling my car and am traveling by foot or bike or bus or whatever, two weeks is more than enough time to plan."

The idea came to Dutcher when he began looking at some old boxes stored in his Mather Street apartment. The boxes contained old pictures and cards and letters he had saved throughout his life.

"I spent a full day looking through those boxes, looking at the pictures of my parents and my childhood and the short time I was married and my friends and I realized one thing. That I have had a

wonderful life." He smiled. "An incredible life. And since I have the ability to leave now, since no one needs me right now—no parents that need me or a wife that needs me—I need to go," Dutcher said. "No, that's not it," he corrected himself. "I owe it to them, to everyone that was ever in my life, to go and see a few things. They would want me to. Then I'll come back."

How does one finance a yearlong trip? The same way anyone finances any other year. "You work," Dutcher said, laughing. "You work and you earn money and pay your own way. Only I won't need much because I won't have a cable bill or car insurance or an electric bill. All I'll need is money for a few crumbs and a place to pitch my tent or a simple room while I see what's around me."

Riley Dutcher graduated from Binghamton High School in 1979 and attended Oneonta State University. He was a sales rep for Crowley Foods for nine years and is currently employed by Broome County.

"I grew up here," Dutcher said. "I was raised here and my parents are buried here. This is home and I will return here and will someday be buried right next to my parents in Vestal Hills Cemetery." He laughed. "Hopefully not right away. So now is the time to get lost for a while. To see a little. To take my time and explore and then come back home."

When asked why he is planning to be away for such a long period of time, Dutcher answered, "I have never gone anywhere and I probably won't again, so why not do it all at once and see everything? There's a lot to see."

Broome County Landfill manager Reese Levitt has reluctantly accepted Dutcher's letter of resignation, effective July 17. "When Dutch told me what he wanted to do we accepted his resignation but told him that if we had a slot open he'd have a job waiting when he got back. And we'd better get some postcards and hear from him, too. He's a good guy and we're going to miss him."

"See here," Dutcher said, pointing to a numbered list in his notebook. This list includes resigning from his job, selling his car, giving up his apartment, moving out, purchasing travel equipment, getting his security deposit back, closing bank accounts, and so on. Each one was numbered in the order they need to occur. "I've done the first six and only have three things left to do before I can leave."

Riley Dutcher has donated the contents of his apartment to the Salvation Army while he waits to turn in his apartment key. His cousin is storing the important boxes of memorabilia from his life and Dutcher has accepted an offer to purchase his car, which he will finalize after his last day of work at the Broome County Landfill. Then he will begin his yearlong trip.

Dutcher has no true travel plans, but he does know the first thing he wants to see.

"Niagara Falls," he said, embarrassed. "I have lived in New York State my entire life and I have never seen Niagara Falls. From there I don't know where I'll go."

John Steinbeck wrote, "A journey is like a marriage. A certain way to be wrong is to think you control it." And this has never been truer than with the plans of Riley Dutcher.

Randy's fat Chef Boyardee fingers pounded down on the newspaper that he had spread open across the bar, tapping the last paragraph of the article.

"Arrogant SOB, ain't he?" Randy smiled. At first, I thought he was talking about me but then I saw he was talking about his brother-in-law, the guy who wrote the article. "That Steinbeck part was too frickin much," he said, gulping down the last of his draft. "But the rest was real good."

I stood there frozen and then started to read the paper over again. The full-page article was on the front page of the Living section of the Sunday paper. It was in color and was about me and had pictures of me moving some things out of my apartment and one of me going through my list at a table at the Belmar.

"I sound like," I said, "an effing lawyer or something. I don't even remember saying all that stuff to him. Not the way he wrote it in there."

"Yup, he painted ya real pretty, Dutch." Randy laughed, pushing his glass to the end of the bar for Sheri to pick up and refill. "Ya'll probably be elected dog catcher when ya come back."

Sheri laughed and placed Randy's beer on his coaster, then leaned over the bar and read the article upside down.

"Yeah," she said. "You'd make a hell of a dog catcher." She pulled the newspaper off the bar and looked at the page. "I liked that last part. That Seinfeld part."

"Steinbeck," Randy said. "Not Seinfeld."

"Whatever. You'll stop here on Friday after work before you leave," she said for the zillionth time—this time not really asking me but telling me. "You promised." Sheri had several years of being disappointed by my promises and she was smart to expect that I would break this one, too.

"Yeah, I will," I said, staring at the paper she was holding and waiting for her to put it back down again.

When I had met Randy back at the Belmar, after dropping off the bike at the church, I told Randy about my plan. About me leaving. And Randy gave me his *You are an idiot* look. He asked me questions about the plan and I answered. He asked me more questions and I gave him more answers and then that *You are an idiot* look sort of went away. He asked more questions and we talked some more. Randy and I talked for a long time and I had three beers (I told myself I can have up to three beers and I had just three—it was so cool). And then Randy reminded me of stuff I'd need to do that I forgot about, like having my mail forwarded to general delivery at a city that I'll be at down the road and keeping a small road atlas handy. Randy told me some tricks about camping and ways to cook cheap and quick. We talked for a long time and afterward I knew Randy was my friend and I wanted to be a friend to him back. (That's the part about friendship that I'd never done before. That friend-back part.)

A few days later, Randy called me at work and told me to meet him at the Belmar, that there was somebody who wanted to meet me. I showed up and there was his brother-in-law. His idiot brother-in-law that he was always making fun of. The one and only Brandon Mosely from the *Binghamton Press*. I had never met him before and we talked and he took pictures of me. Some of the stuff he got wrong—like, I never said I'd be gone a year. He asked me how long I'd be gone and I told him I didn't know and then he asked, *A year? Two years?* And I said a year, maybe, probably not two. Otherwise, he makes me sound different than I really am. Weird. But Randy likes the article and that's part of all that being-a-friend-back part. So that's pretty cool.

Well, I got to get to work. Only eleven days left.

Later.

July 16, 1992

Okay, this is getting weird. This is getting really effing weird. (A good weird, but still really effing weird.)

I think it's around ten o'clock at night, but I ain't sure. I gave my clock to the Salvation Army (ha), along with my coffee maker, a bunch of clothes, my microwave, and some pots, pans, and dishes. That's everything I had in here, but Brandon Mosely's article made it sound like it took ten U-Hauls to cart all my stuff away (ha).

Hold on, let me check what time it is.

Okay, it's 10:51. I was pretty close. I'm sitting in my chair (my chair and my bed came with the apartment and they're all that's left). I'm decompressing.

I like that word, *decompressing*. I've heard it before and I was sort of, like, jealous of the word. Like it was a word only normals use. Normals could go away and decompress, to think everything over and charge their brains back up. We drunks don't have to do nothing like that because we just drink as soon as any need comes up. Up time, down time, worried time, bored time—it's simple: Drink. One pill for everything and one size fits all.

But decompressing is different. It's a word that says not only are you spending time to think about something to, like, review it all, but you've got something to decompress about. Something has to actually kind of happen for you to go and decompress. You don't wake up from a nap and say, I need to go decompress (ha). You finish a project, you come back from a trip, you work through something, and then you get in your normal car and drive someplace and decompress.

This is the first time I've decompressed (probably the first time I've ever needed to) because things are happening now and that's when you need to decompress. Things didn't happen before. Not for a long time.

Since I moved into this apartment four years ago, things have been the same. It's like every day is the same and the weekends are just a little different from the weekdays but all the weekends are the same as all the other weekends. Nothing has moved in four effing years. A few bumps and bruises maybe, but nothing that would make it not the same and nothing that would make it move in any direction, good or bad.

Then I took the bike. Then I looked in all the boxes (and of course I was sober at the time to think about all this stuff—that helped, ha). And then I gave the bike back and now . . . *It's like everything is different*. EVERYTHING.

Randy called me a bunch of times at work yesterday and today. (Reese don't mind if I take a few calls while I'm working. I've never done it before and he knows tomorrow is my last day.) Randy told me that the article about me had been reprinted in other newspapers besides just the *Binghamton Press*—papers in California and Boston and a whole bunch of other places. Randy called me because people kept calling Brandon Mosely and Brandon was giving them Randy's number to call.

"When did I become your frickin agent?" Randy snapped.

"You were the only one that wanted the job." I pressed the green button and waved the BTI truck in as it rolled over the landfill scale and in through the gate.

"Frickin Brandon is only passing these calls to me instead of you to royally piss me off," Randy said. But I could tell Randy really liked being in charge of all the weirdness.

Randy told me about Eureka Tent calling and wanting to donate a backpack, sleeping bag, and tent for my trip. He told me that Dick's Sporting Goods wanted to donate a backpack, hiking boots—as much stuff as I wanted for under three hundred bucks. Wegmans said they had a hundred-dollar gift certificate for me to use for supplies. Another guy wanted to show me ways to organize my pack and make things light and easy to find. There was a company that had one of them pocket phones that they was gonna give me with free service for a year. And then there was the money. People wanted to give me money for my trip. People were calling in and wanting to donate a few bucks here and there, and it was all adding up.

They saw that guy in the article, that guy that Brandon had made up, that perfect guy that said things the way Brandon did, not the way I do, and they wanted to give *him* money for *his* trip. Not *me* money for *my* trip.

"What the eff are ya talking about?" Randy said. "He prettied ya up a bit, but it's still *you*. Ya came up with the idea. Ya had the balls to see it through. It's *you*. It's his job to write like that, but it's still *you*."

"It's, like, dishonest or something," I said. "Like those 'Will Work for Food' guys."

"What?" Randy snorted. "You're not asking for food to feed your family and then going and buying crack. And ya didn't ask for nothing. Ya told your story and people liked it. It's their way of being, like, a part of it. What's that word?"

Randy thought and I let him, since I didn't know what word he was talking about.

"*Vicarious*," he finally said. "They don't have the balls to just pack everything up and go like you do, so they give ya stuff. You're doing it, but you're doing it with *their* backpack or *their* tent. Like, they get to live, like, through *you*, vicariously. They get to be a part of the effing thing and they never have to leave their couches or put down their remotes."

Randy called a bunch more times and then finally gave up.

"I ain't calling ya no more," he said, in a voice that sounded more tired than pissed off. "I'll write all this crap down. Meet me at the Belmar tonight."

Randy and I sat at the table near the window (we never sit at a table; we always sit at the bar) and we went over all the phone calls that Randy got.

Some of them calls was real weird. One lady wanted me to look for her niece while I was "walking around" because she didn't know where the girl lived. One guy wanted me to see what jobs there were for electricians up in Niagara Falls and set up some interviews for him (since I had all that free time and nothing to do). And another lady said she was going with me (Randy said she didn't ask; she *told* Randy she was going with me) and said she had to bring her cats and wanted to know if I had an extra cat carrier because she only had two.

"What did you tell her?"

"I told her, perfect. I said ya was bringing a bunch of cats and squirrels for food, for when times got tough. So we'd just throw them cats in the bag with the rest of them. She didn't need no carrier."

I laughed and snorted beer through my nose. "What did she say then?"

"I don't know." Randy drained his draft. "I hung up on the old dingbat."

Randy and I talked and planned and it was like it was before. Nope. That ain't true. It was better than it was before. Something had happened to me and I knew Randy was my friend and he knew that I knew it.

I had two beers and was going to have a third (just because I can) and realized I didn't want no more. I sat for a while listening to Randy, watching his big Chef Boyardee face and laughing but getting tired. Then I went home. Cuz tomorrow is my last day of work.

July 17, 1992

I finished my last day of work and I'm leaving Binghamton tomorrow and still no news on the bike. Nothing. I asked Brandon (and I was real careful about it, too). *Hey,* I said. *That article about that stolen bike,* I said. *Did they ever find the owner?*

I asked while talking about other stuff, too, and if Brandon thought the question was weird, he didn't act like he did.

Nope, he said. *No one came forward.*

So ain't that a kick in the head? I stole a non-stolen bike? (Ha.) But I don't spend much time thinking about the bike no more. It's over and I have my own stuff to think about now.

At work today they brought in pizzas for lunch and everybody put some money in a card for me. It was real nice. They gave me $285 and they all said nice things and it was great. It was really cool. And I felt like—like, I had done some good there.

I'm taking a shower now and going to the Belmar like I promised. I leave tomorrow on the 9:00 A.M. bus to Niagara Falls.

Later.

* * *

As I'm sitting in my apartment and writing, it's dark out but the sun is starting to come up between the alley of my building and building 3. I remember now why I drank. It's because of nights like this. Nights at the Belmar, with friends and fun and slaps on the back and jokes and stories. Nights that you never want to end. I still only had my three beers. There were moments when I wanted more but only because I was excited and had to have something in my hands, but I had ginger ale at those times.

I loved those nights—nights like this. The people. And then when the people were gone, I had the booze and I thought it was the booze all along. (I think I wrote all of this before but I'll have to check—yup, I did. Sorry about that.)

Anyways, it was fun. I promised to keep in touch and I said I would, knowing it wasn't a lie this time. I *will* keep in touch. Randy and Sheri are my friends. And they always will be. I won't let them just be some pictures stuffed in a box.

July 18, 1992

This is bad. This is real effing bad.

I can't write for long because she's here. She's here and we're talking and I remember about the bike now. Actually, she's crying and

I'm letting her cry until we can talk some more and I'm writing to you until she stops crying and we can talk about the bike and the other stuff. Why won't she stop crying? The other stuff is real bad. Real effing bad.

I've remembered it all now—all about the bike and the other stuff. Eff. The other stuff is worse than the bike. Way effing worse than the bike.

As soon as I heard her voice, as soon as I heard her call me that name, that other name, when she locked her brakes on Main Street and then pulled her car onto Mather when she saw me. Then I remembered. I remembered it all. Even before she got out of the car and walked to the stoop, I remembered. Like a switch was flipped in my brain and I'd seen it all in my head and it's real, real effing bad!

And now she's sitting here and she's crying and we're trying to figure a way out of all of this. And it's hard because I'm remembering it all like it just happened.

This is real bad. Worse then I ever effing thought. Eff.

JOURNAL 3

WALKER

Chapter 12

Kyle Somebody

| July 24, 1992 |

Okay, here's an example. Let's say you have just won the lottery. You have won . . . hmm, let's go with the life-changing amount of $25 million.

Here's the scenario.

You've just checked the lottery ticket you bought and bam! It can't be. Oh, my gosh, it is. You've won. You've actually won. You can't believe it and you check the ticket again and again in disbelief, but there it is. Boom. A perfect match. You . . . have . . . won . . . the . . . lottery!

You scream and jump up and down and check your ticket seventy-four more times and after making several phone calls, you find out that the next step is to turn the ticket in at the nearest lottery office. You figure out where the nearest lottery office is and you take off.

You drive under the speed limit. You nervously watch every car near you, wondering if they know about the winning ticket and are simply waiting to run you off the road and rip the ticket from your cold dead fingers. But you manage to keep it all together and after checking your shirt pocket every forty seconds to make sure the winning ticket hasn't evaporated—proving you've imagined the whole thing after all—you arrive at the lottery office both alive and still holding the winning ticket.

You run inside and tell the receptionist why you are there. She escorts you in. They quickly verify the ticket and confirm that there was only one winning lottery ticket sold, which means the entire twenty-five million dollars is yours. Congratulations.

You sit in a room as photographers get ready to take the standard lottery winner photographs: the ones with you smiling and holding your huge cardboard check that has your name in bold black type and then a dollar sign followed by a twenty-five and six zeros. The caption under the photograph will read: *John Q. Sixpack, our latest $25 million winner.*

Then there will be interviews with the lottery people asking the normal lottery questions: *What will you do with your $25 million? How does it feel to now be worth $25 million? Did you ever dream you would someday win $25 million?*

And by the next day, the world will read about everything that you're planning to do with your brand-new $25 million. They will read about how you are going to buy a new house for your sister and have a new house built for your mother, how you are going to pay your niece's tuition to medical school. And your friends and your coworkers and family will read about your plans and they will wonder how they will share in your good fortune as they congratulate and encourage and advise and request.

And with the photographs taken and the interviews over, you move on to the good part. The best part. The part where they give you all that money, when they give you all that cash. You now get your $25 million.

You fill out more paperwork and are escorted down a hall to a large conference room where your check is waiting. You sit while a smiling lottery man slides the check across the polished conference table to you. You flip the check over to look at it for the first time, to see your name and all those zeros. You lift it up and see a check made out to you in the amount of $834,000.

You look up at the lottery man.

"What's this?" you ask.

"That? Why, that's your lottery check, sir."

"But I won $25 million," you tell him.

The lottery man is ready for this. The lottery man has dealt with this confusion before.

"Sir," he says patiently. "You opted for the lottery payment option when you purchased the ticket, which means that you will receive $25 million over a twenty-year period. Which means that we have put $12.5 million in an annuity for you, which over the course of twenty years will double and will equal $25 million. We have taken the taxes out for you and you will receive a check for this amount, on this same date, every year, for the next nineteen years. Congratulations."

You stand there and look at your check. You have to admit that $834,000 is still a lot of money. A lot of money! More money than you have ever had at one time before. And besides, you will receive a check like this for nineteen more years and by the end of it you will be worth

$25 million. You sign for the check and walk out of the office happy and excited.

Except that the world has already seen you with that big cardboard check. The world now believes that you have $25 million, not $834,000. And soon you will start to believe that you *do* have $25 million, or at least you soon *will* have that much. And suddenly your house is too small for a multimillionaire like yourself. Your car is too drab, your vacations too plain. Someone of your wealth needs to live a little, to share a little, to pay back the family and friends who were with you back before you were so rich. And remember, you did promise to pay for your niece's college and to build your mother a house. And those preapproved credit cards that keep coming in are clogging up your mailbox. It's okay to charge a few things. Hey, it's not like you don't have the money, right? You're rich now.

And let's not forget those friends and family. Friends and family that now feel—no, now believe—that they are entitled to a part of that $25 million. You don't want to seem greedy. You don't want to disappoint them.

And then, four months before the next $834,000 check is set to be cut, you notice that things are getting a little tight—hey, you quit your job months ago, remember? And the minimums on those credit cards are pretty high and then there's the taxes on the three houses you own and Suzie's next tuition payment is due. But hey, you'll weather the storm somehow. Borrow a little to bridge the four months until your next check comes in. It's okay. You're a millionaire. It's not like you don't have the money. It's not like you're not rich, right?

Only here is the rub. You're *not* rich. You *don't* have the money. You're *not* a millionaire. You're an eight hundred thirty-four thousandaire. You're the same as that executive who earns that same amount every year, only he has one advantage over you. He knows he's not rich. The world knows he's not rich. But you, my fine friend, have forgotten that you're not rich. You and your family and your friends and the strangers at restaurants who think that asking you to pick up their dinner tab is normal because you got so lucky with the lottery and all—everyone believes you *are* rich.

And this, my dear reader, is exactly where I am now.

How so, you may ask? Well, allow me to explain.

Bugby left me $19 million, right?

Wrong.

Bugby left me his estate, with an estimated value of $19 million: an apartment complex, the storage units, something called PB Holdings, and a huge liquor store. It's an estate that is worth $19 million, but only if you sold it all and received top dollar for all the property, all the equipment, and all the land. Then, and only then, did Bugby leave me $19 million. What he *did* leave me was a net income from all of his businesses of approximately $145,000 a year—if everything goes as well as it did in his day and I don't mess up what Bugby created.

Not that $145,000 isn't a lot of money. It is. But it's not the $19 million that the world thinks I have. I can't put my hands on $19 million—right now, I could only put my hand on thirty thousand dollars, which was what was in Bugby's checking account.

And this amount, this $145,000 a year, is *only* if I don't screw everything up—only if I know what I'm doing and keep everything running the way Bugby did. And right now I am not doing such a great job of it. In order to afford to keep everything that Sonia and Victor and Bugby himself worked so hard to put together, I may need to tear it all down and sell it. I may need to destroy it all myself on purpose, before I destroy it all by accident.

Ah, it's the paradoxes in life that make things interesting.

But hey, it's not like I don't have the money, right? It's not like I'm not rich. It's not like I'm not a millionaire.

Now, I will now get to the point of all of this and get to the good part. Well, the bad part—the really bad part.

The bad part is—well, it's more of the evil part than a bad part—I don't normally use that word, *evil*, but it's the only one that fits. Angry. Vengeful and evil.

Since I haven't written, I haven't talked at all about the police and the media and about me being a "person of interest" in Bugby's death, so I guess I need to go back to that first.

Well, I *was* a person of interest, but the police are officially no longer interested in me. It's difficult to continue a murder investigation when there is no murder.

It was quickly determined that Bugby fell out of his raft and into the Shubenacadie River, where he hit his head on the bottom. This was witnessed by three different rafting groups at the time—local media hadn't gotten to that part of their reporting yet—and they witnessed Bugby being tossed from his raft and into the tidal bore. In fact, two other rafters had dived in to try to save him but could not get to him in time.

Accidental death. No investigation.

However—and I am *not* making this up—the prosecuting attorney, Mr. Dillon Harris, was interviewed by the *Erie Times News* about Bugby's death. This article was picked up by the wire services and printed nationally, where Harris discussed my "obvious" involvement in the matter. He said, and I quote, "Just because there wasn't a crime doesn't mean he didn't do it."

You can't make this stuff up.

So here comes the bad part. The evil part.

Now, there is obviously some negative feeling toward me since I got out of prison—concerns that I have written about here and concerns that still, three years later, hang in the air like stale cigar smoke. I deserve those concerns. And I deserve the shame that comes with them. But let's mix in the evil part to this bitter soup. Mix in that change that occurs when money chooses only one in the pack. Mix that with the anger and the hunger of $19 million sitting somewhere, just waiting to be taken.

Here are some quick nuggets of history.

In 1988, lottery winner William Post's brother was caught trying to hire a hit man to kill him so he would inherit the winnings.

In 1991, Ibi Roncaioli won $5 million in the lottery and was poisoned by her husband.

In 1990, David Brushingham murdered his sister so he would not have to split his aunt's inheritance with her.

Seeing a pattern here?

So am I being paranoid? Delusional? Overly cautious?

Three days after it was announced that Bugby had left me everything, there were several calls to Holy Cross Day Camp from a man pretending to be me, asking when my girls would be getting out that day. The school thought this was strange, since I had pulled the girls out of school myself and sent them to Ohio to keep them safe. The police believe this was a possible kidnapping attempt. There was another call to the school the next day.

As for myself, I've received three death threats by phone and a handful by letter—I'm not counting Clyde's hate mail; sure, they've kicked up a notch but nothing new.

Each day I receive at least twenty messages on my answering machine—I know it's around twenty, because that's when the tape gets full and turns off—demanding—*demanding* is a strong word; maybe *forcefully suggesting*?—that I *donate, loan*, and mostly *give away* the $19 million. *Especially with what I did.* That's almost always the end of most of the calls—"with what you did."

Also, Bugby's office on State Street was broken into. Yup. All the computer equipment was stolen, along with some petty cash, a few phones, anything the burglar could carry. On the wall, the burglar had spray-painted the words *FELON* and *THIEF*. Ah, irony.

Kyle Somebody—he told me his last name but I can't remember it anymore—from building C stopped me a week ago. He introduced himself. Then he told me that he had figured out a way to fix some of the financial issues caused by his recent divorce. He explained that if I would take over his truck loan and let him stay here rent-free—I am now the landlord, remember—then he could not only afford his back child-support payments but could also buy a boat, something he desperately needs in order to relax from all the stress of the divorce.

At first, I thought this was funny. I thought he was really funny and it felt nice to laugh. It felt absolutely amazing. Then I saw that Kyle Somebody wasn't laughing. Nope. Kyle Somebody doesn't seem like the laughing kind.

Kyle Somebody had figured this arrangement all out in his head. He could see it and had already accepted it to be true, and now I was messing things up. I was ruining it. And besides, what does $356 a month in truck payments and not charging rent mean to a guy with $19 million dollars, right?

Kyle Somebody is now upset. He calls me every day to tell me this.

"I had this all figured out," he says on my answering machine. His voice is a mixture of desperation and anger. "So call me and we can still fix this thing." Kyle always adds that he won't be sending next month's rent, since there won't be a need to.

You can't make this stuff up.

And then there's the media. Ah yes, the media. The media are like an insecure pretty girl. When you ignore her, she gets interested. When you continue to ignore her, she gets even.

Because I have not agreed to a single interview, the street value of an interview with me has been increasing, to a point. The longer I hold out, that value goes up, but only until the public loses interest. There is a shelf life for my story—an expiration date after which it will not be nearly as profitable—so soon they will need to do their stories without me. Hey, they have all the facts. What do they need me for? The trick is to ride the wave to the point where the public no longer cares, to get to that haven where they no longer want to know.

Kyle Somebody told my answering machine that the *National Enquirer* offered the zombie paperboy fifty thousand dollars to be interviewed about me, and he wondered how much I thought *his* interview would be worth. He said this as a threat, as though Kyle may possibly soon be forced to spill *all* the dark secrets he knows about me—knowledge taken from our one conversation and the dozen messages he's left me.

I'm not sure Kyle Somebody was on his meds when he heard the news about the zombie paperboy. I canceled the paper so I can't exactly ask the zombie myself and I'm not entirely convinced the zombie paperboy is capable of speech anyway.

On a different front, because of the fear, or the bad feelings, or maybe because they feel Bugby should have left *them* everything instead of me, six of Bugby's fourteen employees have quit. These are the guys and gals who manage the Mega-Liquor Warehouse, Denning Arms Apartments, and the storage units and keep everything moving day after day.

The Bugby business model was designed to click along with little input from him, being managed by others, but many of those others are bailing quickly and the machine is now missing many key pieces.

Dominick Salter ran everything for Bugby. He monitored all the businesses and was the key to keeping everything running smoothly. He was the first to walk, and there were several others who followed him.

I have put out classified ads in the papers to find new people but few are applying. I will probably even consider hiring Kyle Somebody before too long.

I've been told by my accountants—I now have accountants—that if a liquor store, especially such a big one as Bugby's—shuts down even for a few days, people will go to other stores and simply not come back. I guess the booze-buying public is fickle. So I've been focusing all my time on that. I have two college kids who are splitting the day shift until I can get there right after work, and then I stay until the store closes at eleven. Since my girls are still in Ohio, I have nothing else to do anyway, so it's not so bad. And I am quickly learning how to buy, sell, stock, and bag booze.

My parents would be so proud.

I don't want to quit my job at Mathis and Corbin if I can help it. Bugby managed all the businesses with only a few hours of work a week. But I'm not Bugby. I have no one to make it work, so it's just temporary. I really may have to sell it before I destroy it. Victor Bugby, Bugby's dad, knew that if you're going to sell, you should do it while the business is reasonably healthy. And I may need to do it soon.

And now, dear reader, you are officially caught up. Or as caught up as you're going to be because it's past midnight and I'm falling asleep and can't write much more.

The one good thing to come out of all of this is that every day has been so chaotic and weird, so crazy and busy, that I haven't had time to miss the girls. I miss them, of course, but the true pain of their being gone hasn't had time to fester yet. Or maybe it has and I'm just too numb to feel it. Two weeks is the longest I've been without them since I got out of prison. Right now, two weeks feels like a lifetime.

Catherine and I worked out an arrangement with a piano tutor in Ohio so Abby and Liz won't miss the last two weeks of lessons from day camp while they are all out there staying with Catherine's mom. The local police are patrolling the house and I've hired a private security company to keep an eye on Catherine, the girls, and only if they have time, on Carla, Catherine's mom—a joke, just a joke—financed by more of the money that I don't really have.

And then, there's Catherine. This has not been easy on her. She has already done a full tour hiding from flashbulbs and creditors, and now there's a kidnapper behind every bush and she's being forced to hide from the bad guys, not to mention the small army of reporters just outside.

And I miss Bugby and I wish he was here.

I wish he was here so I could kick him.

I wish he was here so I could kick him very hard.

And then, when I was done kicking him, we'd sit down and talk. He would rub the bruise on his leg where I'd kicked him. He'd laugh and would ask why I'd kicked him so hard and I'd tell him he was lucky I was wearing sneakers and not boots. Then he'd limp over to his La-Z-Boy and we'd talk about all this.

He'd know what to do and he would tell me. He'd get up from his blue recliner and limp over to the dining room table—besides cleaning out the refrigerator, I left everything in his apartment the way it was—and we'd spread all the papers and files over the table and we would figure this all out.

We'd fix it all. Not just the business stuff, but the media stuff and the stuff with Kyle Somebody and Clyde, and the way people at work stay away from me even more than before—even Phoebe is acting weird—and we would fix it all. All of it.

And it would be safe again.

And then the girls could come back.

And then everything would be better.
And I wouldn't disappoint anyone else.
Wishing well.
Wishing well.
Wishing.

Chapter 13

Abercrombie

| July 26, 1992 |

Hey Catherine,
Per our phone conversation, it looks like things are as well there as they can be—considering. Again, I can't apologize enough for putting you and the girls through all this. Please consider the Disney idea. I know the girls have always wanted to go and I've called the security service and they have people available to travel with you. It might not be a bad idea to get you all out of the house so you won't feel like such prisoners. You might as well as take advantage of this, if that's possible. Let me know and I can make all the arrangements fairly quickly.

Here is the letter I told the girls I would send. If you can give it to Abby, she said she would read it to Liz.

Let me know what else you need.

Walker

* * *

Abby,
Here you go, kiddo. You can read it to Liz tonight.

I love you.

Thelma Dreesly stepped out of her apartment—apartment 3, in building A of Denning Arms Apartments—and let the door shut behind her. She locked the door. She checked the lock, then took the nine steps down the hallway to the outside building door, where she turned the doorknob and pulled.

Nothing happened. The door didn't budge.

Thelma pulled again and this time the door moved slightly—a few inches or so—then swung back closed with a click.

Thelma sighed. She widened her stance and turned the knob again, this time leaning back and allowing all of her ninety-eight pounds to work against the weight of the door. The door creaked open slightly, then a little more and a little more until there was a gap wide enough to swing her foot in and block the door from shutting again. Thelma caught her breath and slipped through the gap.

Part one complete.

While Thelma was in the gap of the door, she pushed back against it, walking backwards until the door was completely open.

Just like cocking a gun, Thelma thought. And when the door couldn't go back any farther, when the gun was completely cocked, she hooked her cat purse—the red velvet purse with the white cat head that she never went anywhere without—around her shoulder and leaned slightly forward.

"Go," she said. This change in weight made the door begin to close, pushing Thelma along with it. Her pink sneakers tried to keep up with the closing door until she got to the spot—the crack in the brick, her launching spot—where she took a slight jump. It was only an inch or so off the ground, but it was enough.

The heavy door snapped shut and propelled Thelma off the stoop like a kickball, firing her straight toward the black lamp post across the parking lot. And just before she was about to crash into the blacktop, just before she was about to be reduced to a collection of old-lady parts, Thelma hooked the handle of her umbrella around the lamp post, which swung her up and sideways into the air, toward the old oak tree near the grassy part of the yard.

Thelma went sailing back up, half the distance of the tree. She arched, and just as she was falling back down, she reached into her purse for the four empty white garbage bags she always carried—just in case, she would tell anyone who asked—which acted as four tiny drag shoots, allowing her to float slowly down to the ground below. She landed right at the bench of the bus stop, right at the spot where she always waited for the senior center lunch pickup.

Thelma smiled and tucked her plastic bags back into her cat purse.

"Why don't you use the umbrella instead of the garbage bags?" a voice behind her asked. "Seems easier."

Thelma froze. She knew this voice. Even with the low batteries on her hearing aid, she knew it. And although the words were fuzzy and came out as "Milo and Bella's dead father made jelly flags for Caesar," the words didn't matter. Even after fifty years, she knew who was speaking to her.

Thelma leaned back on the bench—partly because she wanted to remain calm and partly because her back hurt. She did not turn toward the figure behind her. She kept her eyes forward.

"Caesar's dead," she said.

Now, Thelma Dreesley knew that Ida Burch had not said, "Milo and Bella's dead father made jelly flags for Caesar," but since she didn't know what Ida had really said, it was all she had to go on.

From the shadows of the big oak tree, the Countess of Backwards Clocks moved forward—floated, actually—toward the bench where Thelma Dreesly was sitting. She floated and then stopped a few feet in front of Thelma.

The Countess was big—like a normal person but out of scale, a Barbie doll in a world of those troll dolls all the kids had a few years ago.

The Countess hovered just a few inches off the ground. A soft hum could be heard from behind her. Thelma guessed she was wearing some sort of a thingamajig, some doohickey, something that Ida had probably stolen that allowed her to float instead of walk.

Ida had aged, but not much. Her hair was a little gray around the ears but otherwise it was the same brown it had been back when Thelma, Lila, and Ida had managed to smuggle the device out of Germany—fifty years before.

Ida was dressed in gray: gray pants, gray shirt, but with a short red cape that fell over her shoulders and hid the thing that was humming on her back.

In the few moments that Thelma looked at her, Thelma saw one thing about the Countess of Backward Clocks that had changed. Ida had gotten meaner in all those years. Those are mean eyes, Thelma thought. Even meaner than before.

"Hello, Thelma," Ida said.

Although Thelma heard this as "Low sell much?" she guessed what Ida had said and responded appropriately.

"Hello, Ida," she answered. Thelma sat back onto the bench, a little more relaxed now that she could see where Ida was. But from the inner reflection of her glasses she could also see the shrubs around the trees moving and the outlines of figures gathering just beyond them.

"It's been a long time, but I guess you know why I'm here."

Thelma heard this as "I spent it all on limes so let's play chess in my ear."

Thelma adjusted her cat purse over her shoulder. "I was always a checkers player, Ida, and I never liked limes."

The Countess made a confused expression, then paused. She smiled in a bored but aggressive way.

"Well, I'd love to catch up but I have a town to destroy." The Countess of Backwards Clocks held out her gray-gloved hand to Thelma.

Thelma looked at Ida's empty hand, knowing that Ida Burch had not just said, "Will's rug is made of ketchup, so brown up some decoys." But that was all she could hear. And before Thelma Dreesly could answer, the figures from the bushes were all around her.

The hands that grabbed her were thin but strong. They weren't really hands but the frames of hands. Metal, maybe? When she looked up, she saw no hands at all. She saw no arms or shoulders or bodies, but she felt the hands holding her as well as the arms that were jerking her cat purse off her shoulder.

As the contents of the cat purse were tossed onto the bench, Ida pulled a small flat box from her belt. She waved it over the contents of Thelma's spilled purse. The box whirred and images flashed quickly over its small screen.

The device scanned the prescription bottle from Thelma's purse and within seconds the screen displayed the name of the pharmacist who had filled the prescription. It saw the technician who helped, the doctor who prescribed the medicine to Thelma, and the company that manufactured the drug. From some loose pennies and nickels, the device saw Thelma receiving the change at the grocery store. It saw all the countless faces of the people who owned the money before Thelma and the workers at the mint who converted the raw metal into currency. From a library card, the screen showed the librarian, the factory that issued the card, and the raw plastic being molded.

The machine whirred and clicked and scanned. It scanned the pack of gum, the pen, and the picture of Thelma's grandson playing Little League for Erie. But nothing from the purse brought up anything about the Gopher Queen. Nothing came up about the device that allowed Thelma to talk to the Gopher Queen—which meant that nothing came up that the Countess cared about.

And this made Ida Burch very angry.

The Countess of Backward Clocks clicked the box off and clipped it back on her belt. Then she pulled a short black tube from the other side of her belt. It was flat with a pointed tip, and when Ida pressed a button on the side, sharp metal probes began spinning and cutting through the air.

"Now this won't hurt," the Countess said as she moved the spinning cutting wires closer to Thelma's forehead. "Well, it won't hurt me." She smiled. "For you, however, it will be very painful."

Thelma squirmed but was held still by the guards on both sides of her as the Countess of Backward Clocks leveled the device until it was directly in front of Thelma's forehead. Ida waited until a tone could be heard, signifying that the information needed had been found and the device was ready to drill for it.

"Good-bye, Thelma," she said. Ida pressed another button, releasing the spinning, cutting wires.

The figure to the right of Thelma's arm suddenly snapped back hard into the air. It couldn't be seen but even Thelma could hear the sounds—the clanging of broken springs and gears against the blacktop. Then the guard that was holding

Thelma's other arm was pulled back and a similar crashing sound came as the machine smashed against the oak tree.

And then, just as the wires cut through the air, Thelma Dreesley was able to move out of the way, avoiding the probe that was aimed at her head.

And then, there he was, in front of the Countess.

Abercrombie.

Abercrombie crouched, wearing the red high-top sneakers that his father had cut the bottoms out of—so the suction cups on his toes could grip the ground better. His calves were transparent, showing the strong muscles inside. The same went for his upper legs and torso, where muscle could be seen through his clear skin. He was wearing a pair of cargo shorts and a Celtics basketball jersey. The locket around his neck—his prized possession, which held pictures of his sisters, Abby and Liz—swung back and forth in perfect timing. Like a metronome.

Abercrombie crouched, his arms stretched out and his hands splayed so the tiny suction cups on the end of his fingers could smell the air for change and motion and fear. His ears—his famous Abercrombie cone-like ears that projected from the sides of his head—had already picked up on something. Something coming. Something large and traveling by air quickly but still far away.

Abercrombie blinked and his lids moved in from the sides and he peered all around. He saw the additional figures moving in from the bushes beyond the trees. And he saw Thelma Dreesley gather up her empty cat purse and move to the side of the bench.

"Well," said the Countess of Backward Clocks, retrieving the probes and snapping the weapon back on her belt. "I thought you'd be on some lily pad somewhere eating bugs."

Abercrombie moved slightly to the left, as the Countess moved slightly to the right, keeping her directly in front of him.

"I was eating a Hot Pocket, actually," he said. "I don't eat bugs. I've told you that before, but you're old and forgetful." His voice was soft and trilled a little, as if he were speaking through water. "And fat."

The Countess laughed. "Well, I don't think you are the one to make comments on personal appearance."

"Yeah, I am one good-looking guy."

The Countess moved to the right and Abercrombie countered, like a bullfighter. She laughed.

"Well, this must be the inner beauty that everyone talks about. I suppose you have a nice personality, too."

Abercrombie heard the relay click of the device on the Countess's belt and heard the signal go out to the craft that was moving toward them quickly, very quickly.

"I have a great personality," he said. "I'm also a Capricorn, just in case you were curious."

"I'm not. Actually, I'm quite bored. And in a bit of a hurry."

"No kidding? Me, too. So, I guess I'll just have to embarrass you quickly this time."

"Embarrass?" The Countess of Backwards Clocks laughed, shifting her direction to the left again only a moment after Abercrombie had anticipated and shifted with her. "Embarrass? You're an embarrassment everywhere you go, dear boy. That's why your father keeps you locked up here, away from your darling sisters."

It was getting closer now, the thing—whatever it was—that was traveling toward them. He could hear it. Maybe it was ten miles out. It was moving fast. And it was big. Very big.

"Trivia question for you, Countess. When's the last time you beat me?" Abercrombie circled as he saw the figures gather at the edge of the trees. Twelve of them, he counted. No, fourteen, counting the two on the roof. "Oh, yeah. Never."

He heard the relays and shot to the side of building A just a moment before the driveway exploded in a blast of pure white light. Shards of blacktop rained down in all directions.

As Abercrombie held onto the wall, he heard the figures move from the trees to capture Thelma Dressly. A moment later, the craft was directly above them. A thick metal cable dropped from the craft and Thelma was pushed into a wire box and quickly lifted up.

"Well, I'd love to stay and discuss your deep resentment toward your family," the Countess said, stepping into the second thick metal box that was dropped from the craft above. "But I believe I have a meeting with the Gopher Queen."

The Countess rose up. And then, the fourteen guards around him moved in. Abercrombie leaped forward, propelling off the lamp post, off building A, and then jumping straight up toward the craft. Up, up, and up, until he reached the hard metal side of the transport.

The engines hummed and Abercrombie moved his body in closer to the frame, adjusting all the suction cups of his feet and arms to attach himself to the craft like a barnacle.

A second later, the craft was gone.

CHAPTER 14

ITEM 276

| AUGUST 2, 1992 |

In 1974, bored American millionaire Malcolm Bricklin borrowed $23 million from the Canadian government and formed Bricklin Motors Incorporated in New Brunswick, Canada, which would design, manufacture, and distribute one specific sports car: the Bricklin SV-1.

If you've ever seen a picture of the SV-1—and if you've seen pictures of the car, you would remember it—it was most likely taken with the car's gull-wing doors wide open, giving the car that exotic sports-car feel that Bricklin was going for. If you saw the car in person, or saw pictures of it with the doors closed, you would remember it, too, because the body of the SV-1 looked like a Corvette and a Ferrari had a baby, except for the nose. When looking at the car, your eyes would be immediately drawn to the odd little retracting resin bumper nosing out of the edge of the car, which was one of the safety features Bricklin insisted on.

Safety was the goal for the SV-1; in fact, the car's name stood for *Safety Vehicle One.* It was supposed to be the first safe American sports car, although it was actually manufactured in Canada.

Safety features included the molded frame, the interior roll cage, the cage around the gas tank, as well as the fact that the SV-1 had no ashtray or cigarette lighter in the car—a travesty in 1974—because Bricklin felt that smoking while driving was extremely dangerous.

Between 1974 and 1976, almost three thousand SV-1s rolled off the assembly line and out to the car-buying public. The marketing for the car was vast and included numerous television commercials, magazine ads, and radio ads. The car was even given away on popular game shows such as *Let's Make a Deal.*

But from the beginning, Bricklin Motors struggled. The SV-1 cost sixteen thousand dollars to manufacture but sold to dealers for only five thousand—a loss Bricklin was willing to take to purchase a large market share. He believed he could reduce manufacturing costs later on.

Then there was a political scandal. Bricklin was accused of funneling money into the company from Richard Hatfield's political campaign while Hatfield was running for premier of New Brunswick. The Canadian government denied Bricklin a loan for an additional $10 million in order to keep the company running, and then, to make things worse, there were numerous manufacturing and factory issues with the car.

But all these hurdles might have been overcome and the company might have survived except for one insurmountable issue. The car was a piece of crap.

The Bricklin SV-1 shows up on lists such as *Time* magazine's "Top 50 Worst Cars Ever Made"—even beating out the Edsel and the Corvair. It appears on similar lists by *Forbes, Auto Week*, and numerous others.

Problems with the SV-1 range from that funky little nose—which didn't allow enough cooling air into the engine, causing it to overheat, sometimes after only an hour of driving—to general stability issues. As far as speed and performance, although the car had a 380 V8 engine, it was not strong enough to power the heavy compression panels, resin bumpers, and two-hundred-pound gull-wing doors of the car at a high speed. Even though the car's speedometer went to one hundred sixty miles per hour, *Road and Track* tested it at only eighty-three miles an hour. One reviewer stated that the safest feature of the SV1 was its "sloth-like slowness."

The car also had an inconvenient tendency to catch on fire.

Bricklin Motors declared bankruptcy in 1976. Bricklin himself would claim bankruptcy three more times in his life, but not before introducing the American public to another legend in the auto industry: the Yugo—which, interestingly, places *two* Bricklin creations on the same "Worst Cars Ever Made" lists.

I had heard of the Bricklin—and I think I even saw one or two of the SV-1s in the 1980s maybe, though I couldn't tell you where—but I didn't know any of the details about the car. All the history that I just gave you came from Fleece—yes, that's the guy's name: Fleece.

I placed an ad in the *Erie Times News* that I needed some help cleaning out a large storage unit. I gave up on trying to find long-term help so I pursue it day by day now. The three guys who showed up were named Fleece, Dutch, and Iggy—no, I'm not making this up; these are their actual names. My plan was that all of us together should be able to complete this new task that I need to do in just one day.

I was wrong.

The task I am referring to is the need to document the contents of Denning Self-Storage Unit #1, which is the large sixty-by-sixty compartment that Bugby kept for himself. Since I have inherited everything, I have also inherited the contents of Bugby's storage unit. All this stuff needed to be gathered so a value could be calculated and Uncle Sam could take his cut. So, Fleece, Dutch, Iggy, and I spent Saturday morning moving out boxes and furniture and file cabinets—along with old movie projectors, a grandfather clock, a stuffed moose head, and an old cigar-store Indian—all from the old Hotel Denning.

The attorneys were very specific about how I needed to accomplish this inventory; each item had to be labeled with a number—I was using moving stickers I got at Staples—and then that number needed to correspond with a description of the item so a total value could be calculated.

We were about four hours into the project—including nine cigarette breaks taken by both Fleece and Iggy—when Iggy found the SV-1. It was in the back of the unit, cloaked in a custom-fitted cover and jacked up so that all four tires were off the floor. Iggy had just pulled a cardboard box filled with car wax off a wooden table and then he saw the car.

I had just uncovered a great old desk and was about to explore it further when Iggy yelled.

"Hey," he wheezed. Too much smoking, I guess. "There's a car back here." Iggy handed a box of pool balls to Dutch and moved around the table to see what he had uncovered. "By the shape of it," he said, "looks like a Vette."

Talk of a Corvette being nearby made Fleece stomp out his tenth cigarette and venture back inside the storage unit. He walked through the maze of boxes and furniture until he reached the white-covered car.

"That ain't no Vette," Fleece said, moving to the front of the car and lifting the cover off to reveal that funky little Bricklin nose. "No frickin way," he said. He began to frantically pull the cover off the car, like a kid with Christmas frenzy. "No frickin way," he repeated.

And there it stood. The SV-1. Jacked up off the floor. All fluids drained and battery disconnected and placed in a perfectly preserved auto tomb.

It was then that Fleece told us all about the Bricklin. He told us about Malcolm Bricklin and the plant in Canada and *Let's Make a Deal* and the scandals surrounding the car. He told us about how every kid in the world, including himself, had wanted one. He told us about the speed trials and the bankruptcy and the fact that the car did not have an ashtray or lighter.

"I can't believe the color is still so bright," Dutch said, pointing to the shining cherry surface of the car.

"That ain't paint, that's why," Fleece snapped. "The entire car has the color mixed into the pollinate and then molded."

And I listened to the history of the car, all I could think was, *Great. Now I need to pay taxes on a two-seater sports car that I will never drive unless I strap Liz to the back and let Abby have the seat as we work on getting where we are going without catching on fire.*

"These doors won't open because the battery is disconnected," Fleece said, but he pressed the door handle anyway. The driver's side gull-wing door opened with a soft hiss. Fleece looked inside the car in confusion, tracing a tube that ran from the inside of the door to inside the back trunk. "No way," he said, pointing to a series of hoses. "This don't have the electric doors; there's an air canister in there. That wasn't standard. We could probably pump the tires up with that, too."

Now, I don't know how this next part happened, but Fleece convinced me that we needed to get the car out of the storage unit so I could get to it when I wanted it. That meant we needed to get the car off the jacks, get the tires pumped up—if they would still hold air after twenty years—and get the car running so it could be taken out, which meant the car had to be filled with oil and fluids and gas and spark plugs and all those other things that cars need.

So Dutch began keeping track of the storage unit list and Iggy began pulling things out of the unit while Fleece and I headed to the auto parts store to get everything he needed to get the car out of its auto coma.

While walking through, filling a shopping cart with oil and power steering fluid and brake fluid and spark plugs and fix-a-flat and a plastic gas can and a new battery and a small air compressor—in case the air tank could not fill the tires—I began to think about Bugby and the car.

The SV-1 had eleven hundred miles on it. According to the receipt we found in the glove compartment, Bugby had bought the car new in October 1974 with only eleven miles on it. He brought the car home. He drove it. A little. Then he tucked it away. And when he placed it in the storage unit, he probably did it with little intention of ever taking it out again. He just put it in to keep it safe and left it alone.

This notion brought a smile to my face. Fleece saw me smiling as he pulled a few tools he would need from metal pegs and tossed them into the cart. "Pretty jazzed about the car, huh?" he asked.

But I couldn't have cared less about the car. I was smiling at the idea that Bugby had purchased something for himself—something he wanted and possibly even dreamed about. That was the interesting thing.

Fleece told me about the hype when the car came out, about how every male under the age of sixty wanted one. They all wanted the car for different reasons: to feel young, to look cool, to own something others couldn't or wouldn't, or to feel special because they owned something special. But one constant remained for all three thousand people who laid down their coin to purchase a Bricklin: In some way, they all wanted the car to make them happy.

Bugby had wanted it to make him happy, too. So he wrote a check and bought the car. And drove it. And he looked at the car and had people look at him while he was driving the car. But *the happy* never came. I know it didn't. Because if it had come, then Bugby would have kept using the car and it would have more than eleven hundred miles on it now. There would be pictures of him in the car. He would have talked about it. But still, when the Bricklin didn't make him happy, he didn't sell it. Or take it back. He simply preserved it, realizing that it would never, or *could* never, give him what he wanted. And as far as I know—from knowing Bugby and then from going through all the papers from Bugby's life—he never tried to *buy* the happy again.

We left the store and Fleece got the car off the blocks and the tires filled and the oil box filled—is that what you call the place where the oil goes?—and gas in the tank and brake fluid and steering fluid and added new spark plugs and all of the rest of the $336.78 worth of stuff that Fleece told me I needed. Then he sat in the car, turned the key, and the car roared to life.

Fleece started that car for the first time in twenty years. And at the first sound of car life, at that sound of that baby V8, Fleece put both hands on top of his balding head and pulled at the short tufts of hair that remained and screamed in pure pleasure.

And just for a moment, I wondered if Fleece had *the happy.* I wondered if Bugby had smiled that same smile inside that same car in that same way. Maybe they both had *the happy.* At least for a little while.

Fleece pulled the car slowly out of the unit and onto the blacktop outside. As I listened to the revving engine, I placed a sticker on the windshield that said "Item 276" and wrote down the description: one 1974 Bricklin SV-1 sports car.

This is the part where my memory gets fuzzy. I remember walking from the storage unit to my Corolla to get more moving stickers. I remember getting to my car and leaning into the window to grab the stickers off the seat. Because my back was to the entrance of the storage unit office, I didn't see the other car that pulled in—I heard it, but I didn't see it.

So I don't remember being shot. I remember this sort of falling, pushing, stinging feeling, but I don't remember being shot. They told me about that later.

And later, when I was awake in my hospital bed, they also told me how Dutch had grabbed the shooter and stopped a second shot from being fired—this one aimed at my head. They told me that Fleece and Iggy had scattered—something about having old warrants and being afraid of police questioning—and that the bullet that went through my leg also took out the right front tire of my Corolla. So the Bricklin was the only car available. Dutch raced me to the hospital in the SV-1, driving with one hand and holding a tourniquet with the other—a tourniquet he made from his belt to slow the blood pumping out of my leg. And he got me here a minute or two before the car caught on fire and a minute or two before I would likely have bled to death.

They told me that Dutch had saved my life.

JOURNAL 4

DUTCH

Chapter 15

| July 18, 1992 |

The cool thing about traveling by bus (not a school bus but a big Greyhound bus like this one) is the being above everything part. You look out the bus window and then down. Down on the spinning road and down on the cars and the motorcycles and the people. It's, like, flying almost, if you lean back.

When you're done looking down at the everything, you can hold your finger out to some point way off and hold your finger real steady and see all them trees and mountains and poles that are cut by your finger as you speed by. Like your finger is a laser that slices it all away. It's like when I used to do the same thing in the back of my dad's station wagon when we'd be headed to Lake Montrose. And I'm nine years old again.

When you're done lasering everything, you can lean back and look out the other windows, too, the ones across the aisle from you, and it's like there are sixty TVs all set on the same channel.

These are the really cool parts about traveling across New York State by bus. These are my favorite parts. Because everything else sucks.

I didn't sleep last night. I had a visitor—I'll tell you about that in a minute—and then Randy was late picking me up (I ain't got a car no more, remember?), so instead of making the 9:00 A.M. bus to Niagara Falls, I had to catch the 11:15 bus. No big deal, right? It's not like I'm on any schedule no more. But the 11:15 bus has more stops, so the ride takes eight effing hours instead of six (and driving by car should take only four).

Then I forgot two important things: to bring something to read and to bring something to eat. The last time we stopped, everyone hit the vending machines at the bus station like buzzards and then you had to make Cheez-Its and a Mountain Dew last for another two hours. And I have to be careful with money since I have very little. I will have to make sandwiches for my next trip.

But the main part that sucks about the bus is the smell. Eff. You would think that a guy who worked at a landfill for years would have no big cares about smells, right? Wrong. As soon as you walk on the bus, that smell hits you. It's like if somebody filled a dirty sock with Chinese food and no matter where you go on the bus that smell follows you. And then when you leave the bus it's still on you, that effing smell. It's, like, part of you now.

But hey, this is the deal, right? This is going to be my life for a while. Maybe not for a year like Brandon Mosely said in that article, but for a while. So things like smells and long rides and Cheez-Its are just little pieces of it.

I made a bunch of copies of Brandon's article and brought them with me. It was Randy's idea and it was a good one. That way, people can see that I'm a traveler and not a bum. Or maybe just a temporary bum (ha).

So okay, I'd better tell you about my visitor last night, huh? And about remembering about the bike. I'm stalling a little because I really don't want to tell you about the bike. I still don't know who the *you* is that I'm writing this all to, but I still don't want to tell you. I don't want to tell nobody.

I will tell you that I didn't steal that bike. Not *really*. Sort of, but not really. You thought I did steal it because *I* thought I stole it because I've done that kinda thing before. But I didn't steal it because it was given to me. But I *sort of* stole it because the person that gave it to me didn't own it, either.

I guess that should make me feel good, huh? That I didn't *really* steal it, but there's worse stuff that I did do that I remember now. I may have only sort of stole the bike, but the other stuff is effing bad. I remember it all now. I remembered it as soon as I heard her voice. When I heard her voice and she called me that name, then it all came back to me.

I was walking up the stoop of my building, coming back from my going-away party at the Belmar, and I heard her lock all four brakes on Main when she saw me. She jammed her little car in reverse and pulled onto Mather. She jerked into a parking spot, then shut off the car and jumped out. Then she called me that name.

"Roy?" she said, part in panic and part in relief. As soon as I saw her face, as soon as I heard the name she called me, I remembered it. All of it.

Like I told you, I don't black out exactly. I just, like, misfile memories and they require a password sometimes to bring them out. A hint. And then I remember. When she said that name, *Roy*, that was enough. The memory of it all splashed out like a movie on fast-forward.

I sometimes use a fake name when I'm *really* drunk. If I meet you when I'm fairly sober, I'll introduce myself with my real name. If I'm pretty much gone when I meet you, and if I'm someplace other than the Belmar—I couldn't get away with it at the Belmar—then I might be somebody else. I'll pick a new name. Then it won't be Dutch that did the stupid thing—it will be Kevin or Ethan or Mack who did it.

That night, that Thursday, I was pretty much gone when I met Valerie and I wasn't at the Belmar. So I became Roy.

I had been at the Belmar earlier, though. Randy wasn't there and a bunch of college kids came in and I was bored. I should've went home because I had a lot to drink already but I just started walking down Main Street, then down Murray, and I was going to go to Clinton Street but I stopped at Hank's instead.

Hank's is a depressing place. I don't go there enough for anyone to know me. It's so depressing, you actually feel good about yourself while you're there. Hey, if you have a job, an apartment, and a working phone in your own name—sheesh, you're in the top twenty percent of the clientele (ha).

I had been there for a few beers and was going to finish up and go home when Valerie came in. Then it got real weird, real effing fast.

Valerie was in her late twenties, I think—I can't tell with girls; she could have been older. She came in and sat two barstools down from me and was already pretty nervous. She ordered a draft and was looking through her purse, looking for cigarettes, then looking for a lighter, then looking for change for the phone. She kept looking at her watch and she smoked and drank like they weren't going to make beer and cigarettes no more (ha).

You normals probably think there is just drunk and then there's sober. Wrong.

I remember my English teacher in eighth grade telling us that the Eskimos have, like, fifty different words for snow—that those Eskimos can see so many different kinds of snow, they've named all of them. We just see snow, but they see all the different thicknesses and colors of snow. There are just as many types of drunk as there are types of snow. And that night I caught a weird one. You can sit the same man down on five different nights and feed him the same stuff and let him drink the same stuff and he will have five different types of drunk. Guaranteed.

That Thursday, I caught a wild, weird drunk. I drank about the same amount as the night before, which was why I woke up and wasn't hung over at all. But it was different. Weird, huh?

I told you I sometimes use different names, and I do. And just then, when Valerie came in, the wild, the stupid, came over me and Roy arrived.

"How we doing?" Roy asked, in a smug voice. Really, it wasn't even my voice—it was Roy's voice.

"I've been better," Valerie answered, looking at her change and then at the pay phone, then draining her draft and placing it at the edge of the bar to be refilled.

Roy is a patient man. Roy is a confident man. A professional man. Did you know he's an engineer? You didn't know that about Roy? Oh yeah, Roy is a big-time effing engineer just slumming it a little tonight after a long day of designing and engineering and science-type stuff you probably wouldn't understand anyways.

By her third draft, Valerie relaxed a little. She started to cry, then she stopped. She laughed once—it tried to be a cry, but then it stopped. And by her fourth draft she began talking to Roy. Roy listened. He scratched his chin and thought them deep, important engineer thoughts and listened.

Valerie told Roy about Vernon. Vernon was the man Valerie had been living with for eight months.

"Eight months is a long time," Roy said, in his deep, engineering way.

And now it was over between Vernon and Valerie. Vernon was leaving her, or actually, since the place they lived was Vernon's, Valerie had to move out. As soon as Vernon came back from his two weeks with the Army Reserves, he was going on a month-long bike trip alone. She had those two weeks until he got back, and she could stay for the month he was on his bike trip if she needed the extra time to find a place. But when Vernon got back from the bike trip, Valerie had to be out. Vernon was a jerk and Valerie hated Vernon. And soon Roy began to hate Vernon, too.

Vernon thought he was so effing great with his fancy bicycle. Vernon and his fancy bicycle and his rich parents. Roy didn't know this for sure but he guessed Vernon was the type of guy that had rich parents. Not like Roy, who had to work his own way all through engineering school himself, with all the rich kids around him who got their school paid for them. Roy knew all about kids with rich parents and he told Valerie about this.

Valerie listened and told Roy that he was right. Vernon *did* have rich parents. The jerk. Well, his parents were better off than her parents were, anyway.

"He probably thinks his parents are better than your parents and that makes him better than . . . makes him better than you."

"He's always thought that," she said, motioning to the bartender for two more shots.

We hated Vernon. Vernon the cocky bastard. The heartless effing jerk. All the Vernons of the world. They all think other people are like things, not people. They just can't decide . . .

"Just effing decide," Roy had said. "When they've had enough of people and just, they can just decide when they've had enough and just throw away people, like, just like . . ."

"Like garbage," Valerie said. "Just like, just like garbage."

Vernon should pay for what he's done.

And we came up with a plan. Roy and Valerie came up with a plan that only in the deepest funk of drunk would you ever even consider, much less really do. But when you're plowed, when you're dead ripping drunk, then reality is as far away as Roy's engineering degree. Right then, the idea is effing perfect.

I told you that the drunk time wasn't the dangerous time, right? It's the time in between the drunks when the robot-you takes over that's bad. It's true. But emotions and feelings and anger—oh eff, anger when drunk is like a super fuel. It's like gas on an effing fire.

Vernon would pay.

The house was Vernon's house. The furniture, the decorations, and that damn bicycle were all Vernon's. Valerie had always felt like a guest, like it was never really hers. It was always Vernon's house and she was just allowed to stay there.

"Sick," Roy said. "Just sick."

And we downed another drink for the road and we got in Valerie's car and we drove to her house—well, to Vernon's house.

I've had to close this notebook four times already before I can write this part. It's hard. But I need to tell you what we did. What *I* did.

Valerie and Roy got to the house. Roy looked around and walked to the large TV. Valerie giggled and swayed as she saw Roy standing next to it.

"Nice TV," he slurred, moving closer. "Shame if something happened to . . . if something happened to it." And with both hands Roy lifted the table it sat on up, watching the set slide off and smash, heavy, against the hardwood floor.

They both laughed. Then Valerie walked to the mantel.

"I've always hated this." She picked up a large green vase. "I've always hated this, this vase." And Valerie dropped the vase and it turned into tiny green pieces on the floor. Roy and Valerie laughed some more. It took twenty minutes before they could stop laughing. Then they got up again and walked through the house.

Together they found spray paint on the back porch and spray-painted the walls. They put holes in the Sheetrock. They pulled up carpeting and poured red wine on rugs and pulled nails from the wooden floors. They cut up mattresses and filled the bathtub with Vernon's clothes and poured bleach on it all. They smashed paintings and took doors off hinges, and Roy smiled and looked for other ways to make Vernon pay. It was like, what do they call it? Blood lust? When the hyenas or the sharks or whatever can't destroy fast enough? Room by room. Ripping curtains and tearing up pictures. Wouldn't Vernon be surprised? Maybe this would make it so Vernon wouldn't be such a bastard no more.

Vernon was what was wrong with the effing world. Vernon, the big jerk. The big effing jerk. And finally someone's doing something about all the Vernons of the world.

And they broke and smashed and ripped it all away. They took it all away from Vernon, who didn't deserve none if it. Just like he didn't deserve Valerie.

And then all that was left was the bike. The bike was just sitting there waiting for Vernon, precious Vernon, to ride off into the sunset. The bike was already packed and ready to go so Vernon wouldn't even have to stay in the house very long when he got back. He wouldn't have to talk to Valerie or even see her if he didn't want to. He could just grab the bike and go.

Roy moved toward the bike and then saw the hammer on the floor. It was the same hammer that Valerie had used against the blue and white ceramic tile in the shower. When she smashed the tiles into clouds of dust, Roy laughed with her as they danced around in it all.

Roy picked up the hammer but it slipped out of his hand because the powder from the tiles was so slick. Roy wiped the handle of the hammer on the leg of his jeans and the blue and white pieces of glass jumped, by static, to his arm and shirt and face. Then he moved to the bike. Roy laughed and lifted the hammer and was ready to bring it down on the spokes of the tires when Valerie stopped him.

"No," she said. She was out of breath from tearing pages out of photo albums. "It'll piss him off more," she said, then she stopped and looked around the house. It was as if she had just walked in. "It'll piss him off more, if . . ."

If any of the neighbors heard them destroying the house, they didn't complain or call the police or knock on the door or nothing. We destroyed Vernon's life in complete privacy. Nothing stopped us. And then it was as if Valerie was winding down. Running out of anger.

Valerie stood in the middle of the living room, still breathing hard. She brought her hands closer to her face and looked at them.

"You take the bike," she said into her hands.

And since there was nothing left to break, Roy left. He pushed the bike home, since it had them weird pedals that you need the special shoes for (even if he was sober enough to ride, which he wasn't). And Roy put the bike in the kitchen of the Mather Street apartment, where Dutch would find it two days later. And them little pieces of blue and white glass from Vernon's shower jumped from Roy's arms and face and to the walls and to the bike, and stayed there.

And Roy forgot to file away the memory.

So last night, Valerie came running out of the car that was parked on Mather Street. She ran to the stoop when she saw me. And the full recall was there before she even got to me and I remembered it all.

"Roy," she said again. She was older than I thought she was. Forties, maybe older. Maybe not. Even sober, I can't tell. She looked bad, though, like she'd had weeks of worry and no sleep.

"I've been looking for you." She caught her breath. "I've been looking for you for a month."

Had it been that long? Since the memory of it just came to me, it seemed like all of it had just happened, but had it been a month?

"Valerie," I said.

"I've been looking for you." She folded her hands nervously across her blue T-shirt as she rocked back and forth. We went upstairs.

And Valerie sat on the chair, since, besides the bed, it was the only thing left in the apartment. Valerie had tried to find me. That day after we met, she tried to find me and kept trying to find me. Nobody at Hank's knew me. They didn't know Roy.

"I called all the engineering companies in the phonebook and tried them, and there were three Roys, but not you. Then I thought you might be an engineer at IBM so I went there every day and watched people leaving and coming but I couldn't find you." Right then, Valerie looked over and saw one of my tattoos, the eight-ball one under my sleeve and she frowned even more, like now she was in even more trouble than she thought.

"I don't work at IBM."

"Where do you work?'

"No place," I said. "I did work at the landfill but no more." Valerie cried and I let her. And I went to my backpack and got my notebook and wrote in it while I waited for her to finish crying since I didn't know what else to do. Valerie cried for a long time and then finally she stopped and spoke.

"Is the bike here?"

"No."

She wanted to cry again but she was done crying and she couldn't cry no more. Then she told me what happened after I left Vernon's house that night.

The booze was already wearing off of her when I left that night. She said she could still hear the clicking sound of me rolling the bike down the sidewalk when the clouds of drunk moved just enough for her to see spots of the destroyed house. And she just started to cry until she fell asleep.

She woke up the next morning on the one part of the mattress that wasn't cut up, with the stuffing pulled out of it. That stuffing was all around her, screaming at her through her hangover.

"I couldn't look at it. I just sat in that bed and cried and couldn't look at it. And then I couldn't face it all alone so I tried to find you."

She started to clean the house as best she could but soon she gave up. Just throwing things out, that was all she could do. Just get the pieces out. Even if you could fix the walls and tiles and doors in two weeks, the stuff was all gone.

Two weeks later, Vernon came home. Valerie had called him before—she had told him all that happened but he was still unprepared. He looked around the house, even after the house that had been cleaned and some walls repainted and some stains removed, and he was still unprepared.

"He didn't scream or anything," Valerie said. "He just sort of—sort of looked at it all." And after walking through each room and after looking at the damage and the places where things used to be, he finally spoke.

"I should call the police," he said calmly.

"I know it," Valerie said to her hands.

He retraced his steps and walked through the house again. Then he walked outside and around the house and came in through the back porch.

"Where's the bike?" he asked.

And Valerie, who was all out of lies, told him that she didn't know where it was. She told him about me and how I had done as much as she had. She told him everything.

"Did he call the police?" I asked.

"Nope," she answered, squeezing the ends of her T-shirt into a ball then unsqueezing and squeezing it back again. "He talked about it but he didn't do it. We talked for a good long time and, well, he just didn't do it."

Valerie promised to pay Vernon back and Vernon gave her a look that said, *Yeah, right, like I believe that,* and Valerie was so upset that the look didn't even bother her.

"Is the bike gone, too?" she asked me, with little hope.

I went into my backpack and pulled a copy of the article about the bike and gave it to Valerie.

"He can get the bike back," I said. "He can go to the police and get it back. It's all there, even the money."

Valerie read the article. "Okay," she said.

I told Valerie how I hadn't remembered any of what happened. I told her when I found the bike I didn't remember and how I had tried to find whoever owned the bike and couldn't remember anything about it. I didn't remember nothing until I just saw her. And she gave me a look, probably the same look that Vernon gave her, that said,

Yeah, right, like I believe that. And like Valerie, the look didn't bother me at all.

We talked. And we walked over to Danny's Diner and we talked some more there. And we came up with an idea. Not a solution, cuz with things like this, there is never no magic button, but there are ways to start things. There are, like, beginnings.

Vernon the jerk. Vernon, the heartless selfish jerk, could've called the police. Vernon could have destroyed Valerie (and Roy, too, if he could find him, ha). But he didn't. Vernon the jerk, the heartless selfish bastard, couldn't even collect on his homeowner's insurance because for vandalism there has to be a police report and Vernon wouldn't do that to Valerie.

When we got back to my apartment, I went to my backpack and spread out my entire bankroll on the brown carpet. All the money I have saved, the money from selling my car, from the collections for me at work and the one from the Belmar and the money people had mailed to the *Binghamton Press*: a total of $4,745.67.

I took $745.67 of it and stuck it back in my wallet. I took $375 and put it in an envelope and wrote a note that Valerie was going to move into my apartment and I was allowing her my security deposit, that the landlord didn't have to mail it to me after all, and I was giving him the next month's rent. Then I walked downstairs and slipped the envelope under the super's door.

The rest of the money, $3,625, we put in another envelope. I wrote a note and put it inside, telling Vernon what I had done. I also put in the copy of the article about the bike and wrote that Vernon could call the Endicott police and get the bike back and that it was all there in them saddlebags, even the money. I signed the bottom of the article and signed the letter with the same name: Roy.

As the sun was coming up, Valerie and I walked to Vernon's house. We quietly walked up the steps of his porch, expecting Vernon to be waiting just on the other side and for him to jump out at us. We slipped the envelope under the door. We walked back to my apartment, which was now Valerie's apartment, and we didn't say another word to each other until I left.

When Randy finally showed up to get me, he buzzed the button downstairs. I pushed the intercom and told him I would be right down. I nodded to Valerie, because there was nothing else to say. We didn't hug or even say good-bye because we didn't really know each other. We were just two drunks that trashed a man's house together. I started to pull the apartment key off my ring and then realized I didn't need no keys no more and handed her the whole ring of them. Then I left.

Between buying the bus ticket and some food, I now have $667.78 left. Not exactly the bankroll I was hoping for but . . . I'll get some work soon.

The money I gave to Vernon wasn't enough to put back together his house. It wasn't even my half of the damage I done. I'll send what I can, and I'll send it when I can. And someday I'll pay off Roy's tab. And when I can afford it, I'll pay off Valerie's tab, too.

Chapter 16

| July 19, 1992 |

I'm here. I'm in Niagara Falls. I made it. The bus got here and now I'm writing this while sitting on the top bunk of my bed in the youth hostel I'm staying at. I've heard about youth hostels but since I've never gone nowhere, I've never stayed in one until now.

This hostel is in a house, a house on Spruce Street, which is only three blocks from the bus station, but I'm so tired it seemed like three miles when I walked it. And it's really cool. There's bunk beds in this big room, one room for men and another one for women, and you sleep there and then you have the rest of the house to use. There's a big kitchen you can use and a TV room and laundry room and a library to borrow books while you're here and there's free coffee in the morning and other stuff. But here's the best part. It's sixteen bucks a night. I could've stayed at the YMCA for two dollars less a night but there's no kitchen there and I figured that was worth something, and I read about it in the book I bought—*Youth Hostels of America*—and it looked okay. The rooms at the Y sound like effing jail cells.

I'm staying here seven nights. I told myself that when I get to a place, I want to see it all, to like, be *part* of it, not just blow in and see the main stuff and blow back out. Like, you're checking it off a list or something. If a week ain't long enough to see it all, I'll stay longer. But I made these reservations when I had three grand, not two hundred, and there was a fee if I changed it and it cost $112 for seven nights here and I had to pay that all up front, which means I just started this trip and I have only $555.78 left (ha).

But I'm not going to think about that now. I'm here and I'm on my top bunk at the Trudeau Guesthouse and I'm not going to think about that right now. I'll get some work soon.

There's other people in this room but nobody is here right now. I can see all the other beds taken, with blankets and sleeping bags and other stuff on them. But for now, the other people staying here must all be out because I have the dorm room (that's what they call them, dorm rooms) all to myself.

Hold on, I'm going to take a shower.

Okay, I'm back.

I got the bus smell off me and I'm sitting on the top bunk of my bed and I'm going to crash now and will see the Falls tomorrow. Good stuff.

Later.

July 20, 1992

I'm halfway through my second day as a traveling man (I like that title, *traveling man*) and I have a lot to tell you. I'm sitting here at the Wegmans on Amherst Street in Niagara Falls, eating my lunch and writing you. It's been a very good day.

First, I woke up late (late for me), at a little before 9:00 A.M. I must have been tired because I never sleep past eight. Never. I told you before, I can get in at three in the morning, drunk out of my mind, and still wake up before 6:00 A.M. and then do it again the next night and the next. But it was almost nine when I woke up today and that never happens.

It's kind of cool, though. It felt good to sleep so long, like it's another thing you normals do that I do now, too (ha). I love being up in the morning, being the first one up, like I know something about the day that other people don't know yet, but it felt good to sleep, too. Maybe I'll sleep longer now that I'm traveling. Now that I'm a traveling man.

I was wondering if I would know where I was when I woke up today, and I did. It's been so long since I've been anywhere except the apartment, but still, when I woke up I knew where I was. When I opened my eyes and heard the rain I knew it was Niagara Falls rain and not Binghamton rain.

Randy had this great idea. He told me to bring a pillowcase, not a pillow, and then at night fill the pillowcase with my towel and some shirts and I'd have a pillow. That way, I don't have to take all the space in my pack that a pillow would take up and after I woke up I'd have this pillowcase for a bag if I need it. I didn't know if it would work but it did. Pretty smart. The youth hostel here has sheets but no pillows and no blankets so I use my sleeping bag and now I have a pillow, too.

When I looked down from the bunk, the two bottom bunks were already empty but the guy on the top bunk across from me was still sleeping. So I got up, went to the bathroom, headed for the showers, got dressed, and walked to the kitchen.

This place is so cool. It's like I moved in with another family except that each family member speaks a different language (ha). As soon as I walked down the hall my two roommates—or dorm mates?—saw me. They are two Asian guys with thick accents but their English is very good. They were sitting in the dining room and stood up to say hi when I walked in.

"Welcome," the first one said, getting up to shake my hand.

"Hello," the second one said. We introduced ourselves and they said their names were Ping and Pong. I wanted to make sure I got it right so I asked them again and realized I heard it wrong. It was Ping and Pan, not Ping and Pong (ha). They are both from Thailand and are trying to see as much of the U.S. as they can in a month before they go back to Thailand to start graduate school.

I sat at the table with them and drank a cup of coffee, with half-and-half, not the powdered crap (ha), and I met people as they passed through from the kitchen to the dining room. There was a couple from Spain and there were two girls from Slovenia and I shook their hands and I reminded myself to find out where Slovenia is. Pan told me that there was another couple from Russia here but they are out now and our other dorm mate that was still sleeping is from Peru.

I've lived alone for so long, ever since Grace and me split up, that it's weird waking up and having people waking up around you. It's nice weird, but still weird, and I wonder how long it will take to get used to it. But I won't be around people all the time—I'll be alone, too, so I'll get used to both things.

There are notes all over the house. Notes that say things like, PLEASE PLACE ALL DISHES IN DISHWASHER, THANKS and PLEASE CLEAN MICROWAVE AFTER USE, THANKS. They're not mean notes, just notes to help a lot of people get along in a small house.

I noticed two things about everyone at the house, though. One was that I was the only one from the U.S. there. I was only four hours from home but I felt like I was in a different country. The second thing was that I was the oldest guest at the Trudeau Guesthouse. All these kids were doing what I was doing but they were doing it five or ten years earlier than I was. But that's okay. They did it in their early twenties and I'm doing it in my early thirties, but at least I'm doing it, right?

I keep thinking of all the things that I want to do, that I want to see, but now there is this different feeling. Like I'm supposed to be out here. Like there's something important I'm supposed to do while I'm out here. Weird.

Anyways, we all talked for a while and then Ping and Pan left to go over to Canada to see the Falls from there and Miss Cindy, the lady that runs the house, said I could borrow an umbrella if I was going to walk over and see the Falls. So I did.

There were only two umbrellas left in the big stand near the front door. One was this clear bubble-like umbrella that you lower down over your face and look through. It had yellow ducks painted on it and you have to look around the ducks to see anything. The other umbrella was a bright red golf umbrella that three people could have walked under. I didn't know how long I would be out and didn't want to carry a big umbrella around so I took the bubble duck one and headed out into the rain.

I've never been on vacation, not really. My dad would borrow my uncle's pop-up camper every year and we'd head to Lake Montrose for a few days. Grace and me took our honeymoon in the Poconos and then we went to Ocean City, New Jersey, once, but I never took no big, airplane-riding, weeklong vacation. But out in the rain of Niagara Falls, out on the first day of my trip, I can see what the big deal is about vacations. About trips. It's like all the other stuff is gone. The home stuff that you do every day, the work stuff, the things you have to do and the things you should be doing but don't want to. It's all gone or else it's too far away and you can't hear it no more.

When you're on vacation, you can't put a load of laundry in, you can't look at that wobbly door you should be fixing, you can't see all them bills on the table that need paying, and since you can't do any of that stuff, then all you got is the new things around you now. You have to look at the puddles and the rain and the traffic, and it's like you never saw puddles or rain or traffic before and maybe you haven't seen them because you might have run through rain to get to your car or driven through it but you didn't have time to really *see* it all. And it's different puddles and rain and traffic because it's new and special and important now. Just like the raindrops that race down the outside of a bubble duck umbrella.

I think maybe that's the thing about vacations. It's not the place you go. It's kind of the way you see things. Like you can take your heavy pack off and finally walk around and stretch out your legs and see everything.

A bird at home is just a bird, or probably you don't even see the bird—it's screaming at you but you're late or you're pissed off or you're worried, and that bird don't even exist to you. But on vacation, a bird is magical—it's like a lion or a rhino and you see the colors and hear the sounds of it.

I hope I never lose this feeling. I hope all the time I'm traveling, every day is like this day.

I followed the flow of people and cars down toward the Falls. I didn't know exactly where the Falls was, but I knew it was close because everything was traveling that way, so that's the way I went. I passed little shops and stores and the trees near the roads that have wrought-iron fences around their trunks (I wonder why—so they don't get hit by cars?).

I passed a store that had a sign that said they sold bus passes. Randy and me had talked about this so I went inside. They had two kinds of bus passes—one was the touristy kind that took you to seven or eight places and the other was the city bus pass that went all through Niagara Falls and Buffalo. I bought four postcards and a week's city bus and rail pass. That way, I can go out and find work tomorrow and get anywhere in Niagara Falls or Buffalo for the whole week I'm here. I held the bus pass and read both sides of it. When's the last time you read both sides of something (ha)? But it's like the puddle thing—it's magical if you let it be. And I read the bus schedule and looked at all the places I can go now. Places I never heard of like Lafayette Square, Eagle Canal Harbor, and Fountain Plaza. These places are as exotic to me as Marrakesh or Singapore and I'm only four hours from home (well, eight hours if you go by Greyhound bus, ha).

I was moving down with the crowd and I heard the Falls before I saw them, like a far-off engine. Along with the flow of people, I floated toward the sound. It was raining just hard enough to be under an umbrella and just enough where you'd get wet if you didn't have one but I decided I could go without my bubble and I put the umbrella down. And there it was: Niagara Falls.

Even in the rain, people were there looking at the Falls. Watching the giant horseshoe ribbon of water that pounded to the rocks below. I was wondering what the very first people that saw this thought, just walking along and hearing the rush of water, then following it until they saw this. What did those first people that found the Falls think? And I thought how deep and original it was to wonder this until I heard two other people ask each other the very same question about three minutes later (ha).

I stood there and just watched and listened to the Falls, the great Niagara Falls. I moved to different places to see it from different angles. I watched the other people watching it and then watched it myself and I couldn't tell if the spray I was feeling was from the Falls or from the rain but it didn't matter.

The Falls are like the youth hostel and I was among the few Americans there. There were people with turbans and some wearing bright yellow and green soccer shirts and T-shirts with logos written in different languages. I liked leaning against the rail and looking at the Falls and letting all them languages splash up on me like the rain.

There were two rainbows at the base of the Falls and they just sat there, no matter where I moved.

I saw people trying to take pictures with the Falls in the background and I offered to take their picture and they smiled and thanked me either in English or in their language and I walked around looking for other people to take pictures of.

But the really cool part is not the Falls; it's upstream from it. When you walk up from the Falls, there's this bridge-type thingee and you can see the water as it's getting ready to become the Falls. That's the amazing part. That's the part that's completely effing wild.

You're watching this dark, thick field of wet power and it don't turn off and it don't slow down. It just moves to the edge to die. It runs to become spray and mist and it can't wait to get there.

It's effing hypnotic.

I stood and watched it and I would've stayed forever except the rain started hard again. Really hard now. And I had to go.

Even with the duck bubble umbrella, I got wet as I ran to the bus stop (I was anxious to use my bus pass anyways, so I figured it was a good time to go).

On the city bus there wasn't all the different languages like there was at the Falls because these people weren't tourists. These were locals—like me, I guess. People sat in their seats and didn't talk at all, and since I had no place to go I just rode the bus and looked out the window, and soon the scenery changed from the tourist shops and stores to empty neighborhoods and boarded-up houses.

The rain let up a bit so I got off at the next stop and walked back to where the houses were empty. It was still raining, so with my bubble duck umbrella I walked through the empty streets. It was weird. Only a few miles from the bright lights and traffic and tourists of the Falls there was block after block of empty houses with plywood for windows and doors and graffiti written on the flat surfaces (the graffiti reminded me of what Roy and Valerie had written on Vernon's walls and I didn't like it. Eff.).

Some of the houses had put plywood on all the windows and doors and some had put plywood only on the bottom windows. The ones that put plywood only on the bottom windows had the windows on the second floor busted out and you could see the rain washing in. But the empty houses with no plywood across any windows at all had all the windows still good. Like, there was some rule that busting the windows with plywood was okay but the ones without plywood would've been wrong. Weird.

In another block there were abandoned houses mixed with houses that had people living in them and sometimes the houses that were lived in didn't look much better than the empty ones and sometimes they did. I turned a corner and saw an old factory, then another old, empty factory, and then an empty boarded-up church, and I walked up to a store that still had the sign over it but the rest of the building was fenced and boarded up. This once was H & R Food Market and long ago people came here to buy bread and sandwiches and newspapers, and old men complained and old women gossiped and kids played in the streets. I could see all that in my head when I stood there. I saw an entire apartment building, huge like a brick fortress, that was boarded up, and I saw an empty corner store that had the Pepsi logo over it but the name of the store was faded away.

What makes a part of the city home one day and not the next? I know it's not like these people all died, and I know there's all that economic stuff that has to do with it but one day there was life here and now there ain't. There's life other places, but not here. Once, this was home and now it's empty. It's as if someone drove through the streets and shouted through a bullhorn, *Everybody out!* And they all listened.

I walked through the rain and soon came out to where the city was alive again. I saw a bus stop and got there right as the bus was pulling up. A few blocks later, I spotted a Wegmans and realized I was hungry so I got off.

Wegmans was so bright and colorful compared to the dark and the rain outside. It was alive, unlike all them streets before. There was colored chalk on blackboards telling the prices of tomatoes and that the corn was locally grown. They even had chalk drawings of the corn and the drawings were really good.

I walked through each aisle and looked at everything even though they were things I wouldn't never buy, like diapers and makeup, but it was still fun to look at it all. I walked down the aisle selling hair color and looked at each of the models' faces. On every single box. And each face was pretty and different and happy.

At Wegmans I bought a loaf of pumpernickel bread, a pound of ham, a pound of Swiss cheese, a stick of pepperoni, a box of elbow noodles, a box of assorted instant oatmeal and a bunch of bananas. I was at the checkout and was handing the girl some money when I remembered the gift certificate. The hundred-dollar gift certificate (well, ten certificates worth ten each) that the Wegmans in Johnson City gave me. I used that to pay for it all. So cool. Free groceries!

I made a ham and cheese sandwich and sat down at one of the tables of the Chinese buffet part of the store and ate my sandwich and had a banana (plus, there was spicy mustard packets at the table so I even had mustard for my sandwich—bonus!), and wrote all this to you.

Now you're all caught up.

Later.

July 22, 1992

I swam in the Niagara River yesterday, downstream from the Falls (obviously, ha). *I have now actually swam in the Niagara River!* Which I think is very effing cool!

Miss Cindy told us about this little-known place where you can hike in from the road to the river and swim. She even drew a map for us. The bus don't go that far out, so Ping, Pan, me, and this girl from Austria named Panja that's staying at the hostel too got as close as we could on the bus then walked a few miles until we found the trail from the road that cut through the woods.

Once we found the trail, it was easy. We walked to the end, to the secret beach Miss Cindy told us about, and it was just like she said it would be. It was on the shore of the river and it had a beach with small crushed stones and even some sand next to the clear water. It was kind of a lagoon, so the current wasn't real strong and there was even a rope swing but none of us tried it. Pan jumped in first and when he took his shirt off he was covered in tattoos, a bunch more tats than I have.

We had the whole beach to ourselves. We swam and skipped stones and floated on pieces of logs and dove underwater and flipped rocks to surprise crayfish and laughed and sat on the shore and ate cold sandwiches and drank warm beer (I only had three warm beers, ha).

It was, like, everybody else had the Falls, but this lagoon, this place, was all ours.

Panja found a box turtle and she was so excited you would've thought she found a unicorn (ha). She must have taken twenty pictures of the thing and she kept carrying it around and showing it to all of us, its legs slowly rotating in the air and its head bobbing side to side as if the turtle thought it was actually getting away from her. Panja would let the turtle go and just when it was ready to disappear into the brush, she would go get it again and bring it back to us.

Doss you zee da tur-toll? Look at my tur-toll! Doss you all zee my tur-toll?

She said it just like that (ha).

And the day was sunny and fun and nice and I tried to remember it all. I tried to remember every part of it so I could write it down for you here and then write it again for Randy on a postcard tonight (I can call Randy if I have to, but some things just need to be written down).

Panja didn't cry when she finally let her turtle go, but I almost did—not for the turtle, but because of this one perfect afternoon. This one amazing memory was officially over.

I could come back to this place a thousand times. I could bring friends and a band and lobsters and dancing girls, but it would never be like it was yesterday. Never. And that's the cool thing, I guess.

And that's so we don't . . . oh.

Eff.

I forgot to tell you.

There is a job board here and there was a job listed for some temporary work and I called and I now have four hours of work later today. True. I can't believe I didn't write that to you before. My job, my four hours, is to wave a sign at traffic for an all-you-can-eat buffet.

It sounds like kind of boring work but it's work and it's my first real work while being a traveling man. And I have to meet another guy later today to talk about four whole *days*, not hours, of work at the Buffalo Museum of Science, helping tear down this huge display they have so they can get ready for the next one. That works out well, because then my week will be up here and I'll need to decide where to go next.

Eff, where do I go next?

Eff. I don't know.

Okay, that's it for now.

Oh wait. Slovenia is a country between Italy and Austria. I told you I'd look it up (ha).

Later.

Chapter 17

| July 25, 1992 |

I need to talk about this booze thing. This is important. I haven't written about it lately (ever since the Roy memory came to me, eff) and I don't want you to think the switch has just been pulled and I'll never want to drink again so I don't need to worry about it no more. I may be dumb but I ain't stupid (ha). So we might as well talk about it now and then I can tell you some other stuff.

I do think about it. I think about getting stone-faced, plowed, and I think about it every day. It's not, like, this physical thing you see in the movies where the drunk needs a drink or he will die right there on the spot. And it's not like I can't have just one drink. They used to say in rehab, *One is too many and a thousand is never enough,* but that ain't true. Not for me, anyways. I can have one. I can have three. But having just three, eff, what's the point (ha)? I drink to get drunk. Period. And three won't do it, so three ain't dangerous for me.

It's like, last night, Ping, Pan, and me, went to the Anchor Bar. It was Ping and Pan's last night here. They're heading to New York City, so we went out. The Anchor Bar is one of those *must do* things, I guess. It's the place where the chicken wing was first invented and if you're in Buffalo (which is right next to Niagara Falls, like Johnson City is right next to Binghamton), you have to go the Anchor Bar and you have to have chicken wings, and if you have chicken wings you have to have beer. It's a law (ha).

So Ping and Pan were pounding beers last night. These Thai boys can really drink, almost to my level. They had fourteen, maybe sixteen, beers each. I had three. I wanted sixteen, but I had three.

I woke up this morning, hangover-free and glad I didn't have sixteen beers, but I still thought about it all day. Like I said, it's a thinking thing, not a physical thing. It's like a nagging. A dare. As if there is this voice telling me how much fun it would be to get plowed, just once, and how cool it would be to visit that stoned place I've been living at for four years. And the more I think *not* to do it, the more I think I *want* to do it. It's harder to try and *not* do something than it is to try and *do* something. It's like trying *not* to think of the color orange. The harder you try *not to* think of it, the more you think of it (ha).

The end of the day is a tough time, though. Big time. I don't drink in the morning or afternoon, so those times of the day ain't a big deal. I drank right after work and until I passed out at that night. So that time, that part of the day, is effing tough for me, and I've learned to keep real effing busy. Anything I can do, like, anything I can really throw myself into, where I look up at the clock and go, *Eff, it's ten already?* That's real good. Otherwise, my hand misses having something cold to hold, something made of glass (ha).

But then there's this voice, this other voice. This one is not as loud as the other and this voice says to be patient. That there's a reason I'm out here. That there's something important, something *real,* out here and I'm getting closer to it. Eff, it's not a voice really (I'm not that far gone yet). It's more like a feeling.

Weird, huh?

Okay, so I just wanted to write about that and let you know I wasn't turning my back on this thing. I'm on it. I'm just hearing voices now (ha).

Okay, time to catch you up with a few things. First, I have my last day of work at the museum tomorrow and tonight is my last paid night at the hostel, so here's the plan. This guy Steve, who is moving a lot of this display stuff we've been tearing down, offered me some money to come and help him unload his truck with all of this stuff at the Buffalo warehouse it's going to, and then go with him to run a load of office furniture to a hospital in Erie, Pennsylvania. So, I told Steve no problem but that I would want to stay in Erie and not drive back with him. He was cool with that.

So I got $225 from the museum job coming tomorrow, I made another fifty waving a sign (very boring, just like I thought), and Steve is going to give me another hundred to help him unload the museum stuff, load the truck with furniture, then unload it at the hospital in Erie. And I get a free ride, too. Pretty cool, huh? I know nothing about Erie except I guess it's on the lake and is only a few hours away, but it sounds like a good place to go next.

And I already have a day's work lined up in Erie. Man, I'm good (ha). I went to the library and looked in Erie newspapers and found a guy who needs three or four people to help him unload and inventory everything in a big storage unit. I spoke to him on the phone and he gave me the address and told me to be there at nine on Tuesday morning. So I'll have to find a place to camp out when we're done unloading the stuff in Erie on Monday. I looked in my youth hostel book and couldn't find anything in Erie so I guess I'll find some secluded place to crash that night. Then I'll work the next day for this guy at the storage unit and then I'll find a place to stay the next night.

That's all for now.

Later.

July 27, 1992

There's a good feeling in being totally effing exhausted from work. You're there. You've given it all the effort you got and there's nothing effing left. It's kind of a high. Almost. I'm going to write just a few more lines to you (if I can stay awake that long, ha) and then I got to go crash. I'm totally beat (but I told you that already, huh? Ha!).

So we emptied the truck at the warehouse in Buffalo. We filled the truck up with office furniture and brought it here to . . . what's this place called again?

Hold on.

Okay, I'm back. I just walked over to the lobby wall and looked. This place is called the Hamot Health Center in Erie. It's a little after midnight and we're done loading all the furniture into the new offices here and Steve just left to drive back to Buffalo and now I'm going to go to sleep.

The other good thing about being this exhausted is that I'm going to walk from the lobby I'm sitting in down to a group of trees I saw near the water, and pass right effing out. I'm so tired, I know I can sleep right under them trees and I'll be asleep by the time I unroll my sleeping bag. And it's so late that no one will even know that I'm down there.

Okay. Done. Bye.

July 28, 1992

Good morning.

So, here's my new definition of a traveling man. A *true* traveling man has to not only swim in the Niagara River but also go and spend the night sleeping under some trees behind a boathouse near the Hamot Health Center in Erie effing Pennsylvania (ha).

So, then, a true traveling man would be—me.

I told you I would sleep last night (ha). Man, I was out as soon as I laid down. I was effing out. Bam. I haven't done physical work like that for so long. It felt nice to be totally effing spent.

Then, I woke up at about five this morning to the sound of the water against the docks and splashing against all them boats that was tied there and the sun on my face through them trees. Very cool. And I still knew where I was when I woke up, too. Weird.

So when I woke up, here was the plan. I stuffed a change of clothes, a toothbrush, toothpaste, shampoo, and stuff like that into my magic pillowcase and walked back to the hospital and into the emergency room. I didn't think I'd get too far since there is security all over this place (it's like a city—it's fricken *huuuuge*) but if I could get into the hospital then I could find a bathroom to clean up in real quick and then get out before getting yelled at and go find another place to kill a few hours before I have to meet that guy and help inventory that storage unit (I made a copy of the street map from the library and it's only four miles from here). So that was the plan. But this is what happened.

I walked into the emergency room because them other doors aren't open yet, and expected to be turned right around but the security guard on duty was the same guy from last night and he recognized me from delivering the furniture and he thought I was still working today so he not only waved me right in but gave me *another* contractor badge for the day because of all the paperwork we gave him last night (double ha).

So, I walked in. I found a bathroom down a hall where everything was real quiet. And this bathroom not only had a sink but had an effing shower in it (ha). So I took a quick hot shower, shaved, changed, and then walked back to where I had slept last night and there was this place, this great place, behind a shrub and hidden by this black mesh, probably used to keep weeds out, to hide my pack for the day. It was against a hill and hidden by that mesh. Then I walked back to the emergency room, waved to my new pal, Security Guard Latiani, and walked right in. And since I was all official-like, why not kill a few hours here, huh?

A hospital, especially one the size of a small effing college like this one, is not a bad place to kill some time. Especially when you're there early, when the world ain't arrived yet and you have a vendor badge and you can explore the whole place without someone thinking you're there looking for Valium. I walked between all them different departments. I walked through the emergency room and the cardiac wing and the cancer wing and health center and the smoking cessation classes and the center for digestive health and the pediatrics wing and speech pathology (ha).

I found yesterday's *Erie Times News* that was sitting in the waiting room and I sat in a thick leather chair near radiology and read it all. I also read two pamphlets that was very interesting: one on how to perform the Heimlich maneuver and the other on how to apply a tourniquet. And then, at 6:30, the cafeteria opened and I sprung for coffee with half-and-half (not the powdered crap—ha) and a fried egg sandwich on an English muffin with yellow American cheese (hey, I'm working today—it's all right to spend a little).

And that's where I am now. Sitting by a small table near the window, watching the people in them blue or purple or red or multi-colored smocks (is that what you call them doctor and nurse clothes? Smocks?) walk in and get coffee and start their day. Some don't look at me at all. And some look at me but only see my yellow contractor badge. But they don't know me. They don't know what I am. They don't know that I'm a traveling man (ha).

A little before 7:30, I'll start to walk the four miles to Denning Self-Storage (plenty of time to find it and get there wicked early) to meet this guy Walker and clean out his storage unit. And then I'll come back here tonight, use my contractor badge, and maybe grab dinner in the cafeteria if it's a prosperous day and it's not too expensive (if it *is* expensive, I'll try to find a Wegmans where I can use another gift certificate), and then I'll see about finding a place for the night. It'll probably be too late, though, so I'll sleep by the water again if it don't rain. If it does rain, I'll figure something else out. That's what we traveling men do. We figure things out (ha).

Like I said, there ain't no hostels or YMCAs in Erie, none that I could find in the book or the library, anyways. But the newspaper had a bunch of sublets for the month if I want to stay that long. See, there's all these college students that want to sublet their rooms out for the summer because they have leases and don't want to lose their places for the school year, so any money they can get for the time they ain't there is good. Some of them sublets are cheap: $125, $175, for the month for a furnished room in a furnished house, but you need to be out before school starts back up. And hey, that's fine with me.

So, I'll figure all that stuff about where to stay later. Right now, I'm just enjoying being clean, and being here in Erie. And this awesome egg sandwich.

July 29, 1992

My pen has been a couple of inches above this paper and it's hard to push it down and write something. The pen just sits there and I can't get it to write nothing. I can barely get it to touch the paper. I'm forcing it down now and it wants to jump back and I don't know how to start this and I don't know how to tell you all that happened and I don't know how to tell you the weirdest thing of all . . .

I don't know how, how to even tell myself, how even to let myself believe everything that happened. I'm forcing my pen down on the paper, trying to make all the words come to me, like I'm stalling long enough that if I just keep writing and keep the pen on the paper, the words will come, but the words ain't coming.

So I guess I won't write for now because this pen is too afraid. I'm not going to write this now. I'll try again later.

Bye.

* * *

Starting.

I'm going to try again. Slowly.

Have you ever gone into weird overload? Where one thing was so bizarre, so weird, so effing unbelievable, that all the other little things that would normally be really weird and would normally be real unbelievable, are nothing next to that one big weird thing? All them other things even seem normal next to that one big thing?

Before yesterday afternoon, I didn't, either.

Before that, sitting in a police car covered in another man's blood after being found with the gun that shot him in my hand would be *waaaaaay* up there on the weird scale. Not now. Not compared to that other thing. Or how about driving that same man to the hospital with your belt wrapped as tightly around his thigh as you can get it, and still seeing the blood pump out of him, plop, plop, plop? That would be up there. Not now. Or being a few feet behind the car holding the guys that shot that guy, so close that you could grab the guy shooting before he could shoot a second time because the gun was now aimed down at his head and you end up yanking the shooting guy halfway out of the car so he drops his gun and the car takes off? Is that weird? Nope. Or driving some effing sports car eighty miles an hour through Erie traffic while holding onto the belt that will keep the guy from draining out of blood like a fish? Or how about the police handcuffing me and questioning me for hours until they got a hold of the security tapes from the storage place and saw what happened, then uncuffing me and questioning me for a few more hours? Or how about all them TV people and newspaper people that keep sticking cameras in my face and keep trying to get in here to talk to me and take pictures of me?

Nope. Nothing.

Because the other things are scarier. Weirder. And that other thing. The big thing makes all of that other stuff seem so effing small.

That big thing—I can't write about it yet. I can't tell you yet. I need to talk to Walker first. He's the guy that got shot. He was my boss for the day at the storage unit. I need to talk to him about the big thing. About the big scary thing. And then I'll write it all to you.

They say he's going to be okay, Walker, so I might be able to see him in a few days, and then I can tell you.

I will talk about what happened up to that point, though. I can tell you all that happened yesterday at Denning Self-Storage (hey, I've told everybody else so it's about time I told you, ha). But there's people coming in here again and they want to talk some more—ah, eff, and that weasel lawyer is back now, too.

Eff. I got to go.

July 30, 1992

Slow. Real slow. I'll write this real slow and try to get you all caught up. But the problem is, stuff ain't happening slow—it's happening real effing fast, so by the time I get you slowly caught up there'll be more effing stuff to tell you, so I'll try to get this in before anything else happens.

So, you know I had a job at Denning Self-Storage for the day, right? I told you that part? Let me look back. Okay, I did write that part, so here goes the rest.

I walked over from the hospital to the storage place, right? It was pretty close by and I got there early. I met Walker in the office and we walked over to the storage unit we needed to clean out.

The first thing I need to tell you is—no. No. No. No, I didn't know who he effing was! That's the first thing everybody asks me. Cops, reporters, everybody. *Did you know who he was? Did you think there was a reward? Would you have done it if he was just an average person?* What's effing wrong with these people? I didn't know who he was. I keep telling them that.

And that was the first thing that Randy asked me, too. I had so many messages on my new free cellular phone, it blocked any more from coming in, and most of them were from Randy. When I finally called him, he was screaming at me.

What the eff is going on up there? Ya been gone an effing week and you're all over the effing news! Ya know that guy probably killed his friend to get to all that money, don't ya? Brandon is having kittens. He wants ya to call him for the story but ya can tell him yourself because I'm effing coming up there to get ya and bring ya back here. You're going to stay with me until we sort . . . Blah. Blah. Blah.

Eff.

I know Randy is only worried, but eff. Man, chill.

So I met Walker. He told me all about him inheriting the storage units from his friend and everything had to be inventoried for taxes and stuff. I showed him the newspaper clipping in my wallet, the one Brandon wrote, so he would know I was a traveling man and not a bum (ha). He thought being a traveling man was pretty cool and asked me questions about it. And I told him all the things I'd seen in just a week.

But, okay, I'm skipping the part about why reporters want to talk to me and what Randy is so pissed for.

Slow. Slow. Slow.

I got to the storage units. I met Walker and we walked over to the big storage unit #1. The plan was that everything had to be taken out of this storage thing, labeled, and then listed, then put back in. Simple. I thought it was going to be just him and me for a while, then about 9:30 two other guys showed up. Iggy and Fleece. They drove in together and walked over to the unit to find us.

Iggy and Fleece looked a little rough and it don't surprise me now to find out that they both had warrants on them, but . . . eff. Too fast. Slow down.

Iggy was this big bald guy and smoked like an effing chimney. I think Walker was getting pissed that the dude was stopping so much to smoke but he didn't say nothing. Fleece was skinnier and smoked a little less, but not much less. We were a couple of hours into bringing everything out—bringing out golf clubs and old movie cameras and file cabinets and crap like that. This was a big storage unit and it was packed to the ceiling with stuff. So we were a few hours into it when Fleece found the car. No, wait. Iggy found the car. Yeah. That's right. Iggy sees the car and says, *Hey, there's a Corvette back here.*

Well, eff, as soon as Fleece hears there's a Corvette back there, he hands me the box he's carrying and gets to where the car is, fast. Like Walker is going to effing give it to him or something (ha). He sees this car and takes the cover off, only it ain't a Corvette. It's this car called a Bricklin.

I remember the car's name was Bricklin because that's about all Fleece said for the next five hours. *Bricklin, Bricklin, Bricklin*. He told us all about the car (which actually *was* kind of interesting), about how this rich guy wanted to make a sports car but he done a bunch of things wrong and the car didn't work right, stuff like that. And that they only made this car for about two years and that there ain't a lot of them around.

So Fleece tells Walker that we need to get the car out of there so we can get to all the stuff around it. Which ain't really true. We could've left that car there and worked around it, but it's a good thing we didn't because if the car hadn't been running when . . .

Okay, slow down. Getting ahead again.

So off they go, Fleece and Walker, to go get a battery and gas and stuff for the car. I forgot to tell you this car had been in there since, like, 1976 or something. The car was jacked off the floor to save the tires and all the gas and fluids and stuff was drained out of it. So off they go to get stuff to get the car out of there and me and Iggy stay and keep doing inventory. Eff, I did inventory. Iggy just sat on a desk we dragged out of there and smoked and kept looking at me like I was some kind of effing idiot for still working.

So they come back and Iggy gets up like he's been working all this time (ha) and him and Fleece get to working on the car. They had to get the tires pumped up and the battery in, brake fluids in and all that stuff. So for the next few hours, Iggy and Fleece work on the car and me and Walker get to inventorying everything.

It was actually kind of fun. There was *everything* in that storage unit. There was about thirty pogo sticks. Really, at least thirty of them. There was a grandfather clock and a boat motor. There was one of them old-fashioned cigar-store Indians in there and about twenty deflated basketballs.

"Where did your friend get all of this stuff?" I asked, while carrying out a stuffed moose head (a real effing moose head, ha).

And Walker just smiled. "Got me," he said. "It probably came . . ."

But Walker didn't get to finish what he was going to say, because right then, the car, the Bricklin, started up. And inside that metal room, it effing roared.

Fleece whooped loudly as he shut the car door (this car had doors that you pulled down, not the normal ones that swing open) and slowly jiggled the car back and forth to maneuver it out of the unit. It took about four times until the nose of the car could turn out and the car could pull out onto the blacktop outside. Then he put the car in neutral and just gunned it. The engine screamed and Fleece just yelled.

Even Walker yelled.

As Fleece revved the engine, I walked some empty boxes over to the dumpster in a small alley by where Walker had his car parked (not the Bricklin—his other car, a Toyota, I think) and then things got real weird, real fast.

Walker walked over to his Toyota as I was tossing the boxes into the dumpster. He reached in through the window to get something from inside his car just as this other car was pulling in through the gate. Because I was just inside the alley, the other car couldn't see me. They could only see Walker.

The other car pulled right up next to Walker and I thought they was going to ask him something. As Walker's back was to the car, the passenger stuck his hand out of the window. A pistol was at the end of that hand.

Because Walker had his back to the car, he didn't see none of this. Then the gun fired. Right into Walker's thigh.

It didn't sound like the shots in the movies sound. It wasn't the big thundering boom you hear. It was like a pop. A loud pop, but still a pop. Walker smashed against the car, then crumpled to the ground. He was screaming and rocking back and forth holding his leg. Then the passenger lowered the gun toward Walker's rolling body. Right at his head.

They say in times of stress sometimes your body takes over. They say that your body just does what it needs to do because it don't have time to get permission from your brain. It will apologize later if it has to, but now, now your body has effing stuff to do.

I was right by the passenger door when the shot was fired and the passenger still couldn't see me. Instead of me reaching for the gun (which is what every cop said that I *should've* done—now you tell me!), I reached in through the window with both my hands and grabbed the guy on both sides of his shirt. Then I pulled back toward me with everything I had. I think I was trying to slam the guy against his seatbelt but the guy didn't have his seatbelt on, so when I tugged he was yanked a foot or so out the window toward me. He dropped the gun. When I saw that he was coming out the window, I kept pulling and almost got him all the way out (which every cop told me, again, was a really stupid thing to do because if I had pulled the guy out then he could've grabbed the gun from the ground and shot me, too. Eff!). I had the guy halfway out the window and was still pulling when the driver of the car grabbed the passenger by the waist of his jeans and then gunned the car. The car shot forward and my grip was broken and the guy climbed back in through the window and the car whipped out the gate and was gone.

It was right about that time that my brain sent the signal that it was definitely *not* okay to go ahead and try to stop the guy from shooting (too late). But there were a few bigger problems now. Blood was pumping out of Walker's leg. I mean, it was effing *pumping* out. And the bullet that shot through his leg also shot through the front tire of his car.

We would need to take Iggy and Fleece's car to the hospital, since I don't got no car no more and I walked there.

I looked over and there was Fleece and Iggy. Effing frozen. Iggy was leaning against the hood of the Bricklin and Fleece was just staring at us through the windshield. They hadn't effing moved.

"Go get your car," I yelled, as I pulled my belt off and wrapped it around Walker's thigh for a tourniquet. But Fleece and Iggy didn't move. "Go get your effing car!" I screamed. "We've got to get him to the hospital now."

That did it. Iggy and Fleece got up and ran to their car. The doors of their car opened. The doors closed. The car started. The car peeled out. The car shot through the gate. The car was gone.

Iggy and Fleece had left us.

I think I was more shocked, more surprised at Iggy and Fleece leaving than I was that the guy in the car had shot Walker. I even froze a second or two myself, thinking maybe they went to get help.

Right about then, Walker passed out from the pain.

I don't know why I picked up the gun before I grabbed Walker, but I did. Blood was effing pouring out of him now. I got my hands behind him, under his arms and around his chest, and dragged him backward to the Bricklin. We left a trail of blood. I got him to the passenger side, popped open that weird door, got him inside, and shut the door. Then I got on the driver's side and grabbed the tourniquet again tightly.

The blood slowed down but it was still pumping out of him, all over the seat and all over me. The car smelled like cigarette smoke, probably from Fleece being in it for so long, and I remember thinking the car only had five gallons of gas in it, from the can that Fleece and Walker got on their way in. But the hospital was only four miles away, so that didn't worry me. What did scare me was that this car, this effing Bricklin, ain't seen the light of day in twenty years. Could it last four miles? Could twenty-year-old tires make it four miles?

I drove through the gate and toward the hospital. I'm not a fast driver, but I effing punched it. I figured if the car did quit on us, I might as well get as close to the hospital as I could. (The cops later said *that* was a dumb idea too, ha.) I wove in between cars and I drove on the shoulder. I passed cars on both sides and ran through red lights when I needed to. I was holding onto the tourniquet, but because I didn't have time to put on Walker's seatbelt, the rest of him was bouncing all over the place. When I got to Nagle Road, not far from where my pack was hidden, I saw the flashing lights behind me but I was so close that I couldn't stop. The siren screamed at me and the cop car pulled right in behind me but I didn't stop. I swung around the building and right into the emergency room entrance. I drove right to the effing door and locked all four brakes and there was smoke from the tires everywhere. I stopped the car and ran around and pulled Walker out, the same way I did before, with my arms under his arms and around his chest, and I dragged him to the door. I was screaming my effing head off.

HELP! HEY, HELP! HE'S BEEN SHOT! HELP!

And two guys come rushing out and get Walker and put him on a stretcher and get him inside. He's covered with blood. I'm covered with blood. I started to relax a little for a second until I heard that word from the TV shows. *FREEZE!* That's when I realized I still had the gun in my hand. I had driven the entire way with the gun in my effing hand. One hand on the tourniquet and the other hand holding the gun and driving at the same time. Eff. I don't know how the eff I did it.

FREEZE! PUT THE GUN DOWN! NOW! And I did. And then came the tackling part and then the face in the concrete part as the cops jumped on top of me and got the cuffs on. It was then that I heard the first shot. It wasn't like the pop of the gun that shot Walker. This was an effing boom like from the guns in the movies. And I thought, dead. I'm effing dead. Then I heard the second boom and heard the cops screaming at each other and I didn't think I would hear them shoot me twice, so maybe they was shooting at something else.

Then the cops were dragging me away from the car. That exploding, burning car. And just as they dragged me into the building, the last two tires on the Bricklin blew. Boom. Boom. And they sounded just like the guns in the movies, too. Then the smoke poured out from under the hood and the Bricklin crackled. It actually effing crackled, like a campfire. Then you couldn't see the car no more. Just the fire and the smoke where the car used to be. You couldn't even tell what color the Bricklin was.

And then I was inside the hospital and they took me in a room to check me over, to make sure I didn't get shot, too. And they looked me all over while my right hand was handcuffed to a stretcher. I was checked over by doctors and nurses and more doctors, and cops kept asking me questions and then more doctors and more cops, and then they arrested me.

I don't blame the cops for what they did. They didn't know what happened. And they probably still wouldn't believe me if it wasn't for them security tapes from the storage unit. The tapes showed everything. Even perfect shots of Fleece and Iggy. That's when the cops told me about the warrants on both of them. Fleece's was for car theft. (Hmm, wonder why he wanted to get the Bricklin going, huh?) And Iggy's was for missing child-support payments.

I can't really leave Erie yet. Besides all the questions the cops have for me about the guys that shot Walker, I still have to go to court. Pretty funny, huh? Although the cops say the charges will all be dismissed, I still got a charge of driving an unlicensed, unregistered, uninspected car in a high-speed pursuit while carrying an effing stolen hand gun (ha).

And I've only been traveling two effing weeks (ha!).

They got the security tapes and the cops say it's just a—what's it called? *Procedure*? No, *formality*—that's the word, *formality*. But I can't leave until they get me in front of a judge, which may be today or tomorrow. To get everything dismissed.

It would actually be kind of fun just hanging out here and waiting, except that guy Walker's lawyer is here three times a day. He's this big pushy guy named Benjamin Mott and I don't know how he gets in here, but he does. He just came in one day, introduced himself, and said he was Walker's lawyer and would be the liaison between Walker and me. That's the word he used, *liaison*. He pulled out a bunch of papers and told me where to sign.

"Sign?" I said. "I don't need no lawyer."

"I can't begin the negotiations without getting this paperwork taken care of." He smiled. He's always smiling. It's like he smiled one day and then forgot how to stop. He tried three or four times to get me to sign them papers and now he don't try no more.

"We'll take care of the paperwork later," he says. "After you see what kind of settlement we are willing to give you."

And I always say the same thing. I don't want no settlement and I don't need no lawyer, but he just smiles and leaves. This guy's head is huge. It's like a potato stuck on a pencil (ha).

So now you're caught up with *that* part. I'll tell you all the stuff with reporters and cops later but the weird part, the scary thing, I got to tell that to Walker first. I figure I may only be able to tell it once and if I tell you then I might not be able to tell him. And he needs to hear it more than you do. Way more. I tried to see him today, but he was too weak still. I'll try tomorrow.

July 31, 1992

Looks like I got a few minutes so I thought I'd write (I'm popular these days, ha). I thought I'd write about what all the fuss is about Walker. No, I haven't talked to him yet. He's still pretty out of it, but I wrote before that the first thing all them asked me was, *Did I know who Walker was?* And I didn't know who he was. I do now, but I never told you who he was. So I will now.

I guess Walker was some big-shot film guy a few years back. He made some films that won some awards and then he got caught counterfeiting, making phony twenty-dollar bills. It was serious enough for him to go away for it. And he had to declare bankruptcy and he got divorced and a bunch of other stuff happened.

So he does his time and comes back to Erie and gets an apartment and becomes friends with the guy that owns all the apartment buildings. And this guy owns more than the apartment buildings—he owns a bunch of stuff all around Erie. Then the landlord guy dies and leaves Walker everything. Like millions.

Eff, and if people were pissed at him before, they're really pissed at him now. I looked at a bunch of old newspapers they brought me and people can't stand the guy. Some people say the money he got should go toward all the debt he walked away on with his bankruptcy years ago. Other people say he shouldn't get no money at all because he's a felon. And other people are pissed because they think that Bugby, the guy that left him all that money, should've left all that money to somebody else, anybody else, and other people are pissed off because they think it's too coincidental that Bugby just died like that, since he wasn't sick or nothing, and then left Walker everything. They ain't saying they think Walker killed him, but they ain't saying they *don't* think he killed him. Some people are pissed off because he hasn't made no charitable gifts with all that money. And other people are just pissed off because they're pissed off.

And it's jealousy with a lot of them probably, but still it's intense enough for a couple of boneheads to try to kill the guy. That's more than just jealousy. That's jealousy that's rotted and turned to effing hate.

They still haven't caught the guys—the guys that shot him. I got a good look at the passenger, not the driver, and then I looked through them mug shots for, like, ever, and even sat with a police sketch guy, who drew a picture of him. The security tape showed the license plate was taken off but the cops have the make and model of the car and that's it. The camera didn't get a good shot of the guy when I pulled him out the window.

They got Fleece and Iggy, though. From the security tapes they got the plate number of the car they were driving and they picked them both up that afternoon. I felt a little bad about that, but eff, they shouldn't have left us.

Some cops think the guys that shot Walker will either be back to finish the job or will now try to get me, now that I've seen them. Other cops think those guys are too small-time to do anything like that and think they are probably long gone. Hiding. Who knows?

But the cops are having me stay at a house the city owns (sweet, free rent!). I've been here ever since Walker got shot, so I can be protected, at least for now, and keep looking through mug shots and stuff. I can't leave until this judge thing is all done, anyways. This place ain't fancy, but the price is right (ha).

But Randy thinks them guys that shot Walker will come after me now. He's convinced of it and he's driving me effing nuts about it. Randy's a good guy, but he's taking this too far.

I just cleaned my cell phone messages out this morning and turned it back on now to check it and it's already clogged back up again. There's messages on how Brandon's getting a bunch of calls from reporters and messages on how Brandon wants me to call him. Messages on how Randy wants me to tell him where I am so he can come get me and bring me to his house where I can hide (yeah, that sounds like fun). And then he leaves so many messages, he loads the mailbox back up and then gets pissed at me because he can't leave me no more messages (ha).

And some reporters got this number, too, but I don't talk to them. They're outside the police station all the time, and when I go from here to the house, they always ask me stuff, pointing cameras at me. What am I supposed to say? They know what happened, so why ask me about it? And they always ask dumb questions, too, like, *How does it feel* to be this, or *how did I feel* when I did that? Eff.

I can't watch the TV no more. Every news channel has the same effing thing. The clip from the security camera of Walker being shot and of me grabbing the guy. Stop. Again. Walker being shot and me grabbing the guy. Stop. Again. Then over to the pile of ash that used to be the Bricklin. Then Walker being shot and me grabbing the guy. Again. Background talking, calling people on the phone, experts on this and experts on that, outside shot of the hospital, then outside of the storage place, then Walker being shot and me grabbing the guy. Eff.

I'll call Brandon today and he can talk to them reporters for me. They all make me nervous anyways, like I'm at a fancy wedding and I'm the only one wearing shorts and a dirty T-shirt (ha). I'll call Brandon today and see if he can, like, be the guy they talk to. I'll talk to Brandon but I ain't talking to those other ones. Then I can tell Walker about the scary thing and see the judge and then get back on the road again.

Okay, got to go. Going to court now.

* * *

Well, the judge thing is over. I didn't like it, but it's over.

It's funny, with all the stuff I stole in my life, out of all the bad stuff I've done (like what Roy did to Vernon's house, eff), I've never been in a courtroom before. Well, my divorce, I guess, but that was just a room in the courthouse, not an actual courtroom. At my divorce we just signed some papers, Grace cried (eff), and then it was over.

I was wondering how official this was going to be today and it was pretty effing official. There was a judge and lots of people. Man! There were about three hundred people in them chairs waiting for me. The place was effing packed! I wasn't expecting it, and Tony, or that other cop—I can't remember his name, Roland?—if they knew about it, they should've told me but I don't think they expected it, either.

We drove over from that house they got me staying at to the courthouse, and me, Tony, and Roland walked in through the back way to the courtroom. Tony said it's the way they bring in prisoners from the jail when it's time for them to go to court. I asked Tony if he wanted to handcuff me again, and he said, *Be nice* (ha). *Be nice* is what he says when I remind him that he arrested the good guy.

Me and Tony and Roland sat in these chairs in this little room and waited near this door. When the door was opened, we would walk inside. It seemed like it took forever but finally we heard a click and the door opened.

We all stood up and Tony walked in first, then me, then Roland. I heard Tony say, *Holy cow,* and didn't know why he was saying that until I saw all them people. When I saw the crowd, I froze. I stopped walking and Roland had to push me a bit to get me moving again. We walked to the judge's bench and when we got there, Roland and Tony motioned for me to stay and they walked to the side and sat down.

The bench was where the judge sat but there was like, this fence—like a fence made out of chair legs—that I was supposed to stand next to. I didn't like being there . . . at . . . all. And I was getting all the charges dismissed, so I couldn't imagine being the guy standing there when you weren't sure what was going to happen to you.

The judge asked me my name and he asked me a bunch of other questions. I grabbed the edge of that chair-leg fence thing and tried to answer him without throwing up. At the bench there was the judge and this stenographer typing everything down. That was it. There wasn't no lawyer or prosecutor or nothing and I began to get worried. Like I was being set up and maybe I was in more trouble than I thought.

The judge banged his wooden hammer down on the desk and said some legal stuff. Then he stopped and looked at me. He asked me a few more questions. Then he talked.

"The court has reviewed the evidence of this case," he said, real judge-like. "And we have made a decision regarding the charges against you, based on the evidence we have reviewed. Do you understand this, Mr. Dutcher?"

I said that I did.

"And are you prepared to obey the decision of this court regarding the charges brought against you, in lieu of a trial?"

Right then, this fear came over me. Big time. And I wondered if I *had* been set up. Maybe these guys didn't want me to have a lawyer or nothing because this way, they could send me straight to prison. Boom. I had trusted these people, but maybe this was bad. I looked to Tony and he was talking to Roland so I looked back to the judge.

"I am," I said.

"Very well," the judge said. "Then let the record show . . ." And he went on about more legal stuff. I looked over to Tony and he just stared back at me. *I made a big mistake,* I thought.

The judge began to speak again.

"I have reviewed the security tapes obtained from Denning Self-Storage. I have reviewed the tapes from the two police vehicles. I have reviewed your testimony as well as the testimony of Chester Graham, aka Fleece, and Martin Ignacious, aka Iggy."

I was so scared, I couldn't even smile at the thought of bald, fat, chain-smoking Iggy being named Martin.

"The court finds no evidence that would stand to rebuke your statements in any way."

This is good, right? Rebuke? Rebuke is good?

And then he said a bunch more legal stuff before he went down this list.

"On the charge of reckless driving," he said, and then he listed the charge number. "This charge is dismissed."

"On the charge of driving an uninsured vehicle," he said. And then listed the number for that. "This charge is dismissed."

And he kept going down like this, listing all six charges until he got to the one about the hand gun, and after each one he said that word: *dismissed*.

Then, when it was done, he looked at me and said this part—this part I remember because I had stopped shaking and knew I wasn't going to prison.

"Mr. Dutcher," he said. He took his glasses off and leaned forward in his chair. "The city of Erie, Pennsylvania, has nothing but gratitude to you for putting yourself in harm's way for one of its citizens," he said. "Thank you, and you are free to go."

Then he smacked the wooden hammer on his desk one more time. "Case dismissed."

Everybody stood up and started clapping and Tony and Roland walked over and they were clapping, too. They motioned for me to open the little wooden gate and walk out through the aisle of people.

They want me to walk down the aisle where all those effing people are? Out to the hallway where there's even more people? Are they effing crazy?

I shook my head as everyone was clapping and I motioned to the back door we came in through. They smiled and shook their heads and walked me toward the gate.

I gave Tony a *Please, please do me a favor here, pal* look.

Tony gave me a *Hey, it's against the rules, sorry* look.

I moved in closer, and I could feel that my eyes were wide with fear. "Tony," I said. "Please. Be nice."

Roland laughed but Tony just stared at me. Then Tony smiled. He nodded and then he and Roland walked me toward the back door.

Some people in the crowd didn't like this.

"Hey!" one guy shouted.

"Officer, where are you taking him?" a lady asked.

And we got out before they knew where we were and got back to Tony's police car and he took me here. To the hospital.

I'm sitting here now, waiting to talk to Walker. He can see me as soon as his kids leave the room. My pack is in the trunk of the car and Tony says he'll give me a ride to the bus station when I'm done.

But first I need to tell Walker the very scary thing.

Then, I'm effing out of here.

Chapter 18

| August 7, 1992 |

The Very Scary Thing

Okay, that didn't go as expected. It didn't go bad. Not really. Just different. Very different, because instead of me being on a Chinese food–smelling Greyhound bus, heading to, eff, to anywhere, I'm still in Erie, sitting in Bugby's apartment, at his dining room table, writing to you. (Bugby was Walker's friend, the one that died and left him everything, remember?)

So I'm in Erie for at least another few days. Eff. But that's okay. I have a place to stay and even a few days of work for Walker until we sort this thing out.

It's a good thing the notebook I was writing in only had a few pages left because I'm writing in a second notebook now. Walker has the first one.

Okay, so this is what happened.

I went to the hospital. There wasn't too many reporters there because they were all at the courthouse (ha). I got past where the reporters couldn't go any farther and I got to Walker's room and waited in the hallway. Walker's kids, their mom, and some big guy—a cop maybe?—came out of Walker's room and walked up to me. They told me who they were and they thanked me and I said no problem and was trying to get past them but they kept me there. Especially them girls. The taller one said her dad would've died if I wasn't there and the littler one asked me if I was going to hunt down the guy that did it. Like I was a bounty hunter or something (ha). I told her that every cop in the country is looking for that guy, that the cops have a drawing of him that looks just like him. They'll get him.

She smiled at me and I liked that. I liked saying something that could make her smile.

They kept talking to me and thanking me and the big one hugged me and the little one cried and then they left and then I went in to see Walker.

Walker was sitting up in bed when I got there.

"Hey," I said, walking over to shake his hand.

"Hey." He smiled. He looked tired but a lot better than the last time I saw him (ha).

I sat down on a chair and put my pack on the floor next to me. "How you feeling?"

"Like I've been shot in the leg." He smiled.

"What a coincidence."

We talked for a while about nothing until I got to the point—the beginning of the really scary thing speech.

"I've been wanting to talk to you about something."

"I bet," Walker said, raising the bed higher. "I heard about everything you did."

"That's what I want to talk to you about."

"No need to talk, man. Your attorney told me what you were looking for and I'm working on it."

"Huh?"

"Anything you want, Dutch."

I don't get really pissed off very often, but when I do it's real hard to stop it. What an arrogant SOB. "I ain't here to get paid," I said, probably a little too loud for a hospital room.

Walker was surprised. "Not *paid*," he said, real defensive-like. "A reward. What you deserve. I mean, how much is a life worth anyway?"

"I'm not here for a reward. I'm here to tell you something. Something important, and then I'm gone."

"But . . ." Walker looked real confused. "Your attorney said you were looking for three million dollars."

"What?"

Walker told me about Mott, that big-headed weasel, and said that Mott came to Walker a bunch of times saying I hired him to get me three million dollars for what I'd done.

"He told me," I said, still talking too loud for a hospital room, "he told me he was *your* attorney. I didn't sign nothing with him. I told him I don't need no lawyer."

"He's not my attorney." Walker was smiling again. "I have no use for the guy."

Man, I was pissed.

Walker could see how mad I was, so we talked a bit and I calmed down some. I told Walker I don't have no attorney and I didn't want a dime from him. I just wanted to tell him something important about what happened.

So I started from the beginning.

"Do you know anything about probabilities?" I asked.

Walker's expression went from surprise to fear—maybe he was thinking I was a total effing nut job (ha). I didn't let him answer.

"There's encyclopedias at this place they got me staying at—*had* me staying at—I'm leaving right after this. And I've been looking up stuff on probabilities."

Walker looked concerned.

"This has to do with you, trust me. So do you know what the probability is of you winning the lottery?"

"250 million to 1," Walker said.

Now I was shocked. "Wow. That's right," I said. "So, if you buy a lottery ticket, there is a high probability you won't win, right? It's not impossible, just highly improbable."

"Right."

"So, you buy the ticket and win. Boom. Long shot, but you did it. So the next day you buy another ticket. And you win again. Now the odds of winning two days in the row are in the billions. It's still not impossible, just highly, highly improbable. You with me?"

"Sure."

"Now the third day, you buy another ticket and you win again. Now you've crossed the line from improbable to impossible. The odds get too high that it can't happen. No way. But it *did* happen. And the next day, you win, and the next and the next."

"Congratulations."

"Thanks. So, if you're not cheating, then how can you win all them times?"

"I give up."

"You can't. It's impossible. There is only one way that you could win all them times."

"Okay, how?"

"I'll ask you that in a minute. So let's move to this stuff about you. So, when we were at the storage unit, I was standing right by the car that shot you, right?"

Now I had his interest. "That's what they tell me."

"If I had been any other place else in that lot—anyplace—you'd be dead. I was in their blind spot. A step or two in any direction would've changed everything."

"Okay."

"So the probability of me being right there, right at the exact effing spot (I actually said *eff,* not the real word, ha), the only spot that would've worked, was pretty low. Not impossible, but highly improbable. You're a lucky guy."

"Improbable, not impossible."

"Right. Improbable, not impossible. Now, when I grabbed that guy, I did everything wrong. The cops have told me that a thousand times. I should have been shot, the guy should've come out of the car and got the gun back, the car could've run over me. Whatever. Another lucky break. But . . ." I got up and stood at the foot of his bed. "But it worked. Improbable, not impossible," I said.

I started to pace and was trying to keep the next part clear in my head. "Now, after you was shot, I put a tourniquet on you right away, right? That tourniquet slowed the blood down long enough to save your butt. Do you know how long I had known how to put a tourniquet on?"

"How long?"

"About five hours. I read a pamphlet about tourniquets five hours before you got shot. I read it in this very hospital. What are the odds of me just coming across a pamphlet on something I would need to know later that very effing day? If I hadn't read that, you'd be dead. I wouldn't've even thought to put a tourniquet on you. I would've just got you in the car and you would've bled out on the way. See," I said. "You're now crossing that line from lucky to impossible."

"I don't get it."

"Oh, wait. It gets better. I'd been in Erie about thirteen hours when I went to work for you, right? I got a ride here the night before because I had a few hours of work at this hospital. I know exactly two places in Erie: your storage unit and this hospital. I don't know where the mall is or the post office or the effing library is, but I know where the hospital is and where Denning Self-Storage is. What if everything went the same way, only I got you in that car and didn't know where to go? I would have been driving in circles. Or I would have been driving until the car blew up. You'd be dead."

"So you're saying all of this shouldn't have happened?"

"Nope. I'm saying it *couldn't* have effing happened. It's impossible. But there's more. The Bricklin blew up after you got here. Not before. A minute after. Boom! No more car. And what are the odds of finding a car in that storage unit and getting it up and running just a minute—an effing minute—before we would need it? Iggy and Fleece took off. Your car had a tire that was shot out, leaving—ta-da!—the Bricklin. Running for the first time in twenty effing years."

"So how did it happen, then?"

"What's the only way you could win the lottery five days in a row? If you wasn't cheating."

Walker's smile became a sneer. "Are you saying divine intervention? God?"

"I'm saying it can't happen. But it did."

"Dutch, I believe we got lucky. I got lucky, very lucky, but we're probably making too much out of . . ."

I reached into my bag and pulled out my first notebook. "Look, I'm not making this up and I'm not lying. This is my journal. I've been keeping it for a few months now. There's some personal crap in there but read it all. It will show you how I got here and about traveling this way and about the tourniquet pamphlet and how it was dumb luck for me to even be in Erie and how I got to know the very hospital you're laying in."

Walker took the notebook.

"It's not dumb luck. It's not that you should be dead. It's that you need to be alive."

"Maybe it's just to be a good father? Maybe that's all I'm supposed to do."

"Look, I ain't saying that you're supposed to *do* anything or that there's some big important thing *to* do. And I ain't saying that, like, you're *the chosen one* or any crap like that. I ain't that weird. What I *am* saying is that a bunch of really goofy things had to happen in a very specific way so you'd be here talking and breathing." I smiled. "And maybe this stuff happens every day but I just paid attention this time."

We talked for a while more and Walker asked if I had a place to stay. I told him I was leaving but I'd need to stay now until I get my notebook back. That's when he gave me the key to Bugby's place and he said I could stay here as long as I wanted.

"I don't need nothing from you, Walker. You don't owe me nothing at all."

"No, that's not it. It's more selfish than that. Bugby left me all this stuff and I'm destroying it. I can't find anyone to help me. Look what's happening. The only guys who will work for me are guys like Iggy and Fleece." Walker told me about how Bugby had left him everything but the employees walked out on him and now he was afraid of screwing up what Bugby had built. He was really worried about, like, disappointing Bugby, even though the guy was dead.

Walker reached over to his computer and pulled a disk from the side. "Here. Let's swap. I've been keeping a journal, too. Personal stuff as well, but it says everything about Bugby and what he left me and how I need someone to help." I took the blue square disk.

"And maybe it's not me, Dutch. Maybe it's you," he said. "Maybe you need to stay here a while."

Eff. I put the disk in my pack and Walker told me that Bugby had a computer in his apartment I could use. He gave me directions and then I started to leave.

Walker began reading my journal while I was still there. I got to the door when I told him the last part.

"They told me you got a pretty rare blood type."

"Yeah." Walker was reading. "AB negative."

I put my pack over my shoulder and grabbed the doorknob. "You know, only six percent of the country has that blood type, right? When you first got here, you'd lost a lot of blood. They didn't know if they would have enough of that blood for you."

Walker smiled but kept reading. "Another lucky break, huh? They just happened to be stocked up?"

"Nope," I said. "They didn't have any." Walker raised his head from the notebook and looked at me. "None. They ran out of AB negative blood." I waited a second and then turned my wrist to show him the small Band-Aid that still rested in the crook of my arm. "They ended up giving you O-negative blood anyways, because my blood, my AB negative blood, couldn't get screened fast enough for ya. But that's not the point. It's the same blood."

I turned the knob. I opened the door.

"Scary, huh?" I said. Then I shut the door behind me, leaving Walker, a guy I met less than two weeks ago, to read my most personal effing thoughts. To read about Roy. And Grace. And my dad.

Eff.

Which brings me to here.

Tony gave me a ride here to Bugby's instead of the bus station and I'm sitting writing to you on this dining room table in my second notebook, in a dead guy's apartment (ha). Then I'm going to take this disk into the computer in the other room and try to read for a bit (it's been a while since I've used a computer—I hope I can remember how to do it), and that will give me something to do cuz I'm getting that itchy drinking feeling again.

Then I'll crash.

Later.

JOURNAL 5

WALKER

Chapter 19

Thirty-three Cecils

| August 3, 1992 |

When Abby was five and Rachel and Liz were not quite three, I would tell them a story every night—this was long before the Abercrombie stories began and long before television or a movie would be a tempting alternative. Rachel and Liz would sit on Abby's big-girl bed and we would set the stage with the stuffed animals and dolls and other props we would need for that evening's performance. The stories were simple ones—mostly about castles or magic or secret places you can go to only if you know how.

But one story I told, one story that I made up for them, they wanted to hear over and over again. Almost every night, to the point that I began hating to tell it and would beg to try a new story and or even tell an old one, just to get a short reprieve. Some nights they would allow this. Most nights they would not.

The story they loved was called "Thirty-three Cecils" and it took place in a village called Wensley, which is the town where all the liverwurst in the world is made. In fact, most of the people who lived in Wensley made liverwurst. Oh sure, there was a baker, a tailor, a shoemaker, a blacksmith, and a bookstore, but everything else had to do with the production of, the sale of, or the shipment and packaging of liverwurst.

Now, Wensley was a very old town and the people there had been making liverwurst a very long time. Most of the liverwurst makers in Wensley remembered their parents making liverwurst and *their* parents before them making it. It was assumed that when a young person reached a certain age, he or she would go to one of the factories and start making liverwurst. Because, after all, why would anyone want to do anything else?

And because Wensley was a very old town and because the people did things pretty much the same way day after day and year after year, there were very few things that were different in Wensley from one day to the next. A Tuesday in June was pretty much the same as a Tuesday in October—or a Thursday or a Saturday, for that matter. Things remained the same and there were very few surprises.

In fact, most of the people of Wensley had never even heard of that word: *surprise.* If you were to ask someone on the street what that word meant, most would not know or understand it, even if you explained it to them. Why would something different happen, or why would you even *want* it to?

One day, a stranger came to Wensley. He was a short, fat man with a yellow hat. The short, fat man went to the bakery to get a loaf of bread because he was passing through town and was getting hungry. The man who owned the bakery didn't see very many strangers, so he asked the unknown man his name.

"Cecil," the man said. And he paid for his bread and left.

Cecil? That's a funny name, the baker thought, because the baker had never met anyone named Cecil before and he thought it was very odd to do something you've never done before.

About that same time, a tall, thin man in a red hat walked into the shoemaker's shop. He was passing through the town as well and needed a new pair of shoes. The shoemaker didn't see many strangers in town and when the man picked out a pair of shoes, the shoemaker asked his name.

"Cecil," the man said. And he paid for his shoes and left.

Cecil? the shoemaker thought. *That's a funny name*. Because the shoemaker had never met anyone named Cecil before and he thought it was very odd to do something you've never done before.

Also around that same time, a stranger walked into the tailor shop. He was large man with glasses and a yellow mustache. He was passing through the town and needed a new coat. The tailor didn't see many strangers and as the man picked out his coat, he asked the man his name.

"Cecil," the man said. And he paid for his coat and left.

Cecil? That's a funny name, the tailor thought, because the tailor had never met anyone named Cecil before and he thought it was very odd to do something you've never done before.

The baker told the shoemaker that he had met a short, fat man who was named Cecil. The shoemaker told the baker that he had met a tall, thin man who was named Cecil, and the tailor told both of them that he had met a big man with glasses and a yellow mustache named Cecil.

This was very strange, they all thought, and the three men ran to the mayor's office to tell him what had happened. The mayor would know what to do.

When the tailor and the baker and the shoemaker got to the mayor's office, there were already several townsfolk there. They heard the man from the liverwurst shop telling the mayor that an old man with a beard had come in to buy liverwurst. His name was Cecil. They heard the blacksmith say that a young man riding a bicycle and wearing a bowtie came to his shop to ask directions. The young man said his name was Cecil. They heard an old woman say that a man with curly red hair wearing yellow suspenders said good morning to her while she was hanging out her wash. She asked his name and he answered, "Cecil."

The mayor listened to the villagers.

"Friends," the mayor said. "We are the greatest village in the world, because only a village as wonderful as ours would be visited by six men named Cecil, all in the very same . . ."

Before the mayor could finish, two other men came in with stories about meeting a stranger named Cecil. Then four more came in. Then two after that.

Fourteen Cecils? All in the very same day?

"Quickly," the mayor said, and proceeded to give the villagers instructions.

The large blackboard was taken out of the school and brought to the town square. Villagers were sent from house to house to see if anyone had met any new Cecils, and the number was tallied on the blackboard.

"We will have one hundred Cecils come to our village today!" the mayor said, with great excitement. "And when we have one hundred Cecils, the world will know what a great town Wensley is."

There was shouting and yelling after another Cecil was discovered, and then another one, and the news was brought to the town square. Soon there were nineteen Cecils. Then twenty-three. Then twenty-eight Cecils.

The town band was on the square and ready to play the minute the hundredth Cecil was found. Fireworks were set up and ready to be lit as soon as the tally reached one hundred. The town cannon was loaded and ready to be fired the moment the one-hundredth Cecil was discovered.

Thirty Cecils. Thirty-one. Thirty-two Cecils.

"Citizens of Wensley," the mayor shouted over the excited crowd. "We will be known forever, once we reach one hundred Cecils."

Thirty-three Cecils.

The mayor watched for new villagers running to the square. He watched for news of more Cecils. He waited. The villagers waited. But the news stopped coming.

The mayor scanned the edge of the crowd for more runners coming in. But none did.

An hour passed. Then two hours. But no more news came.

"That's it?" the people asked.

"Only thirty-three?" a woman asked.

"Be patient," the mayor said. "We'll get there."

Another hour went by. Then another. Soon it was getting dark, but no further news came. The band went home to eat. The cannon was unloaded and the fireworks were put away.

"Be patient," the mayor repeated.

"I knew it was a trick," a boy said.

"Only thirty-three? That's it?" the liverwurst factory foreman asked.

Night came, but no more Cecils arrived.

The crowd thinned. People walked away. Then it was only the mayor and a few others. Then, just the mayor and one other person. Then it was just the mayor.

By morning, the mayor stepped off his platform. The blackboard was returned to the school. The mayor walked back to his office.

"We are a very unimportant town," the mayor said to himself. "I thought we were great. But we are not."

And the day ended.

And the next day was just as it had been before.

And so was the day after that.

And so was the day after that.

And nothing ever happened in that town again.

Chapter 20

Benjamin Mott

| August 4, 1992 |

Do you know what the worst thing about being shot is? I didn't know the answer to this question until recently, and since you may have never experienced the sensation, I thought I'd share it with you.

The pain? Nope. They keep you pretty doped up, so life is mostly a hazy, sleepy experience. There's very little pain. So far. But even the pain I felt before the drugs was not the worst thing.

How about the fear of almost dying? Nope. I slept through most of that and wasn't mentally checked in when things were iffy, so I sort of cheated on that one, but it's still not the worst thing.

How about the fact that I will now walk with a limp? No. That doesn't bother me—at least for now. Because this other thing has taken up all of my attention and this other thing is by far the worst thing.

The worst thing is, it's in the knowing, in the proof, that there is at least one person—there could be more, but you now know there is at least one—who hates you enough to want to take your life. It's in the knowing that there is at least one person who is willing to go to prison, is willing to give up their own freedom, or is even willing to die if it means they will have the chance to wipe you out of existence.

That thing, that knowledge, far outdoes any physical discomfort or the inconvenience of a limp. Once you know this, I don't know how you can recover from it. There are no drugs or crutches or therapy that can reduce that pain.

The person who hates me that much is still out there. Dutch gave the police a pretty good description, but he's still out there. Will he try again?

Will he try to get to the girls? I can't think about that. My mind gets all fuzzy and I shut down. No one knows.

Since I've been shot, I've been in and out. I write a little and sleep a lot. I need to get stronger before the surgery on my leg to repair some of the damage. While I wait, I've been able to gather most of the pieces of what happened to me and most of the facts have soaked into my drug-addled brain.

There are people in and out of this hospital room all the time, and each one has told me a little of what happened. No reporters, though—they can't get in—but police and doctors and more police and more doctors and a sleazy lawyer named Benjamin Mott. I don't know how he slithers in past the police but he gets in a few times a day.

Benjamin Mott is Dutch's attorney. Dutch wanted to make sure that he is compensated properly for what he did, so Mr. Mott is here to make sure that everything remains fair. I mean, how much is a life worth anyway? That's what Mr. Mott asks me every time he's here.

"How much is a life worth, Mr. Roe?"

Benjamin Mott is a tall man with a great bald gob of a head. It's as if they ran out of heads his size so they needed to use the next size up. Mr. Mott slides in and reminds me of the danger his client put himself in, in order to save me. He reminds me of the chances Dutch took.

Mr. Mott has identified three major areas where Dutch went above and beyond to save me, and he is asking for one million dollars for each of these areas. Three million total.

"After all, Mr. Roe, how much is a life worth?"

I wish Dutch had just come to me before hiring this sleazeball, but hey, he did save my life. He really did. So I'll try to see if I can find three million dollars. I'll have to sell something fast, and when you sell something fast, you never get top dollar. Even a horrible businessman like me knows that.

The three areas Benjamin Mott has identified are the following:

When I was shot, Dutch was just coming out of the alley where the dumpster was. A car pulled in and shot me in the leg—with a small caliber, twenty-two, otherwise at that range a bigger gun would have blown my leg off. When I fell, the gunman pointed the gun at my head to finish the job. Dutch reached into the car and grabbed the gunman, knocking the gun out of his hand. Then the assailants drove away.

That's the first million.

Dutch quickly applied a tourniquet to my leg. By doing this, he slowed the bleeding to keep me alive until I got to the hospital.

That would be the second million.

After Iggy and Fleece took off, since the first bullet went through the front tire of my car, Dutch had to get me into the Bricklin and drive incredibly fast through traffic to get me to this hospital—just before the car blew up, by the way—therefore endangering his life in an unsafe vehicle under dangerous conditions.

That would be the third million.

After all, how much is a life worth anyway?

Apparently, mine is worth three million dollars.

I wonder if Dutch saved my life simply for the money. Did he think about the money afterward or did he see an opportunity and take it right then and there? If I were penniless, would he have let me die? If I were a billionaire, would he have done even more?

It's not important, I guess. To be able to still be with my girls and watch them grow up, I'd give anything.

Dutch has asked to see me and I sent word—that's the thing we do, we the imprisoned; we send word—that I am too weak right now. I do want to thank him and I *will* thank him, but it's going to be difficult being sincere knowing that he only wants to get paid for what he did. Or that he just wants the publicity. Or both.

Mott said Dutch is going to have a press conference today—a press conference! A few days ago, he was a kid with a few hundred bucks in his pocket working his way around the country. Now he's holding press conferences where they want to announce that we've come to *an understanding*.

I've always liked that legal term: *an understanding*. Not a commitment, not a contract, but an understanding. And with a guy like Mott, an understanding is just as good as your signature on a check.

The Tuesday I was shot, Dutch met me at Denning Self-Storage to help clean and inventory the contents of the large storage unit. He arrived early and introduced himself by showing me a newspaper article he kept in his wallet that had been written about him.

"I like to show people this," he said. "So they don't think I'm a bum. I'm a traveler." He smiled. "A traveling man, but a working one."

The article was from the *Binghamton Press* and was a fairly long piece on how Dutch had quit his job and sold his possessions and was taking a year to travel the country. I was very impressed and even reminded myself to look up the article at the library to make sure it was real—I ended up being somewhat busy that night, what with being shot and all, but while I've been here in the hospital I checked it out, and Mr. Riley Dutcher is indeed a traveling man and not a bum.

An opportunist, but not a bum.

When I see Dutch, I'll tell him. I'll get him the money. But I won't give Mott a commitment or an approval or an understanding. He's Dutch's attorney, not mine.

"I'm very tired, Mr. Mott."

"Which is why I want to get this out of the way for you, so you can recover finally."

"You're so thoughtful."

"Can I go ahead and tell my client to state at the press conference today that we have reached an understanding?"

"You can tell your client that I'm very tired and we'll have to do this another time."

Then Mott left. But he'll be back.

The girls are back in Erie. I told Catherine to keep them safe in Ohio, but she wouldn't listen. They're here to see me a few times a day and are always with one of the guys from the security agency. It's ironic that I've been worried about how to pay for this security service since it's almost two thousand dollars a week, but compared to Dutch's three million, it doesn't seem worth worrying about any longer.

Perspective is everything, I guess.

Chapter 21

Two Good Twins

| August 5, 1992 |

One of my favorite legends—well, maybe *legend* is the wrong term. Myth, maybe? Allegory? Fable?—is the concept of an elite subsection of the American prison system, a reservation-only lock-up known as *Club Fed.* It's supposed to be an exclusive detention center set aside solely for those wealthy senators and bond traders who got their hands caught in the till. This is a place where the well-heeled and powerful can serve out their sentences in relative comfort, all while they chip out of sand traps and work on their backhand.

Although I've read some interesting accounts of such unique places during the 1960s and 1970s, as an alumnus of the American federal prison system, I am here to state, once and for all, that Club Fed—and the common notion of the white-collar prison itself—does not exist.

Yet, this myth continues to be perpetuated. You can't pick up a newspaper or watch a news program concerning some crooked real-estate developer or some stockbroker who bilked retired postal workers out of millions without some reporter mentioning that the convicted felon will be serving his easy time at Club Fed. Which will make another news anchor or reporter generate a story focused on how unfair it is that this evil individual gets to serve his sentence in luxury, simply because he has money and power—because everyone knows that Club Fed is simply a resort that you can't leave until your time is up. It's a place where you play golf and bocce ball with Mafia kingpins and crooked congressmen while guards look the other way when the servants deliver the lobster and the twenty-year-old scotch.

Now, I am here to let you in on the inside track of such matters, and I want to acknowledge that not only does Club Fed not exist, but that these reporters are—what's the right term?—oh yeah, absolute boneheads. Do you see now why I avoid them? Plus, I'm fairly drugged up right now, waiting to have muscle reattachment surgery on my leg, and I am in a pessimistic mood. My apologies.

So, let's look at how this myth is perpetuated as well as how these reporters are either incredibly lazy or are purposely spinning a tale that will anger the public and create a better story, or both. Because it *is* a lazy person's story. Juxtapose a minimum-security prison against *any* standard prison and it's difficult *not* to see the differences. In fact, if you were to drive by a minimum-security prison and miss the sign stating that it was Such-and-Such Minimum-Security Penitentiary, you would not think it was a prison at all. You would assume you were looking at a community college or a senior center or a county office facility.

Now, here is an exercise. Picture in your mind a prison. Got it? See that photo of the prison on the screen of your mind? Can you see all the aspects that make up that picture? Okay, now list the first five things you see. Got it? Okay, I guarantee that at least four of those five things you see would not appear in a real picture of a minimum-security prison.

What did you list? Guards? Stone wall? Fence? Gate? Guard tower? Razor wire? Bars on windows?

Nope. A minimum-security prison would probably not have any of these things. There would not be a guard tower or razor wire or bars on the windows or stone walls. In fact, most minimum-security prisons lack even that most rudimentary wall or fence. And what you *would* see would seem strange as well. There might be well-trimmed lawns and trees and you might see a basketball court and a softball field in the back. These collections of buildings would look more like a place where you would learn basic accounting, take your CPR refresher course, or buy your fishing license than a place that houses convicted felons.

Is this because the inmates inside have an easier lifestyle than the inmates at a maximum-security prison? No. It's because—are you ready? It's because—here it comes—they don't need to have all those walls and towers and fences.

Get caught walking off the grounds or get caught a few days after your escape and you won't be concerned about being dragged back to Lewisburg or Allenwood. Because you won't be coming back. You'll be taken to one of those other places—those more traditional places, the ones with the bars and the wire and the fences, and your time served will be erased and you will start all over again in big-boy prison.

For the majority of us, those invisible fences are stronger then any razor wire could ever be. And the same motivation applies to the relatively low guard-to-prisoner ratio. For example, at a maximum-security prison, you could find thirty prisoners for every guard. At a minimum-security prison, you could find up to three hundred prisoners for every guard. The reason for this is simple: Why spend money guarding people who aren't going anywhere?

I saw one of these news stories—the kind that has me going off on this drug-induced tirade—concerning the cushy life of a recent Club Fed inmate, where—and here comes the lazy part—the reporter did *the entire story*—all of it—from outside the prison.

"As you can see from the rolling hills behind me . . ." The suited, stern-looking, news anchor pointed out the trees and the lawn—they always describe a lawn as rolling hills, as if all the inmates are tobogganing down them and making s'mores when they get to the bottom—and a basketball court and a soccer field. He never interviewed anyone and never actually went inside any of the buildings. Either this guy wanted an end result for his story or he was too inept to get an interview with those connected to the prison—or both.

He even stood on the soccer field for the wrap-up of his story.

"While Carl Gerard's theft has left four families without homes, Mr. Gerard gets to think about his crimes here . . ." Dramatic pause. ". . . during his leisure time . . ." Dramatic pause. ". . . among the well-manicured soccer fields of Tralfaz Blah-Blah Prison. For ABC news . . ." Dramatic pause. ". . . I'm Butchie Shneltzer."

And that's . . .

Wait a minute, who is . . . ?

Oh, good. Dutch's attorney is here. Wonderful. I've missed him.

Anyway, where was I?

Oh, okay, well, probably the single most misunderstood detail about the Club Fed myth concerns the actual term *white-collar prison*. Because that, in itself, is a myth. The truth is that there is no such thing as a white-collar prison.

The myth hints that different prisons exist, that there is a white-collar prison and there is a blue-collar prison. Crooked bankers go to prison A, white-collar prison. Cocaine dealers go to prison B, blue-collar prison. Senators on the take go to prison A. Heroin dealers go to prison B. But in reality, the true deciding factor is not so complex.

The criteria as to whether someone will be placed in a minimum-, medium-, or maximum-security prison are based on four simple factors: the violence of the crime, the length of the sentence, the number of prior offenses, and the level of flight risk.

For a minimum-security prison, you need to be convicted of a nonviolent crime, have a sentence under ten years, have this be your first offense, and be a low flight risk. Most of the people who fall into this category are nonviolent drug offenders. In fact, the ratio is three to one. So, for every guy who thought he was smarter then Uncle Sam, there are three guys whose heroin addiction got bad enough for them to start dealing.

I did seven months at Lewisburg Federal Prison Camp, which is not to be confused with Lewisburg Federal Penitentiary, or what we called "Lewisburg Big"—the maximum-security prison that has housed such alumni as John Gotti, Jimmy Hoffa, and Henry Hill. Lewisburg Big is *the* prison. The maximum-security prison. That one is slated for the most violent and dangerous convicted felons in the country.

I did my time at Lewisburg Federal Prison Camp, or FPC, which is the minimum-security facility next door. Comparing the two facilities fuels the Club Fed myth because, compared to Lewisburg Big, the FPC is a Hilton. This is true—but then again, compared to Lewisburg Big, so was Beirut.

Now, I can't say if I bought into the myth of Club Fed before I was sentenced. I never gave it much thought. I was going to prison; that's all I knew. I was going away from my daughters and my wife. I had humiliated my family. I had lost it all. How much did the details of my accommodations really matter?

I've talked to some inmates about the events that led up to their incarceration. Unlike in the movies, this is actually a very sensitive subject in prison. We don't walk up to each other and say, *Hey, my name's Howard, nine years for cocaine. I like fixing old cars and hunting and I'm a Gemini. So what's your story?*

Broaching what got us there was rarely done; however, it's considered good form if someone tells you what he did that you tell him what you did in return. Otherwise, you respect your fellow inmates' privacy and mind your own business.

Of the inmates who chose to discuss the events that led us to be sharing the same prison, most of us had one thing in common: Most of us did not set out to be crooks.

We broke a seal. Most of the time, we broke that seal out of simple desperation, not greed, but when we did break it, the alarms didn't go off and the lightning didn't strike. So we did it again.

The secret I've been keeping from you is that although I am an award-winning filmmaker, I was never a financially successful filmmaker. Never. The *award-winning* part added to my persona and my credentials, and it was the foundation of the company I formed, Ten Tuesdays, Inc., named after the title of my first film. After I formed my own company, I no longer needed to sell my ideas for films to production companies. I could make any film I wanted and team up with a distributor. And since I'm not a Hollywood guy, a big feature-film producer, I can make my films right from Erie without ever having to touch the West Coast.

My company squeaked by in its first year. Barely. I won a few more awards and got some good reviews, but my projects were never commercially viable. They were documentaries, shorts, film studies. It was good stuff that I enjoyed doing, but nothing was ever a true money-maker.

This all goes back to the lottery example I gave you before. I must be rich; I've won the lottery. And I must be successful; look at those awards—they don't just hand them out to anybody, you know.

The next year was the same. I worked hard and wrote and directed two very good films: one a documentary entitled *Appalachian,* which was a study of the events leading to the secret mob meeting in 1957 that confirmed the existence of the American Mafia. More great reviews. More invitations to speak in front of people. More air time on PBS and some cable channels. And very little money.

The second film I made that year I'm also very proud of. It was an animated short film called *That Walrus Is Not on the Guest List.* That film—as well as the subsequent book—is still one of Abby's favorites. It won the Carnegie Medal for Excellence in Children's Video and it was also shown at the Chicago International Children's Film Festival and was nominated for three awards. It didn't win any—those Canadian filmmakers are hard to beat.

I wracked up a little debt. I worked harder. I wracked up a little more debt and took out some business loans, but I wasn't concerned—look at how successful I was. Have I shown you my awards?

Then, while I was in Chicago speaking to a group of film students, Rachel was hit by a propane truck right in front of our house.

I'm not throwing this in to gain sympathy, but it's part of the series of events that led to my time in prison, because when Rachel died, everything changed. I changed. We all changed.

I am the father. I am the husband. I am the one who was supposed to keep them all safe and I couldn't do it. And now my family is hurting and falling apart and in trouble. When that happens, you want to fix it. You want to fix it all. Your pain doesn't matter; you just want to bring everyone inside, lock the doors, unplug the phone, and fix it all. Keep everyone safe and fix it, fix it, fix it.

After Rachel's death, I called Catherine on the phone a thousand times a day. *Where are you? Are you okay? Where are the girls? Why are you shopping? I'll pick it up on my way home. Go home and rest.* She hated it, but I didn't care. I wanted to put them all in a box. A box that I alone had the key for. A place they would all be safe.

I couldn't think about work—I could only think about keeping everybody safe. I had maxed out all my personal credit cards, so about six months after Rachel died I took three grand from the company account—I stole it, which was easy because I was the sole employee—and I took Catherine and the girls to Montreal for a week. We needed to get away, and I liked having them all where I could see them. I took another grand from the business account and paid Catherine's credit card so she would have a little available credit if she needed anything and then she wouldn't have to worry about money.

Since I paid all the bills, it made sense to have all the bills come to the office and not to the house. That way, I could take care of them all. That's what I told Catherine. The truth was, I needed to keep the mounting bills away from her so she wouldn't worry. I needed to keep her safe.

I didn't have a solid film project that year. I still made the rent on the Ten Tuesdays office space, based on some very thin royalties that came in and the new credit cards I took out—maxing out the cash advance limit as soon as I got them and throwing the cash into my accounts. I needed to keep cash on hand to cover checks that were bouncing back and forth from my personal account to the company account.

When a new credit card application was being processed, I would write a check from my personal checking account—let's say for a thousand dollars—and deposit it into my business account. Now, the business account would be up a grand but that check was going to need to clear from my personal account. So, in a few days, I'd deposit a check for a slightly different amount—let's say twelve hundred—back from my business to my checking. If the money I was waiting for came in, this worked out well. If not, I would need to repeat the cycle and deposit another round of bad checks from one account back to the other until the real money came in.

Now, this practice is known as *kiting*, or creating a paper balance. Although I thought I was the genius who invented it, this is the most basic of all bank frauds, and it's one that banks monitor for very closely.

Later that year, Erie Bank told me that it was probably best if I banked somewhere else. They closed both my business and my personal accounts. I quickly opened a business account and personal account at Marquette Savings, telling Catherine that they had better rates.

For the second year in a row, I did not make a single film. This was partly because I didn't have time—my full-time job now was keeping Catherine and the girls unaware of how bad our financial situation was, paying the office space rent, and keeping the checking accounts from closing. But I also had pawned two of my big cameras and most of my editing equipment, so making a film would have been difficult even if I had wanted to.

Instead of walking into the office and dreaming up new projects, I would walk in and ask myself, *How can I get three grand into the business account by Wednesday so that new round of checks won't bounce? What can I sell?*

It was at one of these moments that I slipped down the very last rung of my moral decay right into the criminal. I was looking at my big industrial Kodak printer, because that was going to be the focus of my work for the day. The plan was to find a buyer for it, no matter how big a loss I might take.

Walking to my file cabinet to find the business card of the man who sold the printer to me years before, an idea flashed. A question. It actually stopped me right there where I stood. Was it possible that I was looking at this all wrong? Instead of getting items *out of* the office to make money, why not use what I already had *to make money there?*

I took out my wallet and pulled out a dollar bill—there were only two in there—and placed it on the copier tray and hit print. The machine hummed, the green light rolled across the edges of the cover, and then the machine gave birth to a perfect copy of a one-dollar bill.

I held the copy next to the original. These new printers were amazing! The color was perfect and the lines were crisp. The paper was all wrong, but the image itself was very, very good.

Now, as a reader, you are probably wondering if I considered this next act wrong, if I saw myself as a criminal. No, I did not. I simply saw it as a project, like any other cartooning or visual art project. When you run such actions through the wonderful filter that desperation and denial provides, things come out the other side clean and exciting and creative.

Within twenty minutes I had a plan. I had a target market and a distribution process, long before I even had a product.

I knew that twenty-dollar bills were the key. Not fifties, not hundreds, but twenties—after all, no one would remember who gave them a twenty, but a one-hundred or even a fifty-dollar bill might be enough to trigger a memory, a description.

A hot dog purchased from a cart would yield eighteen dollars in real change back to the faceless customer without a bit of a trace. A busy bartender wouldn't remember which of the hundreds of customers dolling out twenties gave him the bad one, nor would the T-shirt clerk who sold souvenirs to a thousand faces a day.

The plan was so simple. I would hit a cash area—a place where faceless people were handing cash to other faceless people. A high-traffic place. A tourist spot. A cash world. I would blanket this area over a weekend when the banks were closed, so that the fake twenties would not be discovered until the following Monday, long after the faceless money creator was gone.

Change from a few fake twenties might not seem like enough money to risk a felony arrest, but that's what was perfect about it. It was not the big haul. It was not a high-profile crime. It was small and undetectable. Unnoticeable. It was just walking down the boardwalk, just shopping among the vendors at the fair. It was safe.

I kited a check to the Pathmark supermarket and got two new twenties that would become the parents of my counterfeit family.

I had everything I needed to make the bills—cutting trays to make the edges sharp, and I even made a mold so the bills sat perfectly in the copier. That allowed the front and back of the bill to match. But the texture was all wrong. The copies *looked* real, but they *felt* fake, and when I closed my eyes I could always tell the difference between the two.

After a few more days of experimenting, I discovered that it wasn't the *type* of paper that made the texture feel correct, but what I could add to the paper that did it. I tried using fixatives—the same stuff I spray on the original comic strips I drew to lock in the color before printing—but the paper got too smooth. I finally found that by taking plain office paper stock and coating it with hairspray—Final Net brand works best; a tip to all you kids considering an exciting career in counterfeiting—I could not tell the difference between the real bill and the fake one.

By that Thursday, I was done. I had five bundles of my new bills ready for testing. Five thousand dollars in Walker Roe twenties.

I told Catherine I had a speaking engagement in Niagara Falls and early one Friday morning, long before the sun came up, hours before anything was open, I was pacing Whirlpool Street in Niagara Falls, New York, eager to get started.

Like the true criminal I was becoming, I had a set of touristy clothes that I wore—shorts, T-shirt, ball cap—to blend in with the crowd. One by one, I bought a cup of coffee, a bagel, a map, a T-shirt. Each time I exchanged my worthless twenty for a pile of real change. Never once were my bills questioned. Never were they even looked at. I would take the fake from my right pocket and place the real change in my left.

Every hour or so, I would walk back to the car to empty my bulging pockets and get more of the worthless paper. What I had planned on taking two days took only seven hours. By 6:00 that night, I was out of the fakes and I had $3,987.23 in real American currency.

I drove home. On Monday morning, despite showing up to Marquette Bank to deposit almost four thousand dollars in cash into my accounts to stop the worthless checks bouncing back between them, the bank thought that maybe we should part company. They closed my accounts. I opened two new accounts at Northwest Savings—again telling Catherine that the rates were too good to pass up.

By week's end, all the checks bouncing between the two accounts had cleared, but we were broke yet again. So I cooked up a fresh new batch of my new magic twenties.

The next batch was a little larger: $10,000 in fake twenties that yielded me $8,456.23 from the Ocean City, New Jersey, boardwalk. The batch after that was $20,000, but this took me almost three full days to paper all over Virginia Beach and allowed me to bring back home almost $17,000 in cash.

Although the money was great, I was so far behind with the mortgage, electricity, car payments, and credit cards that the cash was going out of the accounts as fast as I could get it in there.

I made plans for my largest batch yet: $50,000.

The printer was still running when the police arrived.

You already know what the firefall from all of this was. The outcry. The anger. The media frenzy. I arrived at the office one morning at around 5:00 A.M. to get an early start on the new big batch and at 7:35 A.M., three Erie detectives arrived. I've since learned that it's standard operating procedure to serve a warrant first thing in the morning.

They were after me for misdemeanor bank fraud, but what they found instead was felony counterfeiting.

Ten Tuesdays, Inc., and my house were raided. They took all the files and my computer and the mold I had made for the twenties. Soon they had more than enough evidence to lock me up for a long, long time.

I don't remember much of my trial—years later, when I was offered the televised videotapes to watch, it was like seeing it all for the first time because I had mentally tuned out for most of it. I fought for Catherine and the girls when I had to; I would walk to the witness chair and answer the questions and then I would walk back to my chair next to my attorney.

Once I was sitting there, I would astro-travel to my best-of memory collection—there was an entire day of that trial where I had a continuous loop going of when Rachel and Liz were little. In this mental film, I would walk into the room where the two of them were playing. They would look up and I would put my hands on my hips and announce the phrase that would begin the game.

"So," I would say. "Which one is the evil twin again?"

And they would squeal and run in opposite directions.

"I am," Rachel would yell and I would chase her through the room, falling and stumbling over chairs as I tried to stop her reign of terror on civilized society.

"No," Liz would yell, just as I was about to capture her sister. "I'm the evil twin. She's the good twin." And I would change direction and stomp around coffee tables and bump into walls and make any sacrifice necessary to protect the good people of Erie against her. And just before I caught her, Liz would change her mind.

"No. I'm good. Rachel's the evil twin." And I would refocus the manhunt back on Rachel.

I sat at the table during my trial and smiled and replayed this memory, and I was not there, not on trial, but back in my living room chasing my two daughters—not a good trial tactic, however, since reporters from three different networks produced stories on how I "showed no remorse" and "simply smiled smugly through the proceedings."

I was found guilty. The only question that remained was the length of sentence. One of the prosecuting attorneys, Marla Kozina, pressed hard for a sentence of twelve years. This would automatically take my sentence to a medium-security prison because it exceeded the ten-year time frame. Because I had no prior convictions, I was sentenced to fourteen months at Lewisburg. I served seven months when all my good time was added in.

The thing I need to emphasize is that time really doesn't matter in prison. Whether you serve a day or ten years, the damage is done. There is little difference.

Now I'd like to tell you all the great prison stories I have, but there aren't many. Prison is prison. I did see a twenty-something kid named Trey get thrown through a window after an argument over what channel to watch on the TV. I watched another man everyone called Smoke get into a fight with a guy named Kevin on the basketball court. Kevin pummeled Smoke's face so badly, you could no longer tell where his nose used to be. And none of us did anything. We all simply walked away in order to put as much distance as possible between us and Smoke and the guards who would soon be arriving.

We didn't have cells at Lewisburg. We all slept in pods—a bunk bed and a trunk separated by a half-wall like in a barracks. Anything you weren't issued—three sets of uniforms, five sets of boxers, a blanket, and a pillow—you could purchase from the commissary. What wasn't available at the commissary was contraband. Period. Get caught with contraband, and there was time added onto your sentence. That goes for all booze or any food that's not on the approved list.

A prisoner could earn, or have deposited for him, a maximum of $115 a month to be used at the commissary. You could purchase toothpaste, deodorant, magazines, newspapers, candy, notebooks, tuna fish, pasta, extra underwear, sweatpants, gloves, whatever. If you had the means, you could supplement the prison food and make yourself something you could buy from the commissary and prepare on the two-burner stove in the rec area or in the microwave. Anyone caught giving or loaning another inmate anything, even a book or a magazine, got time added on—this removed any element of bribery or extortion.

Catherine and the girls moved into a small apartment when we lost our house. Catherine went back to work as a nurse, and every month, by the first of the month like clockwork, Catherine topped off my account so it always had $115 in it. She didn't visit much—I told her not to—but she kept that account full.

"I don't need it," I'd say over the phone. But she would always change the subject. Twice a week, on Tuesdays and Thursdays, we were allowed to go to the commissary and I would stock up—not too much, because I quickly learned that if you didn't use it or eat it fast, whatever you bought had a tendency to disappear.

Lewisburg is a working prison. If you don't choose a job, one is chosen for you. You work forty hours a week—raking leaves, picking up trash, serving meals, whatever, and you are paid anywhere from sixteen cents to twenty-five cents an hour, depending on the job. Then you come back. You eat. You wait. During your free time, you wait. You can work out or read or run on the track around the softball field—no minimum-security prison that I know of has either a golf course or a tennis court, but we did have a running trail around the softball field—but you are still waiting.

We worked. We slept. We exercised—which is another fascinating aspect of the Club Fed mystique. Criminals come into the prison bloated and pale and leave thirty pounds lighter with a healthy tan, leading many reporters to comment on the health benefits of having no responsibility other than tennis and golf.

We worked, often outside, mowing the lawns of Lewisburg Big and the office buildings, picking up garbage and raking leaves and digging trenches and planting trees for forests and parks and cleaning gutters and building stone walls and trimming hedges and bushes. Most of us hadn't done a day of real work in our entire lives and this was a major change. Then, after finishing the day and eating, we worked out. Why? Simple. Because there was nothing else to do.

It's amazing how important exercise becomes when your only other option is to sit on your bunk. Training comes to take up a large chunk of your day.

Investor tip: If any health club could tap into this—that is, have their members live in an adjoining cinderblock building where they can only sleep, eat, and exercise, with no other options—they would dominate the world market.

Junk food is not what leads to obesity. *Options* lead to obesity.

We lifted weights and pedaled stationary bikes and we ran. We ran on treadmills in bad weather and we ran on the dirt track outside and we ran around the perimeter of the prison. We all ran, either away from something or toward something else, but we all ran.

I couldn't make the good memories of Rachel and Liz and Abby come to me the entire time I was in prison. For seven straight months, I couldn't tune into a single good-memory station. Instead, I was stuck watching a compilation of guilt and pain reruns.

One of the constant loops in my head was a mental film showing the time shortly after Rachel's death, when at least twice a week Liz would wake up crying and run to Catherine's and my bed. She would stand there crying, unable to breathe, unable to speak.

"Are—are—you . . ." She'd gulp great, crying breaths. "Are—you sure I'm—I'm not the—maybe I'm the—maybe I'm the bad twin," she'd say. "Maybe I'm the bad one and Rachel—and I'm the bad one—and Rachel—and Rachel is good—and she's good and—and I'm here and Rachel—and Rachel . . ."

"No, sweetheart," I'd say as I scooped her up.

"But maybe they got—got mixed—maybe I'm—maybe I'm . . ."

"There's no bad one. It was just a game. There's no such thing as a bad twin." I'd lie down with her until she fell back asleep.

I watched that memory over and over for seven months.

Catherine and I were divorced while I was in Lewisburg. I didn't fight her. I saw giving her an easy divorce as the last kind thing I could ever do for her. I don't think badly of Catherine for divorcing me—it's not as if she abandoned me during rough times—and I don't want you to think badly of her, either. Statistics show that most couples who lose a child end up divorced within two years. The theory is that each spouse needs more than the other spouse can give—and with all my doings added in, divorce was simply inevitable.

I thought you should know all this. It was difficult to write, but if you've read this far, you deserve to know what happened—plus, the drugs are loosening my inhibitions, helping me finally get all this down on paper.

I already told you that I did everything I was accused of, but I've been stalling when it comes to releasing all the pretty little details.

And now, dear reader, I have some more tests to go through before my surgery. And I need to get rid of this Mott character, who is excitedly pacing around my bed like a puppy that needs to be let outside.

Mott is waving his envelope at me every time I look away from my computer. Maybe Dutch decided he can't live on only three million and needs a little bit more pocket change.

Chapter 22

Seven

| August 10, 1992 |

Good news. I spoke to Jenny Locke, the Mathis and Corbin human resources director, and the company wants to make sure I don't feel rushed in returning to work once I've recovered. So they have generously offered to fire me.

I believe the official term is *indefinite medical leave of absence.*

"Can I return when I'm recovered?" I asked.

"Well," Jenny answered. "We are eliminating your position, so you're not pressured to return and we are dispersing your responsibilities, but you are welcome to reapply for a *different* position." Then she added, "If one is available at that time."

I'm sure one will *not* be available. Mathis and Corbin won't make the mistake of hiring me twice. Before Jenny gets off the phone, she adds, in her most sincere voice, that she wishes there was something she could do, but *her hands are tied.* In the year I've known Jenny Locke, her hands have been tied so often, I'm surprised her wrists aren't cut right through to the bone by now.

The fascinating twist in this whole plot is Dutch. Dutch the researcher. Dutch the observer. Dutch the sleuth. Dutch, the guy who is *not* the money-grubbing weasel I was led to believe he was.

Dutch and I have spent the last few days working on a few projects together and I will soon enlighten you as to the truth about Mr. Riley Dutcher—Dutch's real name—as well as the truth concerning Mr. Benjamin "Weasel" Mott, who is the true carnivorous mammal in this story, but the screenwriter in me demands that I paint this Mathis and Corbin scene for you first. Especially the part where Dutch comes in. Because scenes this good are infrequent in scripts—and even rarer in reality.

So here is the backstory.

Dutch has remained in Erie and has, in fact, spent the past few days staying in Bugby's apartment. I wanted him to stay there while we sorted some things out, and while he's been in Erie, he has been finishing cleaning out the storage unit and organizing Bugby's apartment.

Now, with that in mind, here's the scene.

INTERIOR HOSPITAL ROOM. WALKER ROE IS USING A WALKER TO TRAVEL FROM ONE SIDE OF THE ROOM TO THE OTHER AS PART OF HIS PHYSICAL THERAPY.

RILEY DUTCHER ENTERS THE ROOM CARRYING A CARDBOARD BOX.

DUTCH: Hey.
WALKER: Hey.
DUTCH: What's up?
WALKER: Well, I just got fired, but I believe the hospital pudding today is banana, so at least the day won't be a total loss.
DUTCH: You got fired?
WALKER: Yup.
DUTCH: From Mathis and Corbin?
WALKER: Yes, sir.
DUTCH: You?
WALKER: Um, yeah. Me.
DUTCH: Wow. (*Smiles and sets his box down*) That must have been, like, awkward.
WALKER: It sucked, but it wasn't awkward. (*Makes it to the end of the room and begins to maneuver the walker for the long trek back*)
DUTCH: No, I mean for them. Like, awkward for them, I mean.
WALKER: I don't think it was awkward for them, Dutch.
DUTCH: No, I mean awkward, like, awkward because of, you know, considering the risk and all. You know, it must have been weird for them.
WALKER: Huh? Why would it be weird for them? It was weird for me, but not them.

DUTCH: I mean because . . . (*Looking at Walker, confused*) You know . . . (*Stops and looks at Walker as if trying to see what the joke is*) Walker, you—I mean, hey. I'm not going to say nothing. You don't have to keep it from me. I know . . .
WALKER: Know what?
DUTCH: (*Looks at Walker*) Man. (*Smiles*) Wow, you don't know, do you? (*He smiles, waits*) Now I get it. (*Sounds almost relieved*) That makes so much sense that you don't know. I just thought you didn't trust me.
WALKER: (*Stops walking and looks at Dutch, frustrated*) Dutch, know what?
DUTCH: Man, you . . . you *own* Mathis and Corbin.

CAMERA MOVES IN FOR EXPRESSION SHOT OF WALKER'S FACE. THEN INSERT BUGBY FLASHBACK SCENE.

BUGBY FLASHBACK SCENE

BUGBY: Someday I'll tell you a few stories about Elijah Corbin. *Wishing well.* It may surprise you.

END OF SCENE

The truth about Elijah Corbin is that there *is* no Elijah Corbin. There never was. Nor was there a Lawrence Mathis.

Mathis and Corbin was the creation, the invention, the nom de plume, for the straw man behind the small Erie publishing company. The two individuals who created these characters—the two people who, in the backroom of the Hotel Denning, came up with these alternate identities—were Clara Popodeus and Sonia Bugby. The P and B of P & B Holdings, Inc.

Clara Popodeus, formally Clara Peck, was born in 1898 in Cleveland, Ohio, where she lived most of her life. She was married at age seventeen to Milo Popodeus, a second-generation Greek immigrant. The two had no children and lived a quiet, happy life together until Milo died.

Clara traveled to Erie in the summer of 1940 on what was intended to be a week's trip to finally come to terms with the death of her husband. After she arrived at the Hotel Denning—and against the odds according to all those who observed the differences between the two women—Clara Popodeus and Sonia Bugby quickly became friends.

No observer could help but notice the contrast between the two, on all fronts. Where Sonia was resolute and self-assured, Clara was intellectual and reticent. Sonia was tall and willowy where Clara was small and buxom, and Sonia had a swift temper—a fact well known to the contractors and employees of the three Bugby businesses—where Clara was patient and long-suffering.

Clara's one-week trip to Erie lasted two months. She remained at the Hotel Denning with Sonia Bugby and Sonia's son, Lester. Victor Bugby was away with the Coast Guard and Sonia welcomed Clara's company—records that Dutch found from old Hotel Denning indicate that Sonia stopped charging Clara hotel fees just one week into her stay.

A routine was quickly formed. Clara and Sonia would make breakfast for the hotel guests, then they would head out for the day's grocery shopping, and then they would take a walk along Lake Erie, bringing baby Lester along with them. When business at the Hotel Denning was slow, the three would picnic at Presque Isle or drive to Niagara Falls for the day. Before the day ended, Clara and Sonia would be sitting in the parlor visiting with the hotel guests, or Sonia would play the piano while Clara sang.

Clara Popodeus would often ask Sonia the question she had come to Erie to find the answer to: What do I do now? Clara's life and plans had always been with Milo and now there was no Milo. There was no *them,* only *her.* So, now what? The two women soon developed the idea of forming a business together. Clara, a former schoolteacher, wanted to do something with schoolbooks or teaching materials, which she had always found flat and uninspiring.

Whatever it was that led the two women to create fictitious names—and fictitious masculine names at that—is unknown. It might have been the "women's place in business" kind of attitude that was prevalent at the time, but somehow I doubt it. Sonia flaunted the fact that she was more successful than any five men.

But for whatever reason, the idea was planted. Within a few months, the doors of Mathis and Corbin were open; manager and editors were hired; and, like the true Bugby business model under which the company had been launched, it was monitored for a while and then, for the most part, left alone. Clara had put some money in the company, Sonia had put some money in, a holding company was created so that profits could be paid to the two owners, and then the two women stepped back. Clara was somewhat active in Mathis and Corbin—she chose book titles and subjects—but Sonia had very little to do with the small publisher once it was moving along.

Clara moved to Erie full-time in 1943 and left her small room in the Hotel Denning to move into a large sunny bedroom in the Bugby house. Clara Popodeus died of influenza in her room in late 1944 and Sonia buried her in the Bugby family plot—I remember now that I saw her headstone at Bugby's funeral. Sonia Bugby would die later that same year, a week after Victor Bugby returned from the Coast Guard.

Dutch assumed I knew all of this about Mathis and Corbin—how P & B Holdings, the company that owned Mathis and Corbin, belonged to Clara and Sonia. At Clara's death, because she had no heir to leave it to, the company had fallen directly to Sonia. At Sonia's death, the company that owned one hundred percent of Mathis and Corbin fell to Bugby, who simply left it alone and had his profit check sent to a money market fund in Canada. Now, at Bugby's death, ownership fell to me as part of his estate.

What Dutch had uncovered in a few days, what he thought was simply part of the backstory, was the stuff that three expensive attorneys had either missed or ignored. And how Dutch found all this out is not as covert as you might think.

I mentioned that Dutch is staying at Bugby's apartment. I'll get to how this happened and why, but first let me say that Dutch has some demons he is battling—what they are, are his business alone and I will not mention them here—but at the end of the day, he struggles to keep his mind clear and his hands busy. The end of the day is a rough few hours for him and a task—any task, any project—that can burn the time from five until ten or so is necessary to bridge that rough patch of the day. So after inventorying the storage unit, Dutch took it upon himself to clean and organize the decades' worth of clutter inside Bugby's apartment—no small task. And that's when he found the box of newspaper clippings.

When you think about newspaper clippings from the 1940s and 1950s, take everything you know about modern journalism and obliterate it. All of it. Those were gentler days, friendlier days—when news of your neighbor's garden, updates on the birth of a new baby, or highlights from a town softball game were only slightly less important than news from the war and greatly more significant than accounts of politics from Washington.

Here is one of the clippings Dutch found:

> Mrs. Milo Popodeus, who is visiting us from Cleveland, Ohio, and staying with Mrs. Victor Bugby of Indian Drive, attended the gathering at the Center Presbyterian Church on Wednesday. Mrs. Bugby enjoyed the lamb and Mrs. Popodeus favored the chicken. A good time was had by all.

This is a real clipping from August 1942—can you imagine what my clippings would have looked like during this time? There are hundreds of cuttings like this. Dutch organized them by date, and in doing so, he created a road map of the friendship between Clara and Sonia, the formation of Mathis and Corbin, and the details of Clara's death. From additional records he found in the storage shed and documents from the old Hotel Denning, he easily filled in the gaps.

When Dutch told me that I owned Mathis and Corbin, my first thoughts were how I could help the company and take Mathis and Corbin to a whole new level, how my experience in film could aid the visual elements of the textbooks we created, not only to explain complex thoughts and ideas but to ingrain them into a student's mind. If allowed, I could create better books for the company. *If* I could cut through the egos quickly and simply get to work.

I would need to explain my ideas gently but firmly. I wouldn't want to get caught up in the whole "who owns whom" and "who fired whom" thing. We would need to hurdle those issues quickly and then get busy.

In my mind, I can see the big conference room at Mathis and Corbin. All of the management and editorial staff would be sitting around the large mahogany table waiting to meet the new owner. They'd be watching the clock. Then they'd look at the door. Then they'd look up at the clock again.

Then I'd walk in.

Mathew Comfort would look at me nervously and signal to Jenny Locke to handle this embarrassing situation with a former employee.

"Walker," Jenny would say, stepping up from the table and motioning for me to follow her outside.

"Hi, Jenny." I'd smile and shake her hand.

"This isn't a good time," she'd say, holding the door open for me to follow her.

Instead of walking out of the room, I'd move toward the people sitting around the large table and greet everyone warmly: Martin, Matthew, Ronnie, Ann, Dean, all of them.

"Walker, let's talk," Jenny would say nervously.

"Sure," I'd say. "I thought I had an appointment."

With that, four hawk-faced attorneys would enter the room, each carrying thick bundles of documents to be passed out to everyone sitting at the table.

"What's going on?" Mathew would bark, looking at the clock nervously. "If you have a legal disagreement with how you were treated, this is not the time . . ."

"Walker," Jenny would say. "If you have a lawsuit, this is not the way to handle it. The new owners are coming any minute. But we can go talk about this right now privately in my office." She'd again gesture for me to follow her out of the room. "We can take care of all of this for you."

"I know the new owners are coming in," I'd say, taking my seat at the head of the table and waiting the customary three film seconds for the dramatic pause to reach its full effect. "*I* am the new owner."

Looks of disbelief would fill the room as attorneys turned on overhead projectors and directed everyone's attention to the presentations they'd prepared. Ownership papers would be pointed out as the lawyers mapped the path of ownership from Sonia and Clara to Bugby to me. Contracts would be read. Documents would be reviewed. Within ten minutes, it would be clear who owns the company. This would be good.

We'd be able to move quickly to the next step.

This would be the difficult part. It would be necessary to be gruff because I'd need the time to shock away any resistance to my groundbreaking ideas. Let them fear for their jobs a bit as my ideas take root. If we're going to salvage a good working relationship, it all hinges on this very moment.

The room would now be very quiet. All of them would look to me.

"Okay," I'd say, putting on reading glasses—glasses that I don't actually need, but in this scene they will make me look more studious, more serious.

"First things first," I'd say, opening a large manila folder and studying the contents. There'd be silence in the room. They'd wait for me to speak. I'd look up and smile, soon replacing their fears with my bold new direction for the company.

"You're all fired," I'd say.

From outside the room, uniformed security guards would rush in and begin dumping box after box of personal effects on the large conference room table. Coffee cups and purses and sweaters and calendars and framed photographs would all spill over the sides. There'd be chaos in the room and boxes would continue to be dumped and people would scream and move to collect their things. Black garbage bags would be handed out to all the former employees as they'd be roughly instructed to gather their things and get out.

One burly guard would have a stopwatch in his hand, and as Dean tried to gather his I HEART SAILING coffee mug, he would trip and fall to the floor.

"Get up, geek," the guard would scream, yanking him by his collar. "Gather up your worthless crap and get out."

At the head of the table, I'd continue to review the contents of the folder in front of me.

"Now, Matthew," I'd say, studying a page from inside the folder. "According to this, you have been borrowing from the company funds a little bit."

With this, the windows would shatter as two SWAT team commandos crashed into the room and rolled across the floor. They'd locate Matthew Comfort and wrestle him to the carpet. He'd be handcuffed.

"So," I'd say, slowly marking one thing off the to-do list clipped just inside of the folder. "These gentlemen will be taking you away for a while."

Matthew would be bleeding from his nose and his tears would mix with the blood. I'd notice that he wet his pants and I'd quickly look away to save him any embarrassment.

"Okay," I'd continue. "Now, Jenny," I'd say, calmly keeping my finger in place on the documents I'm reading.

Jenny would look up from the floor where she's hiding in order to avoid the breaking glass of the windows. She'd be crying and black mascara would be running down her cheeks in two perfect vertical clown lines.

"Jenny?" I'd ask, trying to locate her through the crying and screaming ex-employees in the room. I'd look around the table to the floor and see her hiding behind the chair.

"Oh, there you are." I'd lean over so she could hear me better. Guards would be pushing frightened ex-employees out of the room.

"Let's move it, people," the burly guard would shout. He'd look at his stopwatch and then push Ronnie Laven toward the door. Ronnie would miss the door and crash against the wall, sending his papers exploding into the air.

"Leave it, pinhead." The guard would push Ronnie out of the room. "Get out."

"Jenny," I'd begin again. "I'm concerned that the stress of returning to work after such an ordeal as today might be too much for you. So I have generously offered to help you bridge this difficult time."

Jenny would look up as one of the attorneys helped her stand. He'd lay a contract on the table and place a pen in her hand.

"What's this?" she'd ask, her voice trembling.

"It's standard," the attorney would answer. "It's a contract where you are left fired, disgraced, and unemployable. You will look for a job for years as you watch every position from Random House to Dairy Queen turn you down in disgust and revulsion as you dwindle away every penny you have in the sheer act of staying alive until you are forced to live in a rusting van between two condemned buildings where you will suffer stress-related health problems, including projectile acne and acute gastric discharge, and you will watch one day fall into the next as the sad remainder of your miserable life is dedicated solely to remembering the way you treated Walker Roe and wishing every moment of every day that you could change that one thing and that one thing only. Sign here."

And Jenny Locke would sign. Then the burly guard would take Jenny's elbow and lead her out of the conference room.

"I'm . . ." she'd cry out to me. " I'm so . . . so sorry." Her voice would be quivering as the clown mascara spread, deeper and darker, down her cheeks.

"I know, Jenny," I'd say, closing my folder and looking upon her with disappointment. "I know. But my hands are tied."

And Jenny would be led out of the building where the awaiting media would fire a myriad of questions at her, beginning with what the black stuff was running down her cheeks and ending with why she thought she could get away with firing the owner of Mathis and Corbin.

So sad.

So sad.

But, like I said, there are egos over there, so I'm sure there would be resistance to my new and innovative ideas, now that I own the company.

I'm not a materialistic guy, but I do like saying that: *I own the company. I own Mathis and Corbin.* Owning Divorce Court, the apartment complex, owning the Mega-Liquor Warehouse, and owning Denning Self-Storage, that's all one thing—they're very strange, very bizarre things—but owning the very same company that has been my own employer for the past few years is beyond surreal.

So, Dutch found all of this in passing, not even breaking a sweat. However, there are some other things he had to dig a bit to discover regarding P & B Holdings. I may have been better off not knowing them. Like, how it was not a coincidence that Mathis and Corbin hired me. Bugby knew I couldn't find a job and he forced them to take me, apparently even after Matthew Comfort threatened to quit.

But first, more about Dutch not being the weasel I thought he was.

Benjamin Mott is *not* Dutch's attorney, even though Mott told me he was. Benjamin Mott isn't my attorney, either, even though he told Dutch he was. Dutch doesn't want $3 million from me, even though Mott said he did. Dutch only wanted to talk to me concerning how he saved my life—to tell me what he calls "the very scary thing," and then he wanted to hit the road again. I have him stalled here for a few days as we sort some things out. Dutch has *not* held press conferences and basked in the public attention the way Mott said he was doing. He's actually fairly shy and avoids the press even more than I do.

Mott played both sides against the middle, but what neither Dutch nor I know is how Mott got access to both of us—Dutch while he was in protective custody and me while I've been in the hospital with a cop guarding my door.

I asked Dutch how he thought Mott just walked in to both places as if he had a key.

"I dunno," Dutch answered.

I had so quickly become accustomed to Dutch knowing everything that I was almost disappointed; I half expected him to smirk and respond, *You're kidding, right? You don't know this, either? You don't know that Mott is an ex-KGP assassin-for-hire working for rival storage unit and liquor store owners not only in Erie, Pennsylvania, but throughout most of Erie County and even beyond?*

I do wonder how Mott got in, but most of my time is spent considering the other thing. The very scary thing. I think about that more than I do about Mott or even about what to do concerning Mathis and Corbin.

The very scary thing involves how Dutch saved my life, and I admit, it has me thinking—in fact, I've been working hard *not* to think about it, but it always worms its way back into my brain.

The day Dutch first came to the hospital to see me—when I expected him to swing by after his latest press conference, carrying his three-million-dollar deposit slip—he presented his theory, which made sense, mostly because it didn't make sense.

Now, Dutch had analyzed all the chess pieces that needed to be in place in order for him to have been able to save my life. Odds. Probabilities. Luck and impossibility. He had made a few conclusions and it's those conclusions that keep coming back, itching and crawling and scratching just under my scalp.

Dutch analyzes things. He watches. He is not pedantic about it, where the trivial is the focus and the outside world is unimportant. His process is actually more childlike, as if he's been in a box for the past twenty years and is seeing the world for the first time—and according to Dutch's journal, this is almost the case.

And in this study, Dutch concluded one thing.

It is impossible that I should now be alive.

Not that it is improbable, or that it is incredibly unlikely, but that it is absolutely far beyond the curve of reason that I did not die in any one of seven ways that day at the storage unit.

So, here is the very scary thing:

1. Dutch was in Niagara Falls the day before I was shot. He took a job moving office furniture to Erie and it was a fluke that he even happened to be in Erie—it's a fluke that he's on this yearlong quest in the first place. I got lucky that he was in town. If he wasn't here, I'd be dead, because I would have been shot the second time in the head, or I would have bled to death when Iggy and Fleece took off.

2. The job Dutch took was unloading furniture at Hamot Medical Center, where I currently am, the night before we met. He slept here. He has never been to Erie before, and after seeing my ad in the paper, he walked from the hospital to Denning Self-Storage that morning, so he knew the way from the hospital to the storage units. Dutch knows only two places in all of Erie: Hamot Medical Center and Denning Self-Storage. When Dutch got me into the car after I was shot, I was bleeding badly. The only other place he knew, in all of Erie, happened to be the very place we needed to go: Hamot Medical Center. Dutch has a cellular phone that had been given to him but it was in his pack, hidden in some bushes near the hospital, so he couldn't have called 911. If he hadn't known where Hamot was, I would have bled to death in the car.

3. Dutch read about tourniquets in a pamphlet he found at the hospital the very morning I was shot. He had a few hours to

kill and the pamphlet was just sitting there, so he read it. Prior to that, he would not have even thought of applying a tourniquet, much less known how to do it. If the pamphlet hadn't been fresh in his mind, if it hadn't been sitting on a chair near him or if he had woken up later in the morning and didn't have extra time to kill, I would have bled to death.

4. Dutch was dropping a box in the dumpster when the shooter's car rolled in. Dutch was hidden by the alley. Another step or two in either direction and the shooter would have either seen him or he would have been too far down the alley to get to the car in time. The second shot would have been fired, the one that was aimed at my head.

5. If the shooter had been wearing his seatbelt, both Dutch and I would be dead. Dutch grabbed the gunman's arm after he shot the first time and yanked him halfway out of the car, making him drop the gun. If the gunman had had his seatbelt on, he would not have dropped the gun and therefore would likely have shot Dutch and then finished me off.

6. The first bullet shot through my car tire. Fleece and Iggy took off and Dutch had no car of his own. The only car available was Bugby's old Bricklin. Fleece had gotten the car running not three minutes before I was shot and the car hadn't been run in twenty years. Yet, it made it exactly to the hospital just seconds before blowing up.

And 7.—my favorite: I had lost a great deal of blood and I have a rare blood type: AB negative. Dutch is AB negative, too. The hospital wouldn't allow me to take his blood without it being screened, but still, the rarest blood type there is and we both have it? The very guy who saved me just happened to have the rarest blood type in the world—the same exact type that only six percent of the country has.

Scared yet?

It's not simply one huge miracle. It's not just an implausible longshot. It's seven longshots all in a row. It's the same as rolling double sixes seven times in a row or winning the lottery seven days straight or having lightning strike in the same exact place, at the same exact time, every day from Monday to Sunday.

And this is the annoying thing that Dutch has planted inside my brain. This is the thing that simply won't go away.

I believe that Rachel is in heaven. I do. I can accept that there is a heaven for children who are taken away too early. But a God for adults has never made any sense to me. But still, the fact remains that I should be dead. Seven times over, I should be dead.

Now, the second part of the very scary thing is this. Why? Not only how, but for what reason?

"Maybe this stuff happens all the time," Dutch said. "Maybe I just never paid enough attention before."

Maybe.

Maybe we are immune to the miracles that occur all around us every day and Dutch has now become more aware than we usually are.

Or . . .

Dutch told me about the very scary thing the first time he came to see me at the hospital. It wasn't that I thought he was lying, but I did believe he might have been stretching the truth to make it all fit—kind of like a bad UFO documentary.

In order to confirm the facts he had based all of this on, Dutch gave me his journal to read. His personal—very personal—diary of everything that had occurred over the past few months. Interestingly, Dutch started keeping a journal just three weeks before I started writing mine—another coincidence that's hard to ignore.

When Dutch gave me his journal, I reciprocated by giving him a disk that contained my own writings. I said I wanted him to read it all to prove that I needed his help with the liquor store and the storage units and that no one would work for me. But looking back now, I know there were really other reasons I wanted him to read it, only I'm not exactly sure what they all are just yet.

You get to know a person fairly quickly when you are both reading something you had written for no one else to read. Dutch and I probably know each other better than most friends do right now—we're not ready to pick out silverware patterns yet, but reading someone's most private thoughts does expedite friendship a bit.

It's like a bad infomercial:

> Tired of friendships taking soooo long to develop? Does it take months to feel comfortable enough to share personal thoughts and feelings?
>
> Well, no more!
>
> Now there's *Friendship in a Box!*

With Friendship in a Box, a six-month friendship can be developed in . . . only four hours!

Just fill out this ninety-page personal assessment form. Put it in the box. Then exchange boxes with your new friend.

It's that simple!

"Kelly has been cheating on her husband for over nine years? I never knew that!"

"Bob did time for car theft? I never would have guessed!"

Friendship in a Box makes boring conversation and common interests obsolete by sharing your most intimate secrets, right away!

"I've developed a new best friend in only four hours! Thanks, Friendship in a Box!

And now, for a limited time only, order Friendship in a Box and get our new product, Trust in a Bottle, absolutely free!

Call now!

Operators are standing by!

Dutch's journal not only contained all his personal writings about who he is and what he is trying to do on his yearlong quest across the country, but it confirmed the facts he told me about how he saved my life—you couldn't have faked that notebook in just three days. I thought of that and was skeptical at first, but there was just too much feeling written in those pages and too many details.

There is much more to tell, but I don't have much time to do it right now. I will see my girls in a few days, because it'll be Abby's birthday.

I can't pay Dutch back, but I thought of a way I can help.

Dutch got himself in some trouble back in Binghamton. He and I are going to see if we can, well, not fix it exactly, but possibly make it better.

Then we'll see if we can figure out some of these other things, too.

* * *

When Dutch walked into my room, I was pretty well stoned. I was still dopey from the surgery and then they gave me something for the pain on top of that, but even through the pharmacological fog, I could see that there was a strange look on Dutch's face. A different look. It was as if he had just bought ten pounds of confidence and he'd eaten the entire box in one sitting. I asked him what was up—or I tried to ask him, but it came out as *whassss-go-winun*—and he just smiled. He looked odd—cocky, but confident, and it fit him.

I didn't see the cop behind Dutch at first and I don't know if they came in together or if the cop walked in later or if I imagined him entirely because I fell asleep soon after and the room was empty when I woke up. But right then, Dutch waited—not wanting to reveal his secret right away, as if that feeling he had right then would burn off like dew once he spoke. He paced. He smiled. And I watched.

He sat down next to me, happy in his smugness, and he slid a small photograph from behind him and let it land on the blanket of my hospital bed.

I expected the photo to be an old and faded one, assuming it was another discovery that Dutch had made in Bugby's apartment. But the photo was new—only a few hours old, actually—and in color.

I looked at it, but only for a second. The latest round of painkillers had made my reflexes a bit confused and made my mind want to wander. Then Dutch spoke.

"They got him," Dutch said.

"Yeah?"

"He just effing walked into Bugby's apartment when I was there. Well, eff, he actually broke in and then they got him."

"Yeah?"

"They got the guy that shot you, man. It's him."

And after looking at Dutch for another few seconds, I grudgingly removed my eyes from him and let them slide down to the photograph that sat on my bed, to the picture of the man who had shot me. My brain slowly focused on the booking photo taken as the cops arrested him only a few hours before.

I don't know why, but for some reason, I had expected the photo to be of Kyle Somebody. When I picked it up, I already had that image of Kyle Somebody in my head, and when it wasn't him, it took my drug-addled brain a few seconds to refocus. Then I could see that the photo was of Dominick Salter, Bugby's former business manager and the first guy to quit on me after Bugby died.

"Hi, Dominick," I said to the picture. I even waved at it but it didn't wave back.

Then I fell asleep.

Chapter 23

Hiding

| August 15, 1992 |

When the three of us—Abby, Liz, and I—make up games to play together, we always follow a specific pattern, a certain protocol.

First, there is the general announcement of the theme of the game.

"Let's play store," Abby will say. This is followed by the assignment of game roles. "I'll be the storekeeper," Abby says.

"Okay," I join in. "I'll be the customer."

"Okay," Liz follows. "I'll be the astronaut."

And then we play.

Abby opens her store and I walk in and ask if she has any fresh salmon. Before she can answer, Liz the astronaut comes running into the store with a bucket over her head.

"Quick," she says. "Do you have any rocket fuel?"

"Aisle six," Abby the storekeeper answers. "Next to the cat food."

And the game begins.

When I leave the store after returning a can of bad tuna fish, Liz enters and asks if her space shuttle crew can use the bathroom. When I try to use a three-year-old coupon for Milk Duds, Liz needs to know if this store sells booster rockets or just rocket parts.

"Just the parts," Abby comments, while still considering whether I can use the coupon or not. "Try Tops Market for whole rockets."

"Thanks," Liz says and runs out toward Tops Market.

This is how it goes. When we played hospital, Abby was the doctor, I was the patient, and Liz was the car mechanic. When we played school, Abby was the teacher, I was the student, and Liz was the farmer.

This is just how we played and how we had always played. Liz wasn't being defiant; she was just being Liz.

Abby turned twelve while I was still here in the hospital. She had already chosen a theme for her twelfth birthday party—it would be a jungle theme—so we simply moved the party from the Erie Zoo to the Hamot Medical Center. Catherine and Dutch made some phone calls to parents and, when it was time, Dutch wheeled me down in a service elevator—Dutch has found some clever ways to avoid all the reporters—to a large room that had been converted to a jungle bungalow, and voilà, instant birthday party.

Liz was torn between two costumes to wear to her sister's party: a weather girl or a burglar. She went with burglar.

In a room full of twelve-year-olds in tiger stripes and plastic pith helmets, there was Liz in her black skull cap and a burglar shirt—a white T-shirt on which I had carefully drawn thick black prison stripes—as she peered through the small slits of her burglar mask, shifting her pillowcase of stolen loot from one shoulder to the next as she misappropriated plastic forks and birthday napkins from unsuspecting tables.

According to the National Kid's Birthday Party Rating System, this was not *the* birthday party, just *a* birthday party. Like the children of many divorced parents, my girls would have a dad birthday and a mom birthday, along with a dad and a mom Thanksgiving, Christmas, and Easter. Strangely, I am always the host of the kids' party and Catherine and David take on responsibility for the family party—which is fine with me because I enjoy being with the kids more, and then I get to go to the family party, too—which is never as much fun.

When it was time to blow out her birthday candles, when it was time to lock in her wish for that year, Abby stood at the table that held her hippo-shaped cake—her sister's hand was just visible, rising underneath the table to steal the extra birthday candles that were lying next to the cake—she contemplated her wish. It was then that she stopped, turned to find me in the crowd, located me, smiled, and then went back to her decision-making process. This look was not a *Where is my dad, I want him to see me* look. It was a *Where is my dad, he may have wheeled himself out into traffic again* one.

She stood there bathed in candlelight and thought. And I wondered if what Abby had said about me was true—how I was not a traditional father but a twelve-year-old with a license. Because if that was true, then we would be the same age today. Father and daughter. For one full year, we would both be twelve. And then Abby would get older and I would stay the same.

She was already smarter and stronger then I was, and next year she would be older, with Liz coming up strong behind her.

It was a testament to my immaturity that, if given a choice, I would rather be in a room full of ten-year-olds than have lunch with your average adult. With the exception of Bugby and Dutch, adults generally give me hives.

When Catherine and I were dating, she brought me home for the first time to meet her extended family. There was this huge get-together at her parents' house in Ohio and all of the McNarnys were there: uncles, aunts, her brother's family from Texas, as well as bushels of assorted cousins and cousins-in-law and spouses of everybody. I walked into the room and felt as if I'd been dropped into the deep end of a pool while wearing a suit and formal shoes. I couldn't breathe.

Minutes after we arrived, Catherine turned to introduce me to an aunt and I was gone. Lost in the pool of people. When she found me—an hour later—I was on the back deck playing *Star Wars* with three little McNarny cousins and a few nephews.

Catherine just stood there. Shocked. Hurt. She just stood there, staring at me. She looked like she was about to cry.

"What?" I asked.

"I bring you home so my family can meet the man I'm in love with," she said. "And you're out here hiding with the kids?"

Hiding?

Hiding? How can it be hiding? She should be proud that I like kids. Proud that I'm not afraid to get dirty and play in a backyard.

"Hiding? If you're into baseball," I said, probably a little too defensively, "and a group is talking baseball, you move toward them. I'd much rather play with *Star Wars* toys than talk about what stupid sofa goes with what stupid curtains."

Catherine just stood there, stunned. She was beautiful in her red summer dress and she just looked at me. She wasn't angry. She was wounded. She was disappointed. When she finally spoke, when she finally brushed her long hair away from her eyes—the same way that Abby does now—she told me that what I had done was as bad as if I had shown up drunk. She said I was disrespectful to both her and her family. The other McNarny kids stopped what they were doing and looked up at her. She was speaking to me as if I were one of the children. And it would not be the last time that would happen.

"What?" I asked, again probably too defensively. "Disrespectful?"

I didn't understand it, but I did reluctantly leave my young pals on the back deck to stand around with the adults—becoming uncomfortable and unhappy—for the remainder of the day.

On the drive back to Erie, Catherine and I didn't speak until we had crossed over the Pennsylvania line.

"I love you," she finally said, in her most beaten and frustrated tone. "But you wear me out."

After our divorce, Catherine told me to organize the kids' parties for the girls from now on. I was ecstatic. This was not an insult—not exactly—it was only the tired reaction of a woman I had completely worn out.

He sure do disappoint people, don't he?

Was I hiding with the girls? Was I doing them more harm by keeping them—by keeping all of us—away from the chaos of the world?

When Dutch got me back to my hospital room—without a single reporter finding us, by the way—I told him what I had remembered about when Catherine first brought me to meet her family. Dutch took in the story while helping me to my bed and then he rolled the wheelchair back into the hallway.

He sat down on the chair next to the bed.

"When you go to rehab," he said. "They teach you that you stop growing when you start drinking. It's like . . ." He stopped and gathered his thoughts. "It's like, if you was eighteen when you started drinking, then booze is your crutch, right? It's what you use when you're happy and when you're sad so you don't have to grow up because the booze is what you do every time you're supposed to grow up. The booze is the part you use whenever you're, like, supposed to learn a lesson or grow or whatever. But learning is hard, so you just drink instead. And all that confidence and stuff you're supposed to get when you do the hard things, when you're sad or afraid or in trouble, you don't get. You just skip it. You cheat."

Dutch told me about men who got sober in their fifties and sixties who were behaving like teenagers again—because that's where their growing left off. They were forced to pick up right at the point when they started cheating. These were middle-aged and even elderly men that were now primping for dates, gossiping, playing practical jokes, being hurt by a simple word or look. Their crutch was gone and they were forced to move back to the place on the board where they had left their game piece. They were nineteen in a sixty-year-old body.

I listened to what Dutch had to say. I thought about it and thought of the girls and made a silent vow. I would go back to find my game piece and move along the hard lessons with them, and without cheating. I would grow up with Abby and Liz. I might be only twelve now, but next year I'll be thirteen.

When Abby made her birthday wish, she blew out her candles. She smiled. She pulled her long hair back in a ponytail and she looked again through the crowd to me, but this time not with the concerned look she'd been wearing before. This time, she looked happy. And this time, she was twelve.

CHAPTER 24

LUCKY DAY

| AUGUST 16, 1992 |

The day I called Benjamin Mott and told him I wanted to settle with Dutch for two and a half million dollars, I could feel Mott's cold drool dripping through the receiver.

Dutch was standing right next to me in my hospital room when I made the call. He had to look away so as not to laugh, the same way I did as a kid when my sister would call a random number and ask whoever answered if their refrigerator was running.

"Well, I cannot say he'll accept," Mott lied. "My client was expecting the entire three million and he was very specific . . ."

"I want this thing cleared up," I said, in my best, self-important, big-shot tone. "I spoke to my attorneys and they said if they get a written acceptance today, we can have a cashier's check cut tomorrow."

There was a pause as Mott's reptile brain smelled blood. He moved in closer to feed. "That's good to hear. I would suggest, then, that you . . ."

"So, let's conference call your client in right now and get this thing done. What's his number?"

"Mr. Roe, I'm not about to give you my client's personal information. What I will do is . . ."

"Oh, wait. My attorney gave me the number. Hold on, I have a conference call box right here in my room. I'll conference call this Dutcher guy in with us."

Before Mott had a chance to object, I pushed the pound key for a sound effect and cupped my hand over the mouthpiece.

"Hello?" Mott snapped. "Hello!"

We laughed. Then Dutch wiped the smirk off of his face and pushed the button on the speaker box that Dutch had brought from Bugby's.

"Okay, it's ringing," I said to Mott and a moment later, Dutch pretended to answer.

"You will not . . ." Mott said.

"Hello?" Dutch said, right next to me.

"Hey, Mr. Dutcher, this is Walker Roe."

"Mr. Dutcher!" Mott was practically screaming now. "Please, let me do the talk . . ."

"Hey," Dutch answered. "How are you feeling?"

"Mr. Dutcher, I am on the phone as well and we . . ." said Mott.

"A lot better, thanks. Well, a lot better thanks to you. Hey, before we get started, I just have to tell you that I'm recording this call. Is that okay with you?"

"No!" Mott shouted. "I do not give permission for this. You will stop all recording and you will address this situation to me and allow . . ."

"As you can hear," I joked, "I have your attorney here on the line with us."

"Let's start over," Mott said. "What we will do here . . ."

"*My* attorney?" Dutch said. "He said he was *your* attorney."

"Now, we are going to start this from . . ."

"*My* attorney?" I said. "He said he was *your* attorney and that you wanted three million bucks from me."

"All right, I would like to organize this call differently. So, we are going to stop recording and I will . . ."

"Mott, did you tell Dutch that you were *my* attorney?" I asked.

"Three million bucks?" Dutch said. "I never said I wanted any money. 'Specially no three million bucks."

"For the record, I am not confirming or denying anything these two gentlemen are stating. This recording is in no way . . ."

"Mott?" I snapped. "What's going on here?"

It was here that Mott saw the trap. He stopped. He waited. Then he spoke in the softer tone you use when you realize you've just lost thirty percent of a three-million-dollar windfall.

"Do you find this amusing?" Mott asked. "Wasting my time like this?"

"In fact, I find it downright entertaining," I said. "But I'm not wasting your time."

"Are you threatening me?" Mott said.

"You've got it all wrong," I said. My voice was different now. Unrecognizable, even to me. It was low and calm and powerful. I listened to my voice. To my words. I could feel the old circuits and fuses in me sizzle and snap and pop and burn. It was happening. I was changing. I was rewiring. I would do things differently from now on. I would see things more clearly.

We would turn this thing on itself. We would let those who were fighting us fight themselves, and we would no longer be afraid.

"I want you to listen to me," I said calmly. "Because this is the luckiest day of your life."

And then I told Mott about the plan Dutch and I had come up with.

And he listened.

And he loved it.

And he joined up right then.

JOURNAL 6

DUTCH

Chapter 25

| August 8, 1992 |

Time is this really weird, weird thing. It speeds up and slows down and it's real effing moody. It can change, too. The time you use when you're in a dentist chair ain't the same time that you use up when a pretty girl pulls up next to you and asks directions (ha). Time can be different when it wants to be and it can slow down or speed up. It can even just effing stop if you really piss it off.

I remember a speech class in high school where this teacher, Mrs. Ainsworth, said, "If you don't think thirty seconds is a long time, try sitting on a hot stove for that long." Time is different on that stove (it's slow and dragging and lumpy) than it is while you're sitting with Randy at the Belmar and having a beer (where time is soft and running like cold water from an outside faucet).

This is what I mean. I've been gone from Binghamton for twenty-one days, right? That's it, just twenty-one days. In normal time, that's just twenty-one twenty-four-hour buckets of time, three weeks, and it's no big deal. Them twenty-one days would pass by when I lived on Mather Street and I wouldn't even notice. I never even turned my calendar pages over until the next month was almost gone (ha). Each day was like the day right before it and each one of them days would just, like, melt into the next day until you get this big clump of melted days, kinda like when you leave chocolate in your pocket. And then you reach in your pocket and all that chocolate is like one big mess of days and you can't believe it's effing October already.

But in this weird time, in this different time, them twenty-one days is like ten effing years because in them twenty-one days I've seen Niagara Falls and swam in the Niagara River and met Ping and

Pan from Thailand and had a picnic with a pretty Austrian girl named Panja that likes catching turtles.

I never did nothing like that in Binghamton in the last twenty effing years. I don't have no stories like that from before, or even stories at all. Everything was the same.

But in these new twenty-one days, I walked through an abandoned city in the rain and imagined what it was like before when people still lived there and I looked at them empty buildings through the clear plastic of a duck umbrella. I found out I can find work anywhere and sleep real good, all protected in bushes, if I'm tired enough. I saved a guy's life. I got arrested. I spent days in a police safehouse thingee and met this big-headed attorney named Benjamin Mott who tried to hose Walker out of three million bucks. I've been in handcuffs for the first time in my life and I learned to make great sandwiches out of pumpernickel bread and Swiss cheese and pepperoni cut right off the stick.

I drove a twenty-year-old Bricklin sports car through Erie traffic at eighty effing miles an hour being chased by police cars and I watched the car blow up twenty feet from my head (ha). I've been on every effing news channel there is and I've had them reporters and newspaper people effing tracking me and Barbara Walters herself has been calling for an interview with her! (Can you effing believe that? Ha.) I met Walker Roe and told him about the very scary thing and I've stayed a night in Bugby's apartment (he's the guy that died and left Walker all his money). While I finish cleaning out the storage shed for Walker, I get to stay here for free.

I found a Greek diner in Erie where you can buy a big plate of olives and cheese and bread for only four dollars and you can sit at the counter and eat it and talk to the waitress whose name is Yoda (that's her real name, only it's spelled with a J but sounds the same as Y, ha) and she'll tell you about her son, Marco, who has a fishing boat on Lake Erie. I found a park where you can sit at a stone table and write postcards to Randy and watch ducks on the water and sometimes there are old men playing chess and dominoes on tables and you want to ask them old men to teach you, but you don't ask. You just watch and try to figure the games out for yourself.

Bugby has all these videotapes of old movies in his apartment. I never thought I liked old movies but they're so different than the movies I've seen. I like watching them. I've watched *The Maltese Falcon* and *Citizen Kane* and *Mutiny on the Bounty* and *The Magnificent Seven*. That one's real good, *The Magnificent Seven*. I watched it twice so far.

All them things can't fit in just twenty-one days. It's too effing much and the bag will bust if you try to put all that stuff in only twenty-one effing days. But it doesn't bust and the time, it, like, stretches or something and all them things fit in the new weird time bag (ha).

And you end up here, on day twenty-one, sitting at Bugby's table in his apartment and writing and not believing all the things you did in only twenty-one effing days.

I'm writing in the yellow notebook now but I got my red one, the first notebook, back from Walker after he read it. Now I have them both and that's another thing. I never in my whole life wrote enough to fill an effing notebook before. Never. And now I'm starting book two (ha).

Walker gave me his computer disk with his journal on it. He's a good writer. It's like reading a real book when you read his stuff and I knew he'd be disappointed when he read mine, if he can even read my chicken scratch (ha). But the gist of his journal is that he's done some bad stuff and he's sorry about it. He wants to move on, but some people just won't let him. He loves them girls of his and he loved Bugby but now Bugby is dead and people are pissed off because Walker got Bugby's dough instead of them getting it. There's other stuff in there, too, personal stuff, but I wouldn't be able to write it down the right way, so I won't even try.

It's weird reading somebody's personal thoughts and having them read yours. Maybe Walker is the *you* I've been writing to, huh? (Ha.) That would be very funny and even scary at the same time.

The other weird thing is I have to watch where I am now, all the time, and look to see who's following me or trying to take my picture. I don't effing like it. Them newspaper and TV people haven't figured out where I am yet so they don't bother me here, but when I go to the hospital I have to walk past them and they yell and stick cameras in my face. If I see Security Guard Latiani's blue truck in the parking lot, then I can knock at the loading dock and he'll let me go in the back way, through the break room and up to Walker's hospital room. If he ain't working, I need to try to sneak into Walker's room through emergency—never through the front lobby. Sometimes the reporters see me and yell and sometimes I walk right past them. It really pisses them off when I walk past them (ha), like who the eff am I not to be willing to talk to them (ha). But they always look for me to drive up—they never look at the bus stop where I get off (ha).

But Brandon is going to fix some of this TV stuff. He promised. He's going to write something and get it out there so all these reporters leave me alone.

I told Walker I'd go over tonight to see him again at the hospital. Until then, I said I'd go through all these boxes and stuff. I've got that itchy feeling again, and besides Walker said he'd pay me if I went through all this stuff of Bugby's, since I'm almost done with the storage unit stuff. Hey, that's not trying to take his money—that's work and work gets paid, so it's okay.

Later.

August 9, 1992

I went to church today.

Do you believe that? (Ha.)

The very scary thing has got me thinking. A lot. I have all these questions so I went to the Garden Heights Baptist Church.

It wasn't like churches in the movies. It was this big white room with chairs instead of pews and no stained-glass windows or candles or nothing like that. I was wearing jeans and a button-down shirt, and I wasn't the only one. There was people there with jeans and T-shirts and some with shorts and T-shirts. There was no organ but there was guitars and a drum set and there was a stage up front where the band played. The music was weird. Good weird, modern, and you didn't sing from books. The words were projected on a screen and you just sang along.

It was cool but I didn't get to speak to no one. People shook my hand and told me that they was glad I was there but I didn't get to talk to no one about the very scary thing.

* * *

Eff, there's a lot of stuff here at Bugby's place. It's all like a puzzle. This newspaper clipping from this box goes with that receipt in that other box and it all goes with the photo album in that other box (ha). But after putting all this stuff together (and I still ain't done yet—there's a lot here), there is something that pisses me off. Why does Walker have to lie to me? After getting to know the guy and after reading his journal, it kind of makes me mad that he had to lie. If he don't want to tell me stuff, he don't have to, but don't lie about it, eff. I'll be gone soon, so what do I care? Lie to them reporters and stuff but why bother lying to me?

The only reason to lie to me is because he don't trust me, and if he don't trust me, then why not let me get back on the road? Why all this effing crap about needing my help and how nobody will work for him and then putting me in this place where the truth is kept and then lie about it? Eff.

Walker says that he gets, like, a hundred grand a year or so from all that Bugby left him if he don't sell nothing. Bull. It's all lies. All that money from the publishing place alone is going into this brokerage bank in Canada. It's got, like, over four million bucks in it. Bugby never touched it. He just signs something every year and it keeps growing. I've got the latest statement right here. $4,564,342.76. Eff. Broke, huh? I don't think so.

I mean, I guess I know why he lied about owning the place he works at. I guess I'd be embarrassed if the only place that would hire me was my friend's place and only after that friend forced them to take me. Even as pathetic as I am, I got my job at the landfill on my own. I saw the letter from when Bugby called this guy, Matthew Comfort, from the publishing place and told him to give Walker a job. The guy wasn't too happy about it and according to the letters he even threatened to quit. Bugby said, go ahead, but the guy never did. It was just a lot of talk.

But it's no big deal. Walker lied for his own reasons and it ain't nothing for me to worry about. I'll finish all this for him and get it all organized, spend a few more rent-free nights here (hey, it's part of the job and nothing to be ashamed of), and then I'll hit the road.

I'm thinking about traveling to Ohio next and then maybe south a bit, but not having a direction has worked out pretty good so far. Hey, I got a free ride to Erie, didn't I (ha)?

The phone keeps ringing here. I don't pick it up. It's Bugby's phone and maybe people are calling for him, but it ain't my phone. There it goes again. Maybe it's them reporters and if I answer it, I might as well open the door and let them in. And that ain't happening.

It'll be really good to get away from them. They are just mean. Effing bossy. Like, how dare you not talk to them, who the eff are you, don't you see I got an ID around my neck and a microphone (ha)?

Yoda with a J, the lady at the Greek restaurant, figured out who I am and now I can't go there no more. I saw she looked at me different when I walked in and I sat at the counter and then her son, Marco, sat down next to me and started asking questions. He sat right down and leaned into me and said nothing for a while. Nothing. Then he said that I looked familiar and I knew he figured out who I was and then he asked if I knew him. When I said no, he asked again. And then he asked a bunch of weird questions.

Where's all the money? How much did you get? Have you got it all yet or just a little bit? How much? Did you know them guys that did it?

And this is the one that really pissed me off. Marco said—eff, he said, "Hey," he said. "Did you *really* save him or was it something you cooked up with the other two guys? In the car? Hey, if you did, it's effing genius. You could blackmail them. Roe gets what he deserves and you can get some of that cash he won't let go of. I'm just curious. So how much reward did you get so far . . ."

And he goes on and on like that and Yoda with a J just stands there smiling, like she wants to know, too. Then this guy Marco leans in and says, "Hey, look. You're good at secrets," he says. "And so am I. So maybe I can help . . ." And he goes on but I stop listening after that. Yoda with a J brings out the plate with the olives and cheese and the bread but I don't touch it. I just walk out.

I wanted to slug the guy, but that would have been a big mistake. Plus, eff, I never slugged nobody in my life. In fact (ha), *slug* is a word I picked up from all those old movies of Bugby's (ha). *Slug* and *simoleons* and *gams* and *heater* (ha).

Anyways, Randy and me have a plan. I'm supposed to get a conference call with Walker and Brandon and me, and Brandon's going to fix some of this. A press release or whatever. He says you got to give the press a little or else they want it all. So we're going to do this call and Brandon can do his thing. Then I'll leave.

I'm still pissed about Walker lying to me, though. He's a nice guy and after reading his journal I got a lot of respect for him. But eff, I'm not going to touch your money, Walker. I found my conscience (ha).

August 11, 1992

So, when the guy broke into Bugby's apartment (I forgot to tell you, ha), he was real surprised to see me sitting there on the couch. And he just froze. Like his eyes wasn't working right and he was giving them time to adjust to what he was really seeing and not what he *thought* he saw. As soon as he opened the door (well, eff, if you're using a tire iron to open the door, it's not really *opening*, then, is it? Ha!), he just froze. He just froze there in the doorway of Bugby's apartment and stared at me.

And I stared back. And then I smiled. And this is the effing amazing part. I smiled just the way Charles Bronson smiled at Rosenda Monteros in *The Magnificent Seven*. I smiled because I knew that guy at the door. I hadn't seen him since he shot Walker, but it was him. No effing doubt about it. I just smiled that Charles Bronson smile. I smiled that *I couldn't give a flying eff* kind of smile.

He teetered there, like you do just before a race. Not sure what to do and when to do it. He teetered. And I smiled. Then he took off, like the deer that finally jumps back into the woods, and before I knew it, I was running after him.

I chased him down the steps. I actually effing chased him. And I'd like to tell you how I tackled him and slammed him until he dropped the tire iron. I could tell you that and you might even believe me, but that ain't what happened.

This guy, who I now know is named Dominick Salter, ran down the steps as fast as he could go, skipping two and three steps at a time. He ran out the building door and right into the car of . . . wait for it. Ha. Wait for it. He runs right into the car of (ready?)—Tony the cop, who had been patrolling the apartment every night since he dropped me off.

Dominick hit that car hard. Wham! And he rolled over the hood and fell on the pavement. Then Tony the cop got out of the car and grabbed the guy off the ground before he could get up, just as I came running out of the building. And when I told Tony who the guy was, when I told Tony that he was on top of the guy that shot Walker and that I was sure of it, then we both smiled. We both smiled that same Charley Bronson smile.

* * *

"If I ever commit a crime, Dutch," Tony the cop told me, "I want you to be the sole effing witness to it."

Dominick Salter was born in Erie. He went to school here and was married here and had kids here. This guy was in clubs and was on committees and had neighbors come to his house for effing barbecues. He had friends and knew so many people that he couldn't go into a bank or a store without someone saying, *Hey, Dominick, how ya doing?*

Yet, after Walker was shot and the police sketch of Salter was shown on every effing TV station and in every newspaper around the world, nobody said, *Hey, don't that picture look like Dominick Salter?* Nobody even thought of him.

Know why?

Because that drawing sucked.

How often do you look at a person (especially a person you're trying to pull out of a car after they just shot a guy) and say, *Hmm, he has a pointed nose and a flat chin*? Or, *Wow, that guy's eyes are the average distance apart but his ears are bigger than normal*. You don't (or maybe *you* do, but I effing don't). You look at the face and say, *Yup, I got it*. But then later, when they ask you about the pieces that face is made of, you think, eff, just show me the face again and I'll tell you (ha).

When I sat with that police sketch guy, he asked me questions like, *Was his face long or round? Was his nose flat or wide? His eyes, was they oval or pointed?* I dunno. I looked through them mug shots for hours trying to see the guy again, knowing I'd recognize him once I saw him, but I couldn't tell you about his nose shape. Eff, I couldn't tell you about *my* nose shape (ha).

So the sketch they had of Salter was really bad. And nobody, of the thousands of people that knew Salter, even thought of him. But as soon as he broke open that door at Bugby's, as soon as he stood there frozen and staring at me, I looked at the guy. I looked at him and I smiled and I thought, *Hey, his nose IS pointed* (ha).

In the words of them old movies of Bugby's, when they questioned Salter after they arrested him, *He cracked like an egg*.

"The guy was in bad shape," Tony the cop told me. "Paranoid. Worried. He hadn't slept in days. He was unraveling fast."

Salter had been stealing from Bugby for years. He was skimming, like, sixty grand a year every year and he kept the amount constant so nobody noticed. Tony the cop told me they figure he got away with about three million over all the years he worked for Bugby.

But here's the good part. Salter is pissed that Bugby didn't leave him nothing and that he now has to work for Walker—Walker, who is this ex-con, this local joke, and everyone in Erie knows his story. So Salter sends this memo to the managers of Bugby's other businesses.

You can do what you want, Salter says in this memo. *But I have an ethical dilemma and cannot work for an organization whose principles are questionable.*

So Salter quits and a few other guys follow him.

Now, soon after Salter quits, he realizes that a) he's out the extra, tax-free sixty grand he steals every year, and b) when they start looking at the books they might finally see that extra, tax-free sixty grand a year missing.

Wow, what an ethical effing dilemma to be in. What to do, what to do?

So Salter breaks into Bugby's offices on State Street. He breaks things and does the graffiti thing and steals some stuff, but mostly he does it just to get all them files—all the files showing the accounts he draws from, where he parks the money, and how he pulls it out. And when he gets the files and destroys them, he feels a little better. For a while.

Then, Salter begins to worry again. He hadn't worried in years, but he's making up for it now, big time. With Walker trying to run everything, might there be files he missed? What happens when the earnings are up sixty grand for the first time in twelve years? Does Bugby have extra copies of the files? The worry starts to eat at him and he can't stop it.

"He figured there were so many people after Roe," Tony the cop told me, "that they would never suspect him. And with Walker gone, Salter figured the businesses would just collapse and be sold off separately and then he'd be safe."

So Salter and the driver (this is the only part of the story Salter isn't telling yet—who the driver was), they try to knock off Walker and, eff, you know how that turned out.

The funny part is, the only person in the effing universe who thought the police sketch looked like Salter was Salter (ha). Every time he saw that thing on TV or when he saw the copies they got taped up in stores, his nerves stretched a little tighter. He thought the world was just a step behind him.

"He wanted to make sure there were no more files in Bugby's apartment," Tony the cop said. "Then he was going to trash the place and then check out Walker's apartment and trash that, too. To cover it all up."

When Tony and I first told Walker that Salter was the guy who shot him, Walker had just come out of surgery and was pretty well stoned (ha). He probably don't even remember it. But when I told him again, it sunk in real good.

I thought Walker would be happy once he knew the guy was caught. But he just looked at the picture of Salter. He just stared at it when I told him what happened. I felt bad for him then, like it's almost better *not* to know who tried to kill you.

Walker gets out of the hospital in a few days and tomorrow we're gonna have some fun with Benjamin Mott. Walker and me have this idea. It's weird but it could work if this call with Mott goes well.

By the way, Walker wasn't lying to me about owning that publishing place he worked at. (They fired him, by the way. That's funny too, huh?) He just didn't effing know. (Ha.) An extra four million laying around and he didn't even know it.

He just didn't effing know.

CHAPTER 26

| AUGUST 15, 1992 |

I think there is this thing, like, well, the only way to describe it is a sober hangover (ha). It's like when something happens and you would normally drink to get away from it, but you can't now, so you deal with the slap in the face instead. Deal with the hurt of it. Normally, the booze would just take the pain away but you can't do that now. Not if you want each day to be different. Now you just got to belly up and take it.

It's funny when you drink to get away from stuff—that thing, that worry or that trouble is still there, but it don't hurt no more when you drink. It's like all the venom was taken out of it. You can sit there and go, oh yeah, I'm getting evicted tomorrow, or yup, they're going to find out about the money I stole from the cash box as soon as they open in the morning, or uh-huh, my car isn't registered or licensed and I'm going to get caught soon. Yup. I know.

And you see it and it's almost funny. Like a horror movie with the sound turned off (ha). It ain't so scary no more when that creepy music and screaming ain't there.

So here's what happened to make me write all this. Walker had a birthday party for his daughter, Abby. (Her real name is Abigail, but she *hates* being called Abigail, ha.) We had the party at the hospital. Isn't that effing wild? They was supposed to have it at the zoo, but Walker wanted to go to the party and was going to just call a cab and go to the zoo when the doctors came up with this idea. They moved the party to a small conference room off the cafeteria in the hospital. That hospital is like an effing city and you could have a hundred parties and still not run out of places to have them.

So Walker's ex-wife and me started calling parents to change the place where the party was. Some of those parents were nice but most of them were royal jerks. One lady snapped at me, telling me that you can't just change plans like that, people have lives, you know! Eff, like there is a birthday party rulebook someplace and I wasn't doing it right. And some other people used it as an excuse to get out of the party. You could tell. They was nervous about sending their daughter to a party where the birthday girl's father just got shot. Out of the twelve parents I called, five of them backed out, two snapped at me, and five said, sure, no problem.

So here is the sober hangover part. I had to sneak Walker out of his room in a wheelchair and down to the party without them reporters finding out. Security Guard Latiani met me in this service elevator and we got Walker down to the main floor. What we did was cover Walker's face with bandages as we walked him through the hall and to the conference room in case anyone nosy was walking around (ha), and then we took the bandages off when we got to the room.

Smart, huh?

So we got to the conference room and the party started. There was a bunch of girls dressed in jungle stuff playing in a conference room that was decorated to make it look like a jungle shack. And as soon as I got there, I got this feeling. I got this big lump in my gut.

That party reminded me of all the parties my parents had for me. It reminded me of the party for my twenty-first birthday that I blew off, that I didn't even go to, and now I would do anything to see my folks again, now that I don't get to have no more parties with them, or even have them in the same room as me. I dissed them when they was alive, I wasted the time with them, and now there ain't no more time left.

I can't fix it. I can't tell them all the things I done in the last twenty-eight days. I can't blow out no candles while they take pictures. I can't give them no presents or open presents from them.

And that's what really, really, really sucks.

I told you time traveling is dangerous. Once you get traveling back to the shouldas and wouldas, it's straight to the Belmar for you.

And the effing weirder thing is, just when I'm ready to find the nearest bar, just when I want to find a couple dozen bottles to effing crawl into for a month, that's when this other voice says something.

It's that newer voice I told you about. This voice is still softer than the other one—it ain't as loud and bossy—but it's getting louder—no, not louder, just easier to hear. And just when it's getting bad in my head, there's a squeak, like that other voice is clearing its throat, not wanting to be rude (ha).

This voice tells me that I'm looking at it wrong. All wrong. It shows me all the birthdays I had with my parents. It runs the videos of all them times when we were happy and the things I did right and all them times I'd forgotten. It tells me how lucky I am to have had great parents even for a little while and to remember each second, each smile, and each word. It shows me the times when I did good, and the times when my dad was proud of me. It tells me that—and here comes the effing weird part—my parents were lucky to have *me* and that I must be an all right person to have parents that loved me that much.

I like this new voice. And the more I listen to it, the better I feel.

* * *

Walker and me are friends now. We talked for a long time last night. Long after visiting hours was over but the nurses don't care.

Walker and me have a bunch of ideas and the first one involves giving me some money. At first I said no to Walker, but he said, *Wait, hear me out*. So I did. I listened and thought about it and he's right. It's not a bribe or a gift. It's just fixing something. Just rewinding and fixing.

I told Walker I'd sleep on it (that's another thing we normals do—we sleep on things, ha). We think about them.

I told Walker I'd let him know in the morning.

August 16, 1992

I wish I could've been there, but I can see it in my head so that's almost as good (hey, sometimes it's even better but this time it's almost as good). I can see it in my head and I described it to Walker so he could see it in his head, too.

Walker sat in his chair by his hospital bed. He smiled and he listened.

I told Walker about it. I told him about Louis, the contractor from Binghamton that Walker and me hired over the phone, and how we never met Louis but I got this image of him in my head of how he looks.

"Like the Brawny paper towel guy," I said. "That's exactly how I picture him."

I can see Vernon, too—the guy who owned the bike—who I never met neither but I saw photographs of him in his house so I know what he looks like. I can see Louis knocking at Vernon's door. Rap. Rap. Rap.

"You think he knocked three times, huh?" Walker smiled. "Not four or two?"

"Nope. It was three."

Louis waits and then Vernon opens the door. Louis tells Vernon that Roy has hired Louis's contractor company to fix Vernon's house.

What does Vernon do when he hears that? I can't tell. Maybe Vernon's eyes get real wide when he hears that name. Roy. Roy, the bastard. Roy, the drunk. And maybe Vernon wants to shut the door in Louis's face, but he don't. Louis shows Vernon the contract he has with Roy and maybe Louis even shows Vernon a copy of the cashier's check, so he knows Louis has already been paid. I'm not sure. But anyways, Vernon lets Louis in.

"He's actually doing pretty well with getting started," Louis said to me over the phone. "From the way you described the damage, he's got it pretty much gutted. That's a good place to start."

Louis is invited inside the house and he sits down with Vernon.

I don't know where they sat in the house exactly, because I busted all of Vernon's dining room chairs and Valerie smashed the table with an effing ax, but Louis told me they sat someplace. And when they sat down, Louis went over what he calls *the scope of work*. That means a written-out plan of what he is going to do. The scope here is pretty simple: to make the house the same as *or better* (Walker added in that *better* part) than it was before. Before what Roy and Valerie did to it.

Not just to erase it. Not just to rewind it, but to rewind and edit, making it new and improved.

"Like Vernon's house, now with Retsyn," Walker said. "Vernon's house, new and improved."

Louis told Vernon they could start the next day on the work. He told Vernon that he had a full crew ready and they could have it all done in three weeks or so and that wasn't just for the construction part, neither. They would move in the furniture, television, computer, the home goods (that's what they call dishes and coffee makers and stuff). Everything.

"It will be like a new house," Louis told Vernon.

It was probably right then that Louis gave Vernon the check.

"Probably," Walker agreed. "That's when I would have given it to him."

"This check is to replace the other belongings in the house that were damaged," Louis had said. "Clothing, personal items, and so on. Everything else."

Vernon opened the envelope and looked at the check. I know what Vernon said because Louis told me, but I picture him waiting a few minutes before he said it.

"This is too much," Vernon said, handing the check back.

Louis smiled. I picture him smiling and crossing his arms over his Brawny-man red-flannel shirt.

"I've been doing this for twenty years," Louis says to Vernon. "And it's never too much. You always forget something, or items cost more to replace than when you first bought them."

"He took the check?" Walker asked.

"Yup," I answered. "And here's the best part."

Vernon walked Louis through the front door. They had agreed to begin work first thing the next morning. I can see Louis taking a few steps down the front steps of the porch before Vernon spoke, just like in the movies.

"Hey," Vernon said.

I can see Louis stopping on the last porch step and turning around to hear what Vernon had to say. "Do me a favor," Vernon said. "Tell Roy something for me."

This is where I see Vernon pausing for a minute, like Yul Brynner did in *The Magnificent Seven* right before he said the line about protecting the people in the town. Then Vernon speaks: "Tell Roy he's doing a good thing here. With all of this."

"That's what he said?" Walker asked.

"Yup." I smiled. "That's what he said."

Walker waited. "Wow." Then Walker got that distant, weird, thinking face he sometimes gets. And then he looked up at me.

"Well, maybe there's hope for Roy after all." He stood up from his chair. He limped a few steps to get the kinks out of his leg. "And if there's hope for Roy, then we all have a shot, huh?"

"Yup."

August 17, 1992

That weird guy Marco from the Greek restaurant was parked outside Bugby's apartment today. I was brushing my teeth and looking out the bathroom window when I saw him. He was just sitting in his car smoking cigarettes and looking up at Bugby's window. When I got to the living room and opened the curtain to see him, he just drove off. I don't like that guy.

Walker and me talked to Mott, the weasel attorney. Walker has this idea, and (ha) it's a great idea and Mott is part of it. It's an effing amazing idea and it's going to change some things.

Eff, it's going to change everything.

JOURNAL 7

WALKER

Chapter 27

John Lennon

| August 25, 1992 |

If you were to stand on Grandview Boulevard in Erie and ask everyone who sped by to tell one story—just one—about Wanamaker Studios, you'd better have a pen. A few pens. A stenographer would be helpful because that old studio has been around here for decades.

In fact, at least a third of my childhood memories are set at the Erie waterfront or at Wanamaker Studios. My first kiss happened while I was walking Margot Dempsie home from a birthday party. We took a shortcut through the waterfront near the studio and she got scared. My dad taught me to drive a stick shift down in the lot across from Wanamaker, and my first real fistfight happened when I was thirteen years old on the path between the old studio fence and the shore.

The one memory that is stronger than all the others occurred in 1980. I was driving home from a trip, while listening to the Patriots playing the Dolphins on the radio, I heard Howard Cosell announce that John Lennon had been killed. I pulled over right where I was—which happened to be at the studio fence. I put the car in park and just listened. I focused on the sleet slamming against the broken Wanamaker Studios sign and I listened, not believing that John was gone.

And although I have many powerful and emotional recollections of the place, I am embarrassed to say that most of my early memories about the old place involve vandalizing it.

As kids, we would always scour the shore for rocks or rusted bolts or pieces of metal that were the right size to throw over the fence, to not only make contact with the rusting old Wanamaker sign, but also to take out one of those huge white bulbs screwed into its frame. On one glorious day when I was twelve, I became a neighborhood legend by not only breaking nineteen of the bulbs of the sign—impressive enough—but by hitting nineteen bulbs . . . in . . . a . . . row.

For all of us who grew up in Erie, Wanamaker Studios has simply always been there. Always. Our memories are piled in and all around it.

The physical structure of the place is not all that impressive. It was fairly standard for its time—it has a rounded metal Quonset hut arrangement that most film studios adopted right after World War II when war surplus materials were cheap and you could put up a prefab structure in a day or so. Then there is that fence—that military-style fence that's just high enough to show the place's importance and make it seem forbidden. Mythical. But it's the sign that stands out. That great Wanamaker sign that arches around the front of the building and spells out WANAMAKER STUDIOS.

Every Erie kid has heard rumors about the place. Each generation comes up with even new and better stories, but the basics are always there. There was one story that said the studio was owned by the military to make top-secret films instructing agents how to assassinate everyone from Hitler to Castro to Kennedy. There are the stories that Wanamaker's was a porn studio in the 1940s and 1950s. Then, there was a rumor that the studio *still was* a porn studio—a concept that drove every adolescent male in Erie to make at least one pilgrimage to watch the few women who worked at the factory walk in or out, while wondering, *Is she one, you think? How about her?*

We were told the film *Caligula* was made at Wanamaker. So were *Eraserhead* and *The Rocky Horror Picture Show,* along with some film that didn't have a title because everyone who had watched it died before it was finished—it was supposedly one of the many films the military was developing there as a weapon.

As kids, we came down to the Erie waterfront every chance we got. The place had all the trappings that enticed our curious American blood: rusting ships, train cars, water, as well as adults telling us how dangerous it was.

"Yup," we'd say to some cute girl at the swingset during recess. "I've got to get a Band-Aid for this cut I got here . . ." We'd nonchalantly point at a microscopic tear in the skin. "I got it down at the waterfront last night."

She'd stop swinging. "*You* were down *there*?"

"Huh?" we'd say, trying to remember what it was we were talking about. "Oh yeah, I go down there all the time."

"Have you been to that old studio?"

"Wanamaker's? Of course."

And for the next fifteen minutes, we were the most worldly eleven-year-old there ever was.

Kenny DeLorenzo told us about his cousin—and once we had heard the famous cousin story we made him retell it often—who had climbed over the fence one night and looked right in the window of Wanamaker. Right in! There, he saw dozens of naked women sitting on pillows during their smoke breaks as they waited for new film to be added to the many cameras. It was a great story, but Kenny DeLorenzo also said that his father had invented the thermos, so the source was questionable even back then. On the other side of the spectrum, there were always those kids whose father, or uncle, or cousin, or someone worked at the place and said that the building had nothing but old pipes and tools in it.

Karma is a funny thing. Since Dutch and I bought the sign and the old building—I'll tell you about that in a minute—I am now paying for some of the sins of my youth. Those light bulbs are not cheap. I don't normally look at invoices when they come in but I did get a sick sense of pleasure in noticing how much each one of those bulbs cost—*if* they could even be found—since I am personally responsible for the demise of at least thirty of them.

Dutch and I have had the sign restored—the metal of the curved base sanded and filled in, the bright blues and reds repainted, and those bulbs—man, those elusive fifty-year-old Hollywood bulbs—found and screwed into all their newly cleaned and wired slots that spell out every letter of the name: WANAMAKER STUDIOS.

The tracer of the lights now runs slowly, first lighting up all the letters at once, then going dark for a second, then lighting up each letter one at a time—pop, pop, pop—followed by that 1940s ozone sound, like an X-ray machine had just been switched on.

We bought the studio, too, and it's now our office. I finally got my chance to look inside the place. So now, dear reader, I will tell you the truth about Wanamaker Studios and its elusive past.

Ready?

Wanamaker Studios is . . .

Nothing.

There *is* no Wanamaker Studios. There never was.

Like so much that has happened since I've started writing this journal, there is a building and there is a sign. They just don't go together.

Confused?

So was I. But this is what Dutch found out—he's a bloodhound when it comes to tracing things and doing research.

John Wanamaker was this merchandising and marketing genius who lived from 1838 to 1922. He was the founder of the Wanamaker department store chain and he built his largest store—a ten-story building with over a million square feet—in downtown Philadelphia.

Wanamaker's was the very first department store in Philadelphia and was one of the first department stores in the country. Wanamaker's was also the first department store to have electric lights (1878) and the first to install telephones (1879). In fact, when the *Titanic* sank in 1912, the news was picked up by Wanamaker's wireless station in New York and forwarded to the crowds outside the store.

The store in Philadelphia had the world's largest pipe organ. It took thirteen train cars to carry all the pieces. When the organ was assembled and the sound deemed too small for the grand court, Wanamaker had an organ-pipe manufacturing plant built on one of the floors. For the next three years, the organ was upgraded until Wanamaker deemed it perfect.

In the toy department, the Wanamaker store had a working monorail that took customers to any part of the floor. The furniture department had a full-scale model house so you could see furniture in various rooms. The store had a doctor's office for customer safety, a post office, a theater, its own radio station, and a one-of-a-kind restaurant called the Crystal Tea Room, which could seat fourteen hundred people and whose kitchen could cook seventy-five turkeys at a time.

One of the songs from the 1950 Broadway hit *Guys and Dolls* mentions shopping at Wanamaker's. Jimmy Cagney worked at Wanamaker's as a package wrapper before striking out for Broadway.

Besides these store innovations, Wanamaker insisted on customers being allowed to return merchandise for any reason at all. He also provided free medical care, education, profit sharing, and vacations for all his employees—all absolutely unheard of at the time.

I had never heard of John Wanamaker until Dutch started researching the lot titles before we bought the place—like I said, Dutch is relentless when it comes to things like this, and because of his research we saved . . . well, I'm getting ahead of myself.

So, John Wanamaker died in 1922 and upon his death his son, Rodman, carried on his father's vision for the stores. The stores thrived, but Rodman died only a few years later and in 1928 control of the stores fell to a family trust.

The Wanamaker family trust became a paradox: It supported the family financially but each year the family's needs became greater than what the trust could provide. The trust needed to give more and more.

With the rise of suburban living in the 1940s and 1950s came the need for more car-friendly shopping areas, so shopping centers began to pop up across the country. What better way to inject income than to open some new Wanamaker stores, right? The idea was to create smaller versions of the great store out there in the suburbs.

So, new stores opened across the country. But without the grandeur and mystique of the original Wanamaker's, without the history and the experience of the great place itself, shopping was simply—well, it was just shopping, which meant that without the experience, you could get a version of whatever you needed somewhere else. The stores went into decline.

More capital had to be injected into the chain, so in the Wanamaker store in Philadelphia, floors of the building were sold off. The theater was dismantled to make way for additional leasing space. The monorail, the doctor's office, and all the rest were taken down and sold, stored, or simply built around.

When no buyer could be found for the Wanamaker Studios sign —the theater screen, seats, and vending machines had already been sold— the sign was sent out to Erie as scrap. And once it arrived, it was placed snugly against the front of the Quonset hut and mounted to protect it from the waterfront winds. It fit perfectly. In 1959, the lot was sold to a holding company in Houston, Texas. The company did nothing with the lot, but it cut off access to it from the local GAF factory. And there it sat. Creating rumors. Building a legend.

Until now.

So we bought the studio—well, actually P & B Holdings bought the lot and contents, which included the land and the building.

We had placed full-page ads in newspapers from Erie to New York stating that P & B Holdings had purchased Wanamaker Studios in Erie, Pennsyvlania, and that an auction would be held at the site.

What? Not only was the studio finally going to be opened like the gates of Willy Wonka's factory, but you could actually *buy* the stuff inside?

The fuse was lit. Anticipation grew.

On the morning of the auction, a huge crowd of potential buyers, reporters, and spectators waited. And right at 9:00 A.M., just as promised, the restored Wanamaker Studio sign was turned on—unknown to the crowd, it was being publicly lit for the first time ever on Erie soil.

There was an electric crackle, then that ozone hum, and then the sign came alive. WANAMAKER STUDIOS. On, then off, then the letters lit up one at a time, tracing out the words. Then they blinked twice and repeated the sequence.

The crowd went silent as if the collective breath of everyone standing there had been sucked out at the exact same time. Then there was an explosion of screams and applause and the gates were opened.

Willy Wonka himself could not have done any better.

The crew from Affinity Auctions had organized the day to go as efficiently as possible. The crowd was ushered in and fanned out, quickly filling the two hundred available folding chairs. Most people needed to stand.

Sammy Wright, the auctioneer, stood on the portable podium and watched the crowd file in. He switched his microphone on, tapped it twice, then introduced himself and welcomed everyone. Sammy explained that the studio was going to be made into office space and that there were many items up for sale today. Then, with a nod from Sammy, the studio door was opened and the first item was brought up to the auction stand.

It was an old studio camera—tall on its tripod, and as they brought it out to the yard the shining metal caught the morning sun. What movies had been made with this old piece? What secrets had it been part of?

As the camera was being auctioned, the next item was carried out of the studio, waiting to be brought up next. It was an old film projector. Eyes went from projector to the camera and then back.

The camera was sold. The projector moved up to the block, and then a grandfather clock was wheeled out to go up next.

The process continued. There would soon be a vintage leather office chair, then old filing cabinets, boxes of movie film, a locked safe, various stage props—skis and a stuffed moose head and a factory time clock.

The items kept coming. There was furniture and paintings, glassware and fire helmets. There was a sidecar to an old World War II motorcycle. There were tools, a wooden hot dog cart, and racks of vintage clothing. There were antique shotguns and old army uniforms, and wooden radios; there were books and model ships and Turkish rugs and an old shoeshine stand.

For six straight hours, items kept coming out of Wanamaker Studios. And every single item sold.

At 3:17 P.M., the last item was auctioned off: a brass NCR cash register from the 1950s. And then it was over.

Auctioneer Sammy thanked everyone for coming and motioned people toward the gates where parking attendants would help them get out safely. The crowd reluctantly moved through the gate as crowd control officials monitored everything to discourage anyone from trying to sneak a peek inside the studio building.

"Construction going on in there, folks," Sammy announced to two elderly women as they reached for the studio door. "It's not safe."

"Oh." They blushed, pretending they thought the door to the old studio was the way out.

The crowd moved slowly through the fenced gate. Then the gate was locked behind them. The sign was left on as the crowd drove away.

After we paid Sammy and his team, the auction generated $143,523.50 for us. Which, after paying for the construction, will be a decent start for our next project.

So, dear reader, how did all of these items get inside a studio that never existed? How did a scrap building with a scrap studio sign end up being filled with such incredible treasures?

The answer is, it didn't. The building was empty when we bought it. Well, it held a few pieces of rusted pipe, just like somebody's uncle or somebody's cousin had said so many years before. But nothing else.

The auction was all Dutch's idea. We moved all the items from Bugby's storage unit, all the things from the old Hotel Denning, into Wanamaker's and then we auctioned them off from there.

We never said that we would be auctioning off *the contents of the old studio*; we just said we would be holding an auction *at the old studio.*

Now, in the end, everything that was purchased had a value far above what was paid. All of it will increase in price. We took advantage of no one. But nostalgia and competition are a curious mix, and the event definitely drove the sale prices higher than we could have expected.

John Wanamaker, a man who wanted the events of commerce to be remembered, who wanted them to be an experience rather than just a task, would have been proud.

We had made a profit. But more important, we had preserved a legend. Each item brought out provided further validation of the old studio's long pedigree. And that was the ultimate goal.

There are so few good legends left.

So, we now have our offices: the official corporate office of Gopher Ink, at the Wanamaker Studios building, Erie waterfront, Erie, Pennsylvania.

But that's not the best part. We've formed a company and we have a plan. After the auction, we sent out a press release announcing that our new venture would be moving into the newly constructed offices at Wanamaker Studios.

The reaction was just what we expected. Anger. Phone calls. Kyle Somebody left a message asking me how much of *his* money I had already spent on this company I was creating. I even received a few more death threats, and there was a letter to the editor in the paper calling Dutch an "opportunistic sellout."

Then we let *him* loose.

Him, the one who had been salivating, yanking at his chain, waiting for his chance to attack and run and eat. He, who had smelled the blood of opportunity and lusted to get at it.

And Dutch and I sat back and watched him.

Within a week, the tide had shifted. It became its own tidal bore, defying the flow and smashing against the normal path. And then the waters moved the other way.

We did not attack those who threatened us; we let those who were fighting us fight each other. We did not brawl; we shifted. We did not clash; we rerouted. And soon the bubbling all around us had stalled and moved counterclockwise.

We are no longer afraid and we will no longer hide. Things are going to be different now.

Mott is seeing to that.

Chapter 28

The Billings Gazette

| August 27, 1992 |

If your vacation plans this season include a visit to the flagship city of Erie, Pennsylvania, then the Erie Tourism Board would like to remind you that although we have a lot to offer our visitors—the Erie Zoo, the Warner Theatre, a fun downtown area—it's important to note that we are not known for our sunny days and fair weather.

I know. Weird, huh?

In fact, just like Cleveland, Ohio, Erie is often referred to as "the mistake by the lake," and for good reason.

The annual rainfall in Erie averages forty-three inches. To give you a comparison, Seattle, Washington—often touted as the gloomiest place west of London—receives only a paltry thirty-eight inches.

And as far as snowfall, Erie acquires roughly eighty inches of snow a year, which is only eighteen inches less than Anchorage, Alaska—or, as we refer to eighteen inches of snow here, "a heavy dusting."

In Erie, it can be sunny and mild in the morning and by early afternoon you might have three feet of the snow—or the equivalent, about four inches of rain.

This is just what happens when you build a city on the shore of a ten-thousand-square-mile lake. But those of us who live here have become accustomed to it. It is simply the way life is here, and as a third-generation Erie native, I am here to tell you that this is how life has always been.

Now, you would think that by living in such extreme weather, we would become hypersensitive to it—that it would keep us ready and alert, like prairie dogs that sniff the air and prepare to slide underground at the first sign of trouble. But it does not.

It's not that we don't notice or care about the weather. We do. It's more like we are immune to it. Unshaken by it. It's as if the weather happens around us, rather than *to* us.

We don't race to the grocery store to buy all the bacon and toilet paper we can carry at the first sign of heavy snow. Nope. What normal person here wouldn't already have bacon and toilet paper stockpiled? We don't search every hardware store for a generator just because the Weather Channel's predicting three feet of snow on Saturday. Are you kidding? What kind of lunatic would live here without a generator? That would be the same as running out to buy shingles at the first sign of rain.

Cloudy skies are simply normal to us. Average. Even the sunny days here, the fair ones, the perfect ones, don't really excite us. This is either from a *don't get too attached* reaction, or merely one of simple indifference; it's like seeing a Porsche or a beach house, or some other luxury you know you will never, ever possess. And since there is no possible way you will ever own a yacht or a Learjet, why get excited when you see one? If you don't get excited when you see one, then the item in question has no power over you. It produces no lust or desire in you.

But I have to admit, there was something about the warmth of the sun as it hit my face that morning when I finally got out of the hospital. There was something about that blue sky and that warm breeze as Dutch rolled me outside that I will never, ever forget. In that moment, all my Erie training, the decades that prepared me to be nonplussed and unfazed by blue skies and warm breezes, failed me. I dared to appreciate the day. To love it.

It was the most beautiful day I had ever seen.

Now, in fairness, it most likely had nothing to do with the nice weather. It's entirely possible that I would have loved lightning, or rain, or locusts, or whatever other conditions were outside that building right then. Most likely, it was not the condition of the outside world that I found beautiful, but the outside itself. It's entirely plausible that my focus was more on what was beyond those hospital walls than the weather. Between the shooting and the surgery and weeks recovering from some kind of unexpected hospital-acquired infection, it felt like I'd been stuck there forever. What was outside held the same power as Bugby's letter to me in prison: It was evidence of something different and new—something that was about to get better.

Things, they were a changin'.

My nurse's name was Brianna, or Bonnie, or Betty, or—well, I'm not really sure, because every time she told me her name I was extremely stoned on painkillers, and after a while—by the time I should have memorized her name, address, and the first, middle, and last names of her entire extended family—I was too embarrassed to ask her to repeat it again. So I just avoided using her name.

Beatrice or Bella rolled me out of my hospital room for the last time, but it was Dutch who got me from the elevator to the front door—in direct violation of hospital liability policies—and rolled me into that resplendent day.

After first being released from the hospital—after going from my bed to the wheelchair to make my exit from the Hamot Hilton—Barbette or Brenda wheeled me to the elevator and Dutch followed.

The police guard at my hospital room was gone. He had been gone for days—there'd been no need for him since Mott got involved—and even his chair had been taken away.

Right when the elevator door shut—when it made that *swooosh* sound—as if on cue, the blood drained from Beth or Blaire's face. Worry and fear and panic bubbled up in her and we could see the true realization of what she was about to do set in.

Her brow furrowed. Her hands tightened on the handles of the wheelchair, and you could witness the concern rising up inside her. Blythe or Brandi was thinking a) that she was now pushing a man in a wheelchair whom people wanted dead; or b) that she was now pushing a man in a wheelchair into an angry mob of people, all of whom wanted him dead; or c) that she was pushing a man in a wheelchair into an angry mob of people who all wanted him dead, and that man could not even remember her name.

It was then that Dutch saw the look on her face. And he took over.

"No sense in you getting caught up in all them reporters," he said, smiling, moving his hand over to take one of the handles of the wheelchair.

Bridgette or Benita did an honorable job of pretending to protest. She told us about insurance procedures, protocol, policy, and all the time her eyes were begging us to find a way to release her and still save her job.

"I'll leave the wheelchair by the door," Dutch said. He placed his hand over the second blue plastic handle. The elevator door opened and Dutch rolled me out. The door closed behind us and Brooke or Babs rode down the elevator, and I never got to thank her for keeping me alive.

We rolled out into the lobby. The empty lobby. The empty and quiet and open lobby, with carpeted floors and tall beams and a wide area that was completely free of reporters and onlookers and police. We rolled through the lobby and toward the large glass doors, and it was then that I saw that sky. That amazing clear blue sky.

There was no one outside. No one. It had all worked exactly the way we had hoped. The vultures were now all feeding on themselves.

The idea to partner with Benjamin Mott came to me only a few days before the auction. Mott was an enigma. A mystery. He was a vulture, yes, but a vulture who could get into a police safehouse whenever he wanted to visit Dutch. He was a vulture who could simply nod at the police guard outside my hospital room and waltz in, day or night. He was a vulture, sure, but a vulture with some viable skills.

"I want you to listen to me," I had said calmly to Mott over the phone that day from my hospital bed. "Because this is the luckiest day of your life."

Mott listened as I rolled out our plan.

The concept focused on two areas. The first had to do with the media—the reporters, the journalists, the people who made a living finding scandals and hype. The second focus was the crowds—the onlookers. The vengeful. Those who preyed upon Dutch and me. Those who called us and threatened and bargained and blackmailed.

They all had to go.

So, here is how it worked.

A standard lawsuit is a simple process. A man slips on a wet floor in a restaurant and falls and breaks his hand. The man is a concert cellist and may never play his beloved cello again. So he sues the negligent business for the loss of his career. The restaurant chain settles out of court—where many lawsuits end up—and the ex-cellist receives a tidy sum of money—minus thirty percent for the attorney who represented him—and he changes careers and buys a bike shop.

That's how it normally works. We, however, wanted to change the process. First of all, we didn't want to sue *anyone*; we wanted Mott to sue *everyone*. We didn't want to be the ones suing. We didn't want to be the one to profit from it; Mott would be.

"Think of it as a franchise opportunity," I told Mott over the phone that day. "We are giving you the financial right to profit from anyone who threatens, blackmails, or generally gets in our way. You are not only the attorney, but you are the party suing. You are the one to manage, to warn, and to settle. You can say you're doing this as a concerned citizen."

"A concerned citizen?" Mott laughed.

"And we will reverse the fee structure. You get seventy percent of whatever you collect and you give us a thirty percent franchise fee."

Mott stopped laughing.

"The key is, you become the front man. You become *the party of the first part.* You are not only the attorney; you are the one suing."

"As a concerned citizen," he said.

"Yup. That's the good news," I said. "The bad news is, the first time someone gets us involved in any of your efforts . . ." I spoke slowly, letting my new, powerful voice kick in. "The first time someone slips by you and gets to us, the first phone call we receive, the first threat made against us . . . game over." I let this sink in a bit. "You'll be done. And we'll find someone else."

Mott was quiet for a long time. And just as I was about to ask if he was still there, he spoke. "I will have something written up today and I will bring it over for your . . ."

"No, you won't," I said. "We'll partner with you, Mott; we'll put our safety in your hands. But we don't trust you. We're not signing anything."

"What? Look, I don't care if you trust me, but there has to be . . ."

"Why would I want an unethical man to write a contract with the very party he's going to profit from? I would need an attorney to protect me from my attorney."

"But there needs to be an agreement that . . ."

"We are not signing anything," I repeated. "This will all be a verbal agreement only, all subject to change at our slightest whim. If we wake up one morning and decide we don't like that cheap aftershave you use, or if Dutch decides he's still pissed off at the lies you told him, then poof. You're gone. You figure out how to make that legal on your end, but neither of us will sign anything. And that is nonnegotiable."

I allowed a few moments of silence to build up.

"But if you don't like that idea, then we can part ways right now and we will call another attorney . . ."

"I didn't say that," Mott snapped. "It's not how I like to do things, but I'm still interested."

Mott was silent—deep in thought, I suppose, for several minutes—no doubt trying to find a way to still screw us as well as the general public. Then he finally spoke.

"All right," Mott said. "I'm in."

"Great," I said. "Then call one of your town meetings, or press conferences, or whatever it is you do, and get to work."

And he did.

Later that day—don't ask me how he put it together so quickly—Dutch and I were camped out in my hospital room waiting for the evening news to begin.

The television screen flickered as we flipped to channel 24 and watched an antacid commercial. Then we watched a promo for *Star Trek: The Next Generation* and then a trailer for the film *The Last of the Mohicans,* where Daniel Day-Lewis paddles a canoe over a waterfall.

"Do you want to see that?" Dutch asked.

"Maybe. I guess. You?"

"I don't know." Dutch watched the images passively. "Maybe."

The trailer ended and the Erie ABC affiliate, WJET, began the 6:00 P.M. news slot. The intro rolled and then the smiling face and flaxen hair of Jennifer Antkowiak filled the screen. She greeted us warmly—as she always did—and then she began with a national story on how the image of the younger Elvis Presley had been chosen over the older Elvis for the new U.S. postage stamp.

"What?" I pushed the button to raise the back of the hospital bed higher. "They don't want the old and bloated Elvis on the stamp?"

"Wow," Dutch said, looking back at the wall clock, then at the mounted television. "Weird."

The clocked ticked. We watched film clips of both fat Elvis and skinny Elvis gyrating on the screen as an unseen voice told us about the countless hours spent working through this difficult decision. Then, at 6:06 P.M., just as Mott had promised, Jennifer's smiling face came back on screen. She shuffled papers, turned to one camera, then the other, and before we could hear what she was saying, the image of Mott's huge head, perched on his tiny shoulders, filled the screen.

"There he is." Dutch pointed.

"Yup."

Mott stood behind a podium and shuffled his own pile of important papers. It was the typical setting for such an important announcement: a large oak podium with several news microphones mounted to it—there were all the local news logos, some national, and even CNN's bold logo was there. A light brown tapestry hung behind Mott, along with both an American flag and a state flag of Pennsylvania.

This setting stated that whoever this man was, whatever he had to say, it must be important. And I could picture it all through Erie—in bars, in diners, in living rooms, in beauty shops—people were seeing Mott's massive head and this setting, and responding with interest and maybe a little fear.

"Shut up," they'd say, and point at the screen. "Something's going on."

Benjamin Mott took a moment to scan the crowd. He shuffled his papers again. And then he began to speak.

"Thank you all for coming," he said, in his gravest tone. "I'll be brief."

What power did Mott possess that he could put on such a show? What photographs did he have in a safe? What favors were owed to him where in a few hours he could pull off such a grand media sensation?

"There comes a time in an attorney's career," Mott began, "when he comes to the crossroads of what is right and what is profitable." The sound of camera shutters clicked in the background.

"We have all been at these crossroads before," he said. "I have been there many times myself. And I have always taken the easy path—the one paved with safety and security and, of course . . ." He paused. "With profit."

Mott stopped, allowing a moment for the audience to appreciate this revelation that he, a lawyer, had at one time actually been motivated by money. He gathered his thoughts and continued: "I admit that I have always, *always,* chosen the easy path. I have always followed the money trail." Mott paused dramatically and looked at every unseen face watching him. "But no more," he said, shaking his head earnestly. "No more."

"Wow," Dutch said to the television. "Where is he, anyways?"

"Not sure," I answered. "Some press room somewhere."

"So," Mott continued, "it is to the deep regret of my banker . . ." Another pause. "But to the great excitement of my priest . . ." Another breath, as if the big man were contemplating his selfless and bold decision. "That at this time I would like to announce that I am taking a sabbatical as an attorney." Another pause. "Because I have once again come to that moral fork in the road. And for the first time in my career, and possibly in my life, I am choosing the right path. The difficult path."

Mott went on to tell the audience that he—the noble and selfless civil servant—had formed a foundation: the Benjamin Mott Ethical Foundation for Justice—really, that's what he called it—that would protect and secure the rights of citizens. He went on to say that he had been monitoring the public and press manipulation of what he called "the Walker Roe and Riley Dutcher affair." His foundation would not stand for the kind of injustices he had witnessed.

"The Walker Roe and Riley Dutcher affair?" Dutch repeated, walking toward the television.

I located the television remote and turned up the volume. "Sounds like a made-for-TV-movie to me."

"Or like we're getting engaged."

Mott went on to describe what had driven him to make this noble and selfless decision.

". . . the gross misconduct, illegal attacks, persecution, and threats against the safety and personal freedom of these two Americans is revolting." Mott's fist slammed against the podium as flash bulbs popped all around him. "What have they done? What crime have they been accused of? What warrants are being served against them? What laws have been broken? None. None. NONE! The last time I checked, the U.S. Constitution was still in effect. The last time I checked, every American was due the right to face his accuser. Therefore, I have approached these two men and acquired this." Mott waved a thick, dog-eared document in the air.

"What's that?" Dutch asked.

I laughed. "A prop."

"This," Mott said, in much lower, more controlled tone, "is the first of its kind in American jurisprudence. *This* gives average Americans the right to be protected in the same way we protect corporations and special interest groups. *This* will allow me to take on the burden, the ugliness, the dirty work that needs to be done in order to protect the persecuted from the public."

"Hey, we're little guys again," I said.

"It allows *me* to be the fall guy, the heavy, the one willing to do the dirty work for the average citizen and stop the injustices that are taking root in this nation."

Mott explained that he would sue anyone—and everyone—who made a physical, verbal, or financial attack against the two people his foundation was protecting: me and Dutch.

"What is wrong with this country?" Mott wailed. "When we spend millions to save an owl or a seal but we allow human beings to be run over like freight trains and then we can't wait to watch the destruction on the nightly news?"

Before the reporters at Mott's press conference could ask any questions, Mott went on to describe the second phase of the plan. This involved the Kyle Somebodys, the angry onlookers, those people who threatened and pursued us.

Mott went on to describe how he had the right to file lawsuits against anyone and everyone who threatened the life, freedom, or safety of either me or Dutch. In his former life—not now, of course; he was completely different now—he said he had enjoyed lawsuits and had made millions—yes, he said he made *millions of dollars* for his clients.

"Now," he said, waving his prop pile of documents, "I have the burden of being both the one suing and the one who profits from it. And I will oppose with every element of the law anyone who threatens these two men."

The Darwinism of media is very simple—especially where it concerns the bold and the sensational. When some huge story rocks the media world for a few months, all the fish come to feed. The big fish go for the exclusives, using money and pressure to get those important and rare interviews. The rest of the fish nibble around the edges, getting an interview with the gardener, the babysitter, the drinking buddy, or taking a slant from the childhood sweetheart. They all do anything they can think of to get a piece of the prize.

This story becomes a product—an extremely sought after and marketable commodity that needs to be delivered to the public before its shelf life expires. The media have money and influence and pressure to spend. The public is hungry. The people involved in the story know they will need to speak to someone, so why not get the best deal for it?

This is why Bill and Hillary Clinton sit down *only* with Diane Sawyer to give their exclusive at-home interview. Mike Tyson talks *only* to Larry King about the rape charges. He talks to Larry and then Larry is quoted and repeated and cut and diced by all the other media outlets that want to get to Mike. Newspapers and TV channels are now forced to quote Diane Sawyer on some unknown fact that was revealed from her story. A small daily paper in Nashville that wants to take a different slant on the Tyson story is forced to research the details from the Larry King transcript. In effect, the reporter, the interviewer, the one who got the exclusive, now becomes the celebrity. He shifts position with whatever *fifteen-minutes-of-famer* is hot right then and thereby becomes their stand-in.

This is why exclusive deals are so coveted on both ends. The media buy it and package it and sell the pieces. The individual, who found himself in scandal and possibly in some trouble, needs to take advantage of the situation and profit from it. These interviews happen when the right amount of money or pressure is put on the person to be interviewed—or, more accurately, on that person's lawyer or mother or agent or business partner—until it becomes too much, too big, to refuse. This is the world of the exclusive, where only the big boys can play.

It was not going to happen to us.

Dutch and I knew we had to talk to someone from the media. We knew we had to release the pressure or it would continue to grow and everything would just feed around us. The pressure would be on Catherine and the girls, on Dutch's friends, on Bugby's reputation and name. Someone would find a story somehow, and the exclusive would go to whoever could write the biggest check.

So we would give one exclusive interview. And we would do it in a way that would not only reduce the pressure on us, but would actually point the pressure away.

After Mott announced our plan at his press conference, Dutch decided to flip channels and see what the response was on CNN and the local Erie channels. All of them were covering it. Even with the growing saga of Amy Fisher, we were still hot news.

The plan was this: We would give one exclusive interview. Just one. But we would not choose according to who would write the biggest check. Anyone who wanted to interview us could apply and we would choose one. Just one. It didn't matter what size the newspaper or television station, radio station, or media conglomerate was. It didn't matter how inexperienced or how little influence they carried. Everyone would have an equal opportunity and we would give the interview at no cost. If you had a press card, you had a chance. And one news source would be granted the sole interview and would receive all the rewards—and all the curse.

The fallout was bigger than we expected. We upset the media hierarchy. We had thumbed our nose at Diane Sawyer and Larry King and now, the face of Tracy Parrows, from the *Billings Gazette*, could be seen on every TV channel.

Who? Yup, thirty-eight-year-old mother of two Tracy Powers from the *Billings Gazette.*

If it wasn't Amy Fisher, it was us. Then, if it wasn't Amy, it was—Tracy. Tracy was taking our place. Tracy was the Walker and Dutch poster child. We gave her our one and only interview. And Amy Fisher turned into a back-burner story.

Dutch and I sat in the same room where we had held Abby's birthday party and we talked to Tracy, the overweight, nervous reporter from the *Billings Gazette*. And we told her—everything.

Boom. The transfer was made.

And after that, every phone call, every answering machine message, every letter we or Catherine or Dutch's friend Randy received, we turned over to Mott.

The results were quick. We received only two calls the next day.

And after that, there were none.

And then I was rolled in my wheelchair out through the hospital door where I stood and walked under that clear blue sky. The driveway in front of the hospital entrance was empty. There were no protesters or spectators. Our plan had worked. They were all feeding on themselves.

Anthony Robbins wrote that people overestimate what they can accomplish in one year, but underestimate all they can accomplish in ten. And although this might be true, I now know that people underestimate what they can accomplish in a day. Or a week. Or a month.

Dutch saved my life on July 28, 1992. That was a month ago. And in that time, the whole world changed.

In just a few weeks, we had all rewired.

Chapter 29

The Desk

| August 28, 1992 |

Does anyone know where in Erie, Pennsylvania, one might go to get a Viking helmet? A size medium, girl's, not too expensive, original helmet with the fur, and not a plastic copy? Because my daughter *needs* one.

"You *need* one, or you *want* one?" I asked.

Liz stood in front of me—somewhere in front of me. I really couldn't tell exactly because she was standing behind the stacks of new office equipment piled on and around my desk. But I could hear her and I knew she was standing somewhere in the room.

"I *need* one!" she said. I could hear the tone in her voice—it perfectly conveyed that one word: *need.* It was desire mixed with urgency—not pleading, just a burning request for something essential, required, and absolutely necessary.

"Why do you need it?" I asked.

Then she told me. And when she spoke, I knew that Liz did, in fact, *need* a Viking helmet. She needed it the same way old women need sweaters and salesmen need good jokes. And that's why I have to find her one.

See, the desk that was blocking Liz from view was actually too large for such a small room—I don't even know how we got it in there—but it was a great desk and the moment I saw it I knew how important a find it was.

The desk was heavy, blocky, and ugly. It was scratched and pocked with years of use that would have ruined a prettier piece of furniture but gave character to such a strong and industrial boulder of wood. It was also the only item that I scavenged for myself from Bugby's storage unit.

I saw the desk only a moment before Iggy found the Bricklin. Well, I saw a corner of it—the dark oak surface, oiled by decades of hands—and

I was about to remove the clutter to reveal more of the surface when I was forced to stop and focus on getting the Bricklin out of its tomb.

Wait. You know what's funny? Right now, as I write this, my leg has just begun to throb—it happens every time I think of Iggy or Fleece or the storage unit. Every single time. As soon as my mind trips across any of those things, the switch is flipped and the pain begins at the point of the gunshot. Weird, huh?

I've been going to physical therapy, where I get stretched, bent, and beaten up. There are aches and pains but never a consistent dull pain like I get when I think about the Bricklin or the storage unit or Iggy or Fleece. In a month, my mind has already hardwired those memories directly to the point where the bullet entered my leg.

Wow. Is that really all the time it's been? Just a month? That's even more amazing.

But now the old desk is here. At Wanamaker Studios. It was brought here and placed in this new office that smells like fresh paint and brand-new carpeting.

The desk never belonged to anyone important—at least, not in the world's sense of the word. It was not a banker's desk or an attorney's. Most likely, it came from the old Union Station train terminal or the Erie docks or from the Hotel Denning. It was a working man's desk, a desk that had been used to fill out invoices as well as to fix a jammed gearbox or two. I had always been leery of pompous desks, of walking into an office decorated with a truck-sized block of solid, gleaming mahogany that demanded tribute—and therefore demanded that you honor and respect its owner as well. But this piece was different. This was an old desk. This was a working man's desk and it had been used for many years by Erie men.

These men had callused hands and after decades of hard work were finally enjoying the title of foreman or supervisor or chief. These were men who were respected because they had worked alongside the very people they now managed. They were still one of the gang, only now they were in charge.

These men smoked Camel nonfilters and cussed and kept a bottle of Old Forester bourbon in the bottom drawer for hard days and celebrations. At lunch—on those rare, clear days—they would carry a brown bag outside to eat boiled eggs, sliced carrots, and thick ham sandwiches made on bread bought at the Majestic Bakery. They would sit with the very men they managed, while they planned and complained and dreamed.

This desk was Erie. So I saved it and had it brought here—to Wanamaker Studios.

The construction of the interior of Wanamaker Studios began even before the auction—the building itself was simply a shell with a dirt floor. We hired a construction firm called O'Brian's Mechanical, out of Pittsburgh, and we instructed them that we had already paid to have the studio gutted and the old rotted floor removed—this was Dutch's idea, to help keep the building's legend going. We told them we just wanted a new floor put in. Nothing else. Once the floor was complete, we hired movers to take the contents of Bugby's storage unit and place everything inside the studio building instead. Then we hired another company, Woshen Contractors, to design and reconstruct the inside of the studio building once the auction was complete.

And thus, a legend was preserved.

Now, the final construction was fairly simple. It entailed running electric, heating, air conditioning, and plumbing to the building, then repairing and painting the basic structure of the Quonset hut. We added two skylights and four larger windows to bring in natural light. We had carpeting installed and permanent walls put up for offices. Because the building was a Quonset hut—basically just a large curved arch—we did not create traditional offices, just walls and doors without ceilings—no matter where you were in the studio, when you looked up you could see the slow-moving ceiling fans and the large skylights—which gave the place a very artistic look. There was a reception desk and a small lobby and even a kitchen in the back. And within a few days of the auction, we had our base camp. Wanamaker Studios was complete and we moved in.

Now, we don't actually *live* here. I'm still at my place in Divorce Court and Dutch is still staying at Bugby's old place. But we moved our newly formed company—Gopher Ink—here.

We work here now. Dutch, me, and our new office manager, Phoebe—who has taken a leave of absence from Mathis and Corbin to come and work with us.

Phoebe wanted to quit Mathis and Corbin entirely, but we wouldn't allow it. The goal of Gopher Ink—which is more of an "un-company" than a company—is to be completely broke in less than three years. We have a business plan: We will help the people we can and begin the process. We will do what we need to do. We will get the wheels turning. Then, when we are out of money, we will shut the doors—broke and penniless. If our calculations are correct, then that should be in two years, twelve weeks, and four days—give or take.

How's that for a mission statement?

My girls spend a lot of time here. Abby spends most of her time with Phoebe, setting up offices and software, arranging furniture, and basically taking charge of the place. But Liz—ah, Liz. She spends most of her time on patrol.

This is what she calls it—patrol. Every day, she walks along the perimeter of the studio fence—not like a caged animal, like something trapped inside and trying to get out. No, she walks like a warrior princess examining her territory. She is proud. She dares anyone to step across into her domain. Liz is itching for a fight.

Once, I walked past my office window and saw Liz standing outside near the fence with her hands on her hips, staring at the water. At first, I assumed she was preparing for some great attacking horde of ships that she imagined moving toward us. But a few minutes later, when I walked by the window again, I saw her target: An aggressive reporter—a young guy, thin, with Ray-Ban sunglasses and a heavy camera hanging around his neck—stood next to his car near the docks. He would look around innocently—angry that Liz had spotted him—then climb back in the car. Then he would step back out and point the camera at Liz. Then he would step back in his car.

Liz dared the reporter to use the camera and thereby unleash her wrath—and of course, the wrath of Benjamin Mott.

Now, if this guy was a real reporter—someone on the payroll of a news agency—then he would have broken the media agreement we made. If he was a freelancer or just a curious spectator, he would risk a civil lawsuit. Either way, Mott would eat him alive.

Liz stood near the fence. She made overdramatic poses for the poor kid. She had a large piece of cardboard where she had written in chalk the reporter's license plate number—a sign to the poor sap that Mott would find out who he was—and she waved it, like a ring girl at a prizefight.

Phoebe and I watched it all from my office window. The reporter would raise the camera. He would put it down. He would step back in the car and then he would get back out, angry. He did this, over and over, for twenty minutes. Eventually, good sense came over the poor schlump and he drove off. Bested by a nine-year-old.

"When I get my Viking helmet," she said, walking back into the building, "he'll know who I am and he'll tell his friends. He'll tell them to watch out for the little girl with the Viking helmet."

Which is why I have to find her one. To help spread the fear of Elizabeth Roe.

Not all the vultures have given up entirely. Kyle Somebody is still around. And he's gone completely off the rails. Way, way off.

Now, I have to admit, I have actually been . . . well, enjoying Kyle's journey into madness. In fact, I started keeping track of all of his messages so I could see exactly how his mind was linking everything together. It's fun.

Out of the one conversation I had with Kyle—he had obviously imagined many more, conversations where he had me agreeing and committing to transactions I had never heard of—Kyle had, well . . .

Here are just a few of Kyle's messages over a six-day time period:

BEEP. Yeah, this is Kyle. Look, Walker, we need to talk. I need to know when I can get that money. Things are beginning to pile up here and I . . .

BEEP. Hey, Walker. It's Kyle. Call me when you can. Thanks.

BEEP. Yeah, hey, this is Kyle. Hey . . . I'm going to have to (muffled). Have to add a few thousand more to that amount we spoke about, pal. Things aren't too good at work and I . . .

BEEP. Hey, Walker. It's Kyle. Call me. I'll be here all night. Thanks a lot, buddy.

BEEP. Hey, Walker, it's Kyle. Look, great news. I figured something out that's (muffled). That's really cool. So . . . wow, okay, you have, like, nineteen million, right? And I only need forty grand. So, I figured it out and that . . . that's .002 percent. Isn't that cool? That's so good for you. That's . . . *not even a full percent* of the . . .

BEEP. Walker. It's Kyle. Call me.

BEEP. Hey, Walker. If you get this, turn on the TV to Channel 23. Quick. Oh man, the blue boat they are showing at the boat show is the one I was talking about. It's gorgeous. It—is—soooo SWEET! That's the one I'm going to get, buddy. Call me. Whoooo!

BEEP. Hey, Walker. It's Kyle. Call me. Please. Thanks.

BEEP. Walker, this is Kyle. Hey, ya know . . . I've been thinking about that forty grand and . . .

BEEP. Walker, I was just thinking and . . . hey, I figure you—well, this is what I was thinking. . . . Okay, so . . . so, you lived in the building next to Bugby. Right? But I lived . . . I lived in *the very same building as him.* Right? I mean, in the same building and only a floor below him—so. So, yeah. It's . . . It kind of . . . well, makes you see it kind of . . . kind of differently, huh? I mean . . .

BEEP. Hey, Walker. It's Kyle. I went to your apartment but you wasn't . . . you weren't there. So I slipped that paperwork under your door. Did you get it? I have it all figured out how we . . .

BEEP. Hey, buddy, this is Kyle. Hey, give me a call when you get this and we can go grab a beer tonight. My treat. We need this to (muffled), and just kick back and relax for a while, huh? It'll be nice to just forget about everything for a few hours and . . .

BEEP. Hey, it's Kyle. Well, it's official. I've lost my job. Yup. Can you believe . . . after three years at that dump and they (screaming but muffled). Ughh. Losers. So call me, because I am going to need to wrap this (muffled) thing up and . . .

BEEP. Walker? Call me today. I need to . . .

BEEP. Walker. This is Kyle. Give me a call when you get this. Thanks, pal.

BEEP. Walker. This is Kyle. What the hell? Huh? I mean—I just got a letter from the apartment complex saying that the rent is past due. What is this all about? You and I talked about this, remember? And we decided that I wouldn't pay rent no more. Remember? This was all . . .

BEEP. Hey, man. It's Kyle. Call me.

BEEP. Walker, I need to hear from you *today*. Some lawyer is harassing me about contacting you. Threatening to sue me. Sue me? SUE ME?!?! For what? I should be suing—for getting what is mine? And you need to fix this apartment thing. I'm getting . . .

BEEP. Walker. WHERE. THE. HELL. IS. MY. MONEY? Huh? Hey, I'm sorry for being a jerk about this, but come on. This has gone on long enough and . . . you and me had a plan. Remember? And that plan can still work if you . . .

BEEP. (in a very slurred voice) Let me . . . explain this one last, one last time (pause). That money is no more yours than it's the queen of—queen of England's. It's a fluke. It's everybody's. The guy who lived . . . lived in the very next building from me gave it away to . . . to all of us. So what you are . . . going to do today, is . . .

BEEP. Hey, Walker. Sorry about last night. I was just a little pissed because of this—this apartment thing. I'm staying at my mom's for a while. So call . . .

Actually, I'm not so sure Kyle is funny anymore. No. Now he's a little frightening. And he's also a little—missing.

Benjamin Mott—the man who can walk into police safehouses and guarded hospital rooms, and set up multi-network press conferences with a day's notice—can't find him.

"Not a trace," Mott said, in his exhausted, *Look how dedicated I am to you* tone. "No credit card transactions. No ATM records. I even have a man watching his mother's house. Nothing."

"So where do you think he is?"

Mott sighed, as he shuffled papers and ordered underlings around. "Hiding. Drunk. On the run, or all three. Either way, Walker, I don't think he'll be a problem any longer."

But I don't know if that's true. Kyle is furious at us—at me, mostly. He is angry at how Dutch and I are spending *his money*—that's what he calls it. *His money.* Kyle has reasoned that it was simply a random event that Bugby left everything to me and not to him. Just a fluke. After all, he rented an apartment from Bugby just like I did—even though I don't think he ever actually met Bugby—so the money could just as easily have been his. And every day, in every message, his mind convinces him even more that this is true.

And this is part of everyday life here at Gopher Ink—the first company of its kind, by the way. The first true un-company ever.

Un-company.

Un-company is a Dutch thing, and that's what we are forming.

Chapter 30

Gopher Ink

| August 30, 1992 |

We were all exhausted—Phoebe, Dutch, the girls, and me. It had been a long day—a productive day but a very long one—and I'm not sure how it happened but we all ended up lying on the new carpet of the studio with the lights off, looking up at the stars through the skylight. It was Liz's idea to turn the lights off and once we did it, we could not believe how many stars fit in that little window in the corrugated roof. Millions of them.

We were content and sleepy from all the work we had done—and all the pizzas and sodas we had just devoured—and were just lying there. Quiet and happy. Pleased and proud. And then Liz made the request I had been waiting for.

"Abercrombie, Dad."

I let the words hang in the air for a moment—as all good showmen should—then began the story.

ABERCROMBIE . . .

It is a part of worldwide law, in every civilized country in every continent in the world, that legal documents—checks, contracts, agreements—cannot be signed in pencil. The graphite of the pencil is too fragile, too temporary, too unstable. A signature in pencil can easily be erased, altered, or can simply fade off the page. So any document signed in pencil is not considered binding.

For a contract to be complete, it must first be signed by all parties in ink. *This is the law. Ink is permanent. Ink is lasting, and a contract signed in ink is considered complete and in effect.*

But a contract signed in Gopher Ink goes well beyond that.

"What's Gopher Ink?" *Liz Roe peered inside the small glass bottle that sat on the old desk. The elixir inside sparkled and glowed.*

"Gopher Ink is very rare," her father answered. "It can only be made by the Gopher Queen herself."

"What makes it so rare?" Abby asked.

Walker Roe uncorked the bottle and stepped back. There was a slight crackle as a puff of red smoke rose from the opening.

"Is it safe?" Phoebe asked, waving the smoke away from her eyes.

"Safer than that coffee you drink."

"Where did you get this Gopher Ink?" Dutch leaned in to look down into the bottle.

"Oh, I have a connection."

Liz and Abby smiled at each other—realizing that their brother, Abercrombie, was the only "connection" their father had.

Walker reached into the desk drawer and pulled out a small package wrapped in cloth. He opened it to reveal a vintage fountain pen. Walker carefully dipped the tip of the pen into the bottle and drew the ink into the chamber.

"Gopher Ink goes beyond being the most permanent ink in the world. It is the most binding because the ink looks into your intentions."

"My what?" Dutch asked.

"It looks into your heart. If you don't intend to hold true to what you're signing, it won't let you sign."

"How can ink do that?'

"No idea." Walker placed the contract on the desk.

"So it's a . . . it's like a truth ink?" Abby asked.

"Sort of. But it goes beyond that. If you believe you will hold to the contract, but you are actually incapable of doing it—if there is something that will stop you from seeing it through—then the ink won't flow. It won't allow you to sign."

The contract was spread out across the desk. It was the legal charter of their new endeavor and their new life. The world's first un-company. Millions of dollars would be spent over the next few years with no intention to recoup any of it. It was all based on an idea a man came up with while fishing: to simply allow people to step back and be kids again for a few months and see what changed in their lives.

It was a longshot. It was a lark.

"Well, let's see if it works." Dutch took the pen and leaned closer to the paper on the desk. He carefully placed the nib of the pen on the line that required his signature. He held it there, afraid to move it. Then he began to sign. The ink flowed freely.

"My turn," Phoebe said. Again, the ink flowed, as it did for Walker and Abby and Liz.

"Well, that's that."

"No, not really," said a voice from the doorway.

The Countess of Backward Clocks barely fit through the doorway of Wanamaker Studios. She was large and out of scale with everything around her. She was also very pissed off.

"Now, here is what is going to happen." The Countess took a step into the office and the five people inside instinctively took a step back. "I'm going to take the ink that will lead me to the Gopher Queen and you're going to try and stop me, and then that insect of yours will show up. Blah, blah, blah. I'm bored with that."

"Then why don't you . . ." Walker said.

Without looking at him, the Countess of Backward Clocks pulled a weapon from her belt. "I'm going to skip ahead and do something different." She pulled the trigger and fired the gun.

The office exploded with sound. The bullet shot out.

And then . . .

There was a pause. No one spoke.

"And then?" Liz sat up on her elbows. "Finish it."

"Yeah, then what?" Phoebe asked. "Get to the part where I save you all."

"No, Abercrombie will save us all," Abby corrected.

"Finish it," Liz demanded.

"That's it for now."

"What?" she snapped.

"That's it."

"That's it?" Dutch complained. "That's not a story, that's a—that's just a beginning."

"What happens?" Liz barked.

"You'll see."

"What do you mean, you'll see?" Phoebe griped.

Abby laughed. "I knew you were going to do that."

"I hate it when he does that," Liz said.

"Yeah, you suck." Dutch laughed.

Then we all laughed.

And then we all went back to looking at the stars.

And twenty minutes later, we were all asleep.

JOURNAL 8

DUTCH

Chapter 31

| August 18, 1992 |

When you think about it, when you really break it all apart, the whole thing actually makes sense. It really makes *soooo* much sense even though at first it was, I don't know, just another crazy idea. Just like, drunk talk without the drinking (ha). Because all it was, was a . . . what's the word? A notion? No, a whimsy. That's it. Or is it? I dunno. And it wasn't even *my* whimsy. It was one of my dad's goofy ideas that he was always talking about and one I hadn't thought about in years. Decades maybe. But for some reason when Walker and me was talking, I mentioned it. It just sort of popped out. And I hadn't thought about it and it was probably the first time I ever said it out loud to anybody and then we really started talking about it and when we was done, it didn't seem so goofy no more.

"We can do it, you know," Walker said, as he was throwing some clothes in a bag, getting ready to get out of the hospital. And he has a look now, Walker does. Maybe he's always had that look but I don't think so. I think this is a look you get once you've been shot. It's the look of knowing a secret or getting to peek at stuff that other people don't get to see. Like, already seeing a movie and watching it again after you know all the tricks.

"We can do this."

This whimsy was one my old man talked about when me and him was fishing. Maybe he talked about it at other times too, but I only remember it from when we was fishing. My dad used to take me fishing all the time and I hated it but I don't remember why. I just know I'd get to the river and slump down on the bank of the Susquehanna, pissed off that my dad made me come. Most times I even refused to put a line in the water. And he'd just stand there next to me, fishing and smiling. Then he'd light up a cigarette. And then he'd go into his speech.

"When I'm king . . ." he'd say. And that's how it started. And for twenty minutes, or an hour if you let him, he'd go on.

"When I'm king, everyone—no exception—will have to serve two years in the army."

"When I'm king, disputes will be solved on the baseball field instead of court."

"When I'm king, no backyard decks will be allowed to be built, only front porches."

"When I'm king, in order to buy a car you'll have to pass a mechanics course."

"When I'm king, you can buy only one luxury item (a boat, a motorcycle, a camper) and then you have to share and borrow from others if you want something else."

"When I'm king, everyone will have their own garden and grow their own food and you can barter with others with the food you grew but you can't buy any."

He would go on about the details of each of his ideas, like, tweaking them as he talked. Like he was planning for the day when the people of the world would finally wake up and elect him king (ha). But he'd always come back to his first idea. His whimsy. His master idea that started it all.

"When I'm king, every adult will have to take a summer job." And that was the big one—the one he would go on about all the eff-ing details. About how once you get settled in your job and all and once you were a doctor, a teacher, or a mailman, you have to take a summer job at least once. And how this works is he, the king, sends someone else to do your real job. Your job will be done well, you won't get fired or nothing, and your job will be waiting for you when the summer is over. The people you work for can't hire the guy that is replacing you. He's only there for the summer and while he is there you still get all the money from your real job for your bills and stuff because the king pays the guy that's doing your job. But now you got to stop being a doctor, accountant, or a car mechanic, and you got to go take a summer job. You can't go lay on a beach somewhere. You got to work as a bike messenger or on a fishing boat. You got to go be one of them characters at the Renaissance Fair, work at the mini-bike track, or spend the summer cooking barbecue at a roadside stand where guys drink cans of beer and tell you stories as they bag up your takeout. Something simple and fun.

"You'll get to pick your own summer job," he'd say. "And the king will set it up." And my dad would go over every effing detail. Every part of the plan where a fifty-year-old office manager gets to work in a bait store for the summer but is still able to pay for junior's braces (ha).

"Youth is wasted on the young, Riley," my dad would say. "You don't realize how great it is to be fifteen until you're fifty and you've missed it."

So.

That's what we're going to do. Me and Walker. We're going to make my dad's king-plan come true. Not for us, if that was what you was thinking. Nope. For everybody else.

August 19, 1992

I saw that weird Marco guy from the Greek restaurant again today when I was walking up toward the parking lot of Mega-Liquor Warehouse (no, I wasn't buying anything; Walker owns it and we've been meeting in the back room to plan stuff until we finish our office). He (Marco, not Walker, ha) was walking up and just staring at me as I was heading toward the front door. I said "Hey," and he said, "Eff you, I'm not afraid of you. Just do it already. Eff you." (I'm writing *eff*, but he said the real word.)

He really did. He just stared right at me and said, "Eff you." I wish I could say it didn't bother me. But it did. Anytime someone says that to me it bothers me.

And he was coming out of the store but he didn't have nothing in his hands neither.

August 25, 1992

I don't like my tattoos no more. I haven't thought of them in a while and I've had them so long that I can look at them and not even think of them. Not even *see* them. But I've been seeing them lately and thinking about them and I don't like them no more. In fact, I hate them now.

I've never been to prison but that's what they call them—prison tattoos. It's just a name they call homemade tattoos and I've never liked that name, neither. I wish they was just called homemade tattoos but they're not. I have three tattoos that I've had for over ten years and I don't like any of them no more and I wish I could take them off.

When we was moving stuff from Walker's hospital room to the car (Walker is out of the hospital now—I think I forgot to tell you), I was lugging a suitcase into the trunk. Abby, Walker's daughter, was walking down with box of stuff with me. I had a T-shirt on and I was putting the bag in the trunk and when I bent into the trunk she saw the ink under my shirt sleeve.

"What's that?" she asked.

I used to like it when people asked about my ink. Proud? I guess, but probably just fake pride. Just getting attention. I'm not sure. But I had already started to hate my tattoos when Abby asked, so there wasn't even fake pride then.

"A tattoo," I said. I rolled up my sleeve and showed it to her. An eight ball on fire. A two-dimensional, blue, faded eight ball with blue flames on top. "A stupid tattoo."

"What does it mean?"

I told Abby how the eight ball was supposed to be good luck. Because it was the last ball on the table and if you had the ball then you was winning, so the eight ball was like, a reminder, to keep winning in life. But Abby told me that if you hit the eight ball in before you're supposed to, if you hit it in early, you lose. She said you had to stay away from the eight ball. So how is it good luck?

How did that kid know about pool?

"Do you have any more tattoos?" she asked.

We walked back into the hospital and we sat in the lobby by the information desk, where the light was better. I showed Abby the sword tattoo on my lower neck, right below the shirt line. The one that was supposed to look just like the tattoo the girl had in the movie *Heavy Metal* but it looks absolutely effing nothing like that sword.

Then I showed her the tattoo under my right sleeve. This was the tattoo that I always showed people last. This was the one that always got me a few free drinks.

"What is it?"

"It's a Celtic cross," I said. "It's what Saint Patrick used to convert the Druids of Ireland."

For some reason, drunks always liked a good story about Saint Patrick. If I was sitting at a bar talking to somebody, just the mention of Saint Patrick, Ireland, a Celtic cross, or even Lucky Charms would usually get a smile and a drink (ha). As if the Irish demanded it.

Abby looked at the intricate lines of the cross.

"This one is much better than the others," she said. Then she stopped and looked up at me, like she had just insulted me and the other tattoos and wanted to make sure I wasn't mad or nothing.

"Yeah, the guy who did *that* one was sober."

I don't like those tattoos no more. But I can't get rid of them so I have to, what's that phrase? Make peace with them.

And that's what I'll do. I'll make peace with them.

August 26, 1992

There's a bunch I forgot to tell you. Like, the weasel lawyer, Mott, is still a weasel. But now he's *our* weasel (ha). Walker and me have this plan. A bunch of plans actually, but first we needed Mott working for us, not against us. So he is now.

How it works is me and Walker agreed to let Mott sue anybody he wants—reporters, TV stations, people from the crowd, that weird Kyle guy that keeps calling Walker for money (did I tell you about him yet?). Anybody and everybody. And Mott gets to keep most of the money he gets or settles for, and he don't have to give us much of it.

Mott loved the idea and he is as loyal as a front-porch dog (or as loyal as weasel lawyers can get, ha). And when he got started, it was almost like a light switch was flipped and all them people just went away. Poof. Once Mott was on a leash (ha), things got quieter. Real quiet. In fact, when Walker left the hospital there was nobody there. No crowds or nothing. Mott had them all running.

And Mott is doing other stuff, too. Walker told me stories about the old waterfront. Stories from when he was little, so I went down there to see it all. It's really neat. Old buildings and ships and you can see for miles across the water. I just walked around and listened to the waves and the whoosh of the smokestacks. And there's this place, this old metal building that is surrounded by fence. It's an old film studio and Walker told me a lot about it. So I started doing some research on it (that's what us sober traveling men do—we do research, ha).

Did you know you could go down to the city records department and ask to see property records and they have to show you? It's true. Mott told me and I didn't believe him at first, but it's the wildest thing. No appointment. No badge. You just walk in and ask to see the records and they show you to a room and let you loose. Like you was a detective or a lawyer. One day when I was there, a lady even asked me if I wanted coffee (ha).

So this studio, this little block of land on the waterfront, was owned by a holding company. It had a separate deed from the rest of the waterfront. So guess what? Me and Walker bought it (ha). The land, the fence, the building, and that great studio sign. All of it.

It's our new office. A place where we can work on my dad's whimsy and let people take summer jobs if they want. Me and Walker are forming a company. Well, it ain't actually a company because companies try to make money and we'll just be spending money (ha). So, it's an un-company, I guess. But that's what we're going to do. We're going to find people and let them be a kid again for the summer.

I know it ain't like curing cancer. I know it don't seem very important, like feeding starving people or building hospitals in the jungle but that's because it's a whimsy. It's just an effing whimsy. But it's still cool. It's still, well, important.

It may not seem like it is, but it is important.

I mean, I got a second chance. Why shouldn't people have the chance to unplug and take a few months to go back and be a kid again, too? Huh? Why shouldn't they be able to stop being a grownup but still take care of the people they need to and see the world through clear kid's eyes, like I did? Eyes that ain't worried about deadlines and sales quotas. Eyes that can know how important turtles and sandwiches made from pumpernickel bread are.

Our un-company is called Gopher Ink and it will take care of everything. If you take a summer job, your old job is safe. Mott will make sure of that. And your new job will be set up by us. We'll even take care of mowing your lawn or fixing the roof or all the responsibilities you have as a grownup (ha), because your job is just to be fifteen again. Just to work at the hot dog stand on the beach or park cars at the hotel and worry about nothing.

Maybe it *is* just as important as other things. Maybe it's more important. I mean, what happens when a chemist comes back from the summer all refreshed and free and alive? What happens when a businessman gets his fire back or an architect has his first original idea in twenty years?

I don't know if this is all because of the very scary thing. I'm not sure. But I do know that things like that probably happen a lot (probably every effing day) and I never noticed them before. Never. I never saw how all them God-pieces of things fit in.

And I don't know if our new company is part of them God-pieces. But I'm dying to find out.

This is going to be so effing cool.

THIS IS THE END OF THE JOURNALS.

Epilogue

Because of Walker Roe's distrust of the media, in September 1992, shortly after Walker and Dutch's murders, Catherine Woods, the former Catherine Roe, worked with attorney Benjamin Mott to further protect the two men's privacy.

Walker Roe's estate, which automatically fell to his two heirs, Elizabeth and Abigail Roe, was transacted under a closed procedure where an elaborate set of investment companies was established. Because of this, and because Lester Bugby himself had a very complicated estate, many have speculated that there are large amounts of money still unaccounted for.

Catherine Woods and Benjamin Mott also had all documentation concerning Gopher Ink removed from Wanamaker Studios. A police inquiry into the murders led to a search of that studio, which Mott was able to prove illegal. The studio and surrounding fence were locked, and outside of a few public business records and many theories, there was little information about the holdings, charter, or purpose of Gopher Ink. No one entered Wanamaker Studios again until the land was sold to the Erie Waterfront Project. The building was demolished in 2004. The Erie Sheraton now sits on the site where Wanamaker Studios once stood.

Denning Arms Apartments, aka Divorce Court, met a similar fate. The buildings were sold in 1999 to the Pike Group, a Cleveland real-estate development company that converted the apartments to off-campus housing for Penn State students. The buildings were sold three more times and after years of disrepair they were condemned and are currently awaiting demolition.

In a taped confession with Erie detectives, shortly after the journals were authenticated, John "Marco" Stoutman confessed to the September 1, 1992, murders of Riley Dutcher and Walker Roe. Stoutman also confessed to being the driver during the first attempt on Walker's life, on July 28, 1992.

According to Marco Stoutman, Dominick Salter paid him $20,000 to assist in the first murder attempt. Later, Marco Stoutman, who battled cocaine addiction for twenty years, believed that Dutch *did* recognize him from that shooting and was simply waiting to blackmail him.

Dominick Salter, who was convicted of first-degree attempted murder in 1993, was sentenced to life in prison. He will be eligible for parole in 2018.

After over twenty years, "Kyle Somebody" Shustack, the original suspect in the murders of Riley Dutcher and Walker Roe, has been publicly exonerated of the crimes. Shustack plans to write a book and a motion-picture screenplay about his experiences.

Attorney Benjamin Mott, a man who once relished the public spotlight, remained unexpectedly quiet after the murders of Riley Dutcher and Walker Roe. He continued to manage the many lawsuits that were filed but he declined interviews and rarely spoke on the subjects of Dutch, Walker, or Gopher Ink. Mott was killed in a car accident in Boca Raton, Florida, in April 2009.

Elizabeth and Abigail Roe were contacted for their comments on the discovery of the journals, as was Grace Woodcroff, Riley Dutcher's former wife. Through their attorneys they declined to be interviewed.

Randy Bogochek, Dutch's former drinking buddy, suffered a massive stroke in December 2007, which left him unable to speak. He currently resides in a nursing home in Endicott, New York.

One Mather Street, the apartment building where Dutch lived in Binghamton, New York, remains as it once was, as does the Belmar, the bar across the street where Dutch and Randy spent many hours. Once part of a busy block, the Belmar is now the sole square building, surrounded by vacant lots.

As a sign of respect, the night before the release of *Thirty-three Cecils*, three editors from Blydyn Square Books met at the Belmar. We had a drink and we toasted Dutch, Walker, and Gopher Ink.

About the Author

Everett De Morier is the writer and editor of the online magazine www.543skills.com. He is also the author of *Crib Notes for the First Year of Marriage: A Survival Guide for Newlyweds,* and *Crib Notes for the First Year of Fatherhood: A Survival Guide for New Fathers.* De Morier has appeared on CNN, Fox News Network, The Extra Help Channel, PBS, and others. Excerpts from De Morier's books have appeared in *The New York Times* and affiliates, *The London Times* and affiliates, and more than twenty-five Gannett newspapers. He has written articles for *In-Fisherman*, *Florida Keys*, *Bride*, *Parenting,* and other magazines. De Morier is an Amazon.UK bestseller and a Backlist Publisher's Weekly bestseller.

He is also the author of the plays *Dover: A Christmas Story, A Gift to Remember, The Loockerman Letter*, *The Mollywood Tree,* and *Finding Sergio. Thirty-three Cecils* is his first novel.

De Morier lives in Dover, Delaware, with his wife and two children.